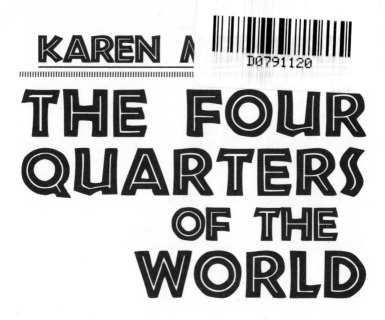

KAREN M[...]

THE FOUR QUARTERS OF THE WORLD

PRESS ®

Silver Imprint
Medallion Press, Inc
Printed in USA

Dedication:

To Sir Richard F. Burton
the brave, bold bandit

I'll never find another hero as singular as you.

Published 2006 by Medallion Press, Inc.

The MEDALLION PRESS LOGO
is a registered tradmark of Medallion Press, Inc.

Copyright © 2006 by Karen Mercury
Cover Illustration and map by James Tampa

Printed in the United States of America

Library of Congress Cataloging-in-Publication Data

Mercury, Karen.
 The four quarters of the world / Karen Mercury.
    p. cm.
 ISBN 1-932815-44-9
 1. Theodore II, Negus of Ethiopia, d. 1868--Fiction. 2. Ethiopia--History--1490-1889--Fiction. 3. Americans--Ethiopia--Fiction. I. Title.
 PS3613.E73F68 2006
 813'.6--dc22

                        2005029009

10 9 8 7 6 5 4 3 2 1
First Edition

Acknowledgements:

The eminent historian Prof. Richard Pankhurst, O.B.E.,
of Addis Ababa, Ethiopia
Who advised me on matters ranging from rice, booze, toilets, and
azmary singing about Monika Lewinsky.
This book is infinitely better for all of your invaluable assistance.
I treasure you dearly.

Jool
Who took breaks from watching the Gladiator Channel to help me out.
Nick Davis says to leave the furry swizzle sticks under the pot of plastic
begonias on your way to Khartoum.
THE LONG VERSION RULES!

Gatlin' Gil Bradshaw, for advice about Victorian armament
And knowing how to blow stuff up.

Kari Noble of Willowbrook Stables for the horse help.

The not terribly bitchy M-H for pardoning my French.

And little angel Mari, who has inspired us with her discussions of
Unkie Dan's butt.

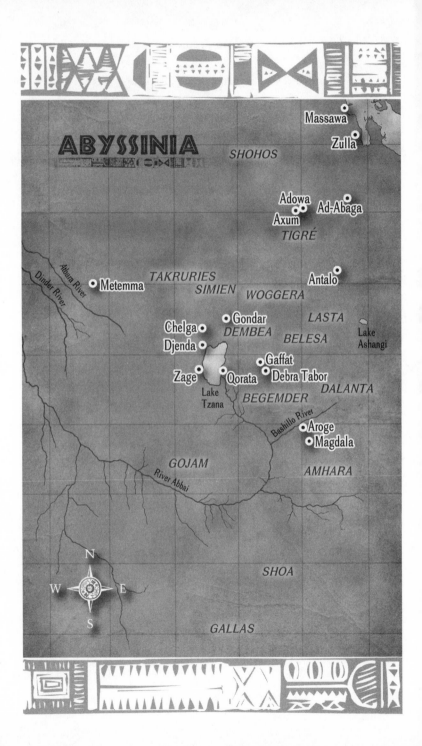

"Cut down the kantuffa in the four quarters of the world, for I know not where I am going."

—Amhara saying

Abyssinia is the only nation in Central Africa bearing the name of Christian, and now, alas, notorious for vice, that may yet become famous for "whatsoever is honest, lovely, and of good report."

—Rev. Henry Aaronstern

PART 1

CHAPTER ONE
THE FIRST JUMMA'S OWN

August 6, 1866
Metemma, Abyssinian Frontier

"COMPANY, FALL IN!"

The Takruries drilled in English. Delphine Chambliss was roused with patriotic zeal to hear her native language shouted in the commodious market square like that—whether zeal for the Stars and Stripes, or the crowned Abyssinian Lion, it didn't matter. "English!" she thrilled, shaking the arm of her towering purple-black consort, the runaway slave Abou Bekr. A formidable, fierce man with starry patterns of cicatrices embellishing his face, Abou was also Takrury, a Soudan pilgrim like the ragtag assemblage of a hundred men who were now commanded to "order arms!"

"Yes," Abou boomed. "They have served in the Egyptian army; that is where they learned to march."

Delphine giggled to see the coarse-haired ragged men with their wild array of old muskets, some shouldering arms, some on their left, some on their right, and some, apparently the conscripts who had never been in the Coptic army, not at all. They forward marched with zesty limbs akimbo, so out of step with one another that they soon jammed up like logs sweeping downriver. The fellows at the tail of the queue stumbled, and stepped upon the heels

1

of the men in front of them, until Delphine was certain the entire row would collapse like dominoes.

"Oh, they're so funny! Are they equally as bad at fighting?"

Abou narrowed his eyes down at her. "They are Takrury, the First Jumma's Own! *Geddai* is the highest proof of courage. You have seen how I fight." For emphasis, he rattled the musket he'd been using as a walking stick, the better to prop himself up and stand on one leg like a stork.

Indeed, Delphine had witnessed the remarkable spectacle of an enraged Abou Bekr running at full tilt at a lion who had been molesting their caravan, thrusting his spear down its throat, and drilling the terrifying creature all in one motion. "Oh, but I do not doubt you, dear Abou."

Abou was not soothed. His shiny forehead furrowed with discontent. "You have not heard my *doomfata*," he grumbled. Since Abou and the gentle and handsome Adam Rajjab had been teaching Delphine the Amharic language, Delphine knew the *doomfata* to be a sort of boasting contest where one sang of one's kills. A man could brag of forty *geddai*, the murder of forty men, but if the other man had killed even one elephant, they were considered even. A lion was good for four men, and rubbing out a hated Galla was sufficient for a whole ballad.

Delphine said, "I should very much like to, as soon as we find another warrior accomplished enough to compete with you."

Again, Abou blessed her with his smile. "Maybe Emperor Tewodros."

The clownish antics of the troops did not dishearten the admiring crowd pressing in on the market square. They whooped and hollered in ecstatic support of their soldiers, the overly zealous among them hoisting spears and marching in imitation, and in a few cases firing off their valuable ammunition.

At the "about face" half the men turned and half didn't, with the result that many banged foreheads, and even Abou finally laughed.

"Did you not get many *geddai* during your war between the provinces?"

For Delphine had told Abou of one man she had been compelled to shoot in Kentucky. She had not told him of the others. "Yes, a few. Not as many as you, I'm sure."

"You are very accurate with your rifle. What about your fiancé? Did he not get many *geddai* in the land of Franks?"

Delphine had taught Abou the word *fiancé*, as it was the closest she could come to describing Anatole Verlaine, Abyssinians not having much concept of love or courting, or even marriage for that matter. They seemed to just come together for lust or convenience. Aside from the Christian marriage performed by a priest which very few chose, the difficulty of divorce putting the kibosh on their ardor, there was a civil marriage, but the bonds were so tenuous as to appear more like concubinage. "Oh, no, Abou. Anatole has not even one *geddai*, of that I am sure. Why, he is a poet from Paris." When Abou remained expressionless, Delphine added, "A poet is a writer of . . . poems. Little stanzas that men recite." Abou raised one eyebrow slightly. "Such as little songs, that one would—"

"Ah! Like verses of the Qu'ran!"

"Yes!" Delphine cried with relief. "He writes little verses."

"And he is so very famous that many people pay him to write verses?"

"Well, no. No, not many people outside of our salon ever fully appreciated the brilliance . . ." Delphine resorted to muttering to herself. "The illuminated genius . . . *une horreur de l'hiver* . . ."

At that, Abou sank back into a consternated silence, and they observed the soldiers take a final half-hearted crack at marching to the rear. Delphine envied the soldiers their simple costume of close-fitting knee-high white breeches and *shammas*, a sort of cotton toga, most with a red ribbon bordering the edge, all in various stages of decomposing from their original white to the desirable and dandified stained black. How she wished she could dress so! She had dispensed with all petticoats but one, and was now in the vanguard of French fashion in nothing more than a skirt and blouse over which she wore a basque-waist with a bolero flair to it, gold buttons, braided trim, and tassels on ropes hanging from the front breast and behind her neck. However, as it was the rain season, the rich chocolate velvet of her basque-waist "hug-me-tight" had sprouted indelible mold that couldn't be wiped away, and though they had moved from monotonous desert to the pleasant green valleys of the Abyssinian frontier, it was still swelteringly hot.

If she only had the gall to travel in the men's trousers that she adored so at home!

"Company dismissed!"

The populace erupted in cries of hysterical cheer, women trilled in the ululating *elelta*, and all went as one body racing onto the parade-ground to congratulate the future victors of Metemma. Delphine and Abou were quite dragged along, submitting with good humor to be nearly borne up into the air. Delphine almost poked out many eyes with her parasol, but the favor was repaid in kind by the propinquity of spears and lances brandished willy-nilly. Large *wancha* cow horns of *talla*, a sort of noxious beer Delphine could not be induced to try, were lifted high. Abou rudely grabbed a horn as it passed him by, as he had, along with everyone else, already paid either a Maria Theresa dollar or bars of salt for his share of the community feast.

Delphine breathed freely once most of the celebrants ran to see a cow killed. Abou was already on his second horn of *talla*, so she tore a chunk off her thick round *hambasha* loaf and handed it to him.

"Every Takrury warrior will eat and drink for his dollar,"

Abou shouted, so as to be heard over the caterwauling that passed for singing.

"We should leave, Abou. The caravan is resting up on the hill, and they will be much more refreshed than us if we keep eating and drinking down here." For the others in their party—some Turkish Irregulars sent by the Pasha to protect their twenty camels, some Portuguese and Indian servants, and some Massawa men for muleteers—were napping in the Imperial Residence, a barn loaned them by Sheikh Jumma.

"Yes, Curd Teeth."

Delphine had protested at this moniker at first, until she learned it was a compliment to be told your teeth were as white as curds.

Adam Rajjab pushed through the crowd, his well-made face the color of asphaltum oil paint lit with excitement, and he pointed.

"Sheikh Jumma!"

Delphine caught sight of her Turkish Irregulars lifting horns of their own over by the dead cow, so she turned to where the Sheikh stood on the roof of a hut, shouting down through a cupped hand. People shushed each other, and Adam Rajjab translated the Sheikh's speech for Delphine.

"We are a strong and mighty people, unequalled in horsemanship and in the use of the spear and shield. The sight of our gunmen will strike terror into every nearby tribe." After some more of the usual long-winded bragging, the Sheikh concluded by suggesting a raid into Abyssinia would be just the thing. "We will take cows, slaves, horses, and mules, and please our master the great Negus Tewodros!"

The resulting roar of approval was so great it hurt Delphine's ears.

✳   ✳   ✳

Djenda, NW Shore of Lake Tzana

RAVI WAS QUITE FOND OF ALITASH for the way her bells tinkled when she moved. Her unblemished skin the color of coffee with milk was soft as an unborn calf, as was her voice, modulated sotto voce so as to excite the most prurient instincts of men.

"Ah, now, my Soft Lips," Ravi growled into the moistness between her breasts. The sun on the red silk tent imbued her with a happy gleam, as though she radiated amber. Most of the silver chains and amulets she wore around her neck were already slung back onto the silk pillows. He had to move the blue cord of her *mateb*, the sign of all Christians, from her bared nipple in order to moisten it with honey that he dipped from a pot. "I heard that you declined to lie with Fitawrari Hasani. Why is this?"

Alitash squirmed and giggled. "Because I only want you, Basha Falaka."

This pleased Ravi, though if it became known one of the favorites preferred only him, he would be in for an extended lecture at least, and all manner of underhanded subterfuge. When he lowered his head to lap at Alitash's nipple, she gave a squeal of joy, causing Ravi to murmur, "Ah . . . El *hazzaz.*"

"Oh!" she squeaked. "That is your Hindoo language of love that I don't understand."

He continued in Amharic, "I have let them see the effect of a subtle shadow, spinning like an ever-busy spider." His penis stiffening again inside her, he began to move ever so slightly. "They said to me 'how long will you go on?' I answered them, 'I will work till I am dead'."

Laughing delightfully, Alitash flung her hands around his buttocks and urged him onward. "You will work till you are dead, Basha Falaka."

"Until I have satisfied *El hazzaz*—oh, *Isgyoh!* What now?"

A Galla eunuch kneeled obsequiously on a carpet inside the tent's door. "I do not mean to intrude, Likamaquas. But Azmach Michael says it is urgent."

"Yes." Ravi turned back to Alitash to utter his regrets, but apparently Azmach Michael imagined his issue of greater urgency, as by the time Ravi had disengaged and was wiping his erect penis with a cloth of rosewater, the annoying muttonhead had already marched his way inside Ravi's tent.

Misha stood solemnly, stolidly, as was his wont, looking as usual completely ridiculous in the *shamma*. Some foreigners could wear it with ease and grace, but Misha wasn't among them. With hands behind his back, he stared at a spot on the tent wall somewhere between Ravi's shield and a wooden liquor cabinet. In English he reported, "Sorry to interrupt, Rav. But there's a situation."

Ravi had stepped into his narrow tight-fitting white breeches, and had his own situation arranging his stiff penis inside the crotch. "This better be important, Misha. Not like that time you swore you saw the hyena wearing the earrings."

"No, this would be entirely unlike that time, Rav."

"Alitash here was just sharpening her pair of tongs."

"Her . . . ? Oh, your Hindoo love."

Donning the long white European shirt, Ravi now nudged Misha to take hold of one end of his belt while he backed across the tent to unroll it. Ravi's own belt was fifteen yards in length, but some chiefs or soldiers in the throes of super-dandyism wore them as long as sixty yards. A warrior was wound up like a top inside his belt from waist to armpit to act as armor against spear or *shotel*. Ravi thought it looked absurd that way, like a mummy who had taken it into his mind to start walking the face of the Earth again, so he wore his around his hips. "Yes, Hindoo love. You can learn a lot from it, Misha."

"No thank you, Rav. You know I have no heart for those strange religions. I'm just here to report that Alemu Mariam has presumed to mount a forage party into Zage."

Having cinched the belt, Ravi twirled toward Misha to wrap himself up. "Zage? Why, in God's name, when we already stayed there for three months just last winter? There's nothing left to forage."

"Exactly, which is why you need to talk to him before he sets off."

"Can you go down and stall him? I'll be right there."

Arranging his toga-like *shamma* over his clothes, Ravi would not be seen in public without the *betoa*, a silver gilt hinged cuff enclosing the right forearm, or his lion's mane mantle, arranged attractively about his shoulders. He wore his Persian *shamshir*, a saber with a blade inlaid in gold with long passages from the Qu'ran. The leather-covered steel scabbard with gold mountings was worn on the right, in other words the wrong side according to Europeans, so as to project out dashingly behind him, like a lion's tail. And of course, even when confronting Amharas of his own tribe, he must buckle at least one Remington into a hip holster.

He squatted next to the reposing Alitash. Lifting her delicate foot to his mouth, his tongue traced a line down her instep stained with *insoosilla*, a root that produced the same red tinge as henna of the East. He shook her foot a little, rattling the girdle of silver bells that encircled her arch and heel. "Stay; rest. I will be right back."

The imperial camp was situated on the most prominent conical hill above Lake Tzana, the great reservoir of the Nile. The Emperor's musketeers and spearmen blanketed other smaller eminences to the very summit. Ravi briefly glanced up at the Emperor's red flannel tent and his white silk pavilion, flanked on the right by the church tent, on the left by his favorite of the day, at the moment Woizero Yetemagnu. Down the hill in descending order of importance were the tents of the Ras Engeddeh, the

Dejazmachs, the martial Fitawraris, and the commanders of the left and right. He saw no sign of stirring save the millings of valets and attendants—he knew it would be so at this time of day, already well into the afternoon. Of late Tewodros had taken to napping after noon, drinking *arrack* and striking fear into those around him, so very few ventured near. One never knew in what mood he would emerge from his tent—ebullient, demanding entertainment, or dark eyes flaring with rage.

As Tewodros's Likamaquas, a sort of chamberlain and commander of horse who dressed as him in battle to draw enemy fire, Ravi was one of the few who still broached the Imperial threshold. Today he didn't bother mentioning Alemu Mariam's expedition to Tewodros, especially as swarms of black-bottomed anvil clouds were sweeping up the valley, casting forked barbs of lightning behind the sunny buttes.

In his horse-tent he accepted his horse from his groom, and loped down the hill past officers' tents, cooking fires, goats and chickens scattering in his path. He found Misha, Alemu Mariam, and about seventy soldiers on the lip of a butte that dropped off into the lake. Hailo brandished a *shotel* obtained from the body of a dead Tigréan, a ridiculously flimsy hooked blade one could only inflict injury with by ducking and bouncing in awkward ways.

"Likamaquas." Alemu Mariam touched his sword to soil and made a small bow. "Azmach Michael says you have some ideas for my expedition. I wish to hear them."

Not bothering to dismount, Ravi bellowed, "That is a new tactic coming from you, Alemu Mariam. I did not see you wishing to hear my ideas when you stood on one leg reciting the Book of Job."

Laughing with new confidence, Alemu looked at the men. "It is well-known that the Likamaquas is not a religious man. He doesn't keep the Sabbath or fast, and he eats hare and wild boar."

Only a few men were bold enough to nod. Ravi smiled imperiously. "That is well-known. There is nothing more savory than a hare stew with cayenne pepper and rice." More men nodded with enthusiasm at the mention of food. "And we will find no hare, nor cattle, nor *teff* flour if we follow this holy man who thinks he can set fire to his enemy's camp a mile away with a cheap burning-glass."

Two dozen soldiers now had the gall to guffaw aloud, Misha among them. "Yes, yes," chortled one, shaking his neighbor's arm. "He thought a tiny glass could start a fire down on the plain."

"Because he burned some ants with it . . ."

"Enough!" snapped Alemu Mariam, rattling his *shotel*, but the men kept chuckling. "What does this have to do with my expedition to Zage?"

Ravi could smell the rain before it hit them. He was fascinated with how it darkened the sheet of lake like an advancing wall of locusts, as though closing the door on the sun. "Because there is no food left in Zage. The good people gave us all they had last winter." That was a neat misrepresentation—they had looted and pillaged the province forty-six ways to Sunday. "There hasn't been enough time for them to grow anything. No, I propose a forage party in a new direction. All men with fire feet meet back here in an hour; we travel in the rain, with no women." He looked pointedly at Alemu Mariam when he said, "The man who handles a lance and does not come to this expedition is a woman and no more a man."

As the pelting deluge passed over the soldiers, they raised their weapons in assent, then scattered running, or kicking their sprightly mules. Ravi turned his horse back uphill, Misha and Alemu Mariam following on their own mules.

"But Likamaquas," said Alemu, "where do you propose to go?"

"Metemma."

Alemu mused, "Metemma . . . That is where you have the

favored Galla slave."

"Exactly!" Ravi agreed.

"But Rav," said Misha. "Who is going to placate the Emperor?"

Ravi reached out and slapped Misha on the thigh. "You are, my boy! Now, who best to tame his moods with serene recitations of psalms than you? I'm certainly no devotee of the scriptures."

"Likamaquas, Likamaquas," a Fitawrari called from the shelter of an umbrella. "We must discuss the ammunition stores!"

Ravi raised a hand in acknowledgement.

Misha wasn't content. His voice even had an undertone of anger. "Rav, you *know* that isn't what I mean! There are times when even scriptures cannot soothe a . . . an Emperor."

Ravi halted and faced Misha, looking so bedraggled in the unremitting torrent with his sodden *shamma* stuck to his skinny thighs. "Misha," he laughed. "He's already arrested every white man in Abyssinia. What are the chances you'll be next?"

He knew his joke was evil, and upset his closest friend, but sometimes Ravi just couldn't resist.

＊　＊　＊

THE SOLDIERS DIDN'T RAID INTO ABYSSINIA; they got drunk. Delphine, an avid member of the Ladies' Temperance Benevolent Society, sat on the roof of the Imperial Residence, first mending clothing, then cleaning her pieces. Abou, having filled two skins with talla, had followed her up the hill to the residence. He had a great talent for excusing most everything with the saying it wasn't expressly forbidden by the Qu'ran. A fierce eater of the most disgusting kinds of filth, Delphine imagined he would have dined on a man with gusto if he thought no one was watching.

It was pleasant on the green hillock after the dry sameness of the desert. The panoply of hills separated by malachite valleys watered by fresh races of rainwater was as though viewing a Garden of Eden painting, the filtered beams of setting sun enough to bring holy tears to one's eyes. To be sure, the townspeople reveled down below, but from this height one could imagine not a bacchanalian scene, but a festival of harvest.

"That is a very handsome gun," Adam Rajjab said for the tenth time, looking slyly sideways at the shotgun stock Delphine had laid down on a rag.

Delphine smiled lazily. "I will give it to you when we reach Gondar." She could hear both Adam and Abou catch their breath and freeze. "Why not? I have my Remington, and my shotgun. I hope I hardly have use for such an arsenal once I'm there." She sighed deeply, commencing to run the cleaning rod down the barrel, sluicing water through it. "We'll go inside churches, and—"

"Ladies may only go in special parts of churches," Abou said. "What will you give me in Gondar?"

"—and walk hand in hand down the cobblestoned streets— they *do* have cobblestoned streets in Gondar, don't they?"

Abou and Adam looked blankly at each other.

"No matter. See the palaces . . ." Bending down, she picked up the shotgun stock and handed it to a reverent Adam. "Here, polish. Can we go inside any of the palaces, or do people still live in them?"

The giant Abou tried to hunch back into the low *alga* couch, constructed of poles lashed together with thongs of cowhides. He grumped, "From Menelik come the Kings of Gondar."

Delphine abruptly stopped her sluicing. "Menelik? I've heard the name."

Abou would not look at her, but continued to grumble, "Makeda was the Queen of the South in Abyssinia. She went over the seas to seek knowledge from the famous Solomon."

Delphine could not comprehend what she was hearing. "To . . .

Jerusalem?"

Abou nodded cynically. "Yes. Jerusalem. She found knowledge, and returned to Abyssinia to give the kingdom to her son, Menelik."

Delphine turned to Adam, who was polishing the stock so assiduously he seemed set to see himself in it. "Is this true, Adam?"

Adam looked up briefly, nodding. "The Kebra Negast tells of it."

Delphine recalled to close her jaw, she was gaping so. "This is astounding! In essence, then, the royalty of Gondar claims to be descended from Solomon!"

Abou drew himself up to his full height and looked down his flaring nostrils at Delphine. "Emperor Tewodros is of that dynasty."

This information did not penetrate Delphine's brain, for Abou abruptly whispered "Halt!" to his companions, sitting erect like a jackrabbit.

They halted, but Delphine soon exhaled and waved a dismissive hand at Abou. "They're just carousing." There were shouts of anger or alarm and a few puffs of smoke from fire-arms down in the dimming market square. "It's nothing. Tell me about Menelik. They're saying that Makeda had a son by Solomon?"

Abou leaped to his feet and ran across the rooftop to shout something in Arabic down the stairs. Rolling her eyes, Delphine poured fresh water into her rifle barrel from a dipper in a bucket, and turned to Adam. "Now, you make sure to take good care of this gun. You must clean it after every use, or it gets full of residue, powder." Drunken revelers pounded in bare feet up the street toward the Imperial Residence, some evidently on horseback as well. Could she ever go far enough to a land where nobody was under the domination of the vine?

Adam's eyes shone with pride. "I will clean it *every day*." Adam did not drink liquor.

"Yes. Treat it as you would a son. Why do you not marry, Adam?"

At this, Adam looked shy. "I . . . I . . ." His free hand fluttered in explanation, but he could not find words.

"That's all right, you don't need to explain. Maybe if you had more money?" The first visitation of a human head appeared over the edge of the roof. "Oh, this is just too much!" Her patience rapidly evaporating, Delphine headed toward the edge, nearly getting trounced by the Massawa muleteers of her party, who all suddenly ran at full chisel across the rooftop. She heard exhortations in Arabic and Amharic, only making out a few words in Amharic such as *shifta*, which was "robber" and *tenesu!* which meant "get up!"

By now an entire row of suspicious heads fringed the rooftop, arms scrabbling in the caulking between the stones. Delphine aimed her barrel at the first head and pumped the cleaning rod, squirting a stream of black powder water right on down the line, soaking every bandit square in the eye, sending them tumbling back down to street level, twenty feet below.

This emboldened her, and she turned to find Adam. She knew this wasn't the usual soused gambit. A horrifying bellowing warrior took giant strides toward where Adam cowered before the couch, frantically trying to put the shotgun back together. In the final minutes of twilight, Delphine saw the warrior's fearsome scimitar flash, and by the time she was there, Adam's head had separated from his neck, and lay face up toward the sky. His neck poured what looked like black blood over the polished gun stock he held in his hand.

The warrior had gone on to better things, giving Delphine one moment to swoop down and grab her Remington, already cleaned and loaded. With no compunction whatsoever, she shot the retreating warrior between the shoulder blades, and he pitched forward with a strangled "*Ah!*" that would have been comical in a different circumstance. "You damned bastard!" she shrieked, suddenly taken out of herself and feeling like a stranger.

She raced back to the edge of the roof, effortlessly tossing over a few men who had managed to scale the wall again, taking great satisfaction in the thudding of their bodies on the dirt below. Seeing a couple of muleteers racing toward the stairwell chased by raw hollering warriors, Delphine dove in between them and was carried down the stairs in a mass of limbs, knocking seven bells out of her on the way down.

Apparently the muleteers were lifted off of her, for when she raised herself up on her elbows to view the inner courtyard, she saw one of the grandest sights of her life—Abou towering above a thrashing vortex of five warriors, swinging wildly with an enormous five-foot-long pestle made from a hollow tree trunk and used for pounding peas. The Abyssinians whooped and shrieked to have such a formidable quarry at hand, but, noting they kept their distance from Abou and could barely touch him with the tips of their curved sword blades, Delphine scrambled to her feet and heartlessly squeezed her trigger, aiming at the chest of one—he fell back, and nobody seemed to notice him dying.

After a momentary sense of poetic rightness, she was slammed from behind with what felt like a massive block of solid wood.

With her breath sucked out of her, she floated in a blissful warm state, up toward the ceiling, as though in a loving featherbed.

Abruptly, to her utter rage, she was lying on her back, and a reeking soldier dripping oily fluid onto her neck from the tips of his hair pinned her to the floor, spraying odiferous phlegm, the droplets which glittered in the light of a country lamp.

She knew the word *ferenje*, white person, and knew they were arguing over her, and she fought with every acidic tendon and sinew she never knew she possessed, but she didn't hold her pistol anymore, and the weight of even the most decrepit Abyssinian was no match for a girl.

Two more men helped him, and she knew then if she just lay

still she might come out unscathed. That was all there was to it. She exhaled, and turned her head to one side, and tried to hold her breath so as not to smell the dead carcasses of a whole herd of cattle wafting down onto her person. Men held her feet to stop her kicking, and with her hands pinned up above her head, her beautiful hug-me-tight jacket was rent down the front, and greasy fingers grappled at her chest.

"Stop."

She heard a large authoritative voice from above, near the ceiling, and all hands ceased to maul her. It was a booming voice that had a shred of reason to it, but perhaps it was her will to live that imagined that.

"Leave." He was heftier than the other men, she could tell by the solidity of his bare feet, and his Amharic was inflected with a patois she couldn't quite put her finger on.

The soldiers scrambled away from her body like spiders, and when two wide feet were planted on either side of her chest, and nothing more happened, Delphine found the will to turn her face to the ceiling.

This one was much broader, more powerful than the rest. If he decided to take her, she'd be doomed. His face was bronzed and scarred, and his naked dark eyes narrowed at her aggressively. But the man wasn't interested in her face, her emotions, and her wild rage. No, he straddled her ribcage and hovered there, thankfully not touching her upon any spot. He reached a hand, oddly enough, to the medal on a ribbon around her neck, now palpitating against her breast.

Of course he was just like the others—oily, only this one wasn't dripping any sort of fluids onto her, but he did have his hair tressed into the myriad of plaits that met at the occiput in one large queue, not hanging down in saturated curls like some—and his hands were larger than most, with tapered fingers that calmed her, in a strange way. Although he had a palpable satanic aura, she felt no threat whatsoever from this commander who studied her medal intently. Even the ragged half-moon scar that followed the curve of his left cheekbone imbued her more with wonder than fear.

He at last looked at her face. His eyes flashed with cruel intelligence.

"Congressional."

What? It was impossible he had said that word in English. "*Tenesu!*" she whispered.

His eyes would not leave her face, and he even took her hand between his massive ones, and yanked her gently to her feet. She was so dizzy it seemed two dozen warriors surrounded her, and when the commander let go of her hand she stumbled back a few steps.

By the time she regained her concentration, she was alone among the dead in the inner courtyard, her Remington at her feet.

CHAPTER TWO
THE SINGING MISSIONARY

"WELL CHRISTOPHER COLUMBUS, RAVI. YOU COME home from a successful raid—successful forage, in a befouled mental attitude, you tell Alitash you don't want to see her for Christopher's sake, then you punched that poor fellow for putting a foreskin on his lance."

"It's a disgusting habit, I fear she has a case on for me and I don't wish to get *us* in trouble, and Jesus Christ, why do you insist on using such babyish euphemisms? If I want to hear infants gurgling I'll take a stroll in the nursery."

Misha Vasiliev snorted with disgust. "I'm merely trying to be prudent."

Ravi snorted too, not taking his eyes from the piece of red cloth spread on the ground between the two men. "Move your *furz*."

Misha was in a lather now. "Why on Earth would I move my *furz*? It's obvious if I move my *furz*, you can come in with your *derr* and pop off this *medak*."

"And who's going to cry over it? It's only a *medak*."

"But you still have four *medaks* left, and I only have this one, and—"

Ravi threw up his hands. "Oh, for Christ's sake!" Getting to his feet, Ravi strode to the other side of Misha's tent and poured himself a cut Venetian glass *barrilye* flask of Hennessey's brandy. Brandy was a luxury both men ensured was always in supply. *"Poichè il dio è il mio testimone . . ."* He knew it irritated Misha when he spoke in languages other than English, Amharic, or Ukrainian, which was precisely why he chose to do so in moments like this. It made Ravi feel more securely at home when Misha stormed about in old duffer's fits over trivial comforting items like *medaks* and foreskins. In a land of feudal lords like Abyssinia, nothing ever stayed the same for longer than two days, so it was important to have comforts.

He carried another *barrilye* over to Misha to pour his partner some brandy. "And what of the prisoners? Has the King of Kings had any messages from them?"

"Well," said Misha uncertainly, staring at the red cloth chessboard. "You know I haven't wanted to get so very close, due to his wrath, and then depriving those three hundred chiefs of their hands and feet."

Ravi sipped his brandy. "Yes, well. His tactics are sometimes unsound."

Leaping to his feet, Misha was now earnest. "It's not that I think them unsound at all, Rav! I mean, look around you, look at this country. I think the tactics are about what you would expect in a place like this. It's his astrologers, those cracked soothsayers who are telling him what to do."

Ravi wagged a pedantic forefinger at his partner. "No, there you're wrong. You know Tewodros would never do something strictly on the advice of another. No, his only lord and master is up here, make no doubt about it." He tapped his own temple with the hand that held the *barrilye.*

"But he's so pious!" Misha sputtered. "Why, just the other day he said to me, 'Without Christ, I am nothing. If He has destined me to purify and reform this distracted kingdom, with His aid who can stay me'?"

"Don't you see, dear Misha?" Ravi cried. "He's just utilizing this pompous jackass jargon to make everyone think a power higher than himself has willed it."

"But it has!" A shadow came over Misha's earnest visage then, and his silly elfin features turned dark, like a nefarious gnome's. "Lately you've appeared to be losing faith, Rav. I don't like to see this, and I'm sure Tewodros will take note."

Ravi burst out into a round of laughter that wrenched his innards. "Oh, is that so? And what will I do then, Misha, run cowering before his might? Did I not sleep in his tent's doorway for years to protect him, and do I not still dress as him in battle? Misha, he may be the King of Kings, but I am Basha Falaka, speaker of twenty-three languages, pilgrim of Mecca and Medina, Knight Errant of—"

Misha had his face up against Ravi's, "You might want to keep your voice low!"

Simply to be contrary, Ravi guffawed even louder. "We're speaking in English, my dear boy!" His laughter carried him back over to the low inlaid table, where he poured more brandy. Misha certainly had a screw loose at times!

Misha sidled over. "You never know . . . these walls have ears. Tell me about Metemma."

Metemma. The joy fell from Ravi abruptly, and he suddenly longed to be back in his library tent, undisturbed, going over manuscripts, or out on a rise where he could take readings of the stars. "Oh, you know, we plundered—or sorry, we *traded* for—about three hundred pounds of *teff* flour, some seven thousand head of cattle; we got the European stores for the captives, and then . . . we returned."

Misha stood behind him, resolute in his absurd *shamma*

hanging from his undeveloped and paltry frame. "No, Rav. No. Something happened."

Ravi drew himself up. They were both tall men, over six feet high, but Ravi being so much broader and more muscular was by far the more domineering figure. "Why do you keep insisting that? It was just an average raid."

"You've been acting so odd ever since returning."

"Well, let's see. We ran into a herd of elephants just off the Dinder River. They were docile, one cow was tossing her young in the air with her trunk, but the men were hungry, so I shot one. Unfortunately, this caused the death of Shetou, when he was squeezed against a large rock—"

"OK, OK, OK!" Misha waved Ravi away with a disgusted hand. "You don't have to tell me anything. Criminy knows I am barely ever privy to any of the important things that happen around here."

To placate Misha, and to forestall the act of the abused party Misha was about to delve into with gusto, Ravi chuckled casually. "Ah, now, Mikhail . . ." He casually meandered to the opposite side of the tent. Cooks and valets chattered outside by the fires that lit the tent walls with lambent silhouettes. Cattle lowed, their long clattering horns knocking together. It was comforting and secure in the tent, and Ravi was certain none of his close servants understood much English, other than the occasional "bastard" or "god-damn."

"There was one strange event. I saw a white woman in Metemma."

"A white woman?" Misha shrieked quietly behind Ravi's shoulder. "A missionary?"

Ravi turned, allowing his brow to become lined with enough concern to make it appear he had only just now recalled this incident. In truth, the memory of the woman had been griping him every step of the way back from Metemma. He couldn't figure the origin of her accent from her few Amharic pleas, but she was a stunner of the highest degree, even in her bedraggled condition, with some of those hyenas that passed for men pinning her down. "No, I doubt she was a missionary. She didn't have that Sunday go to meeting air, especially not when she drilled old Yessous dead center in the torso." He rolled the brandy around his mouth.

"She drilled him?" Misha shouted in a whisper.

"Yes, with the heftiest forty-four Remington this side of the Nile." He allowed his look to become soft and dreamy, and he described the scene with a hand as though polishing a newel post. "I must say, Misha, she had the most exquisitely proportioned breasts, solid and round, not hanging sacks like so many you see."

"Exquisite breasts?" Misha continued to gape.

At last Ravi looked at his partner and frowned. "If you don't shut your jaw, a scorpion is going to build a nest in your mouth."

Misha shook his head hard. "It seems you were involved in a raid where she had the gumption to stand up for herself. Well, good! Good for her."

"I couldn't agree more."

"What else did she say? Where is she from, where is she going?"

"Ah. We didn't talk, my friend. It was a violent encounter, and she wasn't disposed kindly toward me, and the men were all over her like weeds. I only got close enough to . . ." He felt Misha's breath on the back of his neck.

"To what? To see her exquisite breasts?"

Ravi exhaled. "Yes. That's it. That was the entire encounter."

"And? You left her there?"

"Did I have another option?"

"*You left her there?* How many of her party were left alive?"

Ravi shrugged. "None, I don't believe. No. I'm certain. None."

"*You left her there?* How could you do that? I've known you to commit some fairly harsh acts in my time, Ravinger Howland, but

I've just heard a bellyful!" Misha commenced following Ravi about the tent, hovering about like a fly at a raw beef banquet. "It's one thing to leave Ethiopians lying around, but God is going to punish you for leaving a white woman at the mercy of savage Turks!"

Ravi squeezed his eyes shut with patience. "Oh, is it so much more heinous? Do you think God differentiates between skin tone when it comes to acts of cruelty?" It was an admirable crack at leading the conversation astray, but Misha would not back down.

"So you admit that it was a cruel act! If this woman wasn't a missionary, then she was a traveler who is bound to have other *ferenje* men in her party, and they're going to come looking for you!"

Ravi twirled around to face Misha. "Right you are! She must have had other men in her party, therefore I did *not* abandon her to the hyenas."

"You should have talked to her, Rav. What kind of callous oaf leaves a white woman surrounded by dead bodies? You should have said hello, my name is Ravinger Howland, I'm from Boston, Massachusetts, I'm a captain with the U.S. Army Corps of Topographical Engineers, I designed the steam snag boat, and I'm not nearly half as heathenish as I look—"

Flinging back a fold of his *shamma* over his left shoulder, Ravi displayed an enameled eight-pointed Maltese cross medallion pinned to the European shirt over his heart. *"She had one of these!"*

At last, Misha was silent. In the Abyssinian fashion, his palm flew to his forehead where he held it, palm facing out, to express amazement. The two men continued their standoff for a few more moments, Misha huffing with residual indignation, Ravi with self-righteousness. They both broke at the same precise time.

"Now you see why—"

"I still don't see why—"

"Basha Falaka." It was Walde Nebra, Ravi's shield-bearer, who stole in the front flap of the tent.

"What is it?"

"There is a *ferenje* from Gaffat who wishes to see you."

"Gaffat?" Misha whispered. "If he hasn't been arrested, he must be one of the missionaries working at the foundry."

Ravi raised one eyebrow pointedly. "Or a very suicidal adventurer. Let him in, Walde Nebra."

The Gaffat man was fair with honey-colored hair, clad in a spotless white *shamma*. He had the ice-blue eye of the nearly lunatic, as though he would start wailing at the moon at any moment. His features were pleasant, with a cherub's bowed lips, and delicate nose that came to an urchin point. He bowed low, first to Ravi, then to Misha. Ravi scorned him for being of that pale sort whose soft muscles had the consistency of blancmange. Still, if he worked at the Gaffat foundry, and had made it this far into the mountains, that alone earned Ravi's reluctant respect.

The man smiled, a captivating sight that Ravi knew had already won over the naïve Misha. "I must introduce myself." Ravi was shocked to hear the romantic flat tones of English spoken with a Gallic accent. "I am Monsieur Anatole Verlaine of Paris, now of Gaffat, Abyssinia." He looked only to Ravi as he spoke, and he paused, as though waiting for an aghast expression of surprise and admiration. When none was forthcoming, he withdrew from the folds of his *shamma* a corked bottle, and handed it to Ravi. "I have just come from the tent of the Emperor where we were discussing the deplorable state of affairs for the poor British prisoners. He told me there is a *ferenje* Likamaquas here who is his commander of horse, and I must come over and present myself."

The bottle of Château Lafite spellbound Ravi. "Ah, but I've had this once!" He slapped Misha across the chest with the back of his hand without taking his eyes from the bottle's label. "You'll enjoy this, Misha! Shall we open it?"

Misha stared rudely at the Frenchman, and when Ravi looked

to the Frenchman for affirmation, he could give none. For his gaze was affixed to Ravi's chest in an even ruder manner, the spittle on his lower lip gleaming in the flickering light cast by one lantern, his crazy eyes glassed over. He lifted his fingers almost to Ravi's chest, and instinctually Ravi backed off a fraction of a step. What was this odd man so hell-fired about?

"I think I'll just open this right now!" Ravi continued in a jovial tone to detract from the strange moment. "Where's your corkscrew, Misha? Ah, but last time I asked you that, you told me you didn't have one. Well, shall we push the cork into the bottle, like yokels from the bushes?"

Anatole foamed over with excitement. "You're a Knight Templar!"

"Yes," Ravi admitted slowly.

Now the blacksmith did reach out and gripped him by both biceps, shaking him in brotherly camaraderie. "I should have known! You have the noble brow and the regal bearing!"

Ravi hefted the wine bottle upon his shoulder like a spear. "Are you a Knight?" he barked.

"Ah, no, I was not able . . . But I have studied them my entire life! 'He is truly a fearless knight and secure on every side, for his soul is protected by the armor of faith just as his body is protected by armor of steel'."

Ravi covered up his medal again with his *shamma*. He took his Egyptian dagger, which he wore shoved into his belt in the Bedouin manner, and tapped the cork into the wine bottle. " 'He is thus doubly armed, and need fear neither demons nor men'."

"Yes!" babbled Anatole. "And I knew you must be a Knight, from what Emperor Theodore has told me about you. He said you are a devil on horseback. You take the enemy spears and bullets, and come out unharmed."

At the mention of the Knights, Misha had sunk defeated into

a low *alga* couch; Ravi could fairly hear him gritting his teeth. Ravi waved Monsieur Verlaine down onto an opposing *alga*, where he sat also, once procuring some glass *barrilyes*. "I wouldn't really say 'unharmed,'" Ravi said grandly, pouring the precious sanguine liquor. "I've had my share of scrapes."

"And what brings you to Abyssinia?" Misha interjected, perhaps to circumvent any potential braggadocio on Ravi's part. "This isn't your ordinary holiday destination, and you are not of the Society for Promoting Christianity among the Jews."

"Ah, no, indeed!" Anatole laughed so brilliantly, his eyes sparkled like lazulite. He was truly a pleasure to gaze upon, unlike the surly and withdrawn Misha. "I am merely a blacksmith, so I came to Gaffat two months ago to help in their foundry."

Ravi raised a skeptical eyebrow. "A blacksmith who happened to be in Abyssinia?"

"Ah, yes, but you see, I am really a poet."

"A poet!" cried Ravi. "An admirable, though not very lucrative, career. Perhaps that explains why you were searching for blacksmithing work. I should like to read some of your work. Has any been published?"

"Well, yes, back in Paris my salon published a thin chapbook. I do not write anymore. I came to Abyssinia to get away from that sort of life."

Ravi chuckled. "Well, you certainly chose the right place. You can't get any more opposite from Paris than Abyssinia."

Misha inserted, "Tell us, how are the *frenjoch* getting along in Gaffat?"

"Yes, who is left who hasn't been incarcerated?"

"There are Herrs Waldmeier, Saalmüller, Moritz, Zander, and Staiger, and that funny fellow Kaspar Nagel."

Ravi nearly spit out his mouthful of precious wine. "That corned potato-head should be arrested simply on the charge of being who he is. God knows people have been detained for less than that. How does he manage to stay above it all?"

"Maybe they know he's harmless," suggested Misha.

"I do not know," said Anatole, "but he is certainly amusing. He juggles, sings, and tells funny stories."

Ravi sighed. "Yes, he does that. He's sort of an *azmary*." An *azmary* was a minstrel or jester who entertained through song.

Anatole continued smiling uncertainly. "You do not have to worry, he is not coming here. He went to Gondar, to see about converting some Jews."

"Good," grunted Ravi. "That's a good place for him."

DELPHINE HAD MADE A REGRETTABLE ERROR.

After the massacre of nearly her entire party, she had insisted on starting immediately for the craggy table-lands of Abyssinia. She wanted to make a start before the Takruries woke up from their drunken spree and realized that, instead of raiding for the benefit of the Emperor, they now had to get revenge on Theodore's men. As Sheikh Jumma was under Theodore's especial protection, and he paid his tribute every year, nobody knew why they should raid Metemma, unless they were particularly starving, especially as nobody sane traveled in the rainy season.

That concept frightened Delphine even more, that Anatole should be starving, so she set out recklessly with only Abou and two cameleers.

The little caravan quickly passed the Ethiopian Rubicon, and soon the ground became interlaced with deep ravines covered over by bamboo around which they had to detour to keep following the path of the Atbara River. They often had to dismount to descend some perpendicular declivity, and Delphine wondered how her mule would climb the opposite lofty wall of rock. But the plucky little fellow made it, with his sensitive feet searching out every step of stable dirt, and sending showers of rock onto the head of Abou below. She had a virulent terror of high spots that forbade her from ever looking down at where she stepped.

Though she was told that the Atbara slowed to a mere trickle in the dry season, at this time of year it coursed with stupendous force, hollowing out a course between two walls of basalt rock, boiling along from the sheer walls of the vast plateau above. They continued their third day's route parallel with the river, over slopes of tall green grass, through woods of acacia and mimosa. Delphine noted from her compass the river had suddenly made a southerly turn, and continued in that manner for some hours. As Gondar lay due east, this gave her a bad feeling. And indeed about the time of the daily outburst of rain that always inundated them, one of the cameleers, having confabulated with a local countryman, declared they would have to cross the river, and that this was the place to do it, the river widening out into a comparatively calm pool.

As a group of locals gathered for this humorous exhibition, it was decided Abou would descend first, Delphine walking at a distance so as not to send rock-baths onto his head. She lost her footing once in a soft spot, and would have gone hurtling completely over the edge had she not grasped the foot of her screaming mule, and she managed to haul herself back onto the shelf. After this fright, Abou shouted to the cameleer not to try to follow. The fellow insisted upon leading the heavily laden animal down the path that was now more like a waterfall, and within a few paces the camel's feet slipped. Delphine saw it ejected over the side of the precipice, roaring with fright, and she hastened back up the cliff, holding onto a rope a local man had tied to a tree. The animal landed on a thin ledge of rock, stopped from plunging farther by a tough bush that emerged from a fissure, and this alone suspended the creature in the air.

Abou had a solution that was perhaps even more terrifying, but it might save the valuable animal's life, so everyone set to work with ropes of strong twisted antelope hide. They trussed the cameleer and lowered him to the shelf, so he could relieve the camel of its burden, tossing great hunks of elephant flesh to a ledge nearly at the river's banks below. They secured a rope around the camel beneath the forelegs, and thus they both were lowered in midair gently down to the water's edge a hundred feet below.

Exhausted and despairing, Delphine sat in the muddy brooks that poured down the cliff face, and declared they should stop for the night. She was content to huddle under her animal skin treated with milk so as to render it waterproof. The river in this wide channel had stretched to a depth of perhaps only four feet, though the ponderous marks of hippopotamus feet in the mud told them there were deeper pools. As it was only shortly after noon, everyone insisted on pushing on. The baggage was made into parcels, perishable items were packed in skins, and Delphine stripped down to her petticoat, though it seemed absurd to protect her sodden garments from being dunked in the water. Some of the Abyssinians of Woggera district had descended the cliff face to assist. Fine-limbed men they were, with skins from nearly black to the shade of the Hindoo, a few with faces that would be considered comely in any sector of the world.

Delphine prepared her bundles, and spoke to a cameleer in the rudimentary Amharic that she knew. He stepped into the river alone, waving his arms like a windmill. "Don't go in, Yakoub," she called. "Wait for the Woggera men to help."

"I am fine!" Yakoub called gaily. "I can swim!"

He was only in three feet of water. "You should wait. They want us to put these poles on our shoulders, and go as a team, two together, do you understand?"

She heard Yakoub no more, and the next time she looked up, he seemed to be attempting to swim on his back, and was setting off downstream in a rapid manner. Delphine jumped to her feet, calling "Help! Help!" to the Woggera men, who all commenced racing downstream. She had to run behind a clump of bushes and canes, and when she emerged, she couldn't see Yakoub. They jogged along the shore for some miles, thinking the torrent might cast his body up on a bank, or he might become stuck by a stump or bough, but it was hopeless.

Judging from the manner in which witnesses had seen his head sink, it was agreed that a crocodile must have gotten to him; such a bottom-dwelling critter could readily have pulled him down. Others said a strong eddy had sucked him into the mud. And one fellow stridently maintained he'd been grabbed by the *gau* water-spirit who drowns proficient swimmers in harmless rivers. Altogether it was a disheartening episode, and Delphine was glad that it was still raining, so no one should see her tears. The Abyssinians seemed to share as deeply of her loss, though they had known Yakoub for only a few hours.

Delphine was proud of her fortitude, having gone through the War back home, and having witnessed revolting sights such as Gettysburg. She managed to raise her spirits by remembering her vow at the time—"I feel assured I shall never feel horrified at anything that may happen to me hereafter." She entered the river with a Woggera man as her partner, weighted down with parcels and rocks, not caring much should a crocodile or eddy snatch her off her feet, but she emerged on the other bank, for the first time in her life wondering if she should become an imbibing woman.

She went behind some bushes, claiming the need of feminine privacy, and opened her medicine chest for a brace of laudanum. Who would mind? She knew it to calm the spirit, and had utilized it in the past when she might have a tendency to become morose.

Once in Gondar, she would get a message to Colonel Merewether in Aden, and send for some more laudanum. After all, Abou was certainly not hesitant in seeking out the jug of *talla!*

They had a rude meal of *hambasha* bread and, as the rain had stopped, decided to make a moonlit ascent of the cliff. There were five now in her party, two Woggera men having decided to guide them to the plateau for a few salts. They had barely gone more than a hundred yards when the sky opened up on them again, plunging them into pitchy darkness, and rendering the path impassable. Thorns and brambles mauled Delphine's arms and chest, and stones cut her feet, as she couldn't see where she was walking. They turned from the path, cutting away thorns with their cutlasses, and lay down on the soggy ground.

Fortunately, hyenas did not disturb them, though the poor mules and camels, depressed from the striking rain, stood motionless all night, and Delphine awoke often with various hooves in frightful proximity to her face.

In the morning they hailed the sun with happiness, and pressed on up the mountainside without a bite of breakfast. Delphine's behind was sore from the ceaseless rubbing against her saddle seat, made of four pieces of wood bound together. Her hands were bleeding from handling the reins made of plaited hippopotamus hide as strong as oak, and her great toes were oozing pus due to the strange method of using small iron rings instead of stirrups.

The sun had burned her face a nut brown, and she slept while sitting up. She dreamed of fried partridges, deviled turkey with drippings, Pennsylvania pudding with raisins, crackling bread with pigskins, a fat possum roasting on a spit. Once or twice she jumped awake in a sudden panic that she could not recall Anatole's face, and she had to strive for several moments before settling on what appeared to be a reasonable replica. Images of their time in Paris floated all in a fandangle like so many phosphenes. Once she had finished recovering at the hospital, they had met often in Anatole's Latin Quarter apartment to scorn the "dead men and imbeciles" of the Parnassian poets who rejected him.

"*Oh, Anatole . . .*" she whispered as her mule plodded on. "I remember . . . your raving about the 'little world . . . pale and flat' and a ballet of known nights and oceans . . . a worthless chemistry, impossible melodies . . . Ah, but Africa isn't like that now, is it? Bourgeois magic . . . a final understanding . . . fog of physical remorse . . ."

It was just as she said "impossible melodies" that indeed she imagined she could hear a melody. It was impossible, because it was not a sublime tune of the heavens, coming more as a croak that feebly crawled then lightly fell over the lip of the canyon rim above. Without opening her eyes, Delphine laughed with a dry, cracked mouth. "How funny that sounds! It sounds like a fellow singing, only out of key, and exhausted like we are."

It gave her something to do, listen to the song and attempt to make it out, as her mule zigzagged up the cliff face.

"Some man sings!" Abou shouted down to her, so she knew she was not imagining it.

Delphine was shocked to understand some of the hoarsely grumbled words.

> *We are a band of brothers and native to the soil*
> *Fighting for the property we'd gained by honest toil*
> *And when our rights were threatened, the cry rose near and far*
> *Hurrah for the Bonnie Blue Flag that bears the single star!*

Eyes wide open now, Delphine kicked her mule into a brisk lope. She rose in her saddle and cried out, "As long as the Union was faithful to her trust, like friends and like brothers, kind were we and just!"

The voice paused, then sang with renewed vigor, " 'First gallant South Carolina nobly made the stand, then came Alabama, who took her by the hand'!"

"Ferenje!" shouted Abou.

"Ferenje!" shouted the Woggera men.

So on the ledge of an Abyssinian gorge, Delphine trotted on, shouting out a song written as an act of defiant secessionism in America's southern states.

SHE BROACHED THE LIP OF THE canyon, jumped off her mule and skipped toward the *ferenje* as they both bleated out the final line of the tune.

"To hoist on high the Bonnie Blue Flag that bears a single star!"

He was an odd man of compact middling stature, satiny hair the color of milk almost to his waist in a pigtail, with impudent, shining blue eyes. A pointed goatee gave him a distantly satanic look. Even odder, he wore striped trousers and a waistcoat with a watch, the chain displayed jauntily from his pocket. He grasped Delphine's hands, and bowed deeply.

"Missus, it is an honor," he said gravely.

"Who are you?" cried Delphine. "How did you come to be in the highlands of Abyssinia?"

He removed his silk hat and bowed again. "I am the Deacon Kaspar Nagel, your humble servant, also servant of the London Society for Promoting Christianity among the Jews; may God be willing, and a citizen of the German state of Würrtemberg."

"But this is incredible! How did you come to be singing along the Atbara River? Particularly a song about the American South."

Deacon Nagel brandished his hat dramatically, the other hand to his chest. "I am a student of all things American! Yes, I wish to go to that country if I ever get out of here. When I heard there was a white woman in Metemma I said to myself 'Kaspar, I am certain that woman is heading toward Gondar. I have a special sense for things like that. It is a sense beyond the sight, beyond the hearing, beyond the—hey now!" He frowned at the Woggera men, who were inspecting the saddlebags of his fine gelding. He shooed them off with fluttering hands, commanding them in rapid Amharic.

Delphine protested mildly. "Oh, they're just hungry, they did guide us up that terrible canyon; do you have any salts to give them, perhaps?"

Herr Nagel looked at her with a face of mystery. "Salt? I have something better!" From his saddlebag he withdrew a *wancha* horn and a jug of *arrack*, pouring it with a grand flourish. Fastidiously, he covered the mouth of the jar with a cotton cloth to filter out the plant matter. He gulped an entire horn himself before handing it around to the eager men, after Delphine declined.

"You do not like *arrack*? *Arrack* is the end and soul of existence in Abyssinia!"

"Oh, I am sure it's fine, it's just that I'm an abolitionist of all things evi—all things detrimental, such as slavery, and liquor. Now, I must beg your pardon, I haven't properly introduced myself. I'm Delphine Chambliss of Cairo, Illinois, not the Cairo of Egypt, though lately I have been of no place in particular at all—indeed, I barely remember Illinois, so much has happened since then. And you came out here just to find me?"

The odd man smacked his lips with gusto. "Yes! I said, 'Kaspar, that would be a good deed to go and help the white woman.' I started wandering about—I enjoy wandering; I even wrote a book once called *Wanderings among the Falashas*, that is how much I enjoy it—and I thought perhaps if I sing, she will hear me." He paused, and leaned in to Delphine with a confidential air. "I *was* singing 'Old Zip Coon'." Leaning back out as Delphine giggled, he proclaimed, "Performed at the Bowery Theater in New York! Have you been there?"

"I'm afraid I've never been to New York; I spent far too much time on the battlefields of Georgia and Kentucky. You see, I'm a nurse."

Herr Nagel's eyebrows shot upward, and he froze in place. "Nurse!"

Delphine didn't normally like to tell people that, as she would then be beset by legions of the ill, or those who imagined they were ill, and people with incurable conditions like elephantiasis or leprosy, and she was weary of doctoring. "Yes, but keep that a secret, can you? I don't have time to treat everyone, for if I did I should never make it to my destination—*Gondar*," she said pointedly.

"Yes, yes, I understand, but perhaps—later on—you can advise me about this painful leg condition. I at first thought it was gout, but then it resembled pleurisy—"

"Let's discuss it while we ride."

After paying off the Woggera men in salts, they set off across a gently up-sloping plateau covered with rich farmlands, grazing grounds for immense herds of sheep and cattle. The air was sweet and dry, and Delphine cheered to pass by olive trees and lemon bushes.

"How on Earth did you hear about a white woman in Metemma, Herr Nagel?"

"Ah, it was one of those things that gets passed from person to person, and eventually comes out on the other end, yes ma'am!"

"It sounds like a dreadful condition. Do you know a rather tall Abyssinian, handsome to be sure, with no great beard or moustache, and rather wider than the average fellow? He would have a half-circle scar on his left cheekbone, like this."

"Why, yes . . . I may have seen someone like that about from time to time. A very untrustworthy fellow! What an ogre to leave you in Metemma!"

"But he actually prevented his men from harming me! Who is he?"

"He is a sort of captain of war for Emperor Tewodros, a barbarian, but do not worry, you will not have to see him. They travel constantly, in great cities of fifty thousand people, plundering the countryside for their own prurient enjoyment—you will enjoy Gondar! I will take you inside Qwesqwam, the home of the former Empress, and inside Fasiladas's castle."

"That does sound pleasant, but you know I've come to meet up with my fiancé."

"Fiancé? What is that?"

"One whom one intends to marry. Do you know him? He's a Frenchman, from Paris, Anatole Verlaine."

At that, Herr Nagel sat up straighter in his saddle, his empty blue eyes staring at a fixed point ahead of him. "I suppose I do. He's a scribbler, is he not?"

Delphine laughed. "Yes, that's him. I had first heard he was in Axum, so from Massawa I started there, but then I heard he went to Gondar. When did you last see him? Is he well?"

"Oh, I believe I saw him a week ago—"

"In Gondar?"

"—in Gondar, and he looked well as ever. I think you had better watch out for that Takrury fellow with you. I have seen him ten times trying to give you the evil eye."

"The evil eye?"

"Oh, even harmless people can give the evil eye. They can hurt you, your children, or your livestock, by looking at you with envy and praising you."

"I understand English, Mister."

Delphine looked to Abou, who had been riding ten feet to her left. "Abou, are you giving me the evil eye?"

"Never, Missus. I wish only the best for you." Abou looked sullen, his lower lip jutting out. "This man knows about evil eyes, because he is a *buda*."

"A Buddha? Isn't that some rotund cheerful fellow from China? Why would Herr Nagel be a Buddha?"

"Because I am not!" roared Herr Nagel. "I am a humble servant of the Lord! Now, I think it is best for you to stay in Islambet, the Mussulman quarter in Gondar. There are many grand empty houses because two years ago the Emperor commanded his Mussulman subjects to convert to Christianity or leave the country. Many stayed, but many left . . . We cannot stay in Herr Flad's house, as it is occupied by some unsavory ruffians whom you do not wish to know, but I believe Consul Cameron's townhouse is vacant . . ."

CHAPTER THREE
THE SAME MOON AND SUN

"I SHOULD LIKE TO RIDE THAT horse." Ravi surreptitiously showed the horse-seller the inside of his *zenar, a leather case around his waist* that contained a multitude of Maria Theresa dollars.

The horse-seller became excited. "In turning he does not change the position of his neck and tail. When galloping, he does not seem to touch the ground."

"Yes, I can see that. He is very spirited." The splendid cream-colored gelding had a black mane, tail, and hooves. He was beautifully caparisoned for sale, with a headstall of white and red leather, and a strap emblazoned with round brass plates with protruding brass spikes running down his forehead and nose. This *benaika* was only lightly secured but not as to prevent it being tossed in the air. A spunky horse that threw its head up continually and flashed the eye of the onlooker was much valued. "Is he a Wallo Galla?"

"Oh yes, Likamaquas."

"Hasn't he been to the markets in Debra Tabor and Efagh before coming here?"

"No, Likamaquas. We came here directly, knowing he would

command a greater price."

As Ravi believed in the horse-seller's slimy logic, he picked up the horse's hoof to inspect its condition, and the sole for old abscesses. "Have you been giving him *kosso* and fresh butter?"

The seller proudly said, "Oh, yes. This is the good time of year to purge them after all the months of lying about."

"You must stop that. *Kosso* and butter are no good for horses. You must exercise them more during the rainy season."

He was accepting the bridle from the seller's groom when an impudent fellow, a belligerent Gondari, insinuated himself between Ravi and the horse. "I have already told him I want to ride this horse!"

Ravi took two steps back, the better to impress the Gondari with his height. "Is that right? And why aren't you with Tewodros's army, if you are so well-prepared for battle?"

This produced the expected moment of silence. The horse-seller shouted at the Gondari, "In the name of the Father, the Son, and the Holy Ghost! Where do you come from, man? I did not make any promise to you. Get out of here!"

The Gondari turned his frustration onto the horse-seller. "You told me five minutes ago I could ride him, you Turk!"

The crowd jeered at the foulness of the Gondari's language— calling someone a Turk was tantamount to calling them a devil. Ravi stepped between the two men and said to the Gondari, "I have a proposal. Let us duel over the horse."

The Gondari looked skeptical. "*Jareed?* With sticks instead of lances?"

Ravi smiled. "No. *Waffo Waggea.*"

The collective hiss of the crowd was as though a giant snake had just entered their midst. The Gondari looked petrified, and behind him Misha said in English, "Why don't you just let him ride the horse, Rav? It'll come down to who has the most money, so you'll win anyway."

"It's the principal of the matter!" Ravi told him crisply. "And besides, I'm bored. What do you say?" He turned back to the Gondari, who looked as though he'd like nothing more than to make a dash for it. "*Waffo Waggea*, but no killing. Whomever knocks the other off his horse first."

The Gondari found renewed zest, and proclaimed, "Yes, by Saint George!"

Ravi's shield-bearer, Walde Nebra, shouted, "Basha Falaka can throw a lance over the great tree and column at Axum!" That bit was an exaggeration, but Ravi was satisfied to hear it spoken.

"Yes," shrilled another fellow, whom Ravi had never seen in his life. "When he charges, it is not a man but the sun bearing down upon the enemy."

"See the lion's tail on his shield? He killed the lion with only his hands, no *spear* or *shotel*."

Ravi prepared his own horse Selpha, a bay with four white legs, and a splash of white on the forehead and nose. He removed the *limoot*, ten brass chains hung around its neck in conjunction with some amulets. He left the saddle extravagantly decorated with filigree gold and silver, as well as the black and white monkey fur attached to the left stirrup, as it was a charm against the evil eye. Being a rational engineer, Ravi did not believe in such things, but then again, he'd been booted from West Point for sword fighting, so perhaps he was not the most sensible judge of things.

Women fetched water and haggled over items in the market. They were pretty women with proud cheeks, feet and hands darkened with *insoosilla* root, and eyes encircled with black kohl. They stared with level intent, unblinking, in particular an ivory merchant's daughter Ravi had noted before. He mounted his horse, taking care to arrange the lion's mane around his shoulders attractively, and allowed his shield-bearer to lead him to the field.

They began in the usual manner, with their round buffalo-hide shields in their left hands, lances in their right. They charged from a hundred yards across the ground studded with burrow holes and *gwassa*, tufts of grass on mounds of earth. The *gwassa* rendered the entire field slippery as sleet, with countless rows of deep troughs, a soil that would have brought about the dismounting of all European cavalry. But the Wallo Galla horses were sure-footed in such soil, and they charged unflinchingly. Right after he passed up the Gondari, Ravi turned suddenly by throwing his horse on its haunches, and the Gondari wasn't prepared when he came up astride him, shoving him rudely by his lance-tip against the fellow's belt of armor, not enough to dismount him, but enough to annoy.

They charged in the same direction, Ravi harassing the Gondari but making no move to unseat him, allowing him to wheel his horse into a half-circle to become the pursuer. Quickly, Ravi feinted at the Gondari's head with his lance, forcing him to throw up his shield before his face, enabling Ravi to again jab with his lance-point against the Gondari's stomach and push, just causing him to teeter and clutch blindly for his horse's headstall.

On his next pass Ravi feinted at the man's legs, and as the Gondari brought his shield down to protect them, Ravi whacked the shaft of his lance down across the back of the man's neck and sent him crashing to the dirt, limbs flailing like a fallen cheetah.

It was an easy triumph, and Ravi galloped out another fifty yards before turning his horse for the victory charge back. He thoroughly intended on clouting the warrior again with his lance, to show he could have killed him not once but twice if he had wanted to, and that's when he saw the white woman.

Though she was surrounded by a group of others, she stood out in sharp relief with her cunning dress of red and black tartan plaid, and it was her face, at once altogether too familiar to him, that instantly sheared itself onto his brainpan. Her skin browned exotically by the sun, her full pale lips had the tiniest lilt of a sneer, and with her dark sloe eyes that looked to be rimmed with lead-gray kohl as native women did, she had the glamorous look of the Malayan half-caste.

She had been inside of his head for an entire week, and now here she stood, perhaps tracking him down, and—

In the next instant, Ravi was soaring through the air. He managed to land all in a pile on his left arm, for to land on his right might have been perilous, as he still wore his *shamshir* on that side. No damage was done aside from extreme mortification, and that his face was jammed into the back side of his shield, probably causing an imprint of the handle on the already-damaged left side of his face.

He guessed what had happened—that tricky Gondari had circled his horse directly into Ravi's path, the two horses clashed, and he had been unseated. It didn't matter to Ravi—in fact, he had no intention of purchasing the horse now—and he tried to shake off Walde Nebra who helped him to his feet.

The Gondari pushed his buttered face at Ravi. "We are even, so we must fight again!" He must have had a gargantuan headache from the big clout to the back of the neck.

Physically tossing aside the well-wishers, Ravi pushed in the direction of the white woman. "Misha, Misha!" he called, though Misha was standing right next to him. "Oh. Did you see her? Did you see her?"

"Of course I saw her," Misha said with disgust. "I assume that's your Metemma girl."

"Yes, yes! That's her!" Ravi grabbed people and shoved them aside. "Come, help me. I've got to find her."

"First you abandon her to savages in Metemma, now you need to find her?" Misha shouted.

"Yes! I've got to find out what she's doing here, what she wants, and keep her away from Tewodros."

"Because of the medal?"

Because of the medal, blubber-head, Ravi wanted to yell. "Because of the medal."

DELPHINE CONTINUED TO PESTER KASPAR ALL the way back to their house in the Mussulman Quarter. "Now if you would just let me see this bee sting . . ."

"Well, you can't see it just yet. It's on my foot."

"But you have *ferenje* shoes on! How could the bee have stung you through your shoe?" For Kaspar still remained in his European costume, to comfort Delphine and make her feel at home, he claimed.

"Yes, it's the oddest thing; it climbed through my stocking—ow, ow! Let us just hope it wasn't a wasp."

They reached the town-house where they were squatting temporarily. It belonged to Captain Cameron, the British Consul, but he had been detained since 1864, chained in Theodore's mountain fortress of Magdala along with the Reverend Stern, Kaspar's superior. It was a two-story Moorish structure of stone and mud, with a flat crenellated roof, quite capacious with its rooms all built around a central tiled open-air courtyard. Horseshoe arches supported the colonnaded gallery, protecting monstrous potted plants that grew in wild profusion, reaching for the sun and rain that came through the compluvium. A stuffed crocodile hung over the front doorway to catch and distract any evil eyes that may be pointed their way. Kaspar said Captain Cameron would appreciate them looking after his house—indeed, Cameron probably never wanted to lay eyes on the house again, if he was ever released from Magdala.

Delphine liked the Mussulman Quarter—Islambet—on the River Qaha; the remainder of the metropolis comprised mostly the round mud *tukul* huts with thatched roofs. Here there were Mussulman merchants, weavers, and tailors, but oddly enough, no shops. One had to go to the daily market in an open square where they slaughtered bullocks and sheep, and the main market on Saturday when crowds of people came from all around. Here one could obtain the ubiquitous butter, corn, red pepper, *teff* flour, honey, kohl, arsenic, glassware, coarse muslins, cotton velvets, calico, Indian spices, and shirting from the Egyptian merchants. Great caravans of gold rings and ingots, elephant's teeth of ivory, cotton, coffee to rival that from Mocha, and slaves left from here to Sennaar, Massawa, and Metemma, crossing rivers by ferrying their trade items on rafts.

Next to the aristocracy and clergy, everyone in Gondar was a merchant, making up the richest and most powerful presence in the country. But Gondar had been subject to the devastation wrought by warring chiefs of the Zemene Mesafint, the Age of Princes, an era when the power of the Emperor had fallen to almost nil before the days of Theodore, and great feudal chiefs known as Rases held power over their own fiefs and continually warred on each other. Ten years before, Abyssinia had been a mish-mash of battling dynasties with a powerless Emperor, and in times of peace, the weekly market was held. In times of war, merchants had to travel at night, and their fortunes declined.

It was a lively and loud city, where in a day of milling about one could watch the craft of book-binders, makers of parchment, harness makers, copper casters, embroiderers, shield makers, *wancha* drinking horn makers, women huddled in their all-encompassing *burqas*, and Falasha Jews who made exquisite pottery. In lieu of shops in Gondar, one could conduct trade in interior hallways of a house, if one became a trusted purchaser, which a *ferenje* always instantly was.

Kaspar walked just fine up the inner courtyard stairs that led to the second story, the living quarters. "You know, Kaspar, if I didn't know better, I would say you just invented that bee sting because you didn't want me accosting that Abyssinian from Metemma."

"Abyssinian from—? I don't have any idea who you refer to, Missus." At this, he burst into song, as he was wont to do. "Beautiful from its beginnings, Gondar, hope of the wretched! Hope of the great, Gondar without measure or bounds!"

"Come now, Kaspar. That tall, rather feral-looking fellow racing the horse."

Kaspar unlocked the large carved door that led to the drawing room. "O dove of John, Gondar, generous-hearted mother!" A high-ceilinged long room awash with sunlight from the shuttered doors they had neglected to latch, the room was decorated with Arabic walnut divans, cushioned chairs, and mosaic occasional tables inlaid with mother of pearl. The floors were thickly lined with carpets of Persian cabbage rose, Hereke prayer rugs, tree-of-life patterns with peacocks, and long narrow Karabakh rugs from the Caucasus. It was a warm, palatial room where Delphine had immediately felt at home.

Kaspar went directly to a sideboard and decanted some whiskey into a *barrilye*. "Oh, the fellow racing? I did not notice, but I suppose he could be the same barbarian. Gondar, never bowed by affliction!"

"Yes, he was staring at me so intently he didn't see where he was going, and smashed right into that other fellow's horse. I demand to know more about him, or I will force you to show me your bee sting!" Delphine strode to the shuttered door that led out onto the front balcony and looked to the street below, as though she would find the barbarian galloping below.

Kaspar joined her at the balcony door. He spoke earnestly. "I have told you, Missus—"

"Please, call me Delphine."

"Missus Delphine. He is Emperor Tewodros's Likamaquas and commander of horse."

"What is his name?"

"Basha Falaka, which, since you have progressed in your Amharic studies, you know means something akin to 'speedy commander.' But I assure you, you do not want to know this fellow. He is a soldier-of-fortune. You must be satisfied that he did not murder you, or worse." Kaspar withdrew his pocket watch, shook it, and frowned. "Why, he ordered fifteen hundred people shut up in Efagh into five large houses which he then had burned! He has been known to amuse the Emperor by splitting a sheep from head to tail with his Persian saber. His wrath is terrible, my dear, and you would do well to stay away from him. I think it wiser if you pursue the course I've set for you, and—ah!" Kaspar waved to a fellow astride a mule down in the street. "Here is my messenger right now, with our invitation from Woizero Attitegeb to visit her at Qwesqwam!"

Patting her on the hand, Kaspar took his leave, and Delphine wandered dispiritedly back to the gallery, where her bedchamber was three doors down, at the back of the house. "Murder me, or worse," she muttered. "Why does everyone always say *that* is worse than murder? *That* is not worse than murder. I've had *that* happen before, and if one detaches oneself and sends one's spirit elsewhere, one can live to forget about it. After all, there is no shame when one is forced."

She had set up a dressing table utilizing a tall looking-glass she had taken from the drawing room, and here she sat to sip her laudanum, the tasty concoction of J. Collis Browne's Chlorodyne. It was a soothing mixture of morphine, ether, cannabis, and treacle, and although she knew she shouldn't take it when she wasn't ill, the dreamlike effect seemed to go well with this land of amulets and women with blue crosses tattooed on their foreheads and arms, their silver anklets jingling as they walked.

She removed the snood she used to tame her thick, glossy bronze hair. As she brushed her hair, she thought of Basha Falaka and his dark questing lion's eyes. He had a physique like a prize-fighter, one could tell that much right away, though he was covered with the toga-like *shamma*. He had pounded his horse across those ruts like a demon possessed, and just to best a man who wanted to take a ride on a horse for sale! She had seen his well-developed thighs in the tight white breeches as he rode, clutching and steering his horse. And, perhaps because she had been apart from Anatole for six months and had not known the comfort of a male hand, Delphine began to wonder what it would be like with a man like Basha Falaka.

Oh, she was wicked, *wicked* to think like that! But the more she forbade herself, the more a duplicitous grin started at the corners of her mouth, and she saw in the looking-glass that she seemed suddenly younger, and she liked it, so she continued to imagine. Would a heathen like that know to kiss? Her legs turned to melted butter when she thought of his chest a thick pelt of soft hair against her cheek, and if she moved her face down his powerfully muscled stomach, what a thick root of a penis he would have jutting out so arrogantly, and—

"My dear Missus Delphine! We have a message from Qwesqwam!" Kaspar stood like a doltish marionette in the doorway, jarring Delphine unpleasantly from her reverie. "We have an audience with Woizero Attitegeb in one hour."

Delphine didn't believe a word about the fifteen hundred people burned in Efagh. Although she was quite enamored of Kaspar's silly buffoonery, she knew of his penchant for prevarication.

"Well, that's ever so lovely! And is she Emperor Theodore's wife?"

Kaspar jangled the paper message as though it were a twenty-dollar banknote. "She is the mother of the Ras Engeddeh, the Prime Minister, and the favorite of Tewodros. Tewodros's wife is in Amba Magdala."

"What? He imprisons his own wife?"

"No, no." Kaspar chuckled. "Magdala is his fortress. He sends everyone there he wishes for . . ."

"Safekeeping?"

"To keep safe, yes. You can wear that pretty piece of fluff the tailor repaired—"

"—and bring Abou?"

Kaspar's empty eyes froze. "Why, yes, I suppose, if we say he is our *tej-asalefech*, our butler and server of mead. That would look very good. Now! I leave you alone to prepare your toilet—"

"Kaspar? One thing."

"Yes, Missus Delphine?"

"Do Abyssinians . . . Do they know the art of kissing?"

Kaspar's face remained impervious. "I would not know," he said to her footstool. "I would not know that at all."

"All right," Delphine said. "Thank you, Kaspar."

And, bowing, he departed. As she took the cameo brooch off her collar, Delphine said to herself in the looking-glass, "What an odd man."

She thought of Anatole, and how lovely his pellucid white skin was, and how comforting it was putting her head on his shoulder. He was a gentleman, and a poet, and a poor misbegotten youth whom the world did not value.

She tried to remember what Anatole Verlaine looked like again.

THE FOUR QUARTERS OF THE WORLD

THE NORTHWEST PASSAGE OUT OF GONDAR lay toward the high mountain of Debra Tzai, Mountain of the Sun. At the base, within the thirty-foot-high walls of the imperial city was the palace of Woizero Attitegeb. Forty-four churches had been built on the eminences where the trees were—African pines, tamarinds, junipers, the giant ancient warka, acacias—and Ravi rode through the denuded valley peopled with the cone-shaped tukul mud huts, the grass carpet the color of Maine tourmaline. In the rainy season, rivulets of fresh water burbled downhill through craggy streambeds, watering wild sweet pea, thyme, clover, and daisies.

Woizero Attitegeb's palace was a two-story structure built in the Portuguese style, adjoined by a round church, all in a ruinous condition from the crumbling of lime mortar in its walls, excessive rain, and poor drainage. The broad bridge over which Emperors had once rode to chapel so that the earth may not soil their royal feet was crumbling away.

The Banquet Hall at Qwesqwam was famed for huge feasts. The Queen Mother had a large complex of servants' quarters that contained colossal kitchens and bakeries, and places for weavers and other servants—as well as, Ravi knew, a room with a sunken bath. Ravi often came here to consult with the "First Lady of Gondar" on methods to reinforce her buildings, but she thought they would just be pillaged again, and she seemed to only want to meet with Ravi for social purposes, to drink *tej*, a honey mead restricted to the aristocracy, and hear word of her son and Tewodros.

Today Ravi wore his rich red brocaded *kamis* silk shirt given him by the Negus Tewodros and, though the usual custom was to ride your mule while your shield-bearer led your horse, today he sat astride his gelding Selpha. Surrounding the castle were the usual scores of followers—shield-bearers, musketeers, or outdoor servants, all with mules that were richly or meanly caparisoned. There were horsemen recently arrived with messages, and worst of all the supplicants who couldn't gain entrance to Woizero Attitegeb's levee, loudly bemoaning their stories of sorrow. The lucky ones had a judge sent out to them, and others were driven off by sticks. Turbaned lay priest *debterahs* milled among beggars, sometimes a man whose eyes had been put out by the Queen Mother's orders, paying court to obtain a pittance of a pension.

As they dismounted, handing their reins to a groom, Misha remarked, "That fellow's sobbing as if he's kicking the bucket!" He gestured at a man who rent a shirtfront that was already in ribbons.

Ravi smiled. "He's just being polite."

"Polite? Hey, you!" Misha shouted at the man in Amharic. "Why do you scream so? Has your child just been murdered?"

The man abruptly stopped wailing and renting, and approached the *frenjoch* on wobbly legs. "Why? I did not want anyone to feel lonely."

"See?" Ravi continued up the path, pushing through the crowd of applicants who beset him for alms in the name of every saint in the annals.

"Lonely? That's ridiculous."

"The people inside the palace get lonely if it's too quiet."

Ravi was let through the modest doorway, and Misha's scrabbling bare feet rushed to catch up with him through the courtyard. "Do you know what, Rav?"

"What do I know?"

"You know more about this country, but *I* like it better."

"Is that so?"

"Well, you have all the book learning, and you play with your theodolite—"

"Survey the land."

"—and you look at manuscripts all night long. But really . . ." Here Misha dropped his voice, as they were nearing the audience chamber, and Woizero Attitegeb's chamberlain greeted them with a toothy smile. "It would be I who would choose to live here forever."

Ravi halted and looked down at his tall friend. "You're completely right, Azmach Michael. You aren't the same desperate, suicidal Russian chef I met on the *Gold Hunter*. I'd venture to say you don't even want to join the French Foreign Legion anymore." For the poor downtrodden man had been about to throw himself over the rail when Ravi had coaxed him out of it with some Kentucky whiskey and tales of faraway lands where they might be kings.

Misha smiled proudly. "That I don't, Basha Falaka!" The emotional imp stood face front before Woizero Attitegeb's chamberlain. "Good afternoon, Yeddee! How have you passed the time since I last saw you? We are here for a private audience with Woizero Attitegeb."

Yeddee sidled up to the *frenjoch* and spoke in low tones. "That is good, and of course you may come in, but I have first to tell you, there is already a *ferenje* inside . . . a *woman!*"

A *woman*? Both *frenjoch* mouthed the words at each other.

Ravi was the first to speak. "Yes, we know that! We are expected."

Yeddee elegantly waved them into the presence-chamber. Favored eunuchs passed to and fro with whispered messages, and groups of noblewomen and dandified men milled with their shield-bearers hoisting their buffalo-hide shields embossed with delicate silver designs. The lot of aggrieved men perspiring in their red silk shirts looked as though they were set for execution with their anxious faces, and all eyes were upon the *ferenje* woman who sat before Woizero Attitegeb on a low *alga*, as demure and unsullied as though she had just wafted in from Boston. Ravi even heard Misha, beside him, catch his breath at the sight of her so proud in her finery, it had been so long since they had seen a *ferenje* woman in other than a *shamma* or a plain threadbare dress.

And what a stunner she was, with her elliptical skirt arranged about her precisely, the hoops of which must have been a good eighty inches wide, as she needed an entire couch to herself to sit. Her dress of iridescent copper silk was embroidered with bows and pine branches, and it showed off what Ravi had already suspected to be her full-blown form to a fine degree. She sat as regally as Woizero Attitegeb, her lustrous bronze hair done up in a 'waterfall,' a cascade of curls held with tortoiseshell combs—all this Ravi knew from his voracious study of women's fashion, poring over the Peterson's magazines the European wives at Gaffat were sometimes brought. For he loved women, and made as thorough a study of them as of Mohammed, Father Lobo, languages, swords, and the heavens.

No, she was no missionary.

Her shoulders, browned by the sun, showed that she often eschewed a parasol, and her dark, assessing gaze that boldly took in his entire height was by no means shy or retiring. Ravi heard her gasp, and her archly puffy lower lip, blooming as though rubbed with coralline salve, remained askew. He kept his eyes on her for some seconds as he strode to Woizero Attitegeb, seated on a special throne *alga* covered by a carpet of red damask with gold flowers. Misha behind him fell upon his knees and his palms, touching his forehead to the floor. Ravi merely got down on one bended knee, his *shamshir* clattering against the stone floor, in order to kiss Woizero Attitegeb's hand, as someone prodded Misha to his feet.

"I have brought you a jewel." He withdrew a scented paper packet from his *zenar*. It was merely one of the baubles Ravi collected in his forays, a filigree peacock brooch from Messrs. Tiffany & Co., but Woizero Attitegeb beamed like a child.

"Please, show me how to wear it."

Ravi had to move aside her profusion of silver chains, the blue cord of her *mateb*, and her jingly amulets in order to pin the brooch to the breast of her calico shirt. "This is from New York," he said, and he felt the *ferenje* woman jump again at the sound of the American city's name. "These stones are emeralds, probably from Granada. The Duke of Devonshire has one in his cabinet, and Mr. Hope of London has the finest of all."

"I have seen these stones, from Upper Egypt. Basha Falaka, you always bring me the finest things. And a great calm comes over me whenever I see you." She waved him off his knees and onto a couch servants had caused to be brought over for the two men. Ravi allowed Misha to sit nearest Woizero Attitegeb in order to be closest to the *ferenje* woman, whose direct assessing gaze was by now so ardent Ravi felt heat spreading over his shoulder and arm.

"We have a guest," said Woizero Attitegeb. "Missus Chamiss of America. She is telling me that the moon and sun are the same in her country as ours. She will tell me where the tablets of Moses are."

Grateful for the introduction, Ravi stood again and bent at the waist to kiss the woman's hand, as there was no room to kneel or sit next to her. "Missus Chamiss," he breathed, allowing his lips to linger a bit too long for propriety. She had a giddy scent of orange blossom that brought to his mind the American South.

"I am *Miss* Delphine *Chambliss*, sir."

And her voice! It was low and well-modulated, smoky—he loathed the chirpy twaddle of some women who sounded like chipmunks, and drove men from them with their shrill descriptions of things. "Captain Ravinger Howland of the United States Army Corps of Topographical Engineers."

He remained bent with his eyes level to hers to assess her reaction, and it was pleasing. She yanked her hand away, whispering, "The U.S. Army!" She called to Woizero Attitegeb, "We have met before, Your Majesty!"

The chamberlain Yeddee interpreted, and Woizero Attitegeb wanted to know where and how they had met.

Ravi decided it would be prudent for him to answer. He stood erect, hands behind his back, and reported in Amharic, "Metemma, a few weeks ago. We were on an errand from Tewodros to get some food for the troops."

Miss Chambliss stood too. "Did you tell her how your men plundered and murdered? They killed one of my attendants, sir! The U.S. Army indeed! Is this how the U.S. Army trains troops, to murder their own people? For Metemma was not at war with Abyssinia, last I looked!"

Ravi wished he could tell Yeddee to stop translating now. He faced Miss Chambliss boldly. "Miss, the men are hungry, and I have long ago given up on telling them they must not seize food from the people. We are not in America now, and a different set of rules prevails."

"Different set of rules . . . ?" she sputtered. "And what *rule* gives a hungry man the right to assault women?"

"I did stop them. And I can see from where I stand that not only did they not hurt you, you were enhanced and invigorated by the experience."

Miss Chambliss looked angelic with her mouth askew like that. Ravi was taken by surprise when she raised a hand, palm forward, as though about to strike him. "Invigorated?" she whispered. "Why, you callous, murdering, raping monster!" She gasped for breath through her anger.

Ravi was awash with shame. He usually selected his words wisely, and this had not come out as he intended. "I apologize, Miss, I didn't mean to imply that you were in any way stimulated by the—"

That oiled potato-head Kaspar Nagel leaped up as though at a husking frolic, his limbs akimbo with indignation, insinuating himself between Ravi and the woman, safe now they were in a room full of men with swords. "You must desist at once, sir! Your cruel ways with women are famous! You are impugning this good woman's character to suggest she would in any way be intrigued by such violence."

Ravi said calmly, "I *meant* that she seems in robust health." He took two steps to the right to address the woman. "As for the men of your party, I am sorry indeed for their demise, but I seemed to have been lacking a few members of my own party. One was discovered dead with a bullet in the back, and I witnessed your alacrity in dispatching my lieutenant."

"*Lieutenant.*" The woman boiled with barely concealed rage. "Is that what you want to call that reeking low-life *creature* who was leading four other men in attacking my manservant?"

Ravi was forced to address the glowering Takrury standing behind Miss Chambliss' couch. "For a manservant you are very well served, Miss. You will never have to fear the horrors of the kitchen, sitting room, or shithouse, as I am sure he will lustily loot, plunder, burn, and raze any room that does not meet your exacting standards." He turned to the chamberlain. "Will you *please* stop interpreting now?"

To Ravi's surprise, the "manservant" spoke decent English. He intoned lugubriously, "There are cures for the hurts of lead and steel; but the wounds of the tongue, they never heal."

During a brief silence every person in the room regarded the black pilgrim, his limpid eyes shimmering with a pride Ravi appreciated.

Woizero Attitegeb, also getting to her feet, spoiled the pleasant interregnum.

"You are all from the same country; you are all *Inglaise*. Can you not exist in peace? As we do with the people of Begemder, Semien, Lasta, Gojam, Tigré, and Shoa, that the Emperor Tewodros has reunited into one Abyssinia."

Ravi cleared his throat. "Ah, actually, Your Majesty. Our

campaign last year to the prosperous kingdom of Shoa was a disaster. We lost not only the province, but a large portion of our army."

Woizero Attitegeb shrugged, waving a dismissive hand at him. "You must be friends with your compatriots. You killed some of her party, she killed some of yours, so you are equal. You must now kiss her hand, to show your friendship."

While Ravi relished this order with a glee that was not altogether hostile, he saw that Miss Chambliss knew enough Amharic to understand the command, for she recoiled from him with a face of horror. Kaspar made a feeble attempt to get between them, but Ravi was swifter, breaching the distance between them with one broad step. He grabbed the hand that she tried to wrench from him, and yanked it to his mouth without bending much, as he enjoyed looking her directly in the eye when he said, "Cut down the *kantuffa* in the four quarters of the world, for I know not where I am going."

He kissed her hand softly with parted lips, reveling in the orange blossom scent of her velveteen skin. Her flashing sloe eyes seemed to go soft around the edges, and she didn't resist anymore. Indeed, she said in a voice of wonderment, "Ah, so you are a poet too. A poet who left me to the dogs in Metemma."

"My dear," Ravi said ever so gently to her hand. "I hope you will never have to know the reason I left you in Metemma."

The splendor of this moment was mitigated by the disgusted sounds of outrage sputtered behind them by both Misha and Kaspar. But the magic was truly ruined when there came a dull thud accompanied by a rustling of silk, and Miss Chambliss and Ravi, still holding her hand, turned to dash to Woizero Attitegeb's side, for she had collapsed on her couch.

"Attitegeb, Attitegeb," Ravi called distantly, placing his hand on her clammy forehead. Miss Chambliss lifted the Queen Mother's feet onto the couch so she could recline, then felt her pulse with her fingers in the pit of her throat. Ravi had assumed a beau had given her the Congressional Medal of Honor she had worn on a blue ribbon around her neck in Metemma, but the truth was always much more complex.

"What is your complaint?" she asked Woizero Attitegeb in Amharic, as an attendant pressed a cool cloth onto The Queen Mother's forehead.

Ravi told her, "She has been known to fall prey to *tej metall*. If you drink liquor outdoors in the sun, the *tej* becomes a dangerous *metall*. It produces what is basically a cold in the head."

"Oh, Jupiter Ammon, I've never heard such swill in my life. And what does she take for it, eye of newt?"

"Her *hakim* has been giving her *gerowa* leaves, dried, pounded, and mixed up in a large *wancha* with honey and butter."

Miss Chambliss snorted skeptically. "While I am certainly a believer in herbal remedies, I do have some arsenicum in my medicine chest at home. If you will stay here with her, I shall go and retrieve it."

"Yes, of course." Ravi was chagrined when the ethereal woman rushed off. He had already in a short space of time become pleasantly stimulated by her presence, which seemed to pique and soothe him at the same time.

"Is this the *hakim*?" Miss Chambliss cried, and Ravi turned to see the doctor approaching them with the *wancha* of melted butter.

"Yes, that's him."

"Well, I don't suppose the *gerowa* will hurt, but do not in any case allow him to bleed her."

Ravi agreed heatedly. He had always held that this abomination had done much more harm than good, leading directly, irrefutably to dozens of deaths. "No, I abhor 'that scientific form of sudden death,' Miss. You can be sure I will protect her."

Ravi cradled Woizero Attitegeb's head in his lap, refreshing the cloth from a bucket of cool water. *What a singular woman is Miss Chambliss*, he thought. *She kills two men, but will not allow medicinal bleeding.*

Woizero Attitegeb stirred. "That woman, Missus Chamiss. You must be friends, Basha Falaka, but not *good* friends."

Ravi stroked her face with the back of his hand. "No, I will not. There is no danger of that happening," he lied. "I will make sure she safely leaves Gondar and goes back to her house in America."

CHAPTER FOUR
THE SAGA OF BURNT NJAL

"YOU'D THINK THE WORLD WAS COMING to an end, Kaspar, the way you're so hard at that awful peppery man." Delphine had her medicine chest before her on the low inlaid mother-of-pearl table. She had quickly found her arsenicum, and was now pondering on a bottle of Dr. Morse's Indian Root pills. "And do stop pacing so; you're making me dizzy with nerves."

"That peppery fellow is a maniac!" Kaspar cried. He broke out of the invisible box on the floor that dictated he pace only within its confines, and strode briskly to a balcony door. He flung a dramatic arm in Delphine's direction. "He is a sensualist of vast appetite, learned in every Oriental vice! Did you know he was ejected from West Point, the prestigious engineering school in your America? Ejected!"

"Ejected for what?" Delphine said vaguely. "Murder and rape, no doubt."

"Dueling! Yes indeed Missus, dueling has been outlawed but such a bloodthirsty bast—rapscallion such as him cannot resist, and he killed his opponent and fled like a skulking dog!"

"Is that so." She spoke quietly as she regarded the bottle. "This is good for scrofula and female complaints, but I suspect it's really got mandrake and gamboge; I suppose I could ask if there grows any nightshade in this country."

"Hey you!" Kaspar bellowed out the window, still in English, as though anyone in town understood that language. "Stop that unseemly screaming! You are causing a pounding in my skull!"

Delphine put her bottles down. "Kaspar, he's a *muezzin* calling his daily prayers." She strode to the window, pulled Kaspar indoors, and shut and latched the shuttered doors. "I rather like that fellow; he's much more melodic than the fellow over by the tea shop."

Kaspar moved next to the sideboard to pour some of his favorite whiskey. "These people are moral Hottentots! It is just deplorable that the only good houses are in this section of town. Now, my dear, we might send Abou back to the palace with the medicine, so you do not need to submit your pristine self to the insinuations of that murderous degenerate."

"I think not. He might give her the entire bottle, and I shall be blamed for her death. Now Kaspar, tell me. What did he mean? You heard what he said, when the Empress forced him to kiss my hand. I've memorized it, for it's curious. 'Cut down the *kantuffa*—'"

"—in the four quarters of the world, yes, yes, for I know not where I am going. That is a proclamation the soldiers of Tewodros make before they march. The *kantuffa* is a terrible thorn that molests them by grasping their long buttered hair and *shammas*. I don't know why he would be repeating it to you. My dear, you *must* allow Abou to deliver—"

"Abou, you are coming, yes? Kaspar, I need you to do an important errand for me. I believe the Empress needs a censer, and I have seen some lovely ones in town, brass with lovely chains, and incense. I've seen rosewater, sandalwood and ambergris in the markets. That would make wonderful incense."

"Miss Delphine, I protest—"

"Here, take this money—" Delphine was already out on the gallery that ringed the inner courtyard, her medicine and necessaries packed into a basket that she handed to Abou in order to retrieve the Maria Theresa dollars from her beaded reticule. Kaspar protested the entire way down the inner staircase, but Delphine was successful in waving the misinformed man off.

As they rode, Delphine ruminated. "Ejected for dueling . . . I'm quite sure that never happened! I wonder why Kaspar despises that man so. As for the *kantuffa*, I have no idea why he'd be telling me that."

Ravinger Howland was the most dangerously handsome man she'd ever seen. She'd seen men in war, men grown hard and brutal through battle. She knew that wasn't the way they really were, but circumstances turned them into these creatures, and once they turned that way, they never turned back. Their only emotions seemed to be anger and lust. Captain Howland had a poetic side, but it was probably only a ruse to ensnare the cultured, such as Woizero Attitegeb. The moment one turned one's back on him, he was probably devising all sorts of rude plots.

Still, she appreciated that he didn't dress his hair with butter as they all seemed to do, and he smelled very clean, like honey, chocolate rum, and pepper. The lingering feel of his lips on her hand had caused a shiver up her back, and she was glad that her frilly undersleeves hid the gooseflesh that rose on her arms.

At Qwesqwam, they were ushered into Attitegeb's bedchamber, whence Captain Howland had spirited her. The large stone room was rendered cozy, generously lined with rugs, and the Empress' high wooden bedstead was canopied by purple and lilac silk. Her only two valets stood distantly at attention, the *hakim* nowhere to be seen, as Captain Howland sat with familiarity on a lion's skin upon the bed, leaning casually forward on one elbow over Woizero Attitegeb's upturned face.

He seemed to be telling her a story in Amharic. Oddly, Delphine heard him speak the names of Njal, Gunnar, and Skarphedinn, and she could somewhat follow the tale of man-slayers murdering slaves, and then making peace, before Captain Howland said, "Ah, but here is the *ferenje* woman with the medicine." Sitting erect, he gestured for Delphine to place her medicine on a bedside table.

She tried to laugh frivolously. "It sounded like you were telling her the story of Burnt Njal, but of course that's impossible. I need a glass of water," she told Abou.

"And why should that be impossible." Captain Howland's voice was serene. His devil's eyes that had flashed with such ire were now limpid and warm in their intelligence. "I'm telling her the Icelandic saga. Everyone enjoys it very much."

"That's a fine saga to be telling Abyssinians. A blood feud that no one can stop, where everyone winds up dead."

"I've been telling it to them for years. It's something they can understand. Why don't you sit down on the bed, Woizero Attitegeb is quite informal with her *hakims*." Insolently, he patted the hindquarters of the lion's skin.

Sitting gingerly on the tail of the critter, Delphine smoothed her palm over Woizero Attitegeb's forehead and smiled at her. She was slightly feverish but nothing that would be imminently mortal, so Delphine turned to Abou and indicated he should place the cut glass *barrilye* of water on the table. "I'm not a *hakim*," she said as she uncorked the bottle of arsenicum.

"Ah, but I would beg to differ." When he spoke in English, he had the resonant and upper crust accent of the great city of Boston. "Your Congressional Medal of Honor would tell me otherwise."

Delphine stirred a spoonful of white powder into the glass and shrugged. "Oh, that medal? They don't give that to women.

Anyone can copy or wear one of those. I just wear it because . . . it looks good, and I thought it might give me respect, and possibly"—and here she gave Captain Howland a low, dark look—"prevent someone from murdering me."

"Ah, that makes more sense," said Captain Howland with raised eyebrows, and he seemed set to believe her when Abou put his oar in.

"Miss Delphine won that medal from the American President, son of John!"

Twirling to face Abou with wide eyes, Delphine whispered, "Abou, no . . ."

But the looming Soudanese would not be hushed. He continued with fervor, "She is a doctor, only allowed to serve as a nurse, but she healed thousands of men in places like the Battle of Cattle Run, Cheekamagga, and Getteeberk!"

Captain Howland leaned in toward Delphine on the lion's skin. "Well, *aha!* If *that* doesn't take the cake! 'The Battle of Cattle Run'!"

Delphine slid her fingers under Woizero Attitegeb's bony shoulders to indicate she should sit up. Captain Howland helped, brazenly lifting the tiny woman by scooping his large hands under her armpits and easing her back onto the silk pillows. "Abou is just repeating diverse stories I've told him about the war. He's confused, and gets them all mixed up. It's true, I'm a nurse of sorts, or was pressed into service as one, but I don't wish the entire community here to suddenly start applying to me for impossible cures for leprosy or epilepsy." The Empress dutifully drank the water. "My time here is very limited; I have a mission, and once that's completed, I shall return to civilization."

She walked to a window framed in dark red stone, pleased that it afforded one a view of the glittering sheet of Lake Tzana, some forty miles to the south. Captain Howland had also jumped from the bed, and she could see from the side of her eye his approach, his powerful arms swinging with arrogance.

"May I inquire as to your mission?"

She sniffed, despising him even more when she saw him withdraw an elongated brass tobacco pipe from his *zenar*. "I'm here to meet my fiancé." She was gratified to see his hands still themselves on the bowl of the pipe, and he looked up at her from under his eyelashes. "Kaspar has sent a messenger to him at a place called Gaffat, instructing him I'm in Gondar."

Suddenly he threw his head back and laughed, a full and booming laugh that had Delphine hypnotized by the strength of his throat muscles. "Kaspar? If that fellow has sent a messenger, you can expect him to go the long way around the Cape of Good Hope, if he doesn't drown in a barrel of *arrack* first."

"I hardly think—"

"So tell me: who's your fiancé? I'm sure to know him, as I'm familiar with every Tom, Dick, and Harry in this country. Tell me, and I shall send a 'fire-foot' messenger who will grab your fiancé and accompany him back here in grand style."

"Verlaine. Anatole Verlaine. He's a—"

"The poet!" This news seemed to clutch at his vitals. He pointed his pipe at her in rapt astonishment before launching into another round of all-encompassing laughter—this time he even had to grip his stomach, to prevent it from falling out with hilarity, she assumed.

While Captain Howland in his mirth held onto the windowsill, Delphine flounced back to the bedstead where she had left her basket of medicine. Angrily she shook some Dr. Morse's Indian Root Pills onto the bedside table, but at last she was able to hold her tongue no more. "If the mere mention of my fiancé's name is such a cause for humor, sir, then please be assured I'm not in need of your assistance. I have every faith in Kaspar Nagel . . . as if my fiancé didn't want to return to me, besides! I am sure he's already on his horse or mule or whatever one rides in this godforsaken country, and—"

"Miss, miss." With merrily dancing eyes, Captain Howland approached and had the nerve to enwrap her forearm in his strong fingers. "My intention isn't to disparage either yourself or your fiancé. Monsieur Verlaine is a fine poet—why, I read some of his scribblings myself and I found shades of Camões in some of his verses, but when I compared him to Lecomte de Lisle, he became very violent—"

"You *do* know him! Oh yes, he *abhors* Lecomte de Lisle! Tell me, Captain!" In her sudden eagerness to hear news of Anatole, she realized only later she had shaken off his hand and placed her own hands against the warmth of his powerful chest. "Where did you see him? When?"

His jollity fell from him, but he didn't move to avoid her touch. He teased her with his condescending beast's eyes, and continued the rest of his sentence. "—and my intention would never be to belittle a fine woman such as yourself, but just the image of the two of you together, why—"

Delphine jumped back a foot and narrowed her eyes at him. "Why what?"

"It's incongruous, is all. Monsieur Verlaine has his head in the sky, and you're obviously very firmly rooted on this Earth. He's a splendid fellow, just rather ethereal, capricious, and altogether unlike the solid firmness of . . . your person."

That was the first time she'd seen the brute seem even the slightest unsure of himself. A soft edge blurred his corneas as he looked down at her, his massive shoulders rising and falling with his excited breath. Delphine brushed off the moment with petulance. "Seeing as how you're the farthest person from a priest in this country, I've certainly not come to ask for your approval on my marriage." She sauntered back to the window to appreciate the luxuriant sunset primed to take place over the escarpment to the right of the lake. "Anatole has come here to *discover himself* and to shake out the bourgeois dust from his soul, and now that he's finished doing that, we may return." She breathed deeply, reveling in the green meadows below the castle window. The shrieking of the supplicants even seemed remotely charming, now they were kept at bay beyond the church.

She felt the heat of Ravinger Howland standing behind her. "Miss, I apologize if I seem importune at times. I'll send a 'fire-foot' to find Monsieur Verlaine. If that'll speed your egress from this country, then I shall be glad to assist. Though I must say, we could certainly use a proficient nurse such as you, now that the only *ferenje* doctor has been imprisoned."

"Yes," said Delphine. "I've heard about the recent misfortune of Mr. Rassam and Lieutenant Prideaux. The men who come to save the prisoners, imprisoned themselves." When she twirled around, she was shocked to find her face mere inches from the heat of his silken chest. Awash in the ochre light, his form was rich and shimmering with life. "You're a good friend of the Emperor. Why is he so fickle and unstable? Why does he imprison so many people who only mean to help?"

Delphine knew this would be a complex question, but even she was surprised at the thoughtful manner in which the Captain laid his pipe on the windowsill, then bore down on both palms to lean out the window and regard Lake Tzana. The silver cumulus clouds that raced over Gondar's valley cast mutating shadows on his excruciatingly handsome face, forming craggier depths to the half-moon scar on his left cheekbone. "Tewodros's spirit does not lie easy with him, Miss. He wishes to keep everyone close to him, for it's his deepest fear to be abandoned. He wants Europe, and most of all England to love him, and so he keeps making overtures that he interprets as being rebuffed. If he imprisons everyone, they can never leave, and so he'll never have to be alone."

"He's insane," Delphine said quietly.

Standing erect, Ravinger looked down at her. "Perhaps. But isn't it in everyone's nature to want to be loved? And do we not go to great lengths to achieve that?"

"But . . . we don't *imprison* those from whom we expect love, Captain."

They stared at each other, both riled for different reasons. The man had gipsy eyes that looked her through, and seemed to see something behind her. "Yes. But don't you sometimes wish that you could?"

Delphine tilted her head. "I suppose it would be comforting to know that the person one loved . . . would never leave."

Woizero Attitegeb stirred and moaned, but even then they didn't stop looking at one another. Finally the heavy wooden door opened and the *hakim* entered, yammering something Delphine could only make out as "medicine . . . too much . . . cold . . . camel's ass . . . nostrils."

Or perhaps she was shaken by her conversation with the Captain. She didn't speak to Abou until they were halfway through the town, and then it was only to say, "Shall we go to the restaurant with the chickpeas and olives?"

HE WAS THE ONE ASSIGNED TO bring the silver Maria Theresa dollars.

He rode through the narrow streets of Islambet accompanied by Woizero Attitegeb's Badjerund, the man in charge of the treasury, and three spearmen. As Christians, they had the right to salute any Mussulman rudely with their left hand, and two of the spearmen did, but not Ravi. The most he did was shout "Step aside!" in Arabic, and as many of the faithful already knew him as a learned *hadji* this was basically unnecessary.

Miss Chambliss' portico was cluttered by an imploring gaggle of folks, seemingly all afflicted by one of the ills to which flesh is subject. They bleated, *"Abiet, abiet; medhanit, medhanit."* *Lord Master, medicine, medicine.* They were so persistent, Ravi had to shove several in the shoulders with the blade of his *shamshir.*

The surly Abou let Ravi and his retinue inside the carved doors. Abou shouted out to the portico, "There is no medicine here! We have told you! Go away!"

Ravi had not been in Cameron's house for a couple of years, and the potted foliage in the courtyard seemed to have grown ten feet. He was pleased to see workmen scraping off some of the Italianate mosaic tiles that comprised the floor, in preparation for replacing them.

"Captain Howland."

She was at the top of the stairs, rigged in the tartan plaid dress of the day of the horse duel, and she did not seem displeased to see him. Ravi wasn't prepared for the surge of excitement and fondness that overcame him when he saw her there. He had no hat to doff, so he bowed low. "Miss Chambliss, I am your humble servant."

She laughed melodiously. "Oh, bosh to this 'servant' business. Please do come up."

As he led the way up the stairs, Delphine queried, "And who are these gentlemen? I appreciate the flattery of an escort, but these overly large spears give me an attack of nerves."

Had it been so long since he'd been in the presence of a refined *ferenje* woman attired in modern dress? As he followed her to the drawing room, he was overwhelmed by her wake of honeysuckle scent. "I left one of them out front to antagonize the hapless pilgrims bowing to Mecca in the street; the other two are for show, and they can stand outside this door."

The drawing room, too, had been tidied, and Ravi felt the feminine hand on things. Tapestries of Damascus had been draped from balcony doors, and tied to the sides with tasseled silk. One sideboard that had previously only displayed dull bottles of Hennessey's brandy now boasted golden and silver pots, kettles, dishes, Bohemian glasses, Sevres china, and Staffordshire pottery. Another sideboard glimmered with wine bottles of Champagne, Burgundy, Greece, Spain, Jerusalem, and bottles of Jordan water.

The woman walked to the liquor sideboard. "Yes, those apostles outside my front door seem to have a mysterious belief that I'm a *hakim* and have *medhanit*. How they could have formed that opinion?"

Her sarcasm made Ravi edgy, a feeling he was unaccustomed to, and he was glad when she turned with a radiant smile, coming toward him holding in two palms a *barrilye* of the burgundy wine. He bowed a little, feeling as though his sword was poking out at all the wrong angles. Did she know it was a sign of an inferior to present anything with both hands?

Ravi accepted the *barrilye* with his right hand. "People talk, miss. I am sure the servants at the palace told their friends, who told their friends, that you had healed Woizero Attitegeb."

"And have I?"

"Yes, as a matter of fact. This morning she was spiriting around her rose garden, she prayed in her icon chapel, and she visited her confessor. She's ordered more censers from the merchant you bought yours from, and has bought up all the ambergris in the city. In fact, she has a grandson she wishes you to call on—"

Miss Chambliss waved him to a divan, taking a seat opposite him on another divan. "Captain, of course I will do as much to heal your friends as you did to heal my friends in Metemma."

Ravi twitched with sudden rage to hear her bring up such an

ancient feud. He slammed his *barrilye* onto the table, but managed to contain his anger. His voice, however, trembled when he spoke. "Miss. I've been sent here by Woizero Attitegeb with a gift." He gestured impatiently at the Badjerund, who had been waiting by the inner door with his velvet-lined box of Maria Theresa dollars. The man came forward, holding the box with both hands proffered toward the woman.

"I've been wondering why this fellow's been standing here. I thought perhaps you'd brought a picnic." But the haughty woman stood too, and inclined her head curiously toward the box.

Ravi's hand tightened on the grip of his *shamshir*. "I have a hundred Maria Theresa thalers from Woizero Attitegeb, as thanks for your kindness. Please accept them."

She leaned over and glanced inside the box the Badjerund held open for her. "I cannot accept payment for doing what any other charitable person would do, Captain. Now perhaps if you would let me get a glass of water, we could drink to the happy engagement—"

Ravi placed a hand on her arm. "You don't understand. Refuse nothing, for then you have a place of authority with the priests and citizens, otherwise you'll be robbed and murdered the first time you venture a mile from home. They'll reckon you have chests of your own silver, or you can make gold, or you bring whatever you want from the Indies."

He saw her lower lip tremble—perhaps, he imagined in his arrogance, she finally saw the weight of his words. She treated him like a countryman from a ghastly burg, the way she sneered down her nose at him. Ravinger was on the verge of leaving, and it was only the echoing trills of a lethargic song of some sort that stopped him cold, his hand still on her forearm.

They both turned their heads toward the gallery door. A large clattering and sounds of a tussle came from the courtyard, then the lusty tenor of song began its travel up the inner staircase. "When the sun comes back, and the first quail calls, follow the drinking gourd! For the old man is waiting to carry you to freedom if you follow the drinking gourd!"

Ravi and Miss Chambliss swiveled their heads to stare at each other, then resumed looking at the gallery door, waiting for the apparition. They were not disappointed by the sight of Kaspar Nagel, still in his European suit, though it was ratty at the edges and bore the signs of several dining mishaps. He didn't appear to see them as he navigated to the liquor sideboard. "The riverbank will make a very good road, the dead trees show you the way! Left foot, peg foot traveling on, follow the drinking gourd!"

Even the Badjerund wrinkled his forehead skeptically as he gazed sideways at Kaspar's back. Finally Ravi was compelled to shout, "If your gourd is quite empty, Herr Nagel, I'll be taking my leave now."

Kaspar was galvanized for a moment. He twirled dramatically to face them, still gripping his *barrilye*. "*You!*" he yelled quietly.

To circumvent any potential harangue, Ravi stepped to the center of the room. "Yes, it's me, your favored nemesis; I've come with silver from the palace, and I'll leave with silver, because your ward here doesn't believe in accepting payment for services, unless you can convince her otherwise."

"*Silver!*" Kaspar breathed.

Miss Chambliss sighed. "Kaspar, I simply cannot accept a hundred Maria Theresas for ten cents worth of medicine. If Woizero Attitegeb were to pay for the building of a hospital, I could see some good in that. The Arabs are miserable doctors—I've seen them treat dogs for distemper by throwing them off a roof, and immunize them against rabies by tossing them into a burning hut. I have experience in setting up hospitals, and I am sure I could convince Colonel Merewether in Aden to send supplies—if only I were staying!"

Ravi recalled his goal to expedite the woman's journey out of the country. "Yes, a hospital would be lost on these people. They would only plunder the supplies and leave the dying patients on the street." He bowed to Miss Chambliss, "Thank you for the glass of Bordeaux wine. It's very rare to find that in these parts, especially since the aphids have nearly ruined all the grapes in France. If you'd allow me to pay you a dollar for the remainder of the bottle . . ."

To Ravi's utter astonishment, the squiffy missionary grabbed the bottle of Bordeaux wine from the sideboard and eagerly handed it to him. "Please take this. Consider it a sign of goodwill. For as we know, 'Give strong drink unto him that is ready to perish, and wine unto those that be of heavy hearts'." Without even asking for the dollar, Kaspar turned to Miss Chambliss. "My dear, you must become very calm. In fact, you must sit down, so as to prevent fainting. Where is the laudanum? You must prepare yourself for the most lovely and shocking experience—"

But Miss Chambliss' eyes shone even brighter at his words, and she did not sit down. "What is it, Kaspar? Could it be . . . ?"

"Oh, for Christ—" Ravi muttered to himself, and was again about to take his leave with his bottle of rare wine when there rose a racket in the courtyard below. Abou must have been successful in keeping the limbs of the dying on the outside of the door, for only one set of bare feet now pounded up the staircase. All animation fell from the woman's face—in fact, Kaspar supported her by the arm—and she moaned, "Anatole!"

The tumble-haired, crazy-eyed poet raced in the gallery door, his *shamma* girded at ease with bare right arm and shoulder. The couple ran for each other, wrapping their arms around the other's necks, and Ravi was stunned at the instant wave of jealousy that swept over him. He had been in solitude in this country for entirely too long! He must find some fresh women from Tewodros's harem tents.

As it would be even ruder to leave now without greeting Monsieur Verlaine, Ravi was forced to watch the ecstatic couple seemingly intent on squeezing each other to death, and the even stranger sight of Herr Nagel standing nearby, beaming with approval. For lack of anything better to do, Ravi uncorked the wine and refilled his *barrilye* before the couple finally unlatched themselves.

After various nauseating terms of endearment, Anatole asked the woman, "Why did you follow me here, Delphine? It is much too dangerous! I never meant for you to come here. You are much too weak and ill."

Miss Chambliss wiped tears of happiness from her face with the back of her hand. "Anatole, I couldn't continue without you! My spirit has so intermingled with yours that after you left, I was stuck with Antoine, Arthur, and George—it just wasn't the same! I was bereft, a miserable skeleton of a human, the only time I felt alive was when thinking of you and reading your poems over and over. Please, *mon cher coeur*, do not be angry with me. I was only getting weaker and sicker in Paris without you. I've become invigorated and enervated in this beautiful clean Abyssinian air."

Still Anatole frowned. "But how could you have undertaken this voyage—alone! If I would have known, I would have forbade it."

Miss Chambliss gripped Anatole's *shamma* in her fists. "But I am here now, and I am not leaving without you. Antoine has arranged for *Hiver Désolé* to be published in the *Revue Pour Tous*, and—"

"It does not matter! Ah, *mon amour*, you cannot stay here. You must return to Paris—no, to America! Immediately."

"As you must! If it's dangerous for me, then it's dangerous for you as well. Did you know this Emperor is imprisoning Europeans all over the place? He's got a screw loose."

Anatole laughed disarmingly, as though the pixilated king were a source of the highest amusement. "Yes, I do know. That is how I got a job in Gaffat at the foundry—there were no men left. It is all one and the same to me—Tewodros loves me, so I don't have to fear."

"But what are you doing blacksmithing, Anatole? You cannot work with your hands—that's work for other men, women, not a poet! You are the equal of Theodore de Banville!"

"Bah! No work is too good for a poet. Poets must learn the growth of the soil, the heat of the furnace, how else are we to know what to write? I certainly learn nothing drinking absinthe in Paris. You must absolutely turn around and go back, *mon amour*. I will take those spearmen outside that door and pay them to accompany you back to Massawa."

Ravi spoke, glad for the chance to break up the insipid quarrel. "I always took you for a wise man, Monsieur Verlaine. Those are the sanest words I've heard all day. This delicate woman"—here he gestured with his *barrilye* at the "frail" woman in question—"cannot take the rigors of the Abyssinian highlands, not to mention the imminent danger of—"

Anatole spun around upon hearing Ravi's voice, and the sight of him caused an expression of awestruck ecstasy to appear on the comely young man's face. He threw up his arms with glee, took four long strides over, and enwrapped Ravi in a hug, nearly lifting the much more muscular man off the floor in the process.

"Ravinger Howland, my Likamaquas, ah, Basha Falaka, *amour de ma vie!*" He withdrew only far enough to pound Ravi chummily on the chest, gaping such a toothy grin it seemed his face would split in half.

Ravi, unaccustomed to displays of affection among men, tried to extricate himself—and besides, Ravi now had splashes of the valuable Bordeaux wine across his silk *kamis* shirt—but Anatole would not allow it, gripping him tightly nearly in a wrestling hold while proclaiming, "*Mon Dieu*, how are you acquainted with this giant handsome beast? He is the reason I love Abyssinia. He talks of Indian philosophy, and strange Negro habits of lust and cannibalism, or tells descriptions of Chinese abomination and Russian self-flagellation until the stars go out! Delphine, you never have met such a fearsome *vigoureux* man—have you seen him shoot, or sword fight, or wrestle on the ground?"

Trying to peel Anatole's arm from around his neck, Ravi scoffed, "Oh, pah. Abyssinians know nothing of wrestling or boxing. It's nothing to beat them." He had seen Miss Chambliss' face fall a degree with each rapturous outburst from Anatole.

"I have not had that happy occasion as of yet," she replied meekly, "but I have had the pleasure of seeing him throw a man off his horse with his lance."

On the pretext of pouring Anatole some of his wine, Ravi managed to disengage, and he moved to the sideboard. "I've no wish to discuss myself now, monsieur. You must make plans with your beautiful and frail fiancée to return to Massawa—I'm sure Tewodros can make much better cannons without an acclaimed French poet, besides."

"No, no!" Kaspar cried. "You must *both* stay here in Gondar, out of harm's way. It's incredibly safe here, and Monsieur Verlaine can write poems, and Miss Delphine can practice her doctoring. Is this not a beautiful spacious home? There is a big bathtub, and fresh air from the Mountain of the Sun, and—"

"Bah!" proclaimed Anatole, accepting the *barrilye* from Ravi. He poked Ravi in the shoulder. "Tell her, Basha Falaka; tell her this is a dangerous place. How do you find Abyssinia?"

"Well. I generally go to Cairo and head south up the Nile."

Although Kaspar and Anatole looked on blankly with their self-same former expressions, Miss Chambliss seemed immeasurably cheered, and she burbled a feminine laugh, though her eyes were still laden with unshed tears. Ravi joined her in relieved laughter, but it didn't last long, for she suddenly blurted, "Why is it everyone is so eager to be rid of me? Kaspar and Abou are my only friends!"

She fled from the room.

Ravi took a few steps to follow her. He realized it wasn't his place to do so, and he turned to Anatole, expecting to see him follow. The poet merely looked at the empty doorway, sighing deeply and smiling, as though he had just experienced a particularly satisfying meal.

"Well?" Ravi prodded. "Won't you go and comfort her, monsieur?"

Anatole graced Ravi with his starry, fluid eyes. "She needs to be alone. It is a woman thing. She is overcome with emotion."

Ravi frowned. "Well, yes she's overcome with emotion, because you showed much more when you greeted me than when you greeted her, and now it appears you're eager, as she said, to be rid of her."

Again a look of excited adoration overcame Anatole's angelic face, and he stepped closer to Ravi. "Do you know? Last week I was talking to the Emperor about taxation in France. He told me 'The people of my country would sooner bury their money in the ground than trade with it or pay me a percentage of it.' I was apop—apal—" He turned to Kaspar. "What is this word? Amazed?"

"I think the word he is searching for is 'apoplectic,' is it not, Captain?"

Ravi turned to the missionary and demanded, "Why do you not go comfort the poor woman, Kaspar? She herself just said you were one of her only friends."

Kaspar held his hand to his chest. "I? Comfort? You have confused me with someone who comforts women, Captain Howland." He chuckled along with Anatole. "Why, I always wind up making them cry even more. Though that is not my main intention, of course!"

"Oh, for Christ's sake!" Ravi slammed his *barrilye* onto the sideboard and stomped onto the gallery.

Anatole told Kaspar, "Yes, when I comfort women, they always run screaming from the room . . ."

In times like this, Ravi was embarrassed to be of the sex that called itself male!

He briefly paused, leaning over the railing to shout to the courtyard below. "Abou! Get up here!" But Abou was occupied with a couple of the afflicted who had managed to break through the barricade, past the Badjerund who had fallen asleep in a chair, one of them a strident woman swathed in a *burqa* who wailed as though they had just taken her firstborn son.

"I cannot come up!" Abou yelled. "Your guards have gone out for dinner!"

"Oh, what in hell . . ." Ravi muttered, continuing down the gallery, opening every door until he found the woman's bedchamber.

  ✸ ✸ ✸

DELPHINE TRIED TO PREVENT SOBS FROM bursting forth from her lungs, but at length she gave up. She reasoned the ululating women in the courtyard would cover up any sounds of mortification emanating from her bedchamber.

She could not believe she had come this far only to find a man who did not love her.

Or, perhaps he did, and was just trying not to be too demonstrative in front of guests.

She alternately tried to cheer herself with memories of his proclamations of love, then sank into bouts of despair imagining him in her drawing room, displaying far more rapture at seeing a despicable captain of war he had probably only taken his leave of a week earlier.

Holding a handkerchief to her dripping eyes, she sat before her dressing table and grabbed the bottle of laudanum. She swallowed freely of the sweet syrup. She thought of Captain Howland and how he appeared to want her out of the country as well. Was she so gruesome? Did she have a *buda's* tail growing from her behind? She was not so old yet as to be termed a spinster and she had always been told she had a fine, proud, upstanding bosom. A man from New Orleans, who was not in any position to lie, had once told her she had a bewitching way about her, that she could charm the pants off the strictest Baptist, that she was a woman who was not aware of her own charms, but they snuck up on a man, and a man was taken by surprise, and when he was struck by her thunder, he was a man forever changed, and—*Oh!*

"Miss Chambliss?"

There was so much caterwauling going on in her house, Delphine could not be sure if she'd heard correctly. She waited for the personage to say again, "Miss Chambliss, may I come in?"

Replacing the laudanum bottle on her dressing table as though it were a handful of dog feces, Delphine wiped her mouth with her handkerchief and called, "Come in!"

In her besotted state, Ravinger Howland appeared like a magical satyr. The warm shadows cast by the lamp threw his features into a diabolical mask that was not unwelcome to her.

It was curious that he shut the door behind him, looking about the room like a furtive lover. "Miss Chambliss, I feel compelled to apologize for the actions, or absence of actions as the case may be, of your fiancé."

She tried to maintain a haughty expression. "He must apologize himself to me for that." But her voice was already faltering, and to hide her upset she arose from her chair and went to the balcony door. At this time of night, although her balcony looked down over an overgrown jungle of a garden, she could only discern the tops of the *ensete* trees, the glossy broad leaves of the Red Abyssinian banana.

The Captain followed; she felt the warmth of his body standing behind her. "I don't think he will, for he doesn't see he acted wrongly. I just can't bear to see women treated with a lack of manners."

He spoke gently, and seemed sincere, though Delphine could have made no end of sarcastic comments about the Captain's own lack of manners with women. Yet when she opened her mouth to speak, an unexpected sob escaped her throat. She covered her mouth with her handkerchief and fairly skipped to her bedstead, where she flung herself down, and didn't do a good job of covering her cries.

"Miss . . . Miss . . ." The Captain stood beside her, beseeching.

If she could stop crying, she would!

"Some men are just not very good in the company of women. Perhaps he was taken by surprise by your presence here, as he was not expecting to get married in Abyssinia. Perhaps he was planning to make a fortune, and return to Paris triumphant, and—"

"Captain," she was finally able to blubber, and she turned her wet face to him. "He wants me to leave the country *without him!* He expects me to rot in Paris while waiting months, perhaps years, for him to return! Or no, he said America, isn't that correct, well Captain I have to tell you there is nothing for me in America!"

Captain Howland sat next to her on the bed, and his body, muscled like a bull, was already soothing to her. He covered her free hand with his. "Now . . . that can't be true . . . don't you have any family there?"

"Family?" she whispered. Then, when the thought of "family" sent her into a fresh round of sobs she didn't try to hide, the Captain must have completely given up in frustration, for he enwrapped her in his arms—much as Anatole had done to him!—

and held her face to his chest. It was extremely calming, and she did not want to get tear stains on his fancy red silk shirt, nor on the lion's fur of his mantle, but she allowed herself to continue shaking with silent sobs.

His deep cultured voice calmed her, too, when he spoke against the crown of her head. "You're an accomplished nurse, Delphine. I've seen what you do, your touch comforts people."

That was his most noble failure at lying yet! "Oh yes, that's the ticket! I may have assisted in saving thousands during the War, but I was not able to save the people dearest to me. As for my supposed 'touch' and the mystical healing powers attributed to me, it's strictly the medicine, no more and no less." She lifted her face to look him in the eyes, and he did not pull back, as he had tried to do from Anatole. He was so warm, so solid and substantial next to Anatole's thin and studied elegance. He only released her as far as he had to, keeping both hands flat against her back. She basked in his honeyed presence, the aroma of pepper and ambergris. "As for 'family,' there is none. I'm an orphan. I had one brother who was murdered in Atlanta, and I was unable to help him due to being under lock and key in a southern prison, so I'm telling you, Captain—"

"Ravi, please."

"—there is nothing for me back in America!" She replaced her head against his chest because it felt good; indeed, it was the only comforting she had received in months. The man rocked her slightly, though she wasn't sobbing anymore. "Your touch is more calming than mine. You've succeeded in giving me serenity, as you did to Woizero Attitegeb."

"Ah, but it isn't the same."

Again she raised her head to look him in the eye. He smiled remotely, as though she were a favorite family pet, and he stroked her cheek with the back of his hand. How she longed to do the same, to feel the ridges of the half-moon scar on his cheekbone! But he was not the one who was upset. She must learn to cool off, or he would just think her an emotional ninny. She tossed her head a little, casually, throwing off the touch of his hand. "Why, yes, it *is* the same—you have a very soothing touch for women."

He still regarded her with amusement. "You're right about that—with women I do."

Delphine stood, though it was unpleasant to remove herself from his presence, and breezily walked back to the balcony doors. It was as dark as Egypt out, and the hubbub of the city had been reduced to the clankings of teacups, a few men in the streets calling each other or their mules like forlorn pilgrims in the night. "I shall stay here. And I shall not leave Gondar without my fiancé."

Ravi spoke more formally again. "That's your decision. I shall remain here myself, building boats for the Emperor on Lake Tzana. In between, I stay at the house of Herr Flad, if you should need anything."

"Oh, Herr Flad? Is he yet another whom your Emperor has ruthlessly imprisoned?" She was immediately sorry she said that, as when she turned to see Ravi, his kind face was back to an illegible mask of stoicism.

"No, Mi—Delphine. Herr Flad is a missionary for the London Society for Promoting Christianity among the Jews. We've sent Herr Flad as an emissary to London, to ask the Queen to send more artisans—engineers, chemists, blacksmiths, and the like. Now I must leave; you appear to be feeling better."

He kissed her hand—warm, lingering, as before at the Palace, all the while looking up at her with a dark portentous look. She tried to be gracious, but he was stirring something in her that wasn't entirely soothing. "Thank you, Ravi."

She followed him to the bedchamber door in order to watch him leave, his *kamis* billowing with a gladiatorial arrogance, the many braided rows of his tonsure gathered about in one pigtail down the middle of his broad back. He didn't stop into the drawing room to see Anatole, but he did pause by the front door where Abou was grappling with three fresh afflicted men, speaking to them in a tongue she didn't recognize a word of, so it must have been Arabic.

She drifted back to the balcony doors, taking her bottle of laudanum with her. Sipping disconsolately, she thought, *what a singular man. He slaughters men without a second thought, but he comforts women who are upset in matters of love.*

"As it should be," she whispered.

CHAPTER FIVE
THE STREET OF SHRIVELED INVALIDS

Qorata

TEWODROS SENT FOR RAVINGER TO RETURN to Lake Tzana.

He didn't want to leave Gondar. He was looking forward to the Feast of the Cross, and indeed he'd already heard criers near the Palace chanting "*Ahho Akhoy!* Awake from idleness! Awake from darkness! Maskal is coming!" During Maskal, bonfires were lit to pass the news from hill to hill that Saint Helena had found the True Cross, and it was always a festive time.

But if the truth was known, Ravi didn't want to leave Delphine.

True, he was still theoretically keeping an eye on her with a goal toward getting her to leave Abyssinia. But since holding her in his arms in her bedchamber, he didn't feel quite as mercenary about her. He had left her town-house changed in his outlook, and was determined to return to encourage her to nurse the afflicted, incurable or not. He had gone there once, but she was out with Kaspar and Abou. The lingering crowd of patients around her portico, some heaving, some out of their heads, some raising the roof with their wails, gave Ravi the creeps, and he had to betake himself back to Flad's house. He had never leaped to court death or illness, which was one reason he'd joined the Corps

83

of Topographical Engineers, to travel and map the West. It was an ironic thing now that the more gruesome aspects of living were the ones he was always party to.

Tewodros's messenger arrived, bidding him return to the Lake, as Tewodros had run into a few wrinkles with the "paddle steamer," more of a massive flat-bottomed boat woven of reeds of great thickness, driven by two wheels that required a hundred men to crank them deep enough to plow the water. He left with Misha, after sending a dispatch to Colonel Merewether in Aden asking that more medical supplies be sent to Delphine.

Tewodros had the loathing of the Bedouin for towns. He worshiped camp life, the fresh wind of the plains, and above all the view of his army artistically encamped around the hillock he had chosen for the imperial pavilion. He had made himself Emperor of all Abyssinia at thirty-five years of age, in the throes of vigorous manhood, brave as lion, adored by all bellicose soldiers. He had said, "I will have no capital; my head shall be the empire, and my tent my capital."

The hill now near Qorata was surrounded by a double line of bamboo fence, indicating Tewodros planned to spend some time there. As the grooms led their horses into the horse tent, Ravi and Misha appropriately girded their *shammas*.

Ravi asked casually, "Misha, who was that new woman we saw just now, the one with the blue *fleur-de-lis* tattoos on her forehead? You know the one; she was chatting with that wood-cutter."

"You have enough women!" Misha said sternly. "Rav, you've got Alitash the chosen one who keeps lingering outside your tent whether you're there or not, and you've got"—here Misha hushed his voice so low not even the flies could have heard him—"Gudit, and Elleni, and Worqit . . ." Standing erect again, Misha cleared his throat and looked straight ahead at the tent flap, guarded by two sluggish Gallas eunuchs. "Then there's your mooning over

Anatole Verlaine's fiancée like such a soaked man-about-town, to use your own terms."

Ravi turned about right. "All right, that's enough, Mikhail Vasiliev! I've had a bellyful of your self-righteously tedious slander!"

"*Ravi*," Misha warned, still gazing obediently at the tent flap.

Ravinger didn't care. Although their presence had been requested by Tewodros, it was customary to be kept waiting for hours outside the tent. There were already two Dejazmachs in front of them waiting, glancing over their shoulders nervously at Ravi's outburst. "I've not agreed to form a business partnership with you simply to listen to you recite a list of my fatal shortcomings."

"*Ravinger.*"

Ravi pointed at Misha's head. "Simply because your lover preferred her husband to you back in the Lower East Side, you fancy yourself an expert on the ways of love. Well I'm here to tell you, Azmach Michael, that I am vastly above getting hot for another man's fiancée."

Still facing front, Misha finally erupted. "You said she had eyebrows of Ethiopian blackness, vermilion lips and tongue, and she 'fought for female as for food when Mays awoke to warm desire.' Now tell me how you know the color of her tongue!"

"I was pickled when I said that! There is some question of those two being actually engaged, Misha. And I got the Ethiopian-eyebrow part from the Sheikh Nefzaoui in the sixteenth century, so I wasn't being original."

Misha broke his soldierly stance. He twirled to Ravi and growled, "You just doubt her engagement because you wish every single woman on this planet were your servant!"

"Listen here, I'm perfectly satisfied for her to imagine she's the fiancée of such an apt pupil of the Cretans and Chalcidians!"

"Oh, I see! Just because I'm not familiar with those poets, you scoff—"

"Basha Falaka, you may enter."

The Ras Engeddeh gestured them toward the tent flap. Ravi elbowed his way past the two Dejazmachs who had been there before him.

Emperor Tewodros, the King of Kings, was seated on a low *alga* raised a foot from the ground by a platform. Swathed in a voluminous yet plain *shamma* that covered the platform from his feet to his mouth, Tewodros uncovered his right arm to show himself as gracious to Ravi. He was a very handsome man of about forty and five, his rich chestnut skin complementing his refined European features, his slightly Roman nose and well-made mouth. His tightly plaited hair fit snugly along the shape of his skull. Although Ravi had known his black eyes to express fire, today they had a deer-like gentleness as he accepted a small horn from the *tej-asalefech* who had already tasted it. Around him gripping double-barreled pistols stood his Grazmach and Kanyazmach, his commanders of the left and right, as well as his faithful valet Paul, a former servant in the employ of the British Consulate at Massawa.

Ravi bowed on one bended knee on the luxuriant carpet. "Jan Hoy, I have returned at your request." He did not lower his head.

Unmasking his mouth to take a sip of the *tej*, Tewodros smiled and indicated Ravi should sit on the carpet, bidding the *tej-asalefech* to hand Ravi the *wancha* horn, an especial mark of favored status.

Tewodros was tireless in business, sleeping only a few hours each night, and he was strangely polite and charming when glad. He was a dashing ruler, invoking great love and adoration in his people when he wished, but all trembled when his ire was raised. In his early years he had shown clemency toward the vanquished, wishing them to be his friends, requesting nothing from them other than arms for his soldiers. He had been free from greed and generous to a fault. Like Peter the Great, he was a king of kings, overflowing with military idealism, a lover of the mechanical arts, possessed of unbounded courage. Yet when his beloved first wife who accompanied him on all campaigns had died, and he had wearied of the endless rebellions always springing up around him, he changed. He took greatly to drink and began exacting revenge upon his enemies in equal part. He burned men, and deprived them of their hands and feet for the slightest insurrection.

"Basha Falaka, my heart is open with joy to see you again. I have just been thinking and praying. I have killed hundreds of people, but I've never had a feeling of remorse for their death, because I know I'm doing the will of my Creator in punishing them as they deserve."

Ravi smiled indulgently, arranging his legs into the Indian position he found most comfortable. "It's good to find a King in Abyssinia proud of his dignity, capable of giving counsel in grave matters, not lightly saying 'yes' to things he doesn't understand." For Tewodros's visionary goal had been to reform Abyssinia, restore the Christian faith, and become master of the world. He had very nearly done that.

Smiling, Tewodros waved a hand at the Ras Engeddeh, seated next to Ravi on the carpets. "You've been in Gondar; how is Woizero Attitegeb?"

"I spent much time with her. She had a bit of *tej metall*, but that was easily cured by some very simple *ferenje* medicine."

The Ras opened his mouth to speak, but Tewodros was bursting with an exciting tale. "Basha Falaka, I have stormed the citadel of the devil and his imps!"

"Yes, Jan Hoy? Which citadel is that?"

"In the heights of Gojam not far from the town of Mota."

"Oh, yes! Devil's Mountain."

"Devil's Mountain, exactly. Do you know the small stream that arises among the precipices and joins the Abbai?" The Abbai was their word for the Nile.

"Yes, yes."

"It is a well-known place of evil spirits. Well, we took some of the smaller cannon they've made at Gaffat, and we bombarded their hiding places! Oh, Basha Falaka, the devil and his imps shrieked and howled, but we just pounded them without fail!"

With raised eyebrows, Ravi looked over to Misha, expecting to share a surprised look of commiseration, but Misha regarded Tewodros with shining eyes. "Did you get them?" Misha asked eagerly.

"Of course, Azmach Michael. I sent men in there to count the dead, they reported none on the field, so I proclaimed the death of his Satanic Majesty! The dead, of course, had run off, knowing they can't destroy men on Earth anymore, and they went to darken the inhabitants of another world."

Ravi nodded. "That is very impressive, Majesty. A considerable feat."

Tewodros beamed. "It was my finest hour all year! By the power of God I have exterminated those enemies."

"Oh, yes!" agreed Ras Engeddeh. "When we returned here, we killed an ox and had a most joyous feast. You should have been here."

"Yes," said Ravi. "I am sorry to have missed that."

Flush with his own success, Tewodros babbled on happily. "I think next I will do the same in Lasta, to show those faithless wretches who is the son of David and of Solomon. I want to capture that slimy swine Wagshum Gobaze."

Ravi lost no time in gently interrupting. "Do you think that's wise? If you take a force of men to Lasta, that will leave this area unprotected. And without your leadership, the factions might splinter even farther, and break off." He risked the Emperor's ire, but he knew it would be suicidal for Tewodros to venture into Lasta. There had been a steady flow of desertions for the past couple of years. In June Ravi had estimated his soldiery at forty thousand souls. In just a few months it appeared to have been reduced by one-fourth. "In fact, when I arrived last night, I heard news there's a rebel force not four miles from here. Perhaps we should go and—"

"Maybe we should go into Tigré and pound Dejazmach Kassa," Ras Engeddeh suggested.

With narrowed eyes, Tewodros gazed distantly at a spot between Ravi and Misha. His pupils had contracted into pinpoints of black sand, and everyone in the tent stopped moving. It seemed as though some even stopped breathing, the *tej-asalefech* holding the jar of *tej* in midair, about to pour into the horn. At last Tewodros said, "Providence wills that some delay should come between my coronation and my perfect success. I cannot just now abandon my people to the vicious Gallas."

There was an audible sigh of relief in the room, and Ravi gestured for more *tej*. "That is wise, especially now with the Feast of the Cross coming upon us. It's so joyous and merry and holy to view the *damera* bonfires, and to celebrate Empress Helena's discovery of the True Cross."

"Ah, yes," said Tewodros, happy again. "The crosses decorated with flowers . . . Basha Falaka, let's go shooting! It's been a long time since we've gone together and shot a good antelope or a river cow."

"Yes. While we do that, we could find out about these reports of rebels."

Getting to his feet, the signal for everyone else to do the same, Tewodros waved an unconcerned hand at Ravi. "It is nothing, just some boys playing at war. I think I will go to Magdala next."

Ravi raised his eyebrows. "Ah. Give my regards to Louisa."

Smiling grandly, with his fluttering hands Tewodros hurried Ravi out of the tent.

As they walked down the rise, Ravi grumbled to Misha, "He's crazy as a bedbug."

"How dare you say that? And why didn't you tell him about the *ferenje* woman in Gondar?"

Ravi snorted. "Now I think you're the pixilated one, Misha. You know what he would do."

"But he's going to find out eventually. Kaspar or Anatole or some random person will tell him. Woizero Attitegeb will tell her son."

"Kaspar won't. He knows why he shouldn't, and kept it a good secret when he went looking for her, unbeknownst to Monsieur Verlaine or me. Hello!"

For he had very nearly collided with Anatole Verlaine, girding his *shamma* as he exited the horse tent. Initially the cherubic poet had a look of irritation, but when he saw Ravi, a wide grin erupted on his face. "Likamaquas! You are exactly the person I am looking for!"

"That's why you're heading for the Emperor's tent?"

Anatole looked on vacantly. "I've just come from a small mission down the River Abbai. I must report to him about the rebel party of Tigréans."

"So he sends you? Why not Alemu Mariam, or a Fitawrari, or someone under the Grazmach or Kanyazmach? You've probably never shot a gun in your life."

Anatole shrugged helplessly. "I . . . was not alone. I brought some soldiers."

With hands on hips, Ravi huffed indignantly. "Why are you even here at all, monsieur? You've left your lovely fiancée alone in Gondar."

"Fiancée? Ah, you have a mistaken belief, Likamaquas. We are not, what is the word . . ."

Misha assisted. "Betrothed."

"Yes, betrothed. We are not betrothed. We are merely friends, that is all. I was very shocked when she followed me here."

Perhaps he saw Ravi's face changing to a darker shade of purple, for he added happily, "She is a very lovely girl! I merely . . . I have work elsewhere."

Ravi stood so close he nearly trod on Anatole's bare toes. "Yes, and your 'work' is in Gaffat building cannons, if you cannot take charge of your—of Miss Chambliss! Now listen here, Verlaine. I'm going on a shooting party with the Emperor, so we can't leave today. But you'll prepare to be ready at the first rays of the rising sun, for we're going back to Gondar. You're going to see that girl safely out of the country."

Anatole did not seem pleased. *"I'sh-shi."* Very well. "I will do whatever you want, Likamaquas. I'm sorry you don't approve of my attempts to serve the Emperor."

"It's not your attempts to serve the Emperor that I disapprove of, monsieur."

As Anatole walked up the rise to the Emperor's tent, the two partners continued downhill to their tents. Ravi said, "What do you make of that, Misha? Why do you think he was trying to hornswoggle us like that?"

"Do you think he was? I see nothing odd in the Emperor sending him on a scouting party."

"In any event. It's true what I conjectured, that he doesn't intend to marry that poor girl, and now he's leaving her entirely unprotected in Gondar. I'll leave tomorrow; you can remain here if you wish."

"You don't suppose . . ."

Ravi chuckled. "No. I don't suppose. She would be a lot more fleshy by now, and she's just a scrawny slip of a girl. All the same, he's obviously compromised her in some way, and he's going to set her straight."

※　※　※

"YOU TAKE AFYUNI." DELPHINE'S AMHARIC HAD progressed to where she could construct simple statements and commands. "You have dysentery. This is very simple. I've given you castor oil and tannic acid." She spoke the medical words in English, knowing the patients didn't know what she was talking about, anyway. The frail man in the blue *timkin* turban looked to be fifty years of age, though he was probably only twenty and five, and he trembled with respect at her words. She had constructed a "hospital" of sorts on the ground floor of Consul Cameron's town-house, allowing a few patients in, while the remainder had to stay in the street crying "*Abiet, abiet; medhanit, medhanit.*"

It was a horrifying yet invigorating state of affairs—her first patients since Georgia—and it gave her a case of nerves treating the first few, but after that it seemed to come natural, laying the citizens down on the *alga.* Just that action seemed to appease them, and her measly medicine chest became a grail upon which all eyes gazed with fervent desire. Every medicine bottle she withdrew was cause for upheaval among the families gathered around in the "surgery room"—all exclaimed loudly in tones of awe, giving Delphine the impression they were the dreaded strolling *azmary* minstrels who, notwithstanding her entreaties, would continue to bawl and shriek until she paid them to stop.

"I have heard that Abbas Kasim has *afyuni* in his house; you must go there and get some. That will help you."

The supine man smiled up at her with a relaxed gratitude. "My children will pay you."

There was a sudden commotion from the portico. A strident *ferenje* voice burst out and echoed throughout the entire courtyard. "*Delphine!*"

Delphine sighed, and looked up at Abou. "I'll be back."

"*Delphine!* What is this? I come home and I see lepers in my *portique!* What is the meaning of this?"

She emerged into the courtyard, wiping her hands onto a towel. Anatole stood in the middle of the courtyard with hands at his sides as though he held lit bombs, his honeycomb hair all in wild disarray about his skull.

"Yes, Anatole?"

"I have heard you are treating sick people again! Do you not know that is bad for your health?"

Delphine exhaled. "These people are needful. If I can give them some succor from my medicine chest, why shouldn't I?"

Anatole grasped Delphine about the forearms. "But you mustn't! Don't you see they will begin to prey on you, like—"

"*Buda!*"

A piercing shriek came from the vicinity of the front door, and both Anatole and Delphine craned their necks to see.

"He's a *buda!*"

There were six or so waiting patients Delphine had allowed into the courtyard, sitting on another *alga*, and at the sight of Kaspar they had all fled until they were pressed up against a wall, making themselves as flat as possible, like rats.

Kaspar screwed up his face and waved a disgusted hand at them. "*Ach, buda* . . . Is that all they can think about? Their depraved hearts and benighted minds know nothing of God or Heaven!" He walked toward the stairs, pausing to regale the multitude. "Do you not believe in the Prophets, and in Christ, of whom all the inspired writers unitedly testify?"

He didn't seem to expect an answer, for he continued up the stairs. Delphine handed her towel to Abou and followed with Anatole. She admonished the huddled group, "Just because he's a blacksmith, it doesn't mean he's a *buda*. Why do they not think you a *buda*, Anatole? You're a blacksmith as well."

Anatole laughed merrily. The sight of his enlightened face was almost enough to restore Delphine's faith in his soundness. "Ah, my hair isn't as white as Kaspar's, and I do not have the crazed look of a *kranked* German."

"You mean cronked. There are plenty of times Kaspar isn't cronked." They entered the drawing room, where Kaspar stood at the sideboard ruminating on the various bottles that beckoned to him. "He's a man of the cloth, Anatole. He's been here since '55. We must respect that."

"Oh, yes!" laughed Anatole. He spoke louder, in the direction of Kaspar. "And if you are such a man of cloth, why aren't you in Djenda converting your Falasha Jews?" For Kaspar's mission that he had founded with the Reverend Stern and Herr Flad was in Djenda, several hours' ride to the south.

Kaspar twirled around, a ruby *barrilye* in his hand. "And why are you not in Gaffat, smithing your cannons, kind monsieur?"

Anatole's response was swift, and heartened Delphine even further. "Because I am here tending to *mon cher coeur*, that is why!" He turned to Delphine, taking her hand and leading her to a red velvet divan, sitting her down as though she were an invalid. "*Mon cher*. We must find a way to get you back to Massawa, and then back to France. Tewodros controls all the roads through Simien; I think you should go through Axum, that is the swiftest way."

Delphine sighed. He was still pondering on how to get rid of her. "Anatole, dear. You needn't feel you have to remain in Gondar on my account. I'm perfectly cozy where I am, and tending to the ill has given me a fresh look at things. Believe it or not, that is what was missing, helping the afflicted. I know you find it a ghastly occupation, but it gives a peace to my mind that I was lacking."

Anatole squeezed her hand. "You said that was what caused your breakdown! You couldn't function after being a prisoner in

Georgetown—"

"Georgia."

"—and so you needed to take a tour of Europe to regain your health! Now you are going to put it in jeopardy again, and all because you wish to give useless medicine to some natives. What is the point?"

Sitting erect, Delphine bristled, and snatched her hand from his. "Anatole. It's not 'useless' to give medicine. Some of it works, and I'm awaiting more supplies. Abou has scared up some friends who will take me into the countryside to gather medicinal herbs and consult with *hakims*. And what is the harm if I can cure or heal a few people while I'm enjoying a serene stay in this town? Why, even that Captain of War of yours said I had a soothing touch."

At the mention of Ravinger Howland, Anatole's face relaxed into a mask of pleasure. "Yes, Basha Falaka is a very intelligent and knowledgeable man. Did you know he's a Knight Templar? I have seen the cross he wears pinned to his shirt, a lot like the medal you wear."

"A Knight Templar? That's just something childish, like being a Mason."

"Yes," chimed in Kaspar. "It's absurd for adult men to walk about in feathery admiral's hats trying to look like Napoleon."

"No, no," protested Anatole. "The Knights Templar was founded in Jerusalem to keep the highways safe for pilgrims. They were the bravest, strongest, most *vigoureux* men. When they got to France, King Philip declared them sodomites, said that they worshiped cats, so he executed most of them. Some escaped to Scotland, where Basha Falaka's grandfather was born, and he handed the tradition down to him."

Delphine sniffed. "That's a perfectly curious tale, Anatole, but I still say it's a silly excuse for men to dress up in outlandish costumes. You must be tired—"

"There are some parts not too outlandish." Kaspar surprised Delphine by agreeing with Anatole. "Christopher de Gama was also a Knight of the Order of Christ. He is said to have wept for joy when he heard of the Land of Prester John in Ethiopia, and landed a delegation at Massawa. They ventured inland, and met the Moor Ahmed Gragn, where his forces were mangled, his head was chopped off, and his body quartered."

"Yes, yes!" said Anatole. "Where his head fell off, a virtuous fountain sprang up, which fixes many incurable diseases."

Delphine smiled indulgently. "Ah! Well then, we should have to go see that, perhaps on our way back to Massawa."

"Ah, yes." Standing, Anatole shook dust from his *shamma*. "But first I have to pay a few calls here in town. Today is Maskal, and I am going to join all the children bathing in the River Qaha, as I am very *dégoûtant*. Please excuse me."

Delphine had never known Anatole to place any stock in cleanliness—indeed, as a poet worth his salt, he seemed to revel in dirt. "What's wrong with him? It's easier and much more private to bathe in the tub here in the house. What is that?"

For it sounded like a band of children, raising their voice in a cherubic wavering song, down in the street below. They chattered and clamored, and Delphine rose and went to the balcony. She smiled widely to see a crowd of Abyssinian children, standing in the darkening twilight, bundles of wood at their feet, their upturned faces entreating her for fagots of wood.

"Oh, they're darling!" Even the infirm on her portico had forgotten their troubles, and the crippled were walking, the mute were howling, the insane were serene.

Behind her, Kaspar grunted. "Those squalling ruffians! They are saying—if you can't understand—that they need the wood to contribute to the illumination, and that in honor of your visit they will encircle Qudus Gabriel—that's a local church—with a belt of fire that will blaze to the heavens and eclipse the very stars in the firmament."

Delphine laughed. "They're saying all that, then?"

"Of course! They're saying that such a flaming demonstration in your honor requires a substantial acknowledgement in return, so they want money—*you confounded children!*—to donate to the saints, of course, and—Stop that! You're not giving them any money!"

Delphine had her reticule, and had taken two Maria Theresa thalers from it. "Why not? I have some, and they have none." She tossed the coins over the balcony, causing a sudden vortex of singing children to dive, and she laughed with delight.

A delegation of children flowed down the street toward the river, shrilling like squirrels and chattering like mice. Delphine nearly choked on her laugh when in their midst rode Captain Howland, suddenly lit by smoky rays of the setting sun between two buildings. His muscular bay with four white legs was beautifully caparisoned with a red and white leather headstall, the round brass discs of the *benaika* sparkling when it tossed its head.

"Basha Falaka! Basha Falaka!"

All the children seemed to know him, and they molested him in their excitement, pulling on his feet, jumping to grab the reins, petting the monkey fur on his iron stirrup. Delphine knew she gazed upon a singular specimen of man as he rode so upright and rigid, as though a cannon could not even unseat him. His red silken *kamis* war-shirt made him stand out even more prominently in the street of shriveled invalids, and Mussulmen all in their robes of dirt and mud colors.

It was like watching the procession of a Prince. Perhaps because she didn't truck much with *frenjoch* anymore, she was unaccustomed to such sights, and she was shamed that a flush of excitement rose in her chest, tightening her lungs so that she felt giddy. Worse, the man looked straight up at her, beaming a victorious smile so dazzling it seemed to suck all the vigor from surrounding parts of the tableau. Everyone in the street became part of the cardboard scenery behind the man; they may as well have been flat trees or umbrella stands for all the importance they held when Captain Howland smiled up at her.

He waved an arm. "Miss Chambliss! May I come up?"

Kaspar smacked himself on the forehead. "*Mein Gott!* Not that dunderhead again!"

Delphine lifted an arm too. "Of course, Captain! Give your horse to our groom—Adan bin Kaushan, are you there?—and come right up."

Racing back to the drawing room, Delphine fumbled for a match safe on one of the low inlaid tables. Kaspar stamped indignantly to the sideboard. "You can't let that brute in again, Missus! He is just here to stir up more trouble!"

Delphine saw her hands were trembling as she set aside the glass hurricane of a lamp in order to light it. "Oh, Kaspar, I hardly think he's half as dangerous as he looks, and besides, you said so yourself—I work too much with the melancholy air of death and disease; it doesn't suit such a vibrant woman as myself, and if I'm shut up with only you and Abou to discuss worldly business with, I shall surely become one of the invalids before long. Oh! Kaspar, be a darling, and lower that chandelier so I may light it."

"By saying you needed company, I had in mind Monsieur Verlaine."

"Oh, bother. Here!" Stuffing the match safe into Kaspar's ruddy hand, Delphine fairly flew out to the gallery, reaching her bedchamber just as the heavy double doors of the courtyard that let onto the back garden boomed shut, indicating the Captain's arrival. She made a hasty toilette, wiping off the worst of the blood smears from her forearms and neck, dotting attar of roses behind her ears, and threading a pair of green glass earrings through her lobes. Her hair was a sweaty mess, and she whispered furiously to herself as she worked to braid it smoothly.

"Why am I making such a fuss for that odious Captain? Well, maybe it's as I just said to Kaspar. My brain is positively atrophying, and if I have to listen to any more of Kaspar's Märchen fables about yonder rheumatic dotards, the upbraidings of conscience, and shivering the chains of superstition, it shall drive me distracted! I'm dying for some fun, and that Captain appears to be capable of it. Now. Where is my hug-me-tight jacket? Shame there wasn't time to bathe . . ."

For the first time in months, Delphine wanted to look pretty, and the reasons didn't matter.

※　　※　　※

"DEACON NAGEL. YOU DIDN'T NEED TO light the gloomy sepulcher on my account. Or has 'Ethiopia stretched out her hands unto God'?"

Kaspar had lit so many lamps, Ravi could see his head swivel toward him and his upper lip curl back from a full twenty feet away. "Howland. You've won already, so why can't you leave me alone?"

Stepping forward, Ravinger blew out a lamp. "I've no wish to be your enemy, Kaspar—I like you. You're a fine, jolly fellow, and you keep me amused."

Kaspar didn't look at the chandelier as he cranked a wheel on the wall to raise it back up. He looked instead at Ravi with a powerful evil eye. "Isn't it enough that you stole Louisa? Now you have to come and conquer the helpless Miss Chambliss, who is the fiancée of another man."

"Even if they were betrothed—which they are not, I have on best authority from the poet himself—I would have no desire to 'conquer' the delightful Miss Chambliss. You're in full agreement with me that it's in everyone's best interests if she leaves this continent immediately."

Kaspar stood at the sideboard, pouring himself some firewater into a red *barrilye*. "I see with your loathsome and repellant personality, you are going to drive her away! Is that your plan?"

Shrugging, Ravi reached for more Bordeaux wine. "Something like that. And you're certainly assisting the cause with your inane *non sequiturs* and wailing American songs like a hyena."

There came the clipping of the woman's little heeled shoes out in the gallery, so he strode to the center of the room. He bowed low to her fuzzy silhouette, eagerly straightening back up to view the woman he'd decided was the most ravishing to ever dare enter Abyssinia. She wore the Algerian vest with the hanging tassels from the night of the raid—he was surprised all the tassels hadn't been yanked off in the melee. Yet her beauty didn't need adornment. Her impish nose turned up at the tip, her face glowed with freshness, and her hourglass shape was fine.

"Captain Howland, so good of you to come. Are you in town for the jubilee?"

He couldn't resist kissing her hand once more. She smelled now of attar of roses, and he noted a smear of blood on the inside of her wrist. It touched him, that she should be nursing the citizens, especially as he knew he didn't have the stomach for it himself. "Yes, the festivities. Can you hear the *debterahs* singing from here? I do hope you'll accompany me into town."

"When Heaven starts accepting sinners, she will!" Kaspar burst out. "They are citing David's psalm, 'O clap your hands all ye nations,' as an excuse to gambol with levity!"

Ravi and Delphine both laughed at him. The woman cried, "Dear Kaspar, why do you want to keep me a prisoner here forever? I'm much safer with Captain Howland than I would be with anyone else." She gave Ravi a low, sooty glance just then. "I've seen how he fights."

Ravi was so taken aback by her allure, he barely took note of the buffoon slamming his booze onto the sideboard and stamping to the door. "I'll be at Abdul's establishment! You have driven me out of my own house!"

Delphine didn't glance Kaspar's way either. "Isn't he a funny man? As though *we* are driving *him* to the saloon!"

Ravi was painfully aware of his burgeoning erection that could have busted a *wancha* horn. "He's an *azmary* clown, all right. When Tewodros arrested his superior, the very Reverend Henry Stern, he didn't bother arresting Kaspar, because he's such a harmless gump. My dear Delphine. Come sit here on the divan and allow me to pour you some of this wonderful wine of Bordeaux."

The woman moved to the divan to sit. "No thank you, Cap—Ravi. I drink only tea brewed from herbs. I try to eschew coffee as well. But you certainly may have some."

"I see you've managed to replenish the supply. Did ol' Charlie Cameron have such a large amount in his storeroom?"

"No. I . . . was given some by an Arab merchant, as a gift for treating an . . . a copulation problem." In a swifter, light tone, she continued, "They think that I, as a *ferenje*, enter into direct communication with heavenly bodies and spirits, and I can drive away storms and hail, can you imagine? They beg me to remain here—important men appeal to me for aphrodisiacs, and sterile women think I can make them fertile."

Ravi politely sat on a divan placed at right angles to Delphine's, but as close to her as possible. He leaned forward, his hands that held the wine between his knees. "This is most interesting. I've made somewhat of a thorough study of aphrodisiacs myself, in my time. And what did you give the lucky fellow?"

"Spanish fly." Quickly she added, "I made sure to tell him the proper amount, and that he was not to come back to me lamenting and howling if his tongue swelled up."

She looked as though she wanted to laugh, to free her nerves and modesty, so Ravi allowed a hearty chuckle to encourage her. "Of course! If he had enlarged kidneys and the bloody flux, he was not to be blamed for taking more than two grains of the *cantharidin!*"

"Well, yes. I can see there are *some* medicines you've studied." Delphine laughed beautifully. "You know, it can also be used for cystitis and gonorrhea; that's why I carry it."

"As long as you don't emulate the honorable Marquis de Sade and poison candy with it to give to whores. Tell me, if you're not a drinking woman, what interest would you have in obtaining more Bordeaux wine?"

"I . . . I thought Anatole might enjoy it."

"Ah, yes. The ostensible fiancé." He gave her an unwavering look, but she just shifted uncomfortably. "I'm glad to see you're treating patients, my dear. As a nurse, it'd be wrong of you to withhold treatment when there's even a slight possibility you can be of assistance."

As hoped, she had a flash of anger in her doe-brown eyes. " 'A slight possibility'! I'll have you know, kind sir, in '55 I graduated from Syracuse Medical College with a Doctor of Medicine degree. I was the only woman in my class."

Ravi raised his eyebrows in appreciation. "That's mighty impressive. Abou told the truth, then."

"Yes! But when I went to Washington to volunteer for the army, I was denied a medical commission, so I had to serve as an acting assistant surgeon." She tilted her head. "Now you're encouraging me to stay in the country, then? You've changed your mind?"

Ravinger loathed to admit it. "Yes. As the Emperor's Lika-maquas, I can order people out of the country. I can have them arrested. Or I can command that they stay, if it's for the betterment of Abyssinian people."

Was it the light from too many lamps, or was the pretty lady's face flushed with new ardor? "Why, thank you, Ravi. That's most accommodating of you. Perhaps you aren't such a miscreant after all."

"Rather, I've informed Colonel Merewether to send you more supplies. Just don't venture beyond the walls of Gondar."

The woman leaned forward so that her fingertips nearly brushed his knees. "Oh, you *are* an angel! And I've asked him for the same thing myself. Well, now I really *will* have to obtain more Bordeaux for you, for you are the only man I've ever seen who becomes kinder for it."

A moment of silence engulfed them. Both of them gazed at each other, each speechless for probably different reasons. Then Ravi said gently, "Ah. The gesture is most appreciated, for it is you who are the angel."

"Now you must tell me. Is it true you were sacked from West Point for dueling, after killing a man?"

Ravi's laugh was full and complete. He slapped his knee. "That old story! I *was* sacked, that much is true; I was supposed to be in class and instead was practicing sword fighting with another fellow. I was showing him—here." Leaping to his feet, Ravi strode down the length of the room to where Consul Cameron or a prior tenant had hung some swords on the wall for display. Ignoring the other *shotels*, *talwars*, and *shamshirs* on the wall, he selected a plain rapier that resembled a claymore with a fantastic basket-hilt. He pivoted eagerly, aghast to find the woman so close at hand. She had followed him, and he handed her his own grand *shamshir* saber that he unsheathed with a flourish from the scabbard at his waist.

"Oh, my," she whispered, stooping a little under the heft of it.

"I was showing him the superiority of the curved blade. In every cut the edge meets its object at some angle, and the penetrating portion becomes a wedge." Covering her hand with his, he waved the saber, cutting an invisible pie shape in the air. "But this wedge is not disposed at right angles with the sword; the angle is more or less oblique according to the curvature, and consequently it cuts with an acuter edge." He stood side by side with her, demonstrating her to hold the *shamshir* at right angles to the ground, with arm extended. "Were the edge to describe a right line, directed at any object, say that—what is that?—statue of a horse copulating with a bush, it would act as a wedge, measuring exactly the breadth of the blade. But the curve of the saber throws the edge forward, and by cutting nearer the point, the increased curvature gives a more prolonged and acuter cuneiform." He placed his right hand around her bare wrist, helping her to move the *shamshir* from side to side, mirroring with the claymore in his left hand. "We see the enormous gain of cutting power."

"Oh, yes." She stared fixedly at his wrist. "I can see the power in it."

"The history of the sword is the history of mankind." He noticed he was somewhat enveloping the lady in the cradle of his shoulders and chest, so he took a cleansing breath and stood erect. "That was the principal I was attempting to show Nichols." He took the saber from Delphine, but she remained staring at his wrist. "He didn't believe me, and so we had it out." Shrugging, he went to replace the claymore on the wall.

The woman sighed. "I wasn't one for geometry; I see things more in tangible forms. But you did kill him?"

"No, I only 'killed' him by slicing off about three inches of his deltoid muscle. That Matthew Nichols—it's no wonder his ancestor fell off the *Mayflower!* No, I was killed ten times over by the Superintendent who also refused to understand the superiority of the curved blade. I decided to join the Corps of Topographical Engineers, to map the west and explore."

"Yes—why were you not engaged in fighting the War? You're from the Boston area, are you not?"

"Yes, from Newport-on-the-River. But my dear, by that time I was in the Orient, in Sindh, in the Valley of the Indus—in Abyssinia."

She walked to the balcony doors. "Oh! I can hear the *debt-erahs* sing!" She turned to him with her face alight like a child. "Kaspar says the priests' voices are a torture when heard in the church, but they are quite harmonious in the hills, in the perfect stillness of the night."

Ravi joined her on the balcony. They both faced town, north over the River Qaha. The dimming cobalt firmament seemed to be lit from below by the bonfires of the town built around the hilltop castles. It had always invigorated Ravi to note that in the wholesome air of the highlands, one could see the opposite, unlit, side of the moon.

He dared to stand close enough behind her that the slight uptake of wind from the street wafted her attar of roses to him. "May I take you over to see the bonfires? After all, you paid your offering for the wood."

Delphine twirled around so suddenly she was almost in Ravi's arms. Her eyes were lit with an inner burning, and she didn't seem to mind that her bosom nudged his chest. "Oh, yes!" He steadied her by holding her upper arms, and she glanced at his throat. "But we must take Abou."

"Of course. And a ravishing woman such as you must have a more ravishing ensemble than this ragged doctoring shirtwaist. Do you have any ball-dresses?"

This caused her to laugh, and she finally looked up at him. "I'm afraid I left my ball-dresses back in Paris."

Smiling, he lifted the back of a hand to her face and touched the softness. He was surprised that, although her skin was shaded bronze from the sun, it still held a satiny moistness, and he lifted his thumb to describe an outline on her puffy lower lip.

He had never before wished his Abyssinian breeches constrained his erection, but he didn't want to want the white woman. This was absurd! It must be his penchant for constant fucking. Perhaps as he got older, and the more he did it, the more he wanted. He was glad when the woman distracted him by saying, "I do have another clean shirtwaist. If you let me . . ."

However, she didn't turn her head, and her lip rubbed against his thumb when she spoke. He had studied falconry in the Valley of the Indus, and infiltrated the forbidden cities of Mecca and Medina disguised as an Arab *hadji*, but he could not gain control of his wayward lust. "Yes, then we shall go," he said stupidly.

Delphine broke away from his touch to return to the drawing room. Ravinger took this opportunity to duck behind the balcony door and rearrange his cock inside his breeches, so stiffened he was able to lodge the head under his tightly girded belt.

CHAPTER SIX
FIRING THE PILES

"WHAT DID YOU MEAN AT QWESQWAM when you talked about cutting down *kantuffa?*"

Delphine rode Ravinger's glorious gelding, so ornately caparisoned every Gondari in town stopped to stare in their pilgrimage to the bonfires on the hill of Qudus Gabriel. They rode across the River Qaha over the stone bridge built by the Portuguese.

How she wished she could lean back into him! How she wished they could gallop as she'd seen him do at the horse market! He would grip her around the waist with one lusty arm, guiding the horse with the other as they thundered across the grass past the castles of Gondar. He'd shown himself not absent of sentience and the intellectual graces of a man who read many books, and this excited Delphine. Still, her dreamy tableaus of Ravinger Howland were merely children's harum-scarum frolics conjured up by her longing for her only love whom she'd been unable to save during the War. She was a child to feel amiable toward the brutish Likamaquas. He may be kind at the moment, made convivial by the merry-makings of the holiday jubilee, but in the next moment he'd be as likely to be murderous again. She would never turn to the first warm nice body that availed itself to her.

His low growling laugh affected her. "Ah yes, the dreaded *kantuffa!* That's a mimosa tree with thorns as steely as nails. They grab the traveler like the talons of an eagle, and as fast as you work one out, another takes hold."

Delphine dared to look back at him over her shoulder. "Silly man. I wasn't asking for the dictionary definition. I meant why did you say that to me when you . . . kissed my . . ."

"It's a proclamation made before going into war. We're so bold and unpredictable that we need to be prepared to attack in every direction, and the enemy had better clear the way for us. But when I saw your face, possibilities opened to me, unbounded realms of unknown glory, and I suddenly felt that you . . . were the world that I needed to explore."

Delphine was pleasantly shocked and flushed to hear the man speak so brazenly. She was unaccountably at a loss for words, and the Captain seemed content to continue riding silently in the darkening roadway, pressed on all sides by blurry chattering figures. His chest against her back was deliciously warm in the cool highland night, and once again his closeness gave her serenity. "I'm unsure how you mean that, Cap—Ravi, but it does sound very beautifully poetic."

"It's meant to be beautifully poetic. I haven't seen any fresh white women in ages—years—and the missionary wives here are hardly as vital and . . . quarrelsome and spunky as you. Besides which, I've decided we could use the nursing—the doctoring skills you are blessed with. And—"

"There's an 'and'? I think you've quite given me enough circuitous insults."

But apparently he had not, for he now switched the reins to his left hand, raising his right and bringing it to her clavicle, touching her with an erotic whisper. Delphine was stunned rigid that he should touch her in a familiar manner like that. Her mortification was confounded by puzzlement at her reaction—she liked his touch. Was she so severely perishing for affection that she would tremble down to her very quim at the merest brush of this man's hand? He slid his rough fingertips over her collar buttons, tickling as though seeking to pleasure her to the very core. He leaned his chest against her and growled against her shoulder. "And: You are the Queen of Sheba."

The ridiculous insanity of his words took a few moments to reach Delphine's brain, she was so busy struggling to feel nothing at his touch. "What do you mean, sir?"

He nuzzled his mouth against her earlobe, speaking with the richness of the professional libertine. "Your medal."

His fingers found the Medal of Honor she had covered with her shirtwaist, outlining its star shape with his thumb. Delphine realized he wasn't trying to make her hot at all, and she felt doubly shamed at her lustful reaction. "Yes; my medal! What was it about my medal that had you in such awe in Metemma?"

He continued to stroke her medal through the muslin, and he spoke seductively into her ear, sending a cascade of shivers down her arms, and stiffening her nipples. "Many years ago, when the Emperor first saw my Knight Templar medal, similar in shape to yours, he declared it was the sign of Solomon. He told me Sheba would be reborn and would soon come to Abyssinia, also wearing the sign of Solomon."

Rubbing her neck with his unshaven face like a feral cat, he at last withdrew and sat back erect, as though satisfied with his cracked story, again taking the reins into both hands.

Delphine huffed with indignation. "Solomon . . . ! I've never heard anything so bizarre in my life! If you're Solomon and I'm Sheba, that means . . . Well! I don't even want to dwell on the implications!" She felt him shrug with flippant disregard. "This is preposterous! Then—is Sheba the same as Makeda, the Queen of the South who went to Jerusalem and . . ."

"And fucked King Solomon, yes," Ravi agreed pleasantly. "The one and the same."

The absurdity! "So what you're telling me then is this glorious Emperor of whom I've heard so much, so many stories of his grand cruel deeds—"

"—and his sagacious visionary ideas for reunifying Abyssinia."

"—is expecting *us* to . . . to . . ."

"To fuck? Not exactly. He won't, anyway, as long as I can keep your existence from his knowledge. You see, my dear, I didn't want you to leave Abyssinia because your breath was foul or your taste in fashion was questionable. I was trying to protect you from my hateful presence, and the idea that I might force myself upon your ravishing figure merely to beget an heir to the throne."

Delphine snorted hotly through her nostrils, like a horse. "Now it's my breath—let me down, sir! I've heard quite enough insults from you tonight!" But the more she squirmed and flailed in his embrace, the tighter he gripped her about the waist with his powerful arm, with its ridiculous silver cuff as though he were a modern Roman gladiator, bringing the horse to a standstill while the flowing crowd of people surged forward around them. He even rubbed his stubbled face against hers again, raising unwanted gooseflesh on her arms.

"Have no fear, Delphine. I find you too much of a delightful treasure to debase for such calculated and dubious reasons."

She stopped struggling, though his luscious mouth and strong hand were doing indescribable things to her innards. "No, you'll just debase me for spontaneous, obvious reasons." Enwrapped between his sturdy and nearly naked thighs like that, she felt the insistent pressure against her lumbar region of what she had suspected for a long while was a massive, well-hung erection.

When she'd thought him an Abyssinian, she had allowed the luxury of imagining him brutally naked, his erect penis jutting proudly like an arrogant satyr, and her performing acts upon his fully male body she had not thought possible since Georgia. But now, the more she came to know of him, the more her delicious dreams terrified her. The power of her desire scared her, for the men she cared for had a way of dying.

"No. I won't debase you at all. I'll protect you from harm with every cell in my body. That means keeping you safe in Gondar, if I have to lock you in your house and hack the Emperor's fingers from your doorknob with my saber."

Delphine sniffed. "Well, what would be so Abyssinian about the absurd notion of us having a child? The supposed 'heir' would be thoroughly American, anyway. That proves the entire notion is complete bilgewater. I shall take my medal and hide it, since no one other than you . . . and Abou . . . have seen it."

Sitting straight again, Ravi pressed his heels to the horse's flank to urge it onward. "Yes, utter bilge! The only part that isn't is the part about your ravishing figure."

Delphine squirmed salaciously. She knew she rubbed her bottom against the giant mushroom head of his penis, which he had tried unsuccessfully to stuff underneath his belt on her balcony after he'd seemed about to kiss her. How she'd wanted him to! She'd imagined kissing him, licking the perfection of those full lips, imbued with the tastes of honey and pepper. At the same time, she was horrified.

She remembered his words when they'd stood before the window of Woizero Attitegeb's bedchamber. He'd said he wished he could imprison beloved ones so that they'd never leave. The notion that he might love anyone was even more cracked than the story of Solomon and Sheba and she began to laugh, relaxing back against his handsomely muscled chest.

He said, "Over there. Did you see Anatole's friends when they went charging past us over the bridge? There they are. Do you know that Said and Abdul are Bedouin Shoho merchants?"

Delphine made out some figures standing atop a knoll not thirty feet distant, but all men looked alike, nearly blending into the night sky behind them, lit up by oil-dipped rag torches, only Anatole standing out in his tousle of curls. "Yes."

Ravinger reined his horse to a halt. "They're *shifta*, bandits. They trade in guns and ammunition. I'd advise you to avoid them. Don't let them in your house."

"What do I care who Anatole's friends are? He had dubious friends in Paris as well. That's part of being a poet."

"A couple years ago, the Emperor commanded every Mussulman to convert to Christianity or leave. Abdul and Said are among those pretending to be of the True Faith so their business isn't interrupted. Once Tewodros finds out, which he will, there will be trouble."

Delphine had to shout over her shoulder at Ravi, as there now arose some serenades accompanied by the beating of *negarits*, big drums pounded when the army marched. "I still don't see the danger, Ravi. They're not my friends. Come, let's join them up on the hill."

They had to step their way carefully, crushed on all sides by torch-wielding pilgrims who waved their beacons in dangerous proximity to Delphine's skirts. "See that Said, the attractive one with his hand on Anatole's shoulder? He would make your fortune could you buy him at your price and sell him at his own valuation of himself."

"Where are we going? I want to stand by Anatole."

For the Captain was leading the horse to a *warka* tree some thirty yards from Anatole's group. "There's no room to stand over there."

Ravi dismounted over the horse's hindquarters like a gymnastic athlete, and took Delphine's hand so she could extricate her skirts from about her legs.

"In America, I was a passionate espouser of women's dress reform," Delphine shouted to be heard over the yelps and songs of the wild and tumultuous mob. "I was arrested once for wearing Turkish pantaloons."

Ravi laughed beautifully. When he encircled her waist with his large hands, she fluttered to the ground gently. He did not back away from her as she leaned up against the horse, and he didn't remove his hands. "I can find you all manner of Turkish pantaloons if you wish, only please don't call them 'Turkish' around here."

Delphine smiled too. The jubilee atmosphere, the hillsides dotted with flaming torches, the alternately melodious and tuneless singing, it all made her a little giddy. "Yes, and I'd wear neckties and top hats."

Ravi's laughter was so full-blown now he leaned slightly in toward her, giving her a lovely view of his muscular, lusty throat, and her innards warmed to breathe in his lemon and ambergris smell. "Well," he finally gasped, "if you're partial to bloomers I can fix you up with a fine woman's *shamma* to wear over them, but please, my dear." He looked down at her, gracing her with his sparkling black eyes. "No top hat. That'll make you look like a chimney sweep."

"Well, certainly. I wouldn't want to confuse people. Can you imagine the problems if Abyssinians started asking me to clean their chimneys?"

Shaking even harder now with laughter, Ravinger wrapped his massive arms about her shoulders, drawing him to her. She didn't pull away, but touched her parted lips to his salty throat, gratified to feel the ridge of his girded penis stiffening against her belly. It gave her a feeling of might to know she could still affect a man in that manner, for she knew now it was a hopeless crusade to get such a response from Anatole, and she was not such a prudish Miss Grundy to feign no desire for it. It was eerily prescient when Ravinger said with his chin balanced on the crown of her head, "Queen Makeda can have anything she desires."

Emboldened, she dared to put her hands on his hips, and she spoke against his jawbone. "There are some things that are completely, spiritually unattainable."

He pulled away just far enough to look down at her. His look was wondering, amused, but just as he opened his mouth to speak, they were both jarred by the resounding arrival of Kaspar Nagel.

"Ho-*ho*! And what do I see here?" His voice boomed right next to their ears.

They jumped as though shot. The horse was even scared, and it skittered ahead a few feet, causing Delphine to stagger back, and Ravinger to raise his right arm. When he saw it was only the soaked missionary, his body relaxed like a deflated scarecrow.

"I'm gone for one hour, and what do I see but a blatant disregard for what you swore your intentions were, sir!"

Probably just for the fun of it, Ravi made an exaggerated swipe for the *shamshir* at his hip, and withdrew it in a blue flash of lightning as he raised it high above his head. "Deacon Nagel," he roared, his fierce face belying the spirit of fun, "and how many times have I told you to *never* scream oaths down the inner canal of my eardrum when I am enjoying a restful moment of peace?"

But when all the folks surrounding them inhaled in one collective gasp and started creeping backward away from Ravi, Delphine got the idea perhaps it wasn't such a festive mood that had overcome the barbarous man. She insinuated herself between the two men, hands up in a conciliatory stance. "Ravi, please, Kaspar's just trying to . . . to . . ."

Behind her Kaspar continued his oratory bawling. "It is *I* who should be brandishing a weapon at *you*, you confounded dunderhead!"

At the sight of Delphine, a sudden calm had come over Ravi. Not only did he lower his arm, returning the saber to the scabbard in one continuous graceful motion without even looking down, but all the rage vanished from his face. He smiled at Delphine. "He's trying to annoy us, is what he's trying to do."

Abou stepped between Delphine and the Captain. "Basha Falaka, never raise a sword against a woman!"

"Dear Abou!" Ravi protested. "Did you not see me replace the sword when this woman stepped in?"

Suddenly Anatole was there as well, shaking Delphine by the arm and pointing into the darkness. "They're about to start firing the piles!"

When everyone rushed forward in their excitement toward the *warka* tree that was the highest acclivity of their particular knoll, Delphine was wrenched back from the crowd's tide by two strong hands she was by now thoroughly familiar with. As she laughed with delight, she felt him effortlessly lift her high, holding both her ankles in one broad palm and perching her like a mermaid on his shoulder so solid it may as well have been a tree limb.

She could easily see over the heads of the mob. Simultaneously at a dozen hills throughout the valley, men thrust torches into the heaps of wood, and the fires soared into the heavens with a hellish boom. Now every man worth his salt unsheathed his *shotel*, clashing playfully with his neighbor. Anatole, not known for his swordsmanship, feebly jousted with a Bedouin.

Although Delphine doubted this was the most pious manner in which to mark the crucifixion of Christ, it was a wondrous sight to see the flames of the *dameras* fluttering three stories high under the crystal dappled sky.

"It's a most inspirational place," Ravi said.

"Yes, it's a very stimulating place to be," Delphine agreed, fully aware of the ambivalence of her statement, for in addition to her pleasure at his warm hand manacled around both her shinbones, she reveled in the heat of his other palm that propped up her thigh.

Ravi allowed her to slide off his shoulder, but ever so slowly so as to produce an unctuous frisson between her thighs as she slipped down his brawny arm.

Kaspar's shrill voice rose above the clamor of the crowd. "Kind sirs," he shrieked in English, "do not smother me with the effluvia of your tallowy *shammas!*"

Slowly, turning her all the while, Ravi lowered her down the front of his body as though she were a *danseuse*. She kicked her legs up behind her, his strength making her feel utterly airy and feminine. He didn't shy away from the shelf of her bosom, pressing his face to her and sighing a heated breath through the fabric of her shirtwaist.

"Kaspar, *sur la garde!* You must sword fight with me!" Anatole sounded as though at the end of a particularly distant tunnel.

"Desist! These incorrigible vagabonds have the tale of their lives written in letters of fire on their villainous countenances!"

When Ravi's hot mouth took a large bite from the delicate side of her neck, she thought she would swoon. She hadn't been touched like this since Georgia, and she nearly burst into tears at the sheer unbridled ecstasy of it. Waves of shivers like fiery ice ran down her spine and the backs of her thighs. Her toes barely brushed the ground, and he suckled the side of her throat, now her jaw, now a little nip at her earlobe that nearly had her flowing with orgasmic waves into a puddle at his feet.

He held her tenderly, with respect, as though she were a geode of hollow filaments. She knew she was panting like a drugged brood mare, but she opened her lazy eyes when he held the back of her skull.

His dark question lion's eyes shivered with lust. "What man foresees the flower or fruit," he breathed hoarsely, "whom fate compels to plant the tree?"

She panted so, she could scarcely speak. "Ravi, I—"

She was glad that he kissed her then, for she hadn't known what she was about to say, and indeed it would have come out stupid and inane anyway, the way her eyes were rimmed with tears.

His kiss was languid, crushing her lips as though lightly bruising an oyster. Delphine kissed his full delicious mouth, licking him with the tip of her tongue, taking voracious joy in such a simple and nearly chaste act. He tasted like lemons and herbs, and the chocolate rum that radiated from the broad expanse of his chest had her feminine senses all aquiver. It was she who brazenly tilted her hips into him to test the impressive length of his phallus against her mushy sex, and she instantly knew that if she was allowed the luxury of merely rubbing against his columnar thigh like a rutting beast she would climax within one minute.

She gulped fresh air, clinging to the front of his *shamma*. Two tears squeezed from her eyes, and Ravinger's hot sinuous tongue licked them from her face.

"Ah, Delphine." Just the feel of his low growling voice against her face set her off into another round of shivers. "You're a priceless treasure . . . Your graceful mouth, your strong neck have quite slain me. I'm overcome with a great thirst for you."

Delphine raised her fingers to the half-moon scar on his left cheekbone. "Your passion scares me." She butted up against something soft and warm.

"Excuse me, Missus." It was Abou. He seemed to have been standing there the entire time, acting as a wall. "Kaspar will get bored very soon, and will come looking for you." He spoke in hushed, confidential tones.

Ravinger straightened Delphine and loosened his embrace. Over by the *warka* tree, Kaspar ranted, "The terpsichorean performance of those capering *debterahs* has me fully convinced this is nothing but a heretic holiday!"

As heartbroken as Delphine was to break the embrace, she was gladdened that Ravi held her firmly by the hand when they turned to face the reveling horde. Men howled and laughed, fell on the ground, and rolled over each other all in a ball on the ground.

"Kaspar, you must get into the spirit of the celebration!" called Anatole, from somewhere within one of the piles.

She delighted in running her fingertips down the steely tendons of Ravi's forearm. "I hope we didn't give any terpsichorean performances."

Ravinger smiled. "No, but I think we may have capered a bit."

Sighing with contentment, Delphine pressed her hot face against Ravi's cool shoulder. It was such a strange reality to be standing on a knoll watching bonfires in the Abyssinian highlands. Her very closest friend back home in Illinois would never believe where she was now.

She shuddered, and Ravi must have misinterpreted it, for he said, "Abou, you're a fine man, and I've seen you fight, so I have no qualms about leaving Miss Chambliss in your care." Turning to Delphine, he took both her hands in his, and kissed them tenderly. "My dear, you should go home before this husking frolic becomes too rowdy. I'll follow you at a few paces, but ride with Abou on his mule."

"How long are you in Gondar?"

He held her hands to his chest. "Ah, my only truth. 'Truth is the shattered mirror thrown into ten thousand bits.' I'll stay until the boats on Lake Tzana are built."

"Good. Then please come calling . . . when you have a moment."

"These public extortionists assail me from all sides!" Kaspar wailed.

Delphine released Ravi's hands and called, "Nobody is demanding that you stay here, Kaspar! We're leaving now; why don't you ride with us?"

Kaspar's molten silver hair emerged first from the inky darkness, then his face. He clutched a *wancha* as though it contained ambrosia from the fountain of youth. Ravi burst into a fresh round of laughter at the sight.

Kaspar didn't appear to notice him, staggering over to Delphine and uttering, "The sword of Islam is seeking to sweep the Cross from the mountain regions of Ethiopia!"

"Yes," gasped Ravi. "They've already extinguished the fires of the Magi in Persia; why not here?"

Pivoting on a foot, Kaspar pointed his *arrack* horn at Ravi. "And uprooted the idolatries of Sabianism in Arabia!"

"Yes, that's true, dear Kaspar. Why don't we continue discussing it at home?"

Abou and Ravi helped Kaspar onto his horse, and the little caravan started back toward home. Delphine heard Ravi continue to laugh almost all the way back to the river.

CHAPTER SEVEN
BEDOUIN GUN MERCHANTS

ADAN BIN KAUSHAN ALREADY KNEW TO admit Ravinger without announcing him. After stabling the horse, he barged through the double wooden doors that led to the central courtyard. The towering false *ensete* bananas that reached almost to the open compluvium were satisfactory to Ravi's elated grand mood, and he bounded up the tiled stairs.

He'd been manically waiting for three days to call on Delphine. Misha tried to argue him out of it, but he may as well have been a fly buzzing around Ravi's head for all the true annoyance that caused. "You're heading down the path to ruin! What will the Emperor do when he finds out?"

" 'Deprive you of your hands and feet'!" Ravi now mimicked his Ukrainian Azmach under his breath as he swung around the top of the stairs. " 'You're done for; a dead duck! You're cutting your own throat'!"

He'd waited three days to give her time to either make it up with Anatole or abandon her fiancée act. He'd thought of little else other than the feel of the woman in his arms, the lusciousness of her lips, how sweet her mouth had tasted, of honeysuckle and molasses. It was even more pleasantly surprising, in view of how prudish and reserved she'd been on their first several meetings, how she'd quickened against him when he'd slid her off his shoulder at the Maskal celebration. She was like a sensitive quaking deer, responding ardently—though she probably wasn't aware of it—to the minutest of touches. When she'd swiveled her hips against his burgeoning erection he'd near about come off in his breeches. That she was a surgeon capable of doing things he would never wish to dream of only increased his desire for her.

She'd said that his passion scared her. It could accurately be said that her passion terrified him.

He'd been with Karachi women with muscles so controlled they could catch a fly between their toes; women of Crete, Somaliland, and Harar; Bombay women with hair japanned with cocoanut oil; and Afghans and Circassians—but he'd never kissed an American woman who was such a leashed tempest.

In the drawing room Anatole lay back on a divan drawing on a tall brass *narguileh*, the water inside the upright copper pipe gurgling with a rasp. The Shoho arms merchant Said had a round frizzled wig so dense he stuck it through with a wooden skewer for scratching his skull. He sat on the rug below the divan and accepted the *narguileh* hose from Anatole.

"Basha Falaka!" Anatole cried with wonder, swinging his legs off the divan.

Ravi commanded, "Let's repair to the parlor."

Ravi hadn't been inside Cameron's parlor in many years, and it had been transformed. All of the bergère chairs of carved wood and moiré upholstery had been pushed back to the wall, and library tables and desks had been pressed into service from other rooms. It was a laboratory now, the tables covered with grasses, flowers, buds, vials, bottles and even a candle-powered Bunsen burner. In the tall, glassless windows bundles of herbs were strung to dry, rotating aromatically in the breeze.

"Ah, see what she's done." Anatole described the scene with his hands, and Ravi saw that the poet was proud of Dr. Chambliss. "This is her medical office."

"Yes, I can see. I'm sure she's a wonderful surgeon. It's just not anything that I could...stomach myself. Now, Anatole. About Said and his friends. I don't want you bringing them around here anymore. Why do you associate with them at all?" He folded his arms across his chest. "Have you been acquiring arms for Tewodros?"

Anatole's lower jaw dropped. His agate eyes were particularly vacant, as though shocked out of all their color. "Basha Falaka, never! Why would Tewodros choose a newcomer and a *ferenje* such as myself for such a task? No, no, no. Do not even suggest it to him, for it might give him ideas, and I am certainly much too weak and *efféminé* to be chosen for such a task." Regaining his color, Anatole made a swipe at Ravi's bicep. "Now, *you* would be an excellent choice for such a thing. You are so much more brave, so much more—"

Ravi held his palms up. "That's good, but I still don't want you bringing them around this house. Can't you just go to a coffee-house to smoke your *afyuni*? I'm sure Miss—Dr. Chambliss doesn't approve, as she certainly doesn't approve of booze."

"Oh no, she does not mind, but Basha Falaka, I wish to return to Theodore's camp." Anatole stuck his lower lip out peevishly. "He wishes me to be there with him."

Ravi sighed. "Fine. Have you told Delphine yet?" Anatole shook his head. "I'd advise you to do that immediately. You must tell her you have no intention of marrying her. Where is the good doctor?"

"I think she went to bathe. We have this big metal bathtub up here, you know; do you have one of those in Flad's house? You are welcome to use ours . . ."

At the sound of Delphine's voice in the drawing room, both men moved beyond the hanging tapestry that served for a door. Delphine stood before Said with hands on hips, frowning, and said in her rude Amharic, "No *afyuni* in this house! Please go to a coffeehouse for that."

Crawling to his feet, Said oozed, "Oh yes, *hakim*."

Spying the two *frenjoch*, Delphine's face lost all irritation, and it seemed to Ravi in his arrogance that she especially graced him with a smile. "There are patients," she explained, happily now. "Some might have diseases that don't respond well to the vestiges of such smoke. Smoking is a foul habit, Anatole, making a foul place, and a foul mouth to the smoker. Besides, it results in insanity and paralysis." She had indeed just bathed. Her damp hair was braided back into a chignon, and a mixture of rose and orange blossom wafted from her person.

Ravinger cleared his throat. "Well. There is something to be said for it. When you're traveling and don't have much food or water, smoking seems to fulfill both purposes." He took a few strides forward and handed her a bundle he'd brought upstairs. "Here, I've brought you a more suitable ensemble."

While Anatole looked quizzically bemused, Delphine unfolded the white calico breeches and with delight held them up against her to test the fit. They were rather loose, but tapered toward the ankle, and Ravi was pleased it looked like he'd described to the tailor the proper size for her.

"Why, thank you!" Delphine said. "This is so very thoughtful. Now I shall be able to ride in comfort. Please, allow me to try them on." She left by the gallery door.

"You buy her men's breeches?" Anatole smiled.

"They're women's," Ravi said flippantly.

"Did you know in Paris she sometimes wore men's clothing? Yes, she was quite the scandal, and also quite the woman of fashion! Of course," Anatole sidled up to Ravi, who leaned against the doorframe of a balcony door. He spoke confidentially. "You do not have to worry about her. She is a lover of men."

Ravi laughed heartily, apparently scaring the Shoho, for he began edging toward the gallery door. "You're right there, Anatole! I'm sure I have no need to worry."

Anatole looked perplexed. "But I tell the truth! She only wears men's clothing to be more comfortable. She says a few women in your War Between the States went disguised as soldiers. She cared for one such wounded soldier who turned out to be a girl!"

Ravi wiped away a tear of laughter from his eye. "Ah, Anatole. You're right. Why can't women just follow their men into war, as ours do, wearing women's clothing and staying behind the front lines?"

"Exactly!" With arms folded before his chest, Anatole's lower lip protruded. "They are not fit to fight. They are women, and much too weak and *efféminé*."

"Oh, yes. Like you? I find it humorous that such an unconventional visionary poet such as yourself would adhere to those traditional ideas, Anatole."

"They should leave fighting to the *guerriers courageux et forts* . . ."

"They told me nursing soldiers was no work for a refined lady."

Both men gasped at the sight of Delphine. She had left her shoes off altogether in the native style. "I told them the idea of making a business of maiming others wasn't worthy of civilized men."

Ravi stepped up to assist her with the belt, as she hadn't wrapped it up properly. "Peace is the dream of the wise; war is the history of mankind."

"I feel naked in this simple shirtwaist." Delphine held her arms aloft.

Ravi walked around her, wrapping her like a pipe stem. "We'll find you some sandals, until your feet become accustomed to walking bare. Now. I'd like you to accompany me on an outing."

"Oh! An outing?" She sounded excited, but then said flatly, "No, I couldn't. I have three cases of scrofula downstairs, and one man hacking with catarrh so bad he's scaring—"

Ravi didn't particularly want to hear the details. "There's no question about your not coming. It's the Sabbath and you shouldn't be working anyway. Right, Anatole?"

"Yes, yes, and abstain from meat."

"We should be fasting altogether," Delphine mentioned as Ravi cinched the belt about her hips. "Right?"

"Yes, quite. But this outing has some medical value. I want to show you the Bath of Fasiladas."

"A bathtub? How amusing."

Chuckling, Ravi took the woman by both shoulders and regarded her squarely. "I suppose it's a bathtub of sorts. It's where Abyssinians go during Timkat, Epiphany."

"Well . . . May I, Anatole? If there's some medical value . . ."

"Yes! Go! You're safe with Basha Falaka!"

Ravi asked Anatole, "You'll be here when we return, right?"

"Ah, yes, of course."

Ravi's shield-bearer hadn't allowed him to take his horse, as the horse was never supposed to be used on the road, instead being led before its master. (For Maskal, he had snuck the horse out, and had had to listen to Walde Nebra raising the roof for a good solid hour when he returned.) Instead he had his mule, which after all had cost more than the horse, being more valued for its strength and sure-footed ways. It was a simple affair for the woman to mount with no encumbrances of unnecessary skirts. He allowed her to place her toes into the iron stirrups, even adjusting them up so she could reach them, wrapping his powerful arms about her person as he lightly held the reins before her lap. He was shocked at the closeness of her body with so few layers of material between them, and he strove to retain a few polite inches of air between their bodies.

The Bath temple lay en route to Qwesqwam, being the place where Fasiladas, while hunting buffalo, came across a hermit who instructed him to found a city here. In January, during Timkat, Gondaris came here to bathe in memory of Christ's baptism. They weren't quite into the season where the mephitic exhalations from still water would breathe the ague into the souls of men, and it was a refreshing crisp ride in the outdoor air. Women sweated under heavy bags of *teff* flour, and balanced crushing leathern containers of honey atop their elaborately coiffed hair. They passed groups of young girls with head-loads of garlic, onions, chilies, and peppers, and passels of donkeys nearly suffocating beneath bales of lowland cotton.

"You're such a hardworking gal," Ravi commented lightly. "I figured you could use a break from the importuning crowd afflicted with amaurosis, exostosis, and nyctolopia."

"That's very good, sir! I'll call on you when I have need of an assistant."

"Oh, that's certainly all right! I may have become inured to the violent methods that sometimes accompany death and maiming, but I have utterly no desire to see what's on the insides of peoples' bodies. Or what's usually on the outsides of their bodies, when it comes to medical matters."

"Yes," Delphine sighed wistfully. "Fully ninety percent of my cases are common syphilis, and I'm very nearly smack and smooth out of mercury, not to mention opium, although Anatole's been helpful in obtaining me some. We went foraging for *kosso* this morning, and did find a sort of holy medicine man. He refused to divulge any secrets to me, although I was presented as a great *hakim*, and he had heard of me."

"They only allow their firstborn son to know their secrets, and even then it's only when they're on their deathbed. They guard their recipes jealously, for most of their 'cures' are bogus concoctions of dozens of placebo ingredients, and if citizens found out the one item in the mix that actually had some value, they'd just go and gather it themselves."

"I daresay I could use a man like you when I go to forage. You might get to the fact of the business with these people. All Anatole's interested in is finding out which herbs might cause euphoria or gunpowder, and Kaspar in bellowing about lazar speculators in the animal and vegetable creation of Ethiopia."

"Any time you wish it, just ask me. I know a few of these medicine fellows, one who has a very good cure for the evil eye, escaping arrest or prison, acquiring money, and learning to play the harp."

"My. He sounds like a useful fellow."

"Indeed." Ravi languished in the serene silence that followed, with Delphine relaxing back against him as they passed droves of cattle heading in to provide *brundo* joints of raw beef to the royal city. She was no withered old spinster, that was for certain—she was full of the vim and zest of a thousand living things, and he wanted to know everything about her, wanted to know how she'd become such a temptress. Perhaps she'd been married before. Her kisses were not the awkward fumblings of a virgin—thanks be to God. "My dear . . . Anatole's mentioned you were ill in Paris. I hope it wasn't anything too serious."

"Yes, that's why I went to Europe after the war. The idea was to take the baths, as I was so debilitated I was barely able to function." She heaved a great sigh. "I was going to set up some hospitals, but then I met Anatole and was distracted by his poetic nature."

"I imagine that losing your brother in Atlanta helped to . . . create a cynical nature about war. You must have been frustrated, being assigned elsewhere and so unable to help."

Delphine uttered a half-hearted laugh. "Yes, I was 'assigned' elsewhere . . . 'I should glory to describe this hell on Earth, where it takes seven of its occupants to make one shadow'."

"Excuse me?"

She looked at him over her shoulder. "I wrote that in a letter to my friend Siobhan in Cairo, Illinois. I was a prisoner in a Confederate garrison. That's why I couldn't help my brother, and why I couldn't help . . . anyone."

That was so frightful, so thoroughly wrought with horrifying implications, even Ravi didn't dare question it further. He recalled when he had held her in his arms in her bedchamber, she had said something about being under lock and key in a southern prison . . .

And he had had the gall at Qwesqwam to insinuate keeping a loved one prisoner might be a good thing! That had probably not been a peaceful idea to bring to her mind. He took both reins in one hand, lifting the other hand to the back of her bare neck, where he caressed her trapezius muscles with circular motions of his thumb. "I'm terribly sorry for that. Your frustration must have been quadrupled, then."

"Once they discovered I was a doctor; they took me out of the yard of certain death and put me to work in the hellhole of the so-called hospital . . . Oh! Look at that castle beyond the wall!"

"That's the Bath." They skirted the walled compound around the corner by the pepper-pot guard tower. "I have nothing but the utmost awe for the medical profession. Particularly in such a fetid and festering sewer as I imagine that prison must have been."

The woman rubbed her face against him pleasantly, like a sun-warmed cat. "How is it you always manage to have exactly two day's worth of beard on your face? No more and no less."

Ravi growled with pleasure. "I can understand your not wanting to relive the horrors of a place like that."

"Oh, who wouldn't want to remember men lying naked and dying and lousy, in the sand and upon boards, and packed as tight as eels in a jar? Of vermin and lice there was a veritable crop there. It was impossible for a surgeon to enter the hospital without having some upon us when we came out, if we touched anything except the ground, and usually if we just stood in one place long enough."

As the notion of bathing only occurred with regular urgency during several annual proscribed holidays, there were no other visitors and the guard at the two-story gatehouse was taking a siesta, leaning back against the stone wall where the serpentine roots of trees made an impression of marble. A gift of a salt had an enervating effect upon the fellow, for he immediately clothed it in his robes and sank back into his nap, and their mule continued toward the stables.

"I'm sorry you had to endure that. Queen Makeda should have the very finest hospital with all the best instruments and medicines."

"Perhaps you see why the clean air and grand vistas of Abyssinia have been the magical cure for me."

"Ah. Just wait until the cholera, smallpox, and typhus break out, usually in June."

The woman tightened, like a block of water suddenly frozen into ice. "Typhus?"

"Yes, but not until June, and only then in the lower areas, such as around Lake Tzana, and only if large populations are allowed to congregate."

He felt her shudder. There was no one in the stables to assist them, so Ravi dismounted and helped the woman down. "When it happened last June, Dr. Blanc told Tewodros to break up his army and send them to higher ground into Begemder Province, and to isolate all fresh cases. The problem was thus solved."

"And who is this Dr. Blanc? I haven't heard of him."

Ravi regretted mentioning the name. He'd just been trying to take the topic off of typhus. He took Delphine's right hand in both of his, guiding her toward the open grassy field that led to the pavilion. "Ah, he's a medical man, and . . ."

She caressed his hand in hers, and seemed to take inordinate delight in the shape of his thumb. "Is he still around? I should like to talk with him."

"You should pray you never do, my only truth." Ravi allowed some moments of silence to convey the import of his words. "Dr. Blanc is imprisoned on Magdala."

Delphine threw his hand away. *"Oooh!"* She stood with hands on hips, spouting sounds of frustration like a teapot. "And will you tell me *why* has this man been sent to the lockup? Did he fail to remove his hat when he breathed the same air as the great Emperor? Or perhaps he didn't say twenty Hail Theodores when he took his morning trip to the shithouse?"

"The reasons are very convoluted, my dear, but they really all come down to some insult that Tewodros feels has been committed upon him. Consul Cameron, for instance, in whose house you reside. His major crime was that instead of delivering Tewodros's letter directly to Queen Victoria, he went through the Soudan, the land of Tewodros's mortal enemies the Turks. He was really just looking into the cotton trade as he was requested to do, since due to our War not much was getting through to England."

The woman allowed him to take her hand again and lead her toward the pavilion. "And Dr. Blanc?"

"You know, I really can't recall the charge against Dr. Blanc."

Delphine snorted. "Just that he's a *ferenje*, and he happened to be standing there, more than likely."

"Yes, more than likely. I think it did involve something about him not removing his hat, now that I think of it."

"Oooh! How can you *bear* working with such a slimy worm as Theodore?"

They continued over the arched bridge that led to the two-story pavilion, built on solid supports in the hundred-foot-long pool. Today the basin was serene, shaded in parts by *wanza* trees with delicate snow-like flowers, several white-faced ducks fluttering their wings in the water.

Ravi leaned against the red stone arch and looked out at the pool. "He does *now* say that Europeans are wanting in sincerity, ill-mannered and ill-tempered. But it's only because he had the highest expectations of us. You have to understand, I came here ten years ago. Things were different then. According to the apocalyptic work Fikare Iyesus, Christ would himself bring Tewodros to power after a long period of corruption, perversity and lawlessness, of the rule of imposters and corrupt Rases. That was the Zemene Mesafint. During Tewodros's reign, the wrath of God would be averted and blessings and mercy bestowed upon the faithful."

"Oh, yes. Don't they all say that, at first?"

"He exhorted the farmer to plough and the trader to trade. He urged thieves and *shifta* to quit their robbery. Wronged people were invited to appeal, the destitute to approach him as their father. He took it seriously, devoting several hours a day to hearing plaintiffs. He also abolished the custom that kinsmen of a murderer or even someone who'd caused an accidental death had to answer with their lives."

"Yes . . ."

"He risked the clergy's wrath by booting all the big fish, saying that each church should have land sufficient to feed only two priests and three deacons, giving their lands to farmers. He's an educated man, Delphine, raised in a convent. He puts some of our countrymen to shame in his knowledge of Shakespeare—he can certainly out-quote me, though I've never had a warm and friendly relationship with that behemoth."

He dared now to look down at her, and he saw she was staring out at the pool with a remote, dazed expression.

"Well. I suppose there are two sides to every person, and no one can be pure evil." She looked up at him. "But why do you not try to secure the release of the *frenjoch* prisoners? You of all people must have sway over the Emperor's will. Tell him you won't protect him in the next battle, or something. Tell him you won't sleep in the doorway of his asinine tent anymore."

Ravi had to chuckle at her simplistic solutions. Taking her arm gently, he led her out onto the wooden balcony perched over the water, so their voices wouldn't echo so authoritatively within the stone walls of the pavilion. "I haven't slept in his doorway for a couple of years. And his arrogance is so final, for the past couple of years I've had to convince him he still needs protection in battle. No, he's the sort of man who strives to do the opposite if he's commanded to do something. He has to feel it was his own idea. And if you mean bribery, that's why Martin Flad went to London. If Victoria sends artisans here, Tewodros will let the prisoners go. You see? Abyssinia is not a land for the impatient."

Her forearm entwined in his, she leaned gingerly on the railing. "But you admit he's wasting this country now. Why do you stay? You seem capable of much greater things than this."

"I've developed a great affection for Tewodros. When he is kind, his generosity knows no bounds, and his compassion flows freely. To leave him now would devastate him. Now," he continued on a harsher note. "I don't expect you'll ever have to discover any of these things firsthand, my dear."

Delphine grinned. "For the very reason that when he's not good, he's very, very bad." She caressed his forearm up to his silver *betoa* cuff, her fingertips tentative. "Yes, I've no interest in locking horns with that monster. Do people swim in this pool?"

"During Timkat they jump in and splash onlookers . . . Here, let's go down to the edge."

He led her back over the stone bridge and around the corner

of the short wall that enclosed the basin. They ducked under an arched doorway and were on the broad steps that surrounded the pool. They walked quietly for a few moments, the dappled sunlight reflected off the waters in Delphine's placid, angelic face.

"I don't think I shall swim." She wrinkled her nose. "I just bathed."

But Ravi hadn't, so he let go of her arm, unfastening his *shamshir* scabbard and *zenar* and letting them fall to the terrace. He made a running headlong dive into the pool, scattering the ducks and slicing through the water lilies. The shock of the fresh chilly water was expected, and he swam underwater for as long as he could, opening his eyes to the sea-green foam and the curious speckled fishes with whiskers. He surfaced at the other end, shaking his head like an otter and pulling himself halfway up the first terraced step while the woman ran along the edge, laughing with delight.

She sat on the step, and apparently didn't mind when Ravi encircled one of her warm ankles in his wet hand. "Is it cold?"

His other hand squeezed the water from the myriad of braids tied back into a queue behind his neck. "About as cold as San Francisco in July."

"Here, I'll join you." Hitching up her breeches above the knee, she sat on the lowest step and dangled her feet in the water. "Your hair! Is it ruined?"

"No, Alitash plaits—the plaits are so tight, they rarely come undone. You really only have to redo them every couple of months, or after a particularly harried battle." Ravi impulsively reached under the water for her foot. She jumped, and tried to squirm from his touch.

"Oh! I thought you were a sea serpent!"

"That's all right. I've been called worse in my time." He persisted, gently taking her foot from the water and holding it like a paper-thin shell. He applied a rotation with his thumb to her instep. "I must get you a pair of those bell girdles for your feet—you've seen those?"

Delphine settled back onto the terrace, leaning jauntily on both her hands. "Yes, those are pretty. On Abyssinian women, that is."

"My only truth, I think you equally as beautiful as the fairest Abyssinian princess. With your eyebrows of Ethiopian blackness, the limpid whites of your eyes, your cheeks of perfect oval, your long throat—"

"And your penchant for pure gas flattery, Captain Howland!"

"—and your lips of vermilion, you are a woman who deserves to be praised."

She appeared truly humbled now, and unable to look at him even in jest, gazing at the water as though she could see clear to the bottom of the pool. "You overestimate my attraction."

"I look at you with those qualities in front and I'm fascinated; from behind, I die with pleasure."

Delphine shook her head, finally daring to look at him sideways. "You're just touched, Ravi. You've been away from the company of white women too long." But she did not jerk her foot from him.

He massaged her large toe, which he knew to relieve pressures in the head. "I have enough vivid memories of *frenjoch* women to know all men cherish a woman such as you."

She lifted her hand to his face, feathering her fingertips around the edges of his javelin scar. "No. Any man stupid enough to care for me always winds up . . . regretting it."

Gently releasing her foot into the pool, Ravi reached up and grabbed her under the arms. She giggled with joy as he lowered her, the bottom just deep enough her feet couldn't touch, pinning her with his thighs as she slid down the stone wall. "Oh, *brrr!*"

"There," he said softly. "I won't muss your coiffure."

She little knew that her squirming, and the manner in which she hitched her ankles around the backs of his knees, far from having a sedative effect upon him, was engorging his prick in the chilly waters. The usual result of brisk waters was much less tumescent.

"You've been to San Francisco?" She hung over his arms as he braced them, gripping the edge of the pool. Her round chestnut eyes mirrored the lily pads and water lettuce that bobbed about in their wake.

"Yes, and Virginia City, Salt Lake City, and as a topographer I surveyed much of the area about the Yellowstone River." With one deft hand he slid open the buttons at her collar.

"And you were training to be a powerful army officer when you were booted from West Point?"

"My father had wanted me to study finance and become a banker, but he learned early on there wasn't much hope in that." He parted the material of her shirtwaist as though exposing a rich vein of precious silver. He felt more than heard her make a small animal sound of satisfaction, and she pinioned herself to him by her ankles even more firmly. "So it was decided to ship me to West Point, where perhaps they could corral some of my unruly tendencies, but I just got far too many demerits."

"Mm. I can't see you as a banker."

Ravi dared to slide a few more buttons free. The flotation of the water enhanced the splendid muscular shadows of her abundant bosom. She seemed justifiably proud of her fine figure, smiling artlessly as she perched above him. "He should have known much earlier when I became frustrated with his attempts to force me to learn violin, and I smashed it over the head of my instructor."

She laughed like a lovely elegant shorebird, with her head thrown back to reveal her full throat. Ravi parted the shirtwaist fabric to display the arc of her finely molded breasts, and he dragged the edge of her camisole and corset down to just almost exhibit the aureoles of her nipples so erect they arrogantly pushed the fabric away.

"Ah, Ravi," she said happily, accenting her joy with an erotic squiggle of the hips that had him pressing her to the wall like the bark on a tree, "I can't see you as anything other than . . . what you are today. The Likamaquas of a dying feudal kingdom."

Pulling her garments down to reveal her statuesque shoulders, Ravi took a large slurping bite from the sun-browned trapezius he had been rubbing so assiduously on the ride up. She uttered a feminine *"ahhh . . ."* and curled her limbs about him. He levered his hips so firmly against her that the rush of pleasure at the mashing of his bursting erection against her nearly caused him to come off at once. He held himself there to be safe, biting and licking her shoulder with great cow licks that elicited a stream of melodies from the pit of her throat. He lifted her hair, licking the damp roots at the back of her neck. "Woman is like a fruit, which will not yield its sweetness until you rub it between your hands."

She clasped her free hand around his neck, squirming all the while like a fish on a hook. "Ravi . . . your effect upon me is so profound. You terrify me with the strength of your passion."

Her eyes were humid and half open. When he lavished a few open sucking kisses on her full lips, she responded with the sluggish vigor of a woman so roused and hot he knew he could have screwed her then and there, but that wasn't his way. Not when he wished to know the woman for more than a week. "What's so terrifying? I've found the delight of you, and I want to imbibe with endless pleasure." Her lower lip glistened like a ripe berry, and he nibbled on it.

"It's . . . *my* passion that scares me, what you bring out in me. I feel as though . . . if we coupled, we'd explode into fire. *Ah!*"

For when she uttered those pleading words, Ravi was so

overcome he laid a sucking trail of kisses down her sternum. She cradled his skull to her as he lifted one breast so that the nipple popped from the corset, proud and stiff. Ravi tickled a slow, tantalizing path with his mouth down the slope of her breast.

"*Oh!*" She jumped like a rabbit when he slurped the nipple up against his incisors, barely touching it between his teeth. "The power of you . . . is squishing me!"

Oh Lord, was he hurting her? She was such a tall majestic woman he'd never feared squashing her like a bug, as most Hindoo women with their little bird's bones. But he must nibble some more at her breast, and feel the fullness of it floating on the surface of the water that sloshed with the whirlpool rotations of his hips against her. She still cradled his head to her breast, her head thrown back over the edge of the pool. Ravi felt as though he drowned in a vortex of sensation, deaf and blind to the outside world.

Her sudden voice in his ear was like the screaming of a particularly venomous god when she whispered loudly, "Jupiter Ammon! Someone's here!"

Normally Ravi would not have cared. He believed whomever occupied a spot first had squatter's sovereignty, and the interloper could just cool his heels until he was finished. This rule seemed perfectly tailored to the present situation. Even *debterahs* come to perform ablutions at the waters would not deter Ravi. His mouth described a slimy snail's trail to the rise of her other breast.

Delphine pushed half-heartedly at his shoulders. "Ravi, it's a *ferenje!*"

"Yes," he murmured. "And so am I."

Just as he dipped his tongue beneath her corset to nuzzle her other nipple, Delphine pushed against him harder, struggling to cover herself with her garments. Ravi straightened up with good cheer, though his pulsating cock felt as though it had melded with her and seared her to the wall permanently.

"Your *ferenje*," Delphine said pointedly.

Ravi sighed, assisting her with her clothing. "Ah, my only truth. You allow such trivial things to get in the way of your lovely *exhibitioniste* nature."

"And you do not stop fucking when your Azmach stands twenty feet behind you, glowering as though you were wringing the neck of his pet canary?"

Ravi thought. No, he did not often stop, even when Misha breathed down his back and cleared his throat loudly. "Hmm. Maybe he is the *voyeur*. All right." Lifting her under the arms, he set her back onto the stone ledge.

Delphine made a sound of appreciation. "So strong," she marveled, kicking her feet in the water like a little girl. "It's the brisk highland air, and the healthy outdoors mode of living." Sniffing, she looked at the sky. "I think I shall stay here."

Ravi vaulted over the ledge to sit next to her, both of them streaming water down the stones. "Now who is not concerned with being watched?"

Her smile of agreement was so guileless Ravi was compelled to kiss her again, languidly tasting the cottony softness of her full lower lip. They feasted sluggishly on each other for several long moments, hands politely in their own laps, while Misha paced obnoxiously behind them, *shamma* swishing.

When at last the woman drew away, she looked at him with great spirit. "You know . . . I don't know how to swim."

Misha took Ravi's hollow-bellied laughter as his cue to break in. "Likamaquas," he started, in his flavorful patois of Ukrainian and American. "I've been sent from Qorata with a letter from Tewodros."

Ravi craned his neck to view the buffoon, but he didn't take the proffered letter. "Misha, really, now. Couldn't this have waited, say, half an hour?"

Misha stood at attention, staring at the temple at the other end of the pool. "I'm afraid half an hour would have been half an hour too late, Basha Falaka."

Ravi savvied the putty-head's meaning. "Your promptness is always evident, Azmach Michael." He assisted Delphine in doing up her buttons, standing then and reaching an arm down to help her up. "I don't believe you've met Dr. Chambliss. Formally, that is."

Delphine put forward a cheerful paw, but the shy man recoiled visibly from her. *"Doctor?"*

Ravi frowned. "Yes, Doctor. I suppose in your back-alley Ukrainian country they don't have such things as women doctors. Well, greet the modern world of America, chum."

"Yes," said Misha tightly through a clenched jaw. "I've heard about your war medal. It's a great honor to meet you." But he wouldn't shake her hand.

"You're a world-weary traveler," Delphine told Misha pleasantly. "To come from Russia, live in New York, and now you're here."

Ravi stepped forward to whip the letter out of Misha's hand that was like a steel claw. He recognized the fancy English calligraphy of the Emperor's Amharic scribe. Tewodros could read and write admirably in Amharic, he used the scribe for *ferenje* letters.

My most esteemed Likamaquas,

In the name of the Father, Son, and Holy Ghost—One God.

From the King of Kings, Tewodros. I have heard that you are in good health and enjoying your stay in Gondar. Be of good cheer; we will soon meet.

Ask Woizero Attitegeb how she has passed the rains, and how is Mr. Flad's house. He will return from England with the Queen's artisans soon.

By the power of God, prepare to meet me in Qorata to journey to Magdala. It is time for you to join with Louisa Bell. Your friends Dr. Blanc, Mr. Rassam, Mr. Cameron, and Mr. Stern are well, and eager to see you again.

You will be coming to me, by the power of God.

"*Isgyoh,*" Ravi breathed. This couldn't be. Not now. Not ever.

He looked at Misha staring at him dolefully, but he couldn't bear looking at Delphine.

Misha intoned, "This was bound to happen, Rav. This is something you should have set to rights a long time ago."

Ravi folded the letter haphazardly, stuffing it into the folds of his damp *shamma*. He looked at the sky, snorting breaths of frustration. "Yes," he muttered. "You're entirely correct, Azmach Michael. I'll go back with you to Qorata, and set this right." Exhaling with finality, he tried to paste a superficial smile onto his face, and was finally able to look at Delphine again.

She smiled, almost as superficially. "I hope everything is OK."

He put his hand on the side of her face, shocked to feel it so perfect, like an obsidian statue. "Tewodros wants me to go to Magdala."

CHAPTER EIGHT
"MAKE HASTE TO QWESQWAM"

IT WAS WELL PAST TWILIGHT WHEN Ravi and Misha arrived back at the imperial camp near Qorata. Anatole had arrived before them, having cut out from Gondar surreptitiously, before Ravi and Delphine returned from the Bath.

Not being particularly eager to confront a pickled Emperor at that time of day, and as Ravi was sure several minions had already raced to inform the Emperor of his arrival, he took his zenith telescope out onto one of his favorite table-lands to enjoy the starry solitude.

He was angry that Tewodros was finally taking him to task about Louisa. Misha was right—Ravi had allowed it to continue on for far too long and he needed to do something about it. Just not right this minute. Not while Tewodros was elevated. Not while his head was stuffed full of visions of Delphine Chambliss.

Doctor Chambliss. He was certain that his vast respect for her had colored his affections. He had known he could never care for a simpering woman with a delicate nature, for even if he'd been living back in America such a woman would be an appallingly vapid spouse. He needed a brave woman, unafraid of the unknown, willing to share a tent with him.

"Spouse," Ravi said aloud with delight as he adjusted the telescope's wyes. What on Earth had caused him to use that word? He had never entertained serious notions of wedding any woman, not in San Francisco, or Bombay, or Abyssinia. Particularly not in Abyssinia, where marriage was of a much more political nature, and you schemed and analyzed the candidates until you were left with the most advantageous one, never the one you truly wanted.

In this case, Louisa Bell.

Tewodros stood twenty feet from him. In Africa, when the moon was nearly full, you could see as clearly as by day. Ravi rose to attention, and saw the teetering Emperor was far from servile, his eyes flashing like a marauding civet cat.

"Likamaquas. I'm not happy to hear you've been keeping important information from me."

Ravi frowned. "It's not so much I've kept information from you as kept it from myself because I didn't wish to think about it. But now I wish to discuss with you that I cannot marry Woizero Bell."

To his surprise, Tewodros waved a dismissive hand. "That was important when I wrote the letter, but I've been informed of something new. Why have you not told me of the arrival in Gondar of the *ferenje* woman? I'm extremely disappointed in you, after all the talks we've had."

Ravi's reaction was immediate. "Who told you that?"

"What does that matter, Likamaquas?" Tewodros seethed now. "Perhaps *this* looks familiar?"

Isgyoh. There was a flash, and a dangling of metal from Tewodros's outstretched hand, and Ravi instinctively grabbed for the Congressional medal. "How did you get this? This is her personal property, and it's obviously been stolen."

"It is the property of the son of David and Solomon!" Tewodros raved, standing so close that his filthy bare feet nearly stepped on

Ravi's and his spittle rained on Ravi's neck. "Unless perhaps *you* think *you* are the son of David and Solomon, and therefore have a right to it?"

"I am the son of Colonel John Howland of Boston, Massachusetts, and *you* . . ." Tewodros's pupils were like holes in the sky from where stars had fallen. "You have no right to take the medal."

The standoff broke, Tewodros falling back with a grand flailing of limbs like the flapping of a demented stork. "No right? No right, Likamaquas? And how many times have we discussed how Makeda, who had kingdoms on both side of the Red Sea, and who carried gold to Solomon, would come again bearing this symbol—"

Here Tewodros made a swipe for the medal, but Ravi held it fast up close to his own face. He even dared to put out a stiff warning arm against the Emperor. "Your Majesty, if this is Makeda's symbol, why then on the back is it inscribed *Presented by the Congress of the United States to Delphine E. Chambliss, A.A. Surgeon, U.S. Army. For Distinguished Conduct after Chickamauga, September 20, 1863?*"

Tewodros lunged at Ravi and this time succeeded in wresting the medal away. "This shows what a fool you are, for what woman would get a medal for distinguished warfare?" Tewodros brandished it up high as though it were a sacrificial infant he was about to dash on the rocks. "Yes, I am crazy. Don't look at my face or take heed of my words when I speak to you, but look at my heart. I have a destiny."

Ravi tried to laugh casually. "I agree completely, but you're mistaken; your destiny isn't with this woman who owns the medal, your true destiny is with the *real* daughter of Solomon and Makeda! She obviously isn't the one, because that medal is made in America and is dated 1863. You can plainly see the red and white stripes, the emblem of the American flag, so you see—"

"There are customs in every country which only the natives of a place understand. You're a foreigner and don't know our rules. You follow your way and I follow mine, and you'll see if I am not right in the end." To Ravi's horror, Tewodros slid the medal over his own head with great ceremonial import. He stood arrogantly, as though the medal had given him new royal powers of farseeing. "How can I trust any European now, after the bad behavior of those whom I've treated like brothers?"

Ravi made a new attempt. "Don't you see? I haven't behaved badly. I was merely withholding *false* information from you, so as not to confuse you. I knew if you found out about the woman and her medal, you'd assume it was the daughter of Solomon and Makeda, and you might make a mistake based upon this bad information, and—"

"Silence, Likamaquas!" Tewodros roared. "I could have you arrested for your heretic actions! But I keep you close to me because I love you, just as I loved Johannes Bell, the father of Louisa who slept in the doorway of my tent. I will forget about this mistake of yours if you go immediately to Louisa Bell in Magdala and wed her in a Christian ceremony, with a priest giving you Communion."

"No." Ravi's low growl could hardly have been audible, but Tewodros's nostrils flared with renewed anger, so he continued. "No, I cannot do that. I can't serve you with the burden of a wife and then most likely children—Remember in my stories of the Knights Templar? They could not wed, or they wouldn't have been able to serve properly. No, I think it a much better idea to give Louisa to Kaspar Nagel, for he has always loved her, and he's correct in saying that since other Gaffat missionaries received the first two Bell daughters as wives, he is next in line for the third daughter."

Tewodros laughed, a cruel hyena sneer. "That *azmary*? He wouldn't know what to do with a proper wife if we forcibly joined them, and gave them your Hindoo love book as a guide!"

Ravi laughed at this fanciful tableau. "That is very true. But don't you agree it's only right, and will show your Gaffat children your faith in them, and keep the Bell sisters together as they've always wanted to be?"

"But you must wed, Likamaquas! It will keep all of my women from asking after you, and making fools of themselves fighting over you, and . . . Who will you wed?"

"No one, Your Majesty! I'm a Knight Templar and cannot wed. I'm very satisfied serving the Elect of God. There is no bigger honor. When do we leave for Debra Tabor? Dejazmach Kantu has told me that some people are tired of eating only peas, and—"

"Do you see this, Basha Falaka?" Tewodros had now stepped forward with shining eyes, his perfectly even and white teeth bared in what could have been a smile. He fingered the blue ribbon of Delphine's medal, nestled in his nut-brown clavicle. "Is this not similar to a *mateb*? It's a blue string just like the *mateb*. That's another sign this is the woman I've been waiting for. She wears the *mateb* as a sign she is different from Moslems, from Jews, from worshipers of trees, rivers, the sun."

"Ah, no. That's a ribbon, not a *mateb*. You can see it was manufactured in America, and—who is that?"

For a horseman galloped up the hillock, churning up clods of mud and *gwassa* in his wake. Ravi was glad for the interruption—Tewodros was easily distracted by fresh excitement.

"Who can that be?" Tewodros cried. "Ah, it's Waldmeier! Why has he come all the way here from Gaffat?"

Theophilus Waldmeier was one of the "Gaffat children" who were relatively free to move about the town's foundry, casting guns and making gunpowder for the Emperor. He had married one of Bell's daughters, and because of his expertise and willingness to at least attempt to craft armament for Tewodros, he was left in peace most of the time.

"Hello, Waldmeier," Ravi called.

The German missionary dismounted his frothing horse all in one motion, and flung himself to his knees before Tewodros. "Jan Hoy," he panted, hoarse like a dog who has barked too long. "I've come in desperation, out of the stormy depths of my soul, to ask you an imperial favor." He paused to catch his breath, his eyes cast down at Tewodros's feet.

Tewodros's face was placid now. He bent and touched Waldmeier's shoulder. "Rise. What is the problem?"

The artisan unfolded his giant body. "My dear wife, my enchantment, the only sun of my eyes, she has fallen very ill with fever. I come . . . I come to request you to allow the British physician Dr. Blanc to attend her." It appeared he was crying, for he raised his large hands to his face.

Tewodros didn't say anything for awhile, but at length, to Ravi's utter surprise, a tear squeezed from the Emperor's soulful eye, and he touched the blacksmith on the shoulder again. "Of course, of course, my friend Waldmeier! I understand." His tone was soft and almost loving. "I will have some spearmen accompany Dr. Blanc to Gaffat immediately—I will have messengers sent to Magdala tonight to tell them." He sighed a hollow, ragged sigh, dropping his arm and turning away slightly. "I can understand how it feels to lose your beloved counselor, the companion of your adventures, the being most loved . . ."

Ravi knew the extent to which Tewodros had worshiped his first wife, who had accompanied him in the field for so many years and then died of fever. He quietly stepped up to Waldmeier and put a hand on his arm. "Theo, you can rely on His Majesty's word. Come to my tent, you've been riding hard and long. It's late. You can be sure the fire-footed messengers will be sent tonight." He turned to Tewodros, who was now staring vacantly at the constellation of the Southern Cross, the picture in the night sky he always saw as the symbol of strength and faith. "Allow me to arrange for the messengers."

The Emperor's shoulders quaked.

"Come, Theo, just let me get my instruments . . ."

The giant man sobbed freely now. "Thank you, Basha Falaka. Thank you . . . my wife thanks you . . ."

✳   ✳   ✳

Gondar

"BUT KASPAR . . . WHAT OF YOUR ADORING flock? How do they fare in Djenda for so long when you've been here in Gondar?" Delphine faced Kaspar across the low Moorish table that held their breakfast of tea, cold meat, and *hambasha* bread. "Aren't you afraid they might lose faith and turn back to Judaism?"

From his waistcoat pocket, Kaspar removed a handkerchief that had been ironed after a fashion, probably by the laundress sitting on it. Shaking it out, he tucked it as a napkin into his collar and regarded the repast with shining eyes. "Well, I have my assistant Karl who lives there in a rude hut, and you know I would never abandon my vow to protect you here in Gondar. No, my dear, we cannot go! I shall continue to write inspirational sermons and have them sent to Djenda to be read aloud, to keep the Falashas on the one true path."

"The one true path," Abou agreed ambiguously.

Delphine sighed, listlessly chewing her dry piece of *hambasha*. "Yes, but you yourself agree that I should come to Djenda, to see what help I can be of, and treat your parishioners."

She had fallen into something of a blue funk since Ravi's departure. She was convinced more than ever now, through no real evidence other than her distrustful mind, that Ravi would comply with Tewodros's directive to go to Magdala, and then he really would never come back, as Magdala was a fortress in the bushes of Lasta, far to the southeast of Gondar. Magdala seemed in her mind like the Black Hole of Calcutta, as far as anyone ever returning from there went.

"It is absolutely out of the question!" Kaspar stuffed his remaining words down his gullet with a fistful of bread.

Abou intoned, "It is too dangerous." He examined his empty stew bowl as though wondering whether the hunter had said the proper Hail Marys and blessed the bullet before shooting the fowl.

Delphine threw her own bread onto the table. "It's just getting so tiresome around here! Why, yesterday in my surgery room they dragged in a poor sheep to carry around the patient's bed three times before slicing its throat! Of course you know the import of *that*. The absolute worst was when they began tossing eggs on the ground. I tell you, as much as I adore it in this absolutely . . . exotic and glamorous . . . *oh!*"

She went to the balcony window. Nobody had opened it to allow the smoky air in this morning, and the day was even dismal, with lowering clouds not black enough to rain, for that would've been too refreshing and dramatic, no, they merely lay low over the valley city, casting a jaundiced pall over everyone.

Kaspar stood behind her, still eating out of the bowl he had carried with him. "My dear," he mumbled. "Perhaps you are missing the other half of your heart."

Delphine twirled around to face him. *"What?"*

His eyes widened and his mouth stopped chewing. He swallowed audibly. "I said, perhaps if your fiancé were to return—"

Balling her hands at her sides, Delphine stalked to the liquor sideboard as though she contemplated drowning her sorrows. *"Ooh!* I dare say, if I'm to be marmed over by the two of you, I may as well just follow the drum in Theodore's camp!"

There came a short silence wherein everyone in the room froze like wax museum figures. Both men leapt to life at once, coming for her with outstretched arms of panic. There was a brief tussle to see who could grasp ahold of her first, Kaspar's stout white arms intermingling with Abou's elegantly black ones, but Kaspar won out by stomping on Abou's bare foot with his brogan.

He shook Delphine. "My dear, you must *never say that!* Just to say that is to invite the inveterate criminaldom of the worst sort of pestilential devils into your soul! Abou, we shall purge the air in this room with incense at once!"

Abou glared at Kaspar, holding his injured foot in his hand as he stood like a stork on one leg. "I thought you said incense was *dumm!*"

"Oh, for—" Shaking off Kaspar's hands, Delphine strode for the gallery door, fully intent on a relaxing jigger of laudanum from her bedchamber, but stopped cold when she heard bare feet coming up the stairs. She knew the fire-footed sound of a runner.

The youth stood in the doorway panting, holding out both hands, as each one contained a missive. Delphine snatched both missives immediately, seeing that they were sealed with red wax and addressed in lovely educated English calligraphy.

"This is for you." Delphine handed Kaspar his letter.

"*Mein Gott!*" Kaspar cried. "It's that devil, Howland!"

"Abou, give the boy some salts." Delphine was already by the balcony window, eagerly tearing open her letter.

My One and Only Truth,

I have some rather sickening news to report. Tewodros is in possession of your Congressional medal.

I don't have time to ponder on the machinations and subterfuge that went into such a pretty stunt; suffice to say, it is Tewodros who fancies himself Solomon, and we must move you to another apartment immediately, in preparation for getting you out of the country.

My only truth, I tried to hide you as long as I could. I am only sorry it couldn't have been long enough for a true reunion des esprits.

His handwriting degenerated toward the end of the letter, losing its exquisite symmetry and becoming spiky.

So now: make haste to Qwesqwam. Go to Woizero Attitegeb and present yourself. I'm sending her another letter by the same fire-footed fellow. I'm sure the bastard who gave Tewodros your medal also told him where you live.

I'll be at your side when I can get away from here.

Your obedient servant,

Cptn. Ravinger Howland

Delphine's hand holding the letter fell numbly to her side. She was remotely aware of Kaspar in the nether realm somewhere hooting and whooping as though at a hoedown, but she ploughed on past him like a steam engine with shoulders set. It was only when she was down the gallery nearly to her bedchamber that she vaguely thought to herself: *What does he have to be so damned happy about?*

Skidding her behind onto the short vanity stool, Delphine lugged her portmanteau out from underneath the bedstead. Her fingers scrabbled to undo the leather latches, and she shoved aside handfuls of worn wool and silk ensembles to fumble for her copy of *Last of the Mohicans*. She could tell before opening it that the book didn't bulge with the thickness of the medal.

She sat for several long moments staring at a paragraph of text. "The Indian had selected, for his desirable purpose, one of those steep, pyramidal hills, which bear a strong resemblance to artificial mounds, and which so frequently occur in the valleys of America. The one in question was high and pre-cipitous; its top flattened; but with one of its sides more than inordinately irregular . . . which might render defence easy, and surprise nearly impossible."

The utterly desolate knowledge of betrayal sank its tentacles into her heart. Betrayal. Again.

"Is every man in this world out to double-cross everyone else?" she cried aloud. She declaimed to the ceiling, "Is that what we're put on this planet for? To whale into absolutely *everyone*, as though *everyone* were our enemy, and we should walk on tiptoe and suspect *everyone* of absolutely *everything* for as long as we shall breathe?"

Exactly *who* had betrayed her, she was too foggy to think on just yet.

She finally allowed herself to breathe. The sudden air caused her brain to expand, and she wobbled with dizziness. The Cooper book fell to the floor, and Delphine tried to get to her feet, to reach the vanity table where her laudanum was.

Kaspar's crazily ringing voice bounced off the courtyard tiles. "*Whoo-hoo*, Miss Delphine! *Dieses ist ein Wunder!* It is a miracle!"

The laudanum rolled like soothing cotton down her esophagus, the effect when it hit her stomach instantaneous. Her head swelled with a pillowy lightness. *Kaspar. Obviously, he took the medal. Obviously, that's what he's laughing about this very moment. Obviously, Captain Howland is paying him somehow for that cruel heartless deed.*

"Miss Delphine!" Kaspar stood at her bedchamber door, waving his own letter about as though he were a spectator in a vicious boxing bout. "I must renege on everything I've said about Captain Howland—he is a fine upstanding man! I have misjudged—I must say some Ave Marias to compensate for some of the names I've called him."

"Oh yes? Is that so?" With a murderous face, Delphine stamped over to Kaspar and rudely whipped the letter from his hand. She rapidly read:

Deacon Nagel,

I've just discussed with Tewodros the possibility of your upcoming marriage to Louisa Bell. He is in full agreement, as long as you borrow my translation of Vatsyayana.

Now—Doctor Chambliss is in danger of being kidnapped. I've arranged for all of you to stay with Woizero Attitegeb at Qwesqwam. Heed my advice, and hotfoot it out of there.

You have my profoundest thanks for watching out for Doctor Chambliss.

Basha Falaka

"Marriage!" Delphine accused, as Kaspar tried to ease his letter from her grip.

He was sheepish, and could not look her full in the face. "Why, yes. I've favored this young maiden for many years, and as you see, Basha Falaka has fixed it so that it might be possible now, and—"

"Oh, but of course! As payment for your treachery in stealing my medal, is that it?"

All the emotion seeped from Kaspar's eyes, and he stood with his nose twitching, like a small marsupial. "Medal?" he chirped. "What is that?"

"Medal! A token the government gives you when you've waded through fields of intestines and limbs for a couple of years!"

Still Kaspar looked blank, and he muttered, "Medal? *Was ist das?*"

"Oh, you know very well what I'm talking about, Deacon Nagel! I used to wear it around my neck, and then I took it off when Captain Howland told me that Sheba was supposed to return wearing a symbol that looked very much like his Knight Templar medal, and—*oh!* Why'd you do it, Kaspar?"

"But I did nothing! I don't even know what is this medal

you're talking about!"

Delphine paced her bedchamber, stopping at her dressing table to take a swipe at her bottle of laudanum. It occurred to her that perhaps Kaspar told the truth. He'd never remarked upon her medal if indeed he'd even seen it. Abou knew she wore it, and what it stood for, but would he know the strange story of Sheba? Perhaps everyone knew the strange story. She cast a malevolent glare at Abou, who stood needlessly on tiptoes behind Kaspar, as the next logical suspect. Abou hadn't known where she'd hidden it, but—

"Might I suggest . . . ?" Kaspar boldly entered her room. "Who else knew where this medal was? Wherever it was, for I didn't even know of the existence of it until just now."

Delphine stepped up to the looming Takrury. "Abou, where were you that day Captain Howland and I went to Fasiladas's bath? I don't keep my bedchamber locked, and you could have easily—" She stopped.

She brought a hand to cover her mouth. Of course. *Anatole.*

She had just been accusing her only two friends in the whole world!

Looking up at Abou with horror, they both whispered at the same time, "Anatole."

Kaspar stated, "Monsieur Verlaine! Of course! He must have known, for he knew you intimately—oh, I don't mean to imply *that*, but he knew—"

Delphine spun around. "Anatole! Of course! How could I have been so blind? The way he left here in such a hurry without saying goodbye, and I did tell him the story of Sheba, and—Oh, please do forgive me my friends for thinking you may have done it!" She twirled back to Abou, wrapping her hands around his silken forearms. "Forgive me!"

Abou smiled. "I'm not angry. Is this medal the reason we

must hide now?"

"Yes, but I'm not hiding." Delphine strode again to her stool, and dragged a leather gun case out from under her bedstead. "Here. I'll arm you, Abou, with this splendid rifle, and Kaspar you can use my shotgun, unless you have an iron of your own. Oh, how could I be such a fool to think that crazed poet was a good man?" She handed the rifle case to the eager Abou, but Kaspar was more hesitant.

"Fire-arms? My dear, I've seen more occasions when fire-arms are turned against the defender, and used against the very people they were meant to protect!"

Delphine proffered the shotgun to Kaspar. "Do you mean you're a bad shot? We shall have target practice every day. Here, take it! And I shall use my trusty Remington. Don't point that at anyone, Kaspar!"

"You stop that, *azmary*, or I kill you!" Abou shrieked in a high falsetto, ducking down low to avoid Kaspar's field of fire.

Kaspar looked as though he'd just seen a *buda*. "Is it loaded?"

Delphine sighed. "Of course it's loaded; why else would I bother having it? I'll give you all the accoutrements, the possible bag, your shot, your powder horns, and caps—where is that darned thing?" She rummaged around underneath the bedstead, speaking to Kaspar's legs. "Perhaps *now* you'll reconsider the idea of going to Djenda, Kaspar? I'm sure if we went there the chance of being kidnapped would go down to practically nothing. Who would think of looking for us there?"

For now more than ever, Delphine really wanted to avoid Ravinger. Before she had known she was betrayed so completely and utterly by Anatole, a man she had thought at least a dear friend, she had been afraid of the eventuality of Ravi betraying her. Hurting from the punch in the gut of Anatole's treachery, she was convinced more than ever that Ravi was destined to commit some mayhem upon her soul—whether by returning, or not returning, she didn't know which. But she didn't want to stay around like a lame sheep waiting to be slaughtered, either way.

"The whole country would think of looking for us there! That's where my mission is!" Kaspar exclaimed. "No, I think the best idea is to follow Basha Falaka's orders and go to Qwesqwam and wait—"

"Here it is." Standing, Delphine handed Kaspar the possible bag she'd found covered with dust balls, but something in Abou's stance by the window made her suspicious. He stood with the rifle balanced on his shoulder, his head and torso craning so far out the glassless window he seemed to precariously teeter like a scale, his center of balance somewhere in his left hip on the sill. Delphine padded over to see what he was looking at.

That slimy Bedouin Said was skulking in their garden! He had somehow passed Adan bin Kaushan at the stables and was now looking from side to side like the utmost caricature of a skulking critter, taking big ostrich steps in the tall grass. Delphine moved to shout at him, but Abou hissed at her and held her arm. Said continued stalking his prey until he reached a sort of shack. But there was a locked hasp on the door that Said shook with apparent frustration, for he now growled some words of consternation.

"Said!" Delphine shouted. She waved her Remington prominently, dangling her arm over the window ledge.

The man jumped, and started to run past the stables, but apparently thought better of it, for he stopped, and smiled. He waved at Delphine.

"Said. Why do you walk in my yard? Anatole isn't here."

Said called back something that approximated, "Oh, Anatole is gone? I'm sorry. I shall just have to continue on my way back home."

Abou shouted some more succinct things at Said that seemed

to involve a lot of threats about his mother, his mule, and a crocodile, but the man rapidly skedaddled out of the yard.

"He is a slithering snake!" Abou said with disgust.

"A misbegotten pig!" Kaspar agreed, backing them up at the window.

"Kaspar," said Delphine. "I was thinking. Perhaps you want to join up with Tewodros's retinue, now that you are betrothed to Louisa Bell."

"*Ach!* I hardly think I should be called 'betrothed'! Now do not go around repeating that sentiment to anyone, do you hear, young lady?"

Which was funny, because they had discovered Kaspar was exactly one year older than Delphine. "Well, the note said Tewodros was in agreement with you marrying her. How much more betrothed can you hope to be?"

"Ah, well, you see . . . I believe, even though it does not follow the traditional societal mores of allowing marriages to be arranged for one, that one should also obtain the agreement of the lady in question."

"Do you mean to tell me . . . She doesn't know about it?"

"Well, er, no, what I mean to say is . . . She is so far away! She's in Magdala."

"You haven't asked her yet," Abou pouted.

"Now look here, my good man! These things take time. I shall need to fast, and pray, and fling the—Oh, my."

Delphine crossed her arms before her stomach. "And what better place to fast and pray than in Djenda, the bosom of your congregation?"

"We stay here."

* * *

"I'M TELLING YOU, MISHA. I'M NOT going to Debra Tabor."
Ravi buckled his lion's mane around his shoulders, checking for
the proper sartorial effect in the cracked looking-glass.

Misha threw up his hands. "You can't just leave, Ravi. You're
the Likamaquas, we need you. It's sacrilege to abandon Tewodros
when he needs you most."

"He *always* needs me most." Satisfied with the lion's mane,
Ravi picked his shield from the tent wall and sallied forth out the
tent flap. "And I have a woman who needs *me* most, in Gondar.
Where is that Walde Nebra . . ."

"Oh, but of course!" Misha cried. "The same woman you were
prepared to leave to the hyenas? The same woman you said was a
zar in a woman's costume come to demand impossible baubles of
you?" For a *zar* was another sort of woman's *buda* that appeared
as nothing more than a spoiled minx.

Ravi shoved Misha's arm with annoyance. "Yes, yes, the one
and the same." He started down the hill past the royal flagstaffs
that depicted the Lion of Judah, fluttering with their horizontal
stripes of yellow, red, and green. From here one could view the
entire six-mile valley blanketed with thousands of white and black
tents. They threaded a line through the rabble of spearmen sharpening their blades, patching matchlocks, throwing daggers into
stumps of wood, preening, and otherwise behaving in a parlous
and jovial manner. "Where is Walde Nebra?" Ravinger asked
many of them.

"Rav, you go back to Gondar," Misha whispered, "and Tewodros
is going to suspect you of leaving his employment. Or that you've
got it hot for Woizero Attitegeb. Neither one of those items is a
particularly good outcome."

"Or that I want to seduce Dr. Chambliss? It's true, Misha,
why should I honeyfuggle about that? You and I both know that
the prophecy—if true—pertains to *whomever is wearing the medal,*

and up until a week ago, those two people were me, and Delphine Chambliss. Where does the Emperor come into it? He doesn't, Misha." He caught the arm of a fellow who was carrying a long cotton coil for his matchlock. "Have you seen Walde Nebra?"

"Oh, criminy! Ravinger Howland! I can't believe you really think that stupid prophecy has one shred of truth to it. Just because the medals have a similar look—a star, for criminy's sake, how many medals have stars? All of them? Why, in Kiev—"

Ravi saw him from quite a distance away, as though looking through a powerful field-glass that compressed all space. The man was directly in Ravi's sights, frozen like a startled deer as intersecting streams of oleaginous-headed men clanging weapons and tools passed to and fro, bringing wisps of cook smoke with them like highland mists. "Misha, it's the simple fact of the business that I find her vastly intelligent, more delicious than a barrel full of oysters, and even you cannot deny her bravery that goes perhaps beyond the bounds of reason." Several wood-cutters heading uphill jumped out of Ravi's path, as he felt his rage inflate him to what was said to be gigantic proportions.

Misha scuttled alongside him. "Yes, yes, but *why her*? You have plenty of women here, why can't you leave her alone? Ravinger, you're just going to get us in trouble."

Ravi did not need to push aside the scores of *tej* makers and grass-cutters that leaped out of his path to stumble over pots, horns, and spears. His quarry was shaking, clearly making a lickety-split decision whether to hotfoot it or not, his useless spear impotently sliding from his paralyzed fist. "*Us* in trouble?" roared Ravi. "Perhaps Anatole Verlaine is the one"—he was rather glad Anatole had frozen stiff, for Ravi merely had to reach out an open hand in the diameter of a very large spear. Yes, his neck was about as scrawny as that; and pinioning the man in his constrictor's grip, he lifted the squiggling worm a full three feet off the ground—"who should be in trouble, big trouble, for sneaking into women's bedchambers and stealing that which doesn't belong to him!" His elephant's roar was enough to send even the bravest warriors scuttling backward like crabs, some pointing their guns defensively at Ravi, most with their palms held facing outward to their amazed foreheads. "What have you to say for yourself, Monsieur Verlaine?"

"I—I—It was only a silly medal!" Anatole shrieked. He didn't even try to deny what he'd done.

"Ravinger, really now!" Misha cowered behind a man.

Ravinger tossed his shield at Misha. "So it was just a pure and utter coincidence that led you to steal the medal, is that what I'm supposed to believe, you louse of a scribbler?"

As Anatole's visage was now turning the shade of the scorched earth when a cloud of locusts descended, Ravinger flipped him to his left fist, loosening the chokehold only far enough for the pitiable rat to gasp, "He just wanted to see it! That's all! I must do as the Emperor commands!"

Ravi rained spittle on Anatole's face when he yelled, "And exactly *how* did he become aware there even *was* a medal to *look at*, you mewling son of a bitch?"

"Please! Listen to me! We were discussing . . . medals, and—"

"I can lay out a saint just as flat as I can a sinner, *mon cher bâtard*." Ravi gripped Anatole's neck as though strangling a crocodile. Men came down the hill behind him, Tewodros's men no doubt, from the sound of their feet stamping in unison.

Anatole's hands scrabbled to remove Ravinger's manacle grip, and his feeble barefooted kicks pelted Ravi harmlessly in the shins. Ravi laughed, but then the *bâtard* reached a hand around Ravi's ribs and yanked his queue of braids so suddenly it snapped his head back, only enraging the beast in Ravi all the more.

An angry young rebel had once slapped Tewodros's face. No sane man would ever touch Ravinger.

It was a simple matter to lean back and thrash Anatole a lusty belt that had the poet's nose audibly cracking against his knuckles with a satisfying crunch. The fellow, instantly flattened like an arachnid specimen, sprawled on the ground as the crowd crawled back even farther at the horror of such an unknown spectacle as a fistfight.

"C'mon, get up, you *sac des plumes sans valeur!*" Ravinger had never hit a prone man, unless he intended to pop him off completely.

Anatole spit out what may have been a tooth, the vermilion spray decorating the front of his *shamma*. "*Et vous êtes un monstre!*" he cried. *And you are a monster of a man.*

"I'm so pleased," Ravi snarled. "It's time you knew that, *tas de merde.*"

To Ravinger's surprise, the soldiers grabbed ahold of *his* arms and were restraining *him*. He could have easily bucked them off, but he was so shocked to see others assisting the traitorous poet to his feet that he turned mildly to Fitawrari Gebraye and said calmly, "What's going on, Fitawrari?"

The cold-blooded General, a favorite of Tewodros's for a decade, spoke with a roiling venom, his *shamma* so buttery that one could have squeezed it out to fry lentils in a pan. "We are not to harm the Frankish scribe." It was odd, he didn't ask Ravi why they'd been fighting.

"All right, just—let me go!" Ravi jostled the men who clung to his person, and they fell away easily enough, like leeches.

Perhaps even odder, Anatole managed to look petulantly offended, even with blood still trickling from his nose and running into his mouth. He looked at Ravinger as though about to cry. "*Et moi qui pensais que vous m'aimiez.*" *And I thought you loved me.*

"*J'ai aimé votre poésie.*" *I loved your poetry.*

With disinterest Ravi turned to Misha. "Let's get out of here. With my luck, they'll arrest me next."

CHAPTER NINE
Spirits of the Georgia Prison Camp

"More water, more clean water."

Delphine was nearly done sawing through the femur.

Her two youthful helpers, Birro and Giyorgis, were both tremendous surgical assistants. She wanted to tell them that during the War, if they had started out as stewards guarding the medicine chests, they would have already graduated to assistant surgeons by virtue of their fearlessness and interest. She knew—her two years of book training in Syracuse and five years of practice hadn't even prepared her for the rank horrors of war—that the boys would turn out to be fine surgeons. Even now, they could gaze in wonderment when she incised skin and muscles down to the bone with her scalpel, and they knew almost all of the American words for the tools in her surgical case.

Delphine and Abou handed the man's leg over to the boys. They sometimes became so absorbed with the surgeries they watched at eye level they didn't hear her rudimentary Amharic orders, but then, they were boys. They certainly didn't ignore the leg, taken off above the knee after an amorous elephant had crushed the poor countryman, spiriting it off to their friends outside the surgery room before returning with zeal. Delphine didn't want to know what they did with the limbs, as long as they didn't pile up inside her building.

And Abou was a powerful assistant surgeon. He did all of the tall tasks such as holding the ether cone over the patient's nose and mouth, and restraining the patient during the excitement phase when they were prone to attempting to leave the table. He now stoically pinched a leg artery shut so that Delphine could tie it off with silk thread. He only demurred at the female tasks, such as those involving pregnant women.

"Ah, if only Eugene could see me now," Delphine mused aloud, almost happily. She knew she had no business feeling lighthearted during such a bloody procedure, but she reckoned long ago she'd become unresponsive to the business of flesh and body parts. "I should think he'd tell me, 'I never saw one make such tiny stitches of such elegant perfection,' and then he'd say, 'Your countenance is giving token of your inward emotion, Del'."

A shiver took hold of her and seemed to shake her like a rag doll so that she stood up straight, looking blankly at the grimy whitewashed wall. Giyorgis grabbed the needle she was finished with from her very fingers, and Abou handed her the metal file from her surgical case.

She shook her head to rid it of what must have been the evil eye, and set to scraping the ends of the femur smooth so that it wouldn't puncture the skin later. "Ah," she whispered. "I mustn't think of him, that's why such a chill went through me. I should think of someone happier, such as Captain Howland. He's an affectionate bear, yet there's such an untamed air about him." But she shivered again. This time the wave of supernatural creeps didn't stop at her tailbone but continued right down her legs. "All right, what is it?"

"It is men entering the courtyard," Abou answered her

rhetorical question.

Delphine filed even harder now, annoyed. "Well you can't be a guard and a surgeon at the same time, Abou. We must make sure Adan bin Kaushan can hire some more guards, or agree to Woizero Attitegeb's offer to loan us some of hers."

Her fingers slipped off the mass of sharp bone and slimy muscle that were just so much palimpsest to her now. *Captain Howland.* Although she had wanted to get away from the eventuality of his impinging upon her again, whether his intrusion be happy or full of ire, she now only thought of him pleasantly. "His piercing eyes," she whispered to Birro's rapt, shining face. "His vivid, picturesque speech makes me feel like . . . he knows what I look like with no clothes on."

She shared a private giggle with Birro, although he could hardly have known what she said.

The echoing clatter of armament in her courtyard caused her to nearly throw down her metal file. Giyorgis eased it out of her hand as she sprayed blood drops on the floor with it. "Oh, for the love of Saint John! As though it were dull as tombs over here, and we absolutely needed some more excitement! Now who's the blunderbuss?"

It sounded as though a battalion of barefooted soldiers marched in formation into the courtyard, then slammed their shields and spears onto the tiles as one.

"Kind sirs!" Kaspar pronounced from the gallery landing. "What is your business here?"

Giyorgis replaced the file in her hand with a fresh needle and silk thread as she struggled to interpret the Amharic reply. "We are here to see Miss Delphine Chambliss."

She turned to the Takrury, who was already holding the skin flap up over what used to be the countryman's knee. "Abou! What do they want?" She, too, positioned the skin flap, her fingers sliding alongside Abou's, without even looking at the leg.

"Sssh," said Abou, as his fingers encouraged her to start stitching.

She concentrated on sewing the slippery flap of skin while Abou translated.

"They are here . . . to see you. They come with a message . . . from Emperor Tewodros."

"The King of Kings!" She could hear Kaspar whisper loudly in awe before proceeding to invite the men to clatter their way upstairs.

Abou bent down low to put his face near Delphine's. "A message from Tewodros! This can only be something bad!"

Birro had his hands in the bucket of isinglass that would form the plaster to cover the wound. "He wants you to come to his palace and fix the sick people."

Abou glared at the innocent boy as though he had just suggested they open a slave market. "She's not going anywhere!"

Delphine jumped, and the needle leaped from her hand, when the rug that served as a door was flung aside and a magisterial man clad in a scarlet silk shirt strode in. Gasping and holding her hand to her bloody apron's breast, Delphine instantly hoped his startlingly blazing eyes and hooked nose indicated he was of the more sympathetic Abyssinian type, rather than the coarse and brutal. "Dejazmach," she said breathlessly. She'd found it helped to address any male in this royal manner, for if they hadn't attained the rank of Dejazmach, it certainly flattered them. "This is a surgery room, you must leave."

The soldier observed the patient's bloody stump with casual disdain and looked back to Delphine's streaked face. "You must come out . . . Now."

"No." She bent to retrieve her needle that was swinging in the air, as the patient was placed upon boards set upon two flat tree sections.

Giyorgis piped, "Ras Engeddeh! By the power of the Father,

the Son, and the Holy Ghost."

The haughty soldier smiled at the boy, and bent down to greet him.

Ras Engeddeh. That name sounded ... *Woizero Attitegeb's son!*

Delphine asked Abou, "Can you do the plastering?"

Abou nodded.

Wiping her hands on a cloth already soaked in blood, Delphine made a respectful curtsy to the Ras, and accompanied him upstairs.

In the drawing room, Kaspar regaled the platoon of musketeers and spearmen with a jabbering Amharic speech Delphine did not bother to grasp. He was apparently pouring *arrack* (not the valuable whiskey, she noted, but rather the strong spirit utilized when the objective was to get swizzled) for the men as they draped themselves about the room, all standing on one leg as they leaned on their matchlocks or spears. They all turned to Delphine when she entered, but the only one who displayed any horror at her sanguine appearance was Kaspar himself. His appalled intake of breath indicated someone standing behind her swung a few severed heads by their braided tresses.

Positioning herself by the aghast churchman, Delphine folded her hands before her apron lap and said in English, "Now. Can you explain your presence in my house. Be fast, for I have much work to do." She reckoned they needed her to doctor someone, for this wasn't the kidnapping Ravi had warned her of.

The Ras explained, and Kaspar translated.

"Tewodros has heard stories ... that you've come from the Red Sea ... bearing chests of gold ... and the symbol of Makeda, Queen of the South. He wishes you to come ... to his palace at Debra Tabor ... to discuss religion with him."

Delphine scoffed so blatantly her lower jaw hung open. "Chests of gold! Wherever did anyone get that idea?"

Kaspar regarded her sideways, skeptically. "I was wondering the same thing."

"Well, tell them it's completely out of the question! I have work to do here, and I like Gondar. I'm not going to go gallivanting about the hills and dales of this—this fine country just because someone orders me to." She shoved Kaspar in the shoulder. "Well, tell him!"

She knew enough Amharic to understand that Kaspar mostly expressed florid sentiments of love for the Emperor in his reply.

Undeterred, the Ras now apparently said, "Tewodros has heard that you are a great healer. He wishes also to discuss medicine with you, and ways of healing his people, for they often become very ill."

Sighing deeply, Delphine stepped obsequiously toward the Ras, curtsying again. She spoke haltingly in rude Amharic. "Thank you very much, Ras Engeddeh, for the message from Tewodros. But I cannot come. I'm a doctor, and have much work to do here."

Fire burned in the Ras's eyes, and he took several additional steps toward Delphine. His speech was so clipped and rapid, she could only make out that this, indeed, was probably the kidnapping of which Ravi had warned her. Her heart sped up its pounding in the pit of her throat, and a sick feeling of doom seeped into her entrails.

"He says no, Miss Delphine," Kaspar said tremulously. "He says you have no choice but to come with them!"

She railed a bit louder in the Amharic terms she knew, in the belief that the Ras would better understand if she shouted. "I have many amputations, cases of scrofula, elephantiasis, syphilis! Ask Woizero Attitegeb—she will not let me leave Gondar!"

The Ras shrilled louder, too. Delphine could understand that staying in Gondar was unacceptable, something to do with fires blazing across the night skies, and the excrement of elephants. His hand was on the grip of his holstered revolver.

"Miss Delphine," Kaspar wailed. "If you resist, I fear they will harm you."

Delphine spread her hands out with palms facing the floor. "Ras Engeddeh. Ask your mother; I may not leave Gondar!"

Apparently he didn't hold much stock in his mother, for he gestured at the musketeers, who came forward. Instinctively, Delphine whipped her Remington from her hip holster and leveled it at the Ras's head. All the grabbing hands stilled in the air, and the collective intake of spearmen's breath seemed to suck all the air from the very room.

"I . . . am . . . staying."

"Men! Put down your weapons!"

At least twelve spears and matchlocks went clattering to the floor at the sound of the rich, authoritative shout. That left Delphine the only person hoisting a weapon, and she didn't waver in the slightest with her dead aim at the Ras's forehead.

"Ravi." She smiled.

Ravi in all his warlike glory, his red silk *kamis* war-shirt, silver *betoa* armlet about his massive forearm, brandishing the *shamshir*. He strode into the room raising the roof masterfully with his angry lingo that reduced the soldiers to quivering wrecks of bones. They huddled together for protection, each man trying to use his brother as a shield. Amhara men, in the best of times with nary more fat on them than a stork, now quivered like a gaggle of shorebirds in the face of Ravinger's rampage.

Delphine could understand some of Ravi's rant. "Men . . . a crowd of rats . . . taking women . . . should have glory in war!"

Loping before her to drive the flock of men against the far wall, without even glancing at her Ravi wrapped his hand around her gun barrel to lower it to the floor, which she allowed with small resistance to show she wasn't cowed. He didn't miss a word of his harangue. "Men . . . should go back to cutting grass . . . sift corn . . . carry water!"

She was overwhelmed to be standing next to him again, and thrilled to the power of his voice, the supreme warmth he exuded that always rejuvenated her as though fresh blood ran through her veins. She would have taken ahold of his arm affectionately had not the quivering eyes of thirty men been upon them.

"Basha Falaka, it is good that you arrived," said Kaspar, quietly for once.

"Out, out!" Ravi bellowed at the men. They groped for their fallen weapons and clattered onto the gallery, their shields shivering before Ravinger's wrath.

Only then did he turn to Delphine, his wonderfully alive eyes fiery no longer, but brimming with passionate concern. He took her shoulders and asked her sweetly, "Are you all right? Those brutes didn't touch you?"

She replaced her gun in its holster, the better to enwrap her hands around his savagely bulging biceps through the thin cloth of his shirt. "No, but they were about to. Can you explain to the good Ras here that I simply cannot leave Gondar?"

He nodded distantly, his eyes scanning her from head to toe as though she might bear the imprint of some loutish fingers. His naked dark eyes had gone from a malevolent glare when he had addressed the spearmen to the adoring caress of a lover. He smiled, smearing her bedraggled hair back from her forehead with his hand. "As long as you tell me you were this bloody *before* they arrived in your house."

"Oh yes," Delphine laughed with delight. "I was amputating a leg downstairs."

A sudden nauseated pall came over Ravi's face. He turned to the Ras, who had remained immobile with the utmost patience, and Ravi apologized for ordering his troops about.

"They cannot take the woman . . ." was the gist of Ravi's statement. "Tewodros . . . She cannot leave Gondar."

Kaspar waved Delphine over to the sideboard. *"Was dieses über die Medaille ist?"* His hands shook as he poured his whiskey, spilling some. "They're here to get you because of that dunderheaded medal?"

Delphine uncorked a bottle of Jordan water. "Yes, but there's clearly been some mistake. The main one being that I am obviously not the Queen of Sheba."

Abou came belatedly roaring down the gallery then, brandishing his rifle as he leaped into the drawing room. But seeing he had no enemy other than five people with blank faces and their hands at their sides, he regained his normal sullen stance and strolled over to the sideboard as Ravi ushered the Ras from the room.

"Did you finish plastering the leg?"

Abou nodded as he poured *arrack* from a jug. "He woke up screaming, then I heard the Ras's men running from your room."

"Those tawny-visaged maniacs nearly kidnapped Miss Delphine!" Whiskey had elevated Kaspar's vocabulary to its former highfalutin level. "They adhere to vagaries and idle superstitions . . ." He shuddered visibly. "I feel a cold aguish sensation creeping over my heart . . ."

Ravinger returned. Brazenly taking Delphine's hand in his, he pressed his hot, generous mouth to it. "Go, get cleaned up. Here are some more items for your toilet."

She took the folded paper bundle to her room, where their housemaid always kept a basin of clean water. Kicking off her sandals, she stripped to her drawers, even throwing her salty chemise into the pile the housemaid would take and later beat threadbare in the river. She washed with a lovely lavender soap Colonel Merewether had sent along with the shipment of medicine.

Turning to the bundle Ravi had given her, she tore the paper eagerly. She expected to find a shirt of Manchester calico as he'd promised, richly embroidered in patterns around the neck, the bosom, and cuffs. Instead she found spilling like water over her hands a long rectangle of shimmering iridescent amber silk that matched her own eyes, she thought with a twinge of illicit excitement. Where had he obtained this? This was certainly not the plain white dress of Abyssinian women, nor the muted earth and sea tones of the Mussulman. But what to do with it? It was four yards wide, much too wide and sheer for use as a belt, one long edge embroidered in tiny silver filigree with infinitesimal bells.

The only other item in the package was a curious silk corset of the same shade, lined unlike the length of cloth. As it had tight short sleeves that barely covered her shoulder, she tried it first one way. She gasped. This couldn't be the correct manner! For there were only three sets of ties, and if she tied one under her arms and the other two below her breasts, the design surely dulled the intention by jutting her breasts out in an even more erotic attitude. She turned it around, instantly finding it more comfortable, the bodice clinking with dozens of tiny little mirrors she discovered she enjoyed shaking with her shoulders in the Abyssinian *eskesta* "shoulder dancing" method.

But this way must be wrong too, for even after securing the ties behind her neck and back, her breasts burst over the bodice even more bountifully. She had planned to use her Abyssinian belt to bind her breasts flat and then drape herself in the long amber cloth. She nearly reached for her belt, then stopped to consider.

Ravi had brought this for her. He wanted her to wear it, even if it was too small. She had to admit, it made her feel voluptuously . . . feminine. She could easily hide her breasts in the shapeless length of silk. He had certainly given her enough of that!

Abou waylaid her on the gallery to accompany her to the back garden.

Ravi waited in a glade, a circular clearing like a verdant dome covered over with thick braided vines. Abou respectfully faded into the bushes as Delphine stepped forward, hoping desperately Ravi didn't laugh at the way she'd arranged her costume—wrong, no doubt.

"Ah!" His piercing onyx eyes observed her with acumen as he came forward.

Delphine was pleasantly stunned when he gathered her in his long athletic arms, pressing his body to hers. She already felt nude, even though she was covered with several layers of the fine silk— she had no chemise, and she felt every ridge of his hard abdominal muscles pressing into her ribs. The lips of her vulva expanded, as though in preparation for accepting the tremendous penis pressing into her abdomen. She, who had always felt such an awkward gangly woman, felt precious and dainty in his arms!

He murmured into her loosely bound hair. "Without care of what began . . . for what shall end."

End? Who was discussing anything ending? Delphine gripped the man even tighter, nuzzling her face into the lemony smell of his clavicle. "I'm so glad you came," she whispered, "although I could have been rid of those soldiers myself."

He squeezed her as though he'd never thought to see her again, pulling away far enough to lay a gentle, wet kiss on her forehead. "My only truth. Never ever pull a gun on the Ras, unless you fully mean to use it."

She backed away. "I meant to use it, Ravi!"

"No. You wouldn't have shot the Ras."

She strolled about the little glade. "Of course I meant to! I only shoot strangers, and I've certainly never been introduced to the Ras! What do I care about those highland heathens? I say let them run about their savage kingdom, but when they come to the city to try to take me, that's where I must draw the line."

When she turned to regard him, he'd folded his arms across his chest warily. "How many men have you killed, Delphine? Including those two of mine in Metemma."

"Including those two? That would make eight."

He was silent for a moment, appreciating her sharpshooter's skills, she supposed. He threw back his head, exposing his fine full throat, and laughed deeply.

Didn't he believe her? She sputtered, "There was one—in Tennessee—I used to go behind enemy lines to tend the wounded—poor people stuck in swamps without homes—and a Reb came upon us, so I shot him. There was another in our camp in South Carolina who tried to raid inside the hospital tent, so I shot him too!" It was the truth!

He gathered her to him again. "I'm not questioning it."

"And another, when a party of men jumped our column—I had to shoot him three times when he refused to die."

He petted her hair as though she were a family dog. "I don't doubt you. That's part of why I call you my only truth."

She tried to squirm from his embrace. "I don't *enjoy* it, Ravi. As a surgeon, I'm supposed to save lives, not take them. But when under attack . . ."

Ravi finally became sober. "No, you're entirely correct. And you're going to need those cutthroat skills the next time Tewodros's soldiers try to grab you. When you're walking down the street perhaps, or at market, or in your own surgery room. I told you to accept Woizero Attitegeb's gold; now they all think you've got plenty of your own, like Makeda. Why didn't you go to Qwesqwam as I instructed you to?"

Instructed. Delphine didn't like the sound of that word. "It didn't seem necessary. Besides. It's fairly apparent that Ras Engeddeh doesn't give a hill of beans what his mother wants. I believe I heard him saying as much."

"You must have heard wrong." He scratched her behind the ears. Now he treated her like a cat! "Let me look."

He stepped back to regard her handiwork with the *shamma* he'd given her. She shivered with vulnerability, as she'd only had enough extra material to toss over her shoulder twice. As a result the outline of the mirrored corset was clearly visible, and perhaps the swell of her bosom as well. To make it worse, he laughed again in that full-throated lusty manner that displayed his muscular throat to such advantage.

"I see I shall have to give you a lesson in how to wrap your *sari*."

"My . . . what?"

Taking her gently by the shoulders, he said, "The *sari* is a traditional Hindoo woman's costume." To her horror he lifted the fabric from her shoulder, stepping around to unwrap her. When he stood before her again, he looked down with regard at the uplifted shelf of her bare breasts.

She tried half-heartedly to grab the material from his hand. "Please, Ravi. I can dress myself. I don't need a demonstration." His passionate look was turning her red-hot. No man had looked at her like that since Eugene, when they had coupled with such furor it was as though demons had overtaken their bodies. It could not happen again—no, it was impossible! It wasn't even a consideration!

"*Isgyoh*," he muttered, holding the silk fast in his fist.

Delphine pouted, taking ahold of the corset underneath her arms and shaking it to demonstrate. "Isn't it supposed to cover a bit more?"

Ravi both nodded and shook his head at the same time, as though his vast intellect had just been sucked up by a tornado. "Usually there isn't so much to cover."

Delphine frowned. She wanted to take command, not to be commanded by this man whose virility stamped his every word and movement. "You can finish dressing me now."

"Ah," he agreed, but his eyes did not leave her form as he finished unwrapping her to her one measly and threadbare petticoat. "You tuck it in like this to your petticoat. You gather several, say seven folds in your right hand. Tuck them into your waist, just to the left of your navel."

It wasn't lost on her the saturated heat that emanated from his long tapered fingers as he stood close behind her and tucked. The sensuous stroking of his fingers against her abdomen sent lascivious rushes of desire coursing through her quim. What would it be like to have such a man mount her? The abandon would utterly destroy her—she would be dashed into ten thousand bits of mirror like Ravinger's dear 'truth'!

She leaned back into him, lolling her head back against his chest. "And how are you so familiar with how to wrap a *sari?*"

He spoke to the shivering nape of her neck. "Because I've dressed so many Hindoo women."

He said it baldly, just like that, as though it were not a thing to be ashamed of! But then what did she expect from a man who knew twenty-three languages, in particular the language of pornography?

His hand grazed her bare abdomen, coming up to hold the part of the mirrored corset that barely covered her breast. "But never such a ripe piece of fruit as you, Delphine. Come."

Pulling her onward as though to take her right there in the undergrowth, Delphine stumbled up against a bench. She thought they would go crashing to the ground like a couple of *faro* dogs, but she fell onto his lap as he straddled the bench, her legs in the pretty *sari* to one side, as though she rode sidesaddle. She pressed her hands against the chest that she longed to love with her mouth.

She needed command, so she said lightly, "You haven't finished dressing me. I hardly think that Hindoo women walk about the streets in a corset like this. Or perhaps they did, in your section of town, once you were done dressing all of them."

Ravi laughed freely, apparently unafraid of her harshness. "It's a *choli*, and it doesn't usually have quite this . . . voluptuous effect. But then I don't think there is a woman in this hemisphere who would have this effect upon a *choli*." He looked solemnly at her now, his humor entirely dissipated, as he brushed the backs of his fingers against the bursting swelling of her bosom.

She didn't try to pull back—in fact, she rather leaned into his hand, because she enjoyed the sense of control such a simple thing as a bosom packed into a *choli* had over the superiorly arrogant man. Yet her heart raced with such fear and excitement she could see its pounding in his trembling hand, because it was entirely too obvious that *he* exerted a power over *her*.

She felt the truth when she squirmed her bottom over his strapping phallus. The more she squiggled, the more she planted her quim squarely over the massive length of it—and indeed, why was she wriggling at all? The detestably handsome man wasn't holding her captive, he was merely fondling her bosom, as he'd been known to do before. He was merely sliding his hand into the armpit of her *choli* and setting her breast free so that it bounced as he bent his head down to slurp her distended nipple into his mouth.

And oh, how she mashed her chest into his face then, wanting the touch of him, wanting that always led to wanting more and wanting more.

She slithered over his stupendous erection because she wanted it inside of her, and that insane desire always meant wanting more. She galloped her hips and sighed, enfolding his face in her chest until he took great big cow licks from her proudly displayed breasts. Needing more and more of the sex of a man, there would come a day when the man wasn't there any longer. What would she do?

She was a glutton that could not be fulfilled, unless *she* took command.

Withdrawing her torso from Ravi's ravenous mouth, she placed a hand of authority against the firm muscle of his pectoral. "A man is like a banana, and it won't yield its syrup until you stroke it between your palms."

How handsome he was, his wild feral eyes all out of focus like that.

Braiding her fingers together at the back of his slick neck, Delphine leaned into him and plied that muscular throat with fat noisy kisses. She licked his lemon and pepper sweat, pleased when guttural moans roiled up through the depths of his chest. Delphine took thorough delight in the tease and the torment until his penis jumped under the bucking ministrations of her bottom. Delving her face lower over his delicious clavicle to lick like a cat and dog both rolled into one, she yanked the red silk shirt down to reveal the satiny sun-browned brawn of his deltoid. His skin tasted as good as it looked as he leaned back onto the bench with one hand, the other fingertips pressing into her shoulder blade.

Delphine moved back only far enough to tear the red shirt from his torso and fling it somewhere into the nearby shrubbery. The man purred like an amenable lion when she lapped her tongue down the flexed plane of his pectoral, taking slurping bites and squiggling her tongue around the erect nipple.

It was delicious to have control over such a delightful animal of a man. Such control to feel that bulging muscular arm caress her head to him so tentatively, as he tossed her up and down with the power of his hips, rolling her saturated sex over the head of his penis. She nibbled and bit his salty nipple, flicking her fingernails over the other until she coaxed an erotic little roar from the pit of his stomach.

She came up against the barrier of his tightly wrapped belt, and all at once she wanted to roar too, and toss him to the ground.

He unwound his belt in a few dozen flashing movements of his hands. He had to sit up to do so, and now he took his chance to lean into her and try to kiss her. But Delphine was faster, and she quickly straddled him, shoving him back onto the bench so he fell back onto both hands. She was the mistress here. There would be no *wanting* him forever. There would be no futile pining for that which wasn't obtainable. Not as long as she remained in control.

His look was pleading. "Delphine. Let me love you. Let me take you."

She knew she had a rapacious gleam of almost evil intent in her eyes. "No, Ravinger. I can't allow that."

Sliding her hand down the tensile surface of his gloriously bared abdomen, Delphine wrapped her hand around the thick root of his penis jutting from the steamy mound of his pubic bone. She was timorously shocked at the massive circumference of it in the grasp of her hand, though she'd felt its breadth many times sliding urgently against her bottom. Now she had his phallus pulsating in her hand—both hands, for she slid the other below to lift his heavy balls into the open air—and she swept her thumb over the straining head to gloss the dribble of semen down its charged length.

His groan was that of a dying lion, and she'd never witnessed a more spectacular sight than Ravinger with his head tossed back, leaning on both elbows on the bench, utterly at her mercy.

She had the Likamaquas of Amhara at her bidding, in her very hands.

Gripping him tightly, she slowly deliberately frigged him up and down the very length of him. He was a gorgeous pulsating animal, galloping his hips to thrust against the pumping of her hands. For she needed two hands to manipulate the phallus, one stroking the root of it while the other squeezed and pumped the tip, her fingers snaking a glissando over the bursting shiny head.

It was like frigging a beast, a wild satyr. He was a monumental male creature with his pelt of silken hair covering his chest, a darker lineation running from between his pectorals down the middle of his ridged abdomen, melding into the sultry mound of his crotch. It was a scene of lushness for the senses to stroke him like that, the way he quivered and twitched in her hands, the lolling of his head back on a boneless neck, the heaving of his silken chest. Such was her ardor she leaned forward to apply great squiggles of the flat of her tongue to that supreme chest while not missing a single lubricious stroke of her hands.

When she bit lightly down on his nipple, he craned a brawny arm and held fast to the back of her neck, and he met his crisis swiftly with an unbridled groan.

And oh, how she lost all ideas of propriety then with the feel of that great pulsing limb in her hands, and she lunged over him to feverishly suck kisses to the underside of his jaw, his throat, his gloriously sleek shoulders.

He convulsed and came for a long time, with guttural exclamations in foreign languages that only enhanced her passion, if such a thing were possible. For at the moment she would have with no remonstrance rolled on the ground with him as though ten barnyard animals in one, rutting in the mud and reveling in the briars.

She slowed her hands down to accommodate his tapering orgasm, and when she blinked the phosphenes from her eyes she found they were both panting like lathered horses having run the entire valley, only . . .

She wanted him even more.

Egad! How had that happened?

No, no, it was her overwhelming passion for all things male, not any sort of strange and misguided 'love' for this man! It was lust, lust was leading her astray.

Lordy, he was hung like a bull.

They panted into each other's mouths as she squirmed her hand down the entire length of his penis, gently fondling his prodigious balls as he twitched and gasped.

She had thought to take charge because to allow his body to love hers would mean her obliteration. But now she had a conundrum. Because *she wanted him even more.* She fairly oozed off the thigh she'd been rocking on for a good while now. This wasn't supposed to happen.

Ravi held her face close to his by grasping a fistful of her hair. "Delphine, *siete una donna fine.*"

They kissed then, that manner of sloppy kissing lovers are prone to, Delphine with her arms engulfing his exquisitely sculpted bare back, her fingertips feeling the wonder of every ridge and contour of his slick muscular torso.

✳   ✳   ✳

"Delphine, you're a fine woman."

He had never seen a woman exude such sensuality, so utterly confident and embracing her own carnality. In particular, he'd never known a *ferenje* woman so unashamed and blatant, a woman who accepted the inevitability of the art of love. Even nautch girls, the Ghawázi dancers of Egypt, and Somali princesses had a sort of detachment, that they were just submitting, or committing acts upon him.

"*Isgyoh.*" He licked her mouth while she purred around him like a giant twining feline. "How is it . . . you've learned to be such a delectably wanton siren?"

She kissed his mouth as though sucking on a delicious fruit. She pulled away dreamily, her eyes swimming with stars. The fragrant pomegranate breeze after the rains lifted her hair about her face.

He thought she'd say something inspirational, something poetic. "In a rebel prison camp in Georgia."

Then, to further confound him, she drew back like an elegant heron, still smiling dizzily at him.

He came to himself enough to stuff his twitching cock inside his breeches, cinch them up about his hips, and sit upright. "But how . . . is that possible?" He frowned.

Gazing happily at a myrrh tree, she flung the silk of the *sari* back over her shoulder. She spoke to the tree. "I was in love." She seemed to be angelically happy, thinking of this love in Georgia, as though the fellow sat on a branch.

Ravi lifted her damp sweaty hair from her neck, but he didn't dare refer to the bold assertion she'd just made. "Were you ever married?" he asked softly.

"No." She whipped her head to face him. "Were you?"

He shook his head. He wanted to know more about the prison camp fellow, but couldn't come up with a suitably polite phraseology. "I have no interest—" he started to say, but she cut him off.

"Nor have I." She turned to face front again.

Her distance was distressing him. He felt they had just been so beautifully intimate and now she was as vibrant as a butcher in a cornfield. He stroked her cheek with the backs of his fingers, and murmured quietly, "I should have abstained from my own pleasure. You must think me the most selfish of all men." On impulse he slid from the bench to kneel on one knee at her side. Still looking into her kohl-lined eyes, his hand rummaged in the leather *zenar* he had dropped to the ground. He withdrew a few leaves that resembled wilted spinach, and presumed to raise them to Delphine's lips.

Delphine smiled indulgently at him. She must have known what it was, for she opened her mouth just enough to snake out her tongue and snatch the leaves, sensuously, like a chameleon. She did this with studied intent looking for all the world like an experienced concubine, then rolled the *chat* leaves about her mouth and gently crushed them.

"Ah," sighed Ravi. "I'm sorry, but normally that would be betel nut. I was out of betel nut." It was a universal rule that no matter how shy or angered a woman may be, she never disregarded a man kneeling at her feet.

"Ah," agreed Delphine, adorably storing the wad of *chat* up between cheek and gum with the tip of her tongue. "That's fortunate—betel nut is nasty, but I've taken quite a liking to this *chat*. I chew it often during surgery—which reminds me, I'd better go see to my amputee."

Cringing, Ravi covered his vitals with one hand. "No, no," he said, running his other thumb along the plump outline of her lower lip. "Dear truth, it is my turn to pleasure you; you've been much too unselfish."

She did look fondly upon him then, and returned the stroking of his face. "Isn't the orgasm known as the *petit mort* in France? If I die, then I really shall think I've seen a spirit when I gaze upon you." She sighed deeply. "You really are the most exquisitely handsome man I've ever known. Perhaps *you* have died, and *you* really are a spirit. I've seen them, you know. Spirits."

As both subjects, orgasms and spirits, were foremost among Ravi's diverse interests, he warmed to the topic. He remained kneeling, as the sight of his naked chest seemed to excite her particular attention. She gazed at his chest, she talked to his chest, she touched his chest. "Ah, yes, I've been intrigued by the spiritualism movement ever since the Fox girls communicated with spirits in New York."

"I saw a spirit in Georgia," Delphine said lightly.

He wanted to say *I am sure you saw many spirits in the prison camp*, but didn't want to refer directly to it. "Is that so? And what did it look like?"

Leaning casually back to retrieve Ravinger's silk shirt that now seemed like such a rag, she said, "Oh, it looked like a man. Like a man standing right next to my bed at three in the morning. I recognized him, too." With the shirt, she sensuously rubbed dry the wet areas that still remained on Ravi's chest and throat. When a section was wet, she gently took a fresh dry section to tend to his throat.

"Yes? And who was it?"

"It was a fellow surgeon, and he was standing there imploring with the most beseeching face imaginable . . . I rushed back to his quarters, only to find he had just . . . expired, and that I had not been there when it happened."

Ravi shuddered. "I'm very sorry. That must have been trying."

"I have a talking board," she mentioned as she shook out the shirt and laid it on the bench beside her. "In Paris we tried to communicate with the surgeon, but I think some of those clods were just joking, and pushed the planchette whichever way they thought would have the most humorous results. It's just a piece of pressed board on which are written the letters of the alphabet, but I've had much success, particularly with Anatole alone. As a poet, I think his spirit is aligned with the other side of the veil more so than a man based purely in the physical." She got to her feet.

Ravinger took that as his dismissal, and he stood too. "Regarding your poet, surely you've calculated now that he was the one who stole your medal."

Delphine looked at the ground, hugging her *sari* to herself. "Do we know that for a fact?"

"He admitted it when he was dangling from my fist like a sack of horse sh—manure."

Ravi's heart nearly melted in two when she looked up at him

from under her kohl-dusted lashes, and he saw she was trying to suppress a smile. "Well, then. I am most definitely not marrying *him* in that case! Now, I really do have to attend my patients."

Awash with relief the woman had finally hung up the idea of marrying that clown, Ravi whisked his red shirt from the bench and followed her through the overhanging vines. "Please, do wear some sort of smock over your *sari*, my dear. I don't fancy seeing bloody guts staining your beautiful ensemble."

"But of course. I shouldn't want to operate wearing a corset. Somehow it wouldn't seem right."

"Good. I shall go find you a good joint of *brundo* and have your cook roast *tibs* for dinner. Unless, of course, you've already developed the Amhara predilection for eating it raw."

"You don't need to stay for dinner. Surely you have more—"

"I'm staying overnight, Delphine. Don't you remember what I said about hacking the Emperor's fingers from your doorknob?"

"But—"

"Have no fear, I'll sleep on an *arat* with some skins. And I've been told I don't even snore. Now, if you'll let me inspect your kitchen for varmints . . ."

CHAPTER TEN
THE VERY EDGE OF THE WORLD

THE NEXT FEW DAYS WERE THE most pleasant of Delphine's life, since days she couldn't quite recall before the War, whose murky mottled images came back at her in odd moments, when bathing in the tin tub, or "making her gun drunk" by rubbing it with butter. She often had visions of Eugene now, not beseeching or chastising her as formerly; no, now he seemed pleased with her, as though her doctoring the downtrodden of the highlands was beneficial to his tortured spirit.

She was nearly as happy as a cricket in those few days. The presence of the Likamaquas in her house was agreeable to her. His existence seemed to shed a salutary aura over the very blood that ran through her. Whether or not it was possible for another's emanations to have such an effect upon one's blood was still debatable among those in the medical trade. But it certainly felt apparent to Delphine whenever she turned a corner of her house and noted him standing there, conversing in his mellifluous Amharic to his shield-bearer, a tigerish man whose many braided tresses spoke of his prowess on the killing fields. Ravi would cast her a sideways glance full of honey and warmth, and Delphine felt that their inner smiles were apparent to everyone—not such an awful thing in a land where the rich and the great practiced polygyny without embarrassment.

Apparently Ravi came equipped with not only a shield-bearer, but also a valet who seemed quite attached to him, with his dolorous cow's eyes that reminded her of her sweet slain Adam. The valet Wubishet lurked in the shadows, prepared to jump out with a *barrilye* of *tej* whenever Ravi so much as lifted a hand, yet retreated into the bushes so as to impersonate a gnarled gum tree flat against a cliff at the sight of Ravi making a movement toward Delphine. His promptness was such that once, when Delphine brought a section of pomegranate to Ravinger's mouth, the valet leaped out with a ready rag to wipe the trickle of juice from his chin.

There were also two or three surly men armed with Enfields and spears who popped up at the oddest times and places. Ravi assured her they were not the men of his party who had murdered Adam, but Delphine still waved them away whenever they loomed too closely.

Yet Ravi hadn't made any amorous motions toward Delphine. He seemed to think that now that he was her protector, his mission was higher and nobler than the sordid exercises of lust. It irritated her no end to be next to his masterful body, and to be discussing something so innocuous as snake priests, or maps of the Royal Geographical Society, or his favorite poet Camões the Portuguese, and to know that when his hand grazed her face, that would be the end of it. He would retire to an *arat* bed in an empty bedchamber, and she had once seen him wrapped up in his *shamma* while his breeches and belt hung over a chair. In this manner she discovered how men loosened their *shammas* about them, using them as bedclothes at night. He lay splayed on his stomach embracing the *arat*, his powerful bursting biceps refulgent of the darkest amber from the sun, bare to the erotic slope of his lower back before it dipped beneath the covering. And his calves, so supremely muscled and molded like a classical statue, the warmth of desire had instantly spread through Delphine at the sight, and she had to forcibly remove herself from the doorway before a swoon overcame her.

Now she knew he told the truth: he didn't snore.

On the evening of the third day, she sat on her bedchamber balcony composing a letter she intended to post to her dearest friend Siobhan, in Cairo, Illinois. It was pleasant on the balcony, the warm fragrant pomegranate breeze rustling the brittle fronds of the red *ensete* bananas. She had just swallowed a relaxing dose of laudanum, and was trying not to think of the milling and moaning of the ill down in the street, or of the Likamaquas. She did not succeed very well in the latter.

My dearest Siobhan,

How do you fare in Cairo? Sometimes I feel that I'm at the very edge of the world, about to be swept over the cliff into a void of nothingness.

Much has happened since my last missive. Anatole turned out to be a rat of the highest order. Thank goodness I never really intended to marry him. As a result, the Emperor of this benighted country sent some ruffians to forcibly remove me from Gondar to his kingly camp—sort of a regiment on the move, with lots of sorry tents and wretched soldiers—and they were only prevented by the heroic actions of that very self-same Captain of War I told you was such a despicable barbarian! How odd things turn out!

He is now living in my house Siobhan, as a protector of course, and I must tell you . . . I do not mean to be saucy, but there has been some canoodling that is very much to my liking, and has really put me to rights. He is not the ghastly heathen I formerly imagined. He is a refined man of great knowledge who speaks many languages—chief among them being the language of pornography I am sure! Please forgive my sauciness, for he has riled me to unexpected heights and it's perfectly maddening. I'm just in a passion, and you know how I get so savage! No one could ever replace Eugene as you know so that is not the intention here—no, I just have eyes for this man.

There could not be a man as opposite from your Fred! I do not think you'd like him much—

"Ah, I'm glad to see you having a break from your medicine."

Delphine jumped a little, but was instantly overcome with ease when Ravi's upper-drawer Newport-on-the-River inflections graced her ears. Looking up with a smile, she slid her hands over her pages of writing. "Please, do sit down."

Seating himself on a wooden bench, Ravi plunked his Bordeaux bottle and red *barrilye* onto a small inlaid table. His obsidian eyes flashed with a devilry when he leaned forward with his arms on his knees and said confidentially, "I know you're a woman of temperance and don't approve of the vine, but I'll have you know, I have demonstrably refrained from imbibing *afyuni* and for that you must be grateful."

Delphine placed an unused sheet of stationery over her written page. "I much prefer the mellow attitude of an *afyuni*-smoker to the belligerent croaking and staggering Virginia fences of the man with a brick in his hat."

"Ah, yes," said Ravi, gazing warmly up at her from under his eyelashes as he poured the wine. "Nepenthe. The 'drug that has the power of robbing grief and anger of their sting, and banishing all painful memories'."

"How do you know? I mean, what is that from?"

"Homer's *Odyssey*. Paris gave opium to Helen after he'd abducted her to make her forget her old home."

"Ah. Well, I don't enjoy the abduction part, but I certainly would like to forget my old home."

" 'Not poppy, not mandragora, nor all the drowsy syrups of

the world, shall ever medicine thee to that sweet sleep which thou owedst yesterday'."

Delphine tilted her head. "That sounds vaguely Shakespearean. I've never enjoyed him. I have to concentrate much too hard to understand what he's trying to say."

Ravi toasted her with his red glass. It seemed to swim with crystals of dazzling cinnabar. "But you must read Shakespeare if you spend any time with Tewodros. He shames many of our countrymen with his knowledge."

"Good." Delphine pouted, an attitude she knew Ravi to enjoy. She was rewarded by the rapacious way he looked at her lower lip, his imperious aggressive eyes she would have thought were unfriendly had she not known better. "I knew there was at least one reason I didn't care to spend any time with Theodore. When are you returning to his camp?"

Ravinger was silent for quite a while, sipping his wine and staring out across the garden. Delphine utilized this chance to fold her letter into thirds and slide it into her battered copy of Swedenborg's *Amor Conjugialis.*

"Perhaps I won't go back," Ravinger said at last. His words swirled voluptuously around his red barrilye, laden with meaning.

"Do you mean just in the next week? Or month?" How she wished he would say *No, I mean ever. I won't ever go back.* For in the short time she'd known him, Delphine could not imagine a day passing without seeing him, without being blessed by the sheer intensity of those flashing basalt eyes—her spirit was already torn asunder by the deprivation of his embrace these past three days, during which she'd felt like a barren skeleton devoid of flesh or purpose, her blood's longing for his emanation was so strong.

His tone was ruminative. "No, I mean ever."

Had she heard correctly? Delphine sat erect, on the edge of her chair. "Ever? You can't be serious. Theodore is your master."

She instantly knew she'd spoken in error by the acerbic way he lifted one eyebrow at her. "Tewodros may be master of the world, but he's no master of me."

"Of course. I didn't mean to imply that you . . ."

Getting to his feet, Ravi came to her. He stroked the side of her throat as she inclined her head. "In Amhara we say that a master is a child. That means it's our duty to soothe him, pet him, advise him, answer him, understand all his actions. There isn't one great man in Abyssinia who hasn't either recognized a master willingly, or been forced to do so in chains. I'm weary of either way."

She looked up at him, nuzzling her head farther into his broad palm. "But Amhara is your life. Your partner Misha, your shield-bearer Walde Nebra, and your servants, and concub—"

She was glad when he cut her off, as she should never have said the last bit, by sinking his fingers into her hair and rubbing her scalp. Her head lolled against his lap as he stood with feet outspread, her face dangerously in propinquity to the heat of his lazily erect penis. "Dr. Chambliss. We came to Abyssinia to be kings, and kings we have been. There are other quarters of the world to conquer. I've long wanted to explore Greenland, which as you know is ice, and Iceland, which as you know is green." He urged her face into the impressive ridge of the phallus that he'd inexpertly tried to cinch under his belt.

Her craving for him so overpowered her she could only breathe in short puffing breaths, and she managed to gasp, "I could not see you as a banker . . . you would have to keep conquering lands . . . of pygmies and aborigines." Her hand reached up and squirmed between his thighs from underneath the folds of his *shamma*. She was stunned by the heat of his firm balls under the flimsy covering of his snug breeches, drawn up tight and hard between his athletic thighs. She fondled him with infinite yet eager tenderness.

How could she ever remain in control if her mouth kept

salivating for the taste of him? He could reduce her to such a slithering pile of invertebrate jam simply by caressing her face to his crotch. Perhaps it was *she* who could retain power over *him* by standing, tossing him to the floor, and—her fingers crawled up over the root of his hulking penis, twining about the trunk of it, worshiping it like a phallic god.

She was whipped from her lusty trance when he grabbed her beneath her arms and yanked her up to face him. The air was sucked from her lungs and the man panted down at her, trembling with lust. The granite bands of his femoral muscles, pressed against hers, were wracked with tremors, and he grasped both her wrists in one broad hand and held them in the small of her back.

"Delphine." His voice was heavy with the shaky tonalities of a lust that was almost drugged. He leaned over her, his free hand delving into her loose coiffure and cradling her skull to his face. "You must let me love you properly. Let me pleasure you with the whole of my body. I can't just get you off . . . We need to unite our desires, to obtain our satisfaction . . . by climbing the tree of each other."

The mere concept that she would obtain satisfaction upon any one part of this man's splendid body was enough to cause Delphine's knees to cave, as though some *buda* had suddenly slid a wheeled wagon beneath her legs. The man was astute enough to capture her sinking body in both his arms, and he flung himself back against the balcony's rickety wooden railing to cushion her against his solid mass.

His eyes remained wild, unaffected by her swoon. "But not here . . . I want to pleasure you in a red tent, upon lions' skins—" His hand caught her jawbone. "What's wrong?"

How had he noticed the brief twitch of her eyes when she saw a flapping of white fabric down in the garden? She didn't want to mention it. She wanted to "climb his tree"—But he embraced her around the waist with one long arm, sliding his Colt's from his holster with the other, as he twisted them in tandem to look out over the garden.

The flash of white fabric came slowly into focus, and she saw it was a man at about the same time that Ravi roared.

"Hey! *Dadab!*" *Idiot!* His swear Amharic words didn't hurt her ears nearly as much as the explosion from his revolver. The Colt's had such a kick that even Ravi's forearm that seemed composed nearly entirely of sinewy iron recoiled back a foot.

Delphine saw instantly that Ravi hadn't meant to kill the man, as even she could have made that shot from that distance. Moreover, if Ravi intended to kill, he wouldn't have shouted a single word. But it appeared that he hit Said's foot, for the shifty snake limped, leaving a red trail across the viridian green of the fallen leaves.

Returning his Colt's to its holster, Ravi bellowed down, "*Yet abat?*" *Where is your father?* One of the most venomous insults one could give. The fire-arms trader didn't whimper a word as he staggered, snarling, from the garden.

Ravinger looked down at Delphine, a slow smile at the corners of his luscious mouth. How could he be so relaxed when he'd just shot a man? She instantly knew he'd draw correlations between this, and her shooting of eight men, but there was a big dissimilitude between the two. Those eight men had been attacking her, or someone in her near neighborhood. Said had just been wandering in the garden.

"He's after something in that godown," Ravi explained almost jovially, as Walde Nebra came jangling into the yard below with limbs flailing, a useless rifle in his hand.

"That shack?"

The valet Wubishet and the looming gunners now crowded them on the balcony railing, much too late to have been of any assistance, shouting and gesticulating down at the empty garden. Ravi coolly said, "Yes, that storeroom down there. You stay here, I'll go look at it."

"Abou must have the key to that padlock."

"Don't move a muscle—stay in your bedchamber," Ravi admonished her. He made as if to go, then turned back, gathering her to him in his arms. Delphine flung her arms about his neck, relishing the rough hemp feel of the myriad of tiny braids he had tied behind his neck. "My Queen of Heaven." Kissing her upper lip with a languid, tantalizing lick, he then wrenched himself away, going through the bedchamber with the clamoring gunners all pushing and stumbling over one another.

Delphine didn't follow Ravi's instructions exactly; she stood at the balcony railing fingering "my food," her affectionate name for the Remington she wore in a hip holster. The little crowd of men, after being assisted by Abou with his key, disappeared into the darkness of the square thatch-roofed storage room. Loud exclamations and arguing then emanated for a good ten minutes.

Queen of Heaven. Did Ravi believe that nonsense about her being the Queen of the South? *Oh Lord, what a thoroughly carnal beast that man is.* Sighing deeply, Delphine shut her eyes for a brief moment and allowed herself to indulge in a vision. His flashing eyes that clearly had a strain of the gipsy in them, how utterly depraved it was to lick the fullness of his lower lip. And when he slept, all gloriously sprawled and bare even of the silver *betoa* cuff that signified he had killed ten men . . . Delphine longed to run her tongue across the deliciously edible slope of his back where the rise of his gloriously muscled haunches dipped beneath the covering of the *shamma.*

Delphine nearly swooned again, and had to sit on her chair breathing deeply until the men were expelled from the godown, a snarling knot of flailing rifles and shouted expletives. Ravinger strode rapidly across the yard, and Delphine skittered through her bedchamber to meet him at the door.

"What is it? I heard many mentions of guns."

Ravinger continued striding back onto the balcony, where he sipped his wine and snorted ferociously through his nostrils. Abou was now there, but he deferred to Ravi to explain the situation. "Because there *are* guns in there. Fifty, sixty old muskets, shotguns, rifles, different makes and models, some as rusty as a chastity belt hasp, but guns all the same."

"Oh, holy . . ." Delphine breathed, and took Ravi's free hand in both of her own.

"My dear." Ravi put his wine down. "I know it isn't your fault; I know you would never willingly have let that shifty Shoho in here, and I'm not leaping to conclude that your former betrothed allowed him to store artillery in your house."

Abou couldn't help himself now, for he burst out with, "Mister Verlaine has the only other key! Unless Consul Cameron escaped from Magdala and returned to his house as a ghost in the night, and put the guns there!"

Delphine was aghast. "Anatole most certainly *did* have a hand in this! Captain Howland, I realize you're trying to be gracious and not hurt my feelings, but now I wish you had tried to shoot him a bit higher than the foot!"

Ravinger said calmly, "Well, be that as it may. I can easily conscript the fire-arms, and send some of my gunners back to Tewodros's encampment, saying that I seized them in battle or some such garbage. Tewodros won't care where they're from, he'll just be elated to have more guns."

"But don't you think Anatole meant to send them to Theodore anyway?"

There came a long silence fraught with a meaning of which Delphine was unsure. Abou looked sideways at Ravi while Ravi looked at Delphine's feet.

"What I mean is . . . Of course he was collecting them to give to Theodore? Correct?"

Ravi sighed, rubbing Delphine's hands in his own. At last he said, "Probably not, my Queen. Said is known to be sympathetic to Dejazmach Kassa in Tigré. There are all sorts of possibilities . . . none of them very uplifting, I'm afraid."

"Oh, God's holy trousers." Delphine collapsed in her chair and stared at the godown in the garden. Her mind had been mulling over something as basic as rutting, all the while she could have been executed for harboring treasonable fire-arms!

Squatting next to her in the Abyssinian manner with hands dangling between his knees, Ravi spoke gently to her. "I'll parley with my men, get our story right. We'll wait for darkness . . ."

"Make people believe they have loads of bananas and oranges," Abou suggested.

Ravi graced Abou with his brutal flashing eyes. "I'll load them up with things nobody will want to touch or steal—animals with teeth in their upper jaw, such as hares, or hyenas."

"*Awnat, awnat.*" *True, true.* "They do not like the animals with fingers on their feet."

Ravi returned his gaze to Delphine, and she was comforted by the instant manner his look transformed from the eyes of a wild beast to an affectionate lover. Gazing upon her seemed to please him. His angry obstinate mouth lost its hardness, and curled upwards into the beginnings of a sly smile. He said something to her in a language so seductive and syrupy her innards quivered, from her heart in the pit of her throat to her trembling quim. She felt certain he would grab her and kiss her then, but he didn't. He rose and strode back through her bedchamber, leaving Delphine to race after him like a schoolgirl in the throes of puppy love.

"Ravi," she called.

Turning, he looked knowingly at her, as though pleased with his enigmatic performance.

"When we were ... When I ..." She had to walk closer to him so she could talk more quietly. "When we were *close* and ... on the stone bench in the garden ..."

"When you stroked me so expertly I came off at once in my own face?" His look was playful, erotic.

"Why, yes. What language were you speaking?"

Ravi made a big show of rolling his tongue around in his mouth and screwing up his face, as though he couldn't recall. Then he said with alacrity, "Slavonic Jaghatic." With a grin, he turned to leave, and she stopped him again.

"And what is that?"

He walked backward onto the gallery as he spoke. "It's the language of the Gipsy Jats, spoken from the Ukraine to Afghanistan."

She couldn't very well detain him any longer by asking what he had said as he'd lain splayed with his member so proudly exhibited. He was in a rush to speak to his men, and he clearly didn't relish or want a repeat performance of the episode on the garden bench. Maybe he felt she was too bold, too forward, and that was unappealing to him. Worse yet, perhaps her technique compared unfavorably to the women he'd known—after all, they were trained concubines and nautch women!

Wandering back to her dressing table, Delphine lifted the laudanum bottle and uncorked it. She had learned all of her lovemaking in the rat-infested chambers of a prison camp. They had coupled like feral pigs, entombed with the broiling stench of the dead entrapped by the high walls and trees, trying to breathe lungfuls of hope into each other, but only felt desperation and despair.

"*Ach.*" Kaspar entered, frowning over his shoulder at the departing Likamaquas. "There is a cross of Gipsy blood in him! He speaks Romany like the Gipsies themselves! I tell you, Missus

Delphine, he is a foul, twisted and quite worrisome man!"

Exhaling laudanum fumes, Delphine stared over Kaspar's shoulder at the empty gallery beyond. "Gipsy . . ."

Kaspar jumped visibly, shrinking back as though a hyena wearing a lady's earring had leaped at him. A wavering feminine sound issued from his trembling lips. *"Die Grausamkeit!"*

Delphine sprang to her feet to see what horrified him. She laughed with relief to see it was only her *choli* and *sari*, draped over the back of a chair. She picked them up and sighed happily at the feel of the silk sliding over her fingers, and Kaspar backed slowly out of the room.

CHAPTER ELEVEN
THE MORMONS OF DESERET TERRITORY

"THERE IS SOMETHING INEFFABLY PLEASANT IN a tropical morn in the Black Highlands."

Ravi cheerfully agreed with Kaspar. "The brisk air of these vast buttes and mesas reminds me of the sandstone monoliths of the Utah Territory."

From the city they had ridden southwest through narrow defilements in the hills that ranged like Cyclopean embattlements around Gondar. They were in search of medicinal herbs for Delphine's laboratory, in particular the purgative bulb *michamicho* that was held to be superior to *kosso* in its laxative effects. Delphine also demanded *endod* buds to wash clothes with, Abyssinia sorely lacking soap. They had pushed onward through acacia forests, then water-carved narrow canyons, and brooks bestride the *wanza* and *warka* trees, emerging onto a rich alluvial field where they lay in soft grass and aromatic herbs next to a pumpkin garden. The shield-bearers and gunners made a fire where they soon had a bubbling pot of peppered pumpkin, and the *frenjoch* stretched their limbs by a larger, smokier fire for their tea.

"Gratitude invigorates the breast, and holy visions gladden—

Utah?" The hand of Kaspar's holding the *barrilye* of *arrack* stilled in midair. "In the United States?"

"Yes, dear Kaspar, I mapped much of that territory from the Wahsatch Mountains to Ogden City and the Great Salt Lake, and took great interest in the pluralistic teachings of Joseph Smith. You might take interest in it as well, Kaspar, for certain of their credos seem perfectly aligned with many of your mottos. For instance, 'Which truth shineth. This is the light of Christ. As also he is in the sun, and the light of the sun, and the power thereof by which it was made'."

Kaspar stood alert, his ears perked like a rabbit's. "I like this Joseph Smith fellow! He must be one of the exemplary Americans who are leading the country into the Utopian future of tomorrow!"

Ravi chuckled. He did so love chatting with the good deacon. " 'Wherefore, let no man glory in man, but rather let him glory in God, who shall subdue all enemies under his feet'."

Kaspar nearly spat forth his mouthful of *arrack*. "Yes, yes! This is astounding! Perhaps . . . could it be . . . that this Smith fellow might join us in Abyssinia, and share his visions with the Emperor? This is astounding! In essence, then, the royalty of Gondar claims to be descended from Solomon!"

"This is what he's been calling for, for men of vision and industry to join him and raise this country to the heights for which it was intended!" His shining eyes were moons that reflected the velvety cumulus clouds above. "And do they have artisans? They must be very industrial people there in Utah!"

"Indeed, Mr. Brigham Young of the Latter-Day Saints is the *Sheikh-el-Jebel*, the Old Man of the Hill, and the 'Zion on the tops of the mountains' forms a fair representation of Alamut. They've been shooting and cutting one another in all directions, and the law is boldly defied everywhere."

"Can we send for them? I shall speak to Tewodros—"

"Kaspar, Kaspar! Joseph Smith also teaches in the Covenants 'Inasmuch as any man drinketh wine or strong drink among you, behold it is not good . . .' "

Kaspar's frozen eyes narrowed a bit. "Well. Perhaps we will not invite this Smith fellow, then."

Placing aside his cup of tea, Ravi stood and reached a hand down to Delphine. "Come." He pulled her to her feet. He said loudly enough for everyone to hear, "There's a fine stream just down that ravine. I'm confident you'll find some *michamicho* there. Or I shall find a wild swine to shoot, and your syphilitics may drink of its blood."

"With the raw liver of the hyena, so you may scare off Kaspar and Abou," Delphine looked at him from under the coy fluttering of her dusky lashes.

"That would be an additional benefit," Ravi replied.

Abou had up until now been loudly slurping his pumpkin stew as befitted any proper man of the Ethiopian plateau. He called out gaily, "I do not get scared easily, Captain."

Kaspar sneered at him. "You would eat the barely braised eyeballs of a dirty hare, you unkempt heathen."

"Thank you for the receipt idea, Kaspar," Ravi waved as he escorted Delphine down the rise. "I'll mention it to Cook tonight."

"You're a terribly saucy man." Delphine hugged his forearm tightly, lodging it directly underneath her breasts. "Why do you hate Kaspar so?"

"Because it's easy enough to do. I actually like the poor misbegotten fellow. It's to his credit that he stays in Abyssinia when he's certainly free to leave. He does have a serious spiritual quest to convert those unfortunate Falasha Jews, and he will absolutely not abandon his mentor, Reverend Stern, as long as he's being held in Magdala."

"He does have admirable qualities, and it's wrong of you to

hate him. I suppose you did speak to the Emperor on his behalf for that girl he wants to marry, that does somewhat redeem you in my eyes."

Ravinger pointed to the gorge. "Ah, here is where you're likely to find your *Oxalis semiloba* bulbs, under that grove of *warka* trees. Step lightly—you must get accustomed to going without shoes."

He helped her down the path wide enough for a goat, but she was nimble, and didn't really need his assistance.

They reached the first shelf of the gorge, where a stand of enormous gnarled *warka* trees grew from the sandy loam. The trees were ancient; Ravi guessed them to date from the time of Christ, with long glossy leaves and sweet white flowers. Nearby there were some green shoots that looked to be the bulbs Delphine wanted, and they both got on their knees to yank them.

"Then you've met with this Brigham Young, and agree with his teaching of polygyny." Delphine glanced up at him, a sharp warning in her dark-rimmed eyes.

He knew his answer would please her. "Oh, their leaders decry sensuality in all aspects. There are extreme penalties for adultery: three to twenty years in prison. A suspicion of immorality is more hateful than a reputation for bloodshed. When I asked Young if I could join the fold, he turned to me and said 'Captain, haven't you already done that sort of thing before'?"

Delphine laughed merrily as she put the bulbs into the skin they had brought. "Oh, I can imagine!"

"He had already read my book on my six months with the Sioux. Ah, dear truth, don't dig that with your hands." Ravi withdrew his Egyptian dagger from his belt. "After, I went as an Arab *hadji* merchant into Mecca and Medina, and then Harar, whence I discovered the kingdom of Tewodros the Second. I took Misha on a journey where all existence was inexplicable."

"I suppose you wrote books about Medina and Harar also?"

"Of course."

"And are writing one about Abyssinia? I've seen manuscripts scattered about on the table near your *arat*."

"Ah, no. And you'd do us a kind favor not to repeat that imaginary idea. No, I won't make the same mistake poor Henry Stern made. I'm merely writing *A History of Weapons in Abyssinia*." He allowed her to sift through the sandy bulbs he'd uncovered.

"He wrote a book?"

"Yes, indeed, a captivating and engrossing edition entitled *Wanderings among the Falashas*. He published it back in England, and had the sincere naïveté to return to Abyssinia afterwards. Tewodros said 'I've had enough of your Bibles' and had him chained, claiming that he was calumniated in the book. He nearly killed him, merely for putting a hand to his face to suppress horror at seeing his two servants beaten to death. Here, let's rest on this rock." Under the dappled olive green shade of the grove, there was a perfectly flat shale rock one could lean against, and be completely snug. He led Delphine there, dragging the skin of bulbs.

"Wait," she said, as he pulled her down into the sand with him. "*Wanderings among the Falashas*? Isn't that interesting? The day I had the fortune to meet Kaspar, he told me *he* had written a book with that title."

Ravi positioned her in the crook of his arm, and slung her long legs over his hips so that she reclined with one arm above her head. "Ah, truth, but it does sound like something Kaspar would write, does it not? And I'm sure he was so embroiled in helping Stern with the manuscript, he might fully believe he *had* written it."

Delphine's open face quested over his as though she regarded a map of a country she hoped to visit one day. The backs of her fingers grazed his unshaven chin. "Ravinger? In your letter you told me it's Theodore who believes himself Solomon, and not you. I think you only told me Solomon was you in order to prevent me from becoming afraid of him."

Ravi sighed deeply. Catching her hand in his, he pressed her palm against the side of his face. "Yes. I didn't want you to know what a danger he posed. In my typical attitude of avoidance, I think I hoped that you would leave before anything happened."

Enchanting how her eyes could smile along with her mouth! "Now it's too late."

He said nothing. A honey-bird whirred in the limbs above their heads.

"Ah, well. Is it all right if I say that I would rather Solomon were you? I can imagine that, can't I?"

He could barely speak. A clot of words and emotions welled up in his throat, and he couldn't allow it all to rush forth at once. His hand gripped her jaw, and he raised himself over her. "It's insane of him to believe anything of the sort, when it's you and I who wore the two medals. If there's anything true in this inexplicable savage country, it's that you and I were meant to join. Our passion and minds have been intertwined."

At this she looked fearful, her eyes darting back and forth across his face. "But I will not beget any son."

He kissed her then, sucking up her full lower lip gently between his incisors. She responded ardently, folding her thighs back over her hips as though prepared to accept him completely as he launched himself over her.

As it was more divine to kiss her than any earthly amount of rutting with well-trained concubines, Ravinger gave himself up utterly to it, reveling in the honeysuckle scent of her hair. It was a delectable treat to worry and lick at her mouth that tasted of the astringent *chat* leaves.

Her fingertips wandered over the cords of his neck to his crescent facial scar, then less timidly over his shoulder to unwrap the fold of his *shamma* so she could slide her hand up his bicep, underneath the white cotton shirt. This emboldened Ravi, even as he remembered what she'd said when they tussled on the garden bench, and he'd begged to take her. "I can't allow that." Was she afraid of having a child? She'd just said something about not having a son, if he could recall, too enraptured licking a trail down her velvety throat to the brown, bared plane of her breastplate.

When Ravinger gathered up the bottom hem of her voluminous shirt in one hand, inching it up toward her hips, she whispered fervently, "Your passion and your mind terrify me."

"That's because you desire me—it's nothing to fear."

He moved to kiss her again, but she pushed him away. "I don't deny that, Likamaquas. I just can't—can't allow—myself to be pleasured."

Perhaps Ravi was so startled his muscles froze for a brief moment, but the woman had soon unraveled herself from his limbs. She sprang to her feet and paced like a proud creature, brushing dust from her shirt.

Ravi sprawled on his behind with all four limbs out like a crab, stunned by her odd revelation. It was impossible! He leaped up, halting her in her oddly manic pacing by wrapping his arms around her from behind. He stilled her tossing head by capturing it between his chin and shoulder, and he growled, "Queen of Heaven, that's just not possible! You must learn to relax; you're much too accustomed to giving pleasure. You must perhaps learn to be a bit more selfish."

"Ah, and that is what I cannot do," Delphine whispered. "My whole life has been occupied in caring for others. I wanted to become a surgeon so I could do the most good, to help people in measurable ways unlike the nebulous 'helping' of charity or preaching. And why do you call me Queen of Heaven? Surely you don't believe in that Sheba bilgewater."

Ravi laughed as he slid one hand down her ribs and hipbone

until he found the hem of her shirt again. "The Queen of Heaven is a . . . position in a Hindoo treatise on love. It was favored by the wife of a king who was more generously endowed than was comfortable for her."

He continued bunching her shirt in his hand, pleasantly shocked that not only did she not recoil from him at such an unromantic revelation, her breathing quickened. She wiggled her behind against his crotch then, and he bit her lightly on her earlobe, the vulnerable side of her throat. "*Ah*. You're saying this is a good position because of course *you* are the one so amply endowed."

"Yes," he admitted, and he dared to slather the whole length of his cock into the cleft of her ass, immediately realizing he had to stop or he'd come off too hastily. She gasped, and jutted out one hand blindly to grasp the trunk of a *warka* tree. "I will certainly challenge any African, and in my time no honest Mussulman would take his wife to Zanzibar on account of the huge attractions and enormous temptations there offered to them." Ravinger was never above bragging, and it seemed to be working, as he felt a fine tremor running through her legs. "Allowing yourself to be pleasured is a monumental gift to the other."

"Ah," she gasped, as his searching fingertips found the bare skin of her belly. "Then men are the most generous and giving, for they are constantly gracing others with such prizes."

With his free arm Ravi gripped her upper body to his, so that her head lolled back against his shoulder. He slid his other fingers beneath the white Soudanese cotton breeches, coaxing choked whimpering sounds from her when he tickled the swollen, succulent outer lips of her quim. "You're right there, my truth. Men are indeed known for being such philanthropists. I'm famous for such acts. But to balance out the yogic life forces, there must be equality of giving, and—"

She caught her breath loudly when he slipped his longest

middle finger down over the distended length of her clitoris. She planted her feet wider apart on the ground, and propped herself firmly against the *warka* tree. Ravinger was thoroughly happy just to bring her to orgasm, knowing the great benefits to be had from toying with a woman, causing her eyes to drop half-open and humid when he placed a line of jewel bites against her exposed shoulder. He sped up his ministrations to the slick core of her, wanting above all to gain for her an unquestionable treat.

She slid one hand around the back of his neck. "Ravi." Just his name like that was enough to send him to the edge with crazed passion—oh, how he wished there were a looking-glass, for he knew she was an unprecedented joy to see from the front, all loose and wide open as she was, heaving deep sighs—and when he clamped down on her nipple between two fingertips through the calico shirt, he knew he had her.

She gasped, and convulsed, and fairly swung from the tree limb of his neck when she stood on the tips of her toes. Slinking his other hand over the slope of her behind, Ravi wiggled his two longest fingers inside her, the better to feel the clamping spasms that rolled down the length of her. It was his favorite part of pleasuring a woman, to feel the powerful contractions he'd brought to bear upon her, as she shuddered like a freshly caught fish, tottering on her toes.

Her powerful contractions awed him—perhaps it was true it had been so many long months since she'd surrendered to a man. Then he remembered that the more often a woman was satisfied, the stronger her climaxes became. He meditated on this dilemma as his fingers describing rapid meridians on her clitoris slowed, and she whiffed in despair through her open lips, as though his touch were a thing of torture.

"*Isgyoh*," he growled with wonder, his teeth champing down on her earlobe.

"Ah! Stop," Delphine said weakly. She gave a feeble shot at moving his hand from her crotch.

"I'm witnessing the violence of the bliss I've given you."

She tried an enervated laugh. "Violent bliss? Indeed."

He allowed her to squirm free now and collapse like a fallen lodgepole against the *warka* tree trunk. He kept her captive by bracing one hand astride her neck against the trunk, while salaciously sucking on the two longest fingers of his other hand.

"Oh, *beastly!*" was her expected cry as she tried to yank his hand from his mouth. "Captain Howland. While it may be a wickedly delightful joy to taste your semen on my tongue, I can hardly imagine kissing you until you have used your cleaning stick on your teeth—and chewed on a mouthful of mint and *chat* leaves!"

Knowing she would even entertain the notion of tasting his semen sent Ravinger crazy as a bedbug. Bending at the knees, he tilted his hips into her and bucked her up several inches against the tree trunk. " 'How can she cease to be on my mind, when she has sown the *naca* plant in my whole body'?"

"Ah, Ravi. Sometimes I think you're more poetic than the *monstre ignoble* of the Latin Quarter."

It annoyed him that she should mention Monsieur Verlaine at such a moment, but yelling was now coming from the plateau above.

"Basha Falaka!" Walde Nebra and Abou shouted in tandem. "Come quick!"

"Stay here." Ravi dashed to the clearing where he could see the two black heads bobbing, Walde Nebra gesticulating with his *shotel*.

Ravi shaped his hand into a horn and yelled, "What's wrong?"

The men above shrieked in oddly wavering, feminine tones.

"Men are leaving Gondar! Running and riding hard!"

"They say the city is being plundered!"

Ravi yelled, "Keep some men there, I want to hear the story!"

To Delphine he shouted, "Grab our skins."

Delphine swiftly gathered up their skins of bulbs and followed him on his scramble back up the cliff.

"Come back, you wayless rapscallions!" Kaspar shrieked, his egg-blond hair all awry like a halo about his head. Three Gondaris mounted upon mules continued down the road toward the granary plains of Dembea, looking frantically back over their shoulders as though escaping from a slew of ravenous succubi.

"Basha Falaka!" screamed Abou. "That one is the Shoho Said who stored fire-arms in our shed!"

Ravi bellowed, "Said! Halt!" The fellow looked him in the face, and obviously recognized him, but continued kicking his mule forward. Ravi withdrew his Colt and this time was compelled to shoot the miscreant in the calf (for better or worse, the same leg he'd shot in Delphine's courtyard), sending a chunk of flesh catapulting across the plateau. As much from surprise as the shot, Said leaped from his saddle and fell to the grass, rolling like a frolicking hyena pup.

Ravi dashed over. "I told you to halt, you execrable dog!" Wrenching the poor sot to his rocky legs, Ravi thrashed him about like a decrepit scarecrow. "What's going on in Gondar?"

"Tewodros!" the arms merchant shrilled. "He's burning the city!"

Another shake had globules of sweat and other liquids spraying from Said's skin. "Why? By Saint Michael, Prince of Angels—"

"Someone told him there were arms!"

Arms! "By Saint George, you damnable donkey!" Ravi shook the wobbly creature some more, then tossed him to the ground, leveling the barrel of the Colt at his head. "And *who* on the face of Allah's planet could have possibly warned you to make your escape? Speak, you camel-eating swine, or I'll make you eat your own brains in a hare stew!"

"We—we—heard them coming, from the Chelga gate! Many other people escaped too!"

While this may have been plausible, Ravinger shot the worthless rat anyway. If he had not been stockpiling arms in Delphine's godown, and if the arms hadn't been discovered in time, it would be they who would be murdered for trading weapons—Delphine, Ravi, Abou, Kaspar, and anyone else connected with their house. He shot him through the forehead with no more compunction than potting a woodchuck, and took Said's *zenar* loaded with Maria Theresas.

More citizens galloped down the road, mostly men associated with Said who could have also been warned about the raid by Anatole. Leaping into the middle of the road, Ravinger leveled the Colt at a man he knew to be an ivory merchant. "Ibrahim! What is Tewodros doing in Gondar?"

"Basha Falaka! He has finally gone much too far, my friend! He is burning churches and throwing priests into the flames! There is no God in Abyssinia if he allows Tewodros to live after burning churches."

Lowering his arm to his side, Ravi spun around to find Delphine. She leaned against her mule, her face wan, the robust color of earlier having been sucked within her. Striding to her side, he lifted her onto the mule and arranged the bulb skins about the saddlebags. "We're going back, it's all right, it's safe. I'll hide you, and then go protect your house."

"Are you sure, Ravi? Don't you think part of this may be retribution for my refusal to go with them?"

"Ah. Ibrahim!" Ravi spoke to the ivory merchant who had not budged a limb from the middle of the road. "I need to purchase your *shamma*. One Maria Theresa?"

Ibrahim was already stripping off his dingy blackened robe. "Two!"

Ravi arranged the filthy *shamma* about the beloved woman, not a single fear skulking on the fringes of his awareness. "There! Now you're a countryman, a *hakim* dealing in herbal remedies and bulbs." He didn't even yell at the half dozen or so men of his party who had already joined the flow of pack animals making tracks in the direction of Lake Tzana.

"Ravi, couldn't we just go hide somewhere until the raiders leave town? They're not going to stay around afterwards and occupy, are they?"

Ravi mounted his own mule. "No, that's not Tewodros's style. They'll pillage, and leave, most likely by tonight. I'm sure he only brought his elite corps of Fitawraris and musketeers, and their main joy is in plundering, not in governing."

"*I'sh-shi*." Delphine was particularly lovely beneath the grime of the *shamma* that Ravi had draped about her head. "I shall trust you to know what's best."

Ravi told a skittish Kaspar, "I'd advise you to hide with Delphine as well. In their ecclesiastical fervor they might snatch you up, as a churchman."

"Yes, and it will be just my wretched luck that those who riot in dissolute habits will throw me into the lockup along with the Reverend Stern!"

"There is no God in Abyssinia . . ." muttered Abou.

Ravi said, "Abou? Are you happy to come with us? I'll hide you in the tunnels of the Royal Enclosure."

Abou opened his eyes balefully. "Once struck off, the human head does not regrow like a rose."

❋   ❋   ❋

THEY DESCENDED FROM THE WHOLESOME MEADOW heights and into a vast amphitheater of castellated mountains. Roiling fog shrouded the rocky heights, creeping from fissures and occasionally breaking to reveal majestic vistas where a lambent cestus encircled a lone scarp. It had been a lovely, refreshing jaunt out that morning, but now the cleft looming before them displayed a vaporous tomb through which they might be sucked to their death.

That Tewodros had sealed off the city was proved by the ever-smaller groups they met on the road, at last merely some women struggling under head-loads of leather honey sacks, and bushels of chilies and capsicum berries. Women were usually much more fearful of speaking out than men, but these irate merchantwomen seemed to know Ravi, and Delphine heard them speak plainly.

"The Abuna Salama has died in Magdala," she understood them to say. "That is his reason for this sudden pillaging. When the Abuna lived, the Emperor would not have dared do this!"

"Ravinger?" Delphine queried when they continued riding. "Who is this Abuna?"

"He has been slaughtered in the name of the blessed Trinity!" cried Kaspar. " 'My soul clings to the dust; revive me according to your word . . .' " He had stooped to reciting the 119th Psalm, oft chanted by the *debterahs* of Gondar.

Ravinger disregarded the deacon. "The Abuna Salama is a Coptic high priest of the Ethiopian church. Abunas are appointed from Alexandria, so the Amharas view them with the same skepticism as all Turks. He anointed Tewodros as Tewodros the Second ten years ago, but . . ."

"But?"

"He wound up accusing the Abuna for being mixed up in politics instead of attending to matters of the spirit, so Tewodros chucked him into Magdala. They used to have the most exciting public arguments. The Abuna would call Tewodros a pretender and apostate, while our King of Kings called the prelate a Moslem and a Turk—which is the worse shall be anyone's decision."

" 'The arrogant utterly deride me, but I do not turn away from your'—His person was sacred to the utmost!" Kaspar babbled. "He lived at Gondar, almost always veiled from public inspection! He ate nothing but the execrable physic *kosso* and he is pure from defilement. The man gave me the permission to preach and hold congregations in every Jewish domain throughout the land."

"Ha!" It was unclear whether Abou was expectorating or laughing. "He wears the very big tall hat."

"The miter!" Kaspar corrected.

"Ah," Ravinger agreed. "Its gargantuan size and outré style reminds me of one I saw on a poor drum major on the Columbia River. He wore it once and then deserted. He was caught, and during his court-martial he gave the only logical excuse for having deserted—the fear of wearing that hat again."

Kaspar allowed the other three to enjoy a bout of glee over that image. "It was the fear of wearing that hat that killed the Abuna."

While Ravi's plan to protect their houses made sense, it seemed an unnecessary risk to take for guarding a few old spears, her laboratory, and a storeroom full of Bordeaux. Delphine's old unease at being anywhere remotely near a person who might take her captive came back at full chisel, and she quelled her fear by constantly shaking the mule's small leather loop that passed for reins. Surely Ravinger could calm the raiders, could steer them clear of her, could direct them back to their encampment.

The last five miles, they met no one on the road, and they circled around to the northern gate, the one closest to Qwesqwam. The guards by the stockade seemed surprised to see a group of people attempting to get in, as opposed to the other way around, and they entered without incident. It was terrifying, the arms and legs of potential refugees surging through the cracks in the gate, and soldiers beating the frightened people about the heads and shoulders with sticks.

Cottony white smoke surged like pond spume into the skies, the wattle and thatch roofs of most *tukul* conical huts and of the palace buildings having ignited like boxes of matches. Men on the distinctive Wallo Galla geldings darted to and fro across the green lawns that separated castles and churches. The soldiers yelped happily, brandishing old muskets and matchlocks, shaking their gay *limoots* of brass chains around their horse's necks. Delphine nearly vomited what little liquid was in her stomach at the sight of two men ruthlessly chasing down a *debterah*. Without breaking stride, they both thrust spears into the man's back and neck, slicing through the jugular like wood through butter, bursting a plume of mercury fluid from the hapless man's throat before he fell on his face like a strange terrified ferret. Abou had once told her that Amharas never throw their lance at any but a living object, the ridiculous notion of "wounding the earth" being the objection against this.

"Likamaquas, let us ride fast to Qwesqwam," Delphine spoke in what she hoped was a convincing baritone.

Ravi's brutal face looked more menacing than ever, his nostrils flaring as he sat erect, utterly composed and prepared to fight or flee. "Yes, I agree." Suddenly frantic, he flung a hand out to grab her arm, yanking her around so she faced Qwesqwam, but not in time for her to avoid the sight of the dismounting spearmen. They tore the dying man's breeches from him with exultant fervor, and one brandished a knife that only had a single purpose. She finally swiveled her head to face front when Ravi commanded, "Toward the palace!"

"I shudder to view such savagery," Kaspar stated, quieter than usual, and even his voice shuddered.

When they passed through the stone walls of the Royal Enclosure, someone blasted away at them. The terrified guard immediately came forward full of apologies to Basha Falaka, his hands shaking so holding the gun Delphine saw it rattle from six yards away.

Walde Nebra, Wubishet, and the gunners stayed with the animals as Ravi hustled the other three inside the courtyard. They were fortunate to quickly find the Chamberlain Yeddee as placid as ever, perhaps recalling the sacking of the city a few years previous, that time under the pretext the inhabitants refused to pay taxes.

"Yeddee, you must hide my friends in the tunnel."

"Yes, yes, Likamaquas. No one will enter—we have too many guards, with guns that have real bullets."

Kaspar jiggled Ravi by the arm. "Howland. Make sure those devils do not disturb my reserve of Schnapps. It is a very valuable and precious commodity, and I utilize it in giving Communion."

Ravi patted the deacon on the shoulder. "Have no fear, Kaspar. I'll protect all of our liquor with every weapon at my side." He turned to Delphine while the other three men politely made themselves unobtrusive by flattening themselves against a wall. Only then did Ravi remove the *shamma* hood from her head. Taking her chin between his fingers, his cruel and now strangely vulnerable eyes scanned her face. "My love. I've sworn to protect you, and protect you I will. Don't have any doubts of that." It was plain he nurtured his ferocious façade. This made it exquisitely more touching when he exhibited a softness of heart.

"I have no doubts, I just . . ." Her lower lip trembled then, and he stilled it with a dab of his thumb. ". . . wish you could stay with us."

His half-smile lifted one corner of his slyly erotic mouth. "I think it much wiser for me to find Tewodros, protect your house, our horses, Kaspar's liquor, and get a report. Though believe me, if I had my choice, I'd spend the rest of my worthwhile days with you."

She gave a little jump then to better facilitate him gathering her into his arms. He was so strong, so warm, so secure! She loved to grasp the back of his powerful neck in her hand, and she licked his full, warm lips with the tip of her tongue. "How I should like that," she breathed, but she didn't really believe him. It just seemed like the sort of lovely utterance a man might make.

He pulled back to murmur in her ear, " 'I have no hat on my head. I have no shoes on my feet. In what a hurry I am when I come to thee'."

"Ah," Delphine sighed at the beauty of the poem, but Kaspar and Abou grabbed her and shoved her in the direction of the low doorway that presumably led to the tunnel.

"Take care of her, men!" Ravi called. "I'll be back within the hour."

His fierceness of eye when he stood with upraised commanding arm was the last Delphine saw of him, before she was enveloped by a cluster of frantically yammering men who shoved the *frenjoch* through the door in their haste to join them.

Delphine felt her way along the slimy walls, lit up only by a few *debterahs'* torches. The boom of the heavy door closing behind them turned her intestines into water, and her heart pounded at the claustrophobic closeness of the air.

"Rancid urine emanates from this tunnel," Kaspar observed.

✳ ✳ ✳

RAVI THUNDERED PAST THE CHURCH OF the Light, where silhouettes of *debterahs* wrestled with spearmen in the battlements, the windows below spewing fire. He was vexed thinking of the fine murals inside being damaged, the seraphic big-eyed angels that decorated the ceiling. That he didn't spend a moment in pondering when a flailing *debterah* flung from the roof landed not fifteen feet from him as a white cloth bag of bones in the street was evidence enough of the ire many countrymen felt for the clergy. Ravi had always been something of an agnostic, although able to cleave his visions to some of the Middle Eastern religions. He shared Tewodros's belief that they needed to reduce the number of priestly bums lolling around the vast tracts of holdings they hoarded. Churchmen had refused to send away men or grant land, and that was the source of Tewodros's conflict with the Abuna.

But, leaving the Royal Enclosure and galloping through the quarter of ordinary people's *tukuls*, he saw many things to which he took umbrage.

Tewodros's men fed branches of the great sycamore and cedar trees into a bonfire near several smaller churches, where other looters ran hither and yon with gold censers, bells, manuscripts, and holy *tabotat*, representations of the Ark of the Covenant. Several soldiers tussled desperately with a white-robed *debterah* who resisted being thrown into the conflagration. Already he had stabbed several warriors with the silver cross that he refused to release.

"Fitawrari Inchael!" Ravi shouted, halting his mule abruptly so close to the bonfire it near scorched his face. Walde Nebra and his other spearmen backed him up boldly.

"Likamaquas!" Inchael quitted his hold on the fighting priest, and came to attention, as did most of the other soldiers.

"What is the meaning of this? Who has given the order to burn priests?"

"By the death of Christ!" Inchael reported obediently. "The Great One has commanded us."

Ravi snorted hotly. "By Saint George, you ignorant dog! Your Likamaquas now commands you to let go of this and all priests! I see it is too late for these unfortunates"—for two melting *debterahs* already smoldered in the pyre, their caved faces emitting the most awesome stink—"but you must not touch this or any other holy men. Also"—and he had to raise his voice to an elephantine bellow in order to impress the scampering looters on the other side of the bonfire—"all looting of sacred articles will *stop right now!* Do you hear me? Walde Giyorgis, I can plainly see you right there with that *tabot.* Give it to this *debterah!*"

There came a brief clattering of devotional objects either dropped or handed over, and Ravi fixed upon one slimy tiptoeing soldier with a silver cross under an arm, trying to sneak around a corner of the church. "You swine! You have heard me! Stop!" But the fellow wouldn't, so with his Colt Ravi shot off the man's cross and one finger simultaneously and turned back to Walde Nebra. "Keep an eye on things with these two men, I'll take the other two to find Tewodros."

But Walde Nebra wouldn't hear of allowing the Likamaquas to sally forth unattended, so Ravi left another man in his stead, and continued down toward the River Qaha.

"I think," Walde Nebra dared to say, "that if it is true, that the Emperor has ordered the burning of priests, then we are safe to say that he . . ." He lowered his voice so that Ravi had to lean far to his left to hear him. ". . . that he truly is not in his right mind."

"Here, here," Ravi agreed in English. "Man alive, now what's this?"

A woman shrieked as though a *buda* was expiring within her as two growling soldiers attempted to pull her toward another bonfire. The forms of several such women were already burnt or perishing in the licking flames. Other women screamed and railed and beat on the soldiers, and there were concise trials and judgments meted out against a blood-splattered church wall. Women were condemned of something, and then just as swiftly beaten about the heads and shoulders with gun butts before being dragged to the pyre.

"Fitawrari Gebraye!" For directing such morbid proceedings was Tewodros's favorite, his most devoted and malevolent General. "What can these women possibly have done that deserves such harsh punishment?"

Gebraye was an archly handsome, proud man to whom women often cottoned. "Basha Falaka! By Saint Michael, prince of angels! These women were singing in the street as we arrived, warning the arms *shifta* to escape the city!"

Alas, the stricken woman was much too weak for the superior mass of men, and she too went sailing into the pile, as Ravi and Gebraye both flinched, and uncomfortably edged their mounts away.

"Yes, I saw one man I knew to be an arms *shifta* running like a coward toward Lake Tzana—the Shoho Bedouin Said, of the Islambet quarter."

Gebraye's eyes narrowed. "And you didn't arrest him?"

"I killed him."

Gebraye laughed violently. "Ah, Likamaquas! I should know, we can always rely on you!"

Ravi wasn't heartened. "Gebraye. I don't believe it was these women who warned them of your arrival—I believe it was someone close to Tewodros who is a traitor. If you would please stop the execution of these women, I'll go find Tewodros and tell him."

Both men swiveled their heads. There were no women left in the street.

Gebraye shrugged. "You will find him in Islambet; he heard there were guns in the *ferenje hakim*'s house."

Not any longer, thought Ravi as he led his men across the bridge over the River Qaha. Halfway across, Ravi was walloped in the shoulder by a whirling black object so heavy it later left a yellow bruise the size of a cooking pot lid—indeed, that was mostly likely what it was, as some profaning women scattered from their stand of bushes by the water's edge.

One of Ravi's gunners shot at her, but Ravi said, "Stop. To these women, we're just more soldiers."

They tethered their mules before the main entrance to

Delphine's house, underneath the stuffed crocodile that was supposed to dispel evil eyes. There were no mendicants here today, as they had all apparently fled in terror from the bustle of soldiers stomping up and down the inner staircase, looting the place forty-six ways to Sunday. Ravi wrenched a sword from one fellow's grip. That was the claymore he'd demonstrated to Delphine, and he finally cracked when he saw it being carried away. Roaring and snarling like a cornered beast, Ravi raised it over the son of a bitch's head with the point directly in sight of his brain, but unfortunately Walde Nebra wrestled his fighting arm, as any good shield-bearer must sometimes do. Ravi gnashed his teeth at Walde Nebra, but the servant was so accustomed to it he merely beckoned him up the staircase.

The Wild Boar of Ethiopia had commandeered Delphine's drawing room. He now paced up and down the length of the room, his bare feet soundless on the carpets. Detecting Kaspar's *arrack* jug had probably been his first priority, for he held a red glass *barrilye* that he swigged from with an air of distraction. His concentration was so great as he paced that he didn't start at the entry of a few more live bodies, just continued his fluid, leonine walk. That attitude Ravi had always thought so majestic now enraged him.

Walde Nebra held fast to his forearm, warning him to proceed with delicacy and tact. Ravi took several deep breaths, then stepped boldly onto the carpets.

"Jan Hoy!"

"Basha Falaka!" Tewodros opened his arms to his chamberlain. "I am so glad you are here! I was told you were out designing maps for more road-building."

Ravi inwardly thanked whomever had been dishonorable enough to craft that lie. He walked into the evil embrace, but only superficially patted the man on the shoulders. "Yes, yes, I was on the Dembea plains surveying for building roads. I've heard the

awful and sad news of the demise of His Eminence the Abuna."
Going to the sideboard, Ravi casually withdrew his Bordeaux
bottle. "I must offer you my deep consolation."

That was when Tewodros changed. He was so mercurial,
shifting with the swiftness of the clouds above, that keeping on
one's toes had become a tireless and grueling chore. "Console me?
You should be congratulating me on my happiness!"

A permeating silence prevailed as the two men stared each
other down.

Tewodros broke first. "If once I have peace from my enemies,
I'll teach those priests that activity and study, not sloth and indo-
lence, are their proper vocation!"

Ravi sighed, and took his first sip of wine. "So now you burn
churches, and throw the priests into the fires."

Tewodros shrugged, and likewise sipped at his *arrack*. "I'll
build better churches."

"People are saying that since you burn churches, there is no
longer any God in Abyssinia. They are turning against you."

"They are godless because they've *always* been godless! That's
none of my concern."

"And what do you seek in this *ferenje hakim*'s house? I have
just killed Said, the *shifta* responsible for storing arms here,
unbeknownst to the *hakim*. She had no part in it, and would never
have willingly agreed—it was the Frankish scribbler, that traitor
Anatole Verlaine, that *buda* blacksmith, who conspired with Said
to store—"

Tewodros nearly flattened Ravi with the enthusiasm of his
revelation. With arm whipped in the air, he waved some papers
over Ravi's head, his sharp kisser in all of its zealous glory so
close that Ravi tightened his grip on the *shamshir*. "I have proof
of her deceit!"

Ravi dared to tear the papers from Tewodros's talons. "And

what is this 'proof'? Oh, this is a missive to base such a verdict on? It appears to be a letter from *Doctor* Chambliss to a female friend of hers, and she discusses the weather—"

Tewodros ripped the pages back from Ravi. He rattled them with even more vigor, if such a thing were possible. *"This is an unauthorized letter!"*

Ravi shouted over Tewodros's words. "She discusses the weather!"

Tewodros bellowed over Ravi's words. "An unauthorized letter!"

"She discusses how much she hates you!"

"Unauthorized! She will love me!"

Ravi noticed Delphine's Congressional medal around Tewodros's neck. "Hates you, as everyone else in this benighted country does, and for the simple reason that you are ruining this country! Ruining this country that you set out to restore ten years ago, to unify, and now you've only pulled it asunder with your hatred and anger and murder!" His love for Tewodros had been vast, worldly, eternal, and now some of that love had transmogrified into hatred.

"Loves me as she can never love *you*, because *I* am the descendant of Solomon and Menelik, and *you* are merely a *ferenje* scientist!"

They both paused at the same time, perhaps regenerating enough breath for the next onslaught. Ravinger tilted back on his heels to avoid the fanatical fervor of the Emperor's sweat. A man standing in the doorway that let onto the gallery had the gall to shift his elbow, and Tewodros spun to face the man. Exhaling with relief, Ravinger went back to the sideboard to pour more wine. He was soon stopped by the strange conversation.

"Alemu Mariam!" For it was the fool who had thought he could kill men with a sixpenny burning-glass. "What news do you have for me?"

"Your Majesty?"

"Yes, yes, I know he is standing right there. Tell me! *Where is the* ferenje *woman?*"

"The Likamaquas went to Qwesqwam where he left the *hakim* and her two—"

"Wait," Ravi breathed, his hand holding the *barrilye* suspended in midair.

"*Ras Engeddeh!*" Tewodros bawled out for his prime minister, who materialized in the gallery doorway. "Do you hear me? Get over to Qwesqwam and find her!"

"Wait," Ravi breathed once more, as an overpowering sensation of weakness sank its tendrils into his very intestines. One sharp quick breath gave his brain some more air. "*Wait!*"

Tewodros sidled over to him, once he'd been convinced that Ras Engeddeh had vanished. "So . . . you admit that there is a *reason* for us to search inside of Qwesqwam? I see you wished to detain the Ras on his errand."

Ravi sipped his wine and shrugged. "You can search all you want." Chortling, he turned to Walde Nebra, who clung to the doorjamb for dear life. "Correct? Walde Nebra was there. He knows that we left the *hakim* back up near Chelga, where we mapped the roads."

Walde Nebra strode into the room, suddenly sublime in his calm. "Yes, yes!" He shrugged helplessly. "She wished to stay to search for roots, but the Likamaquas knew he needed to return here."

Tewodros slid Delphine's tattered letter inside a *shamma* fold. He hissed like an air-filled boar's bladder. "We shall see."

Ravi clapped his hands together jovially. "Well! Let us go to ensure the Deacon Nagel's Schnapps has been guarded."

✹   ✹   ✹

" 'THEN ASA WAS ANGRY WITH THE seer, and put him in the stocks, in prison, for he was in a rage with him because of this.

And Asa inflicted cruelties on some of the people—' "

"Will you please shut up?" Delphine nearly bit Kaspar's head off.

They sat on their duffs in the mucoid slime of the rocky tunnel. They had started out standing up leaning against the mossy walls, but one by one their legs tired, Abou the last remaining standing on one leg, propped by his spear.

Abou withdrew some *chat* leaves from his *zenar*. He handed a few of the wilted things to Delphine, who took them gratefully. "If I am captured," he intoned, "I am taking this *merz*." He surreptitiously showed his friends an airtight leather container.

Delphine's hand shot out and grabbed the *merz*. "You're doing no such thing! I'm ashamed of you, Abou!"

Kaspar's eyes were round. "*Merz* is for making poison arrows."

"Yes, and causes hair and nails to fall off, and is an excruciating and unattractive death besides!" Delphine frowned.

Abou stuck out his lower lip. "Why ashamed? It is very brave to swallow *merz*. I will never be a slave again!"

Kaspar inserted, "We must have a plan for if that duplicitous devil Howland has double-crossed us."

"Kaspar!" cried Delphine. "Don't even say that! I think I am a decent judge of human character, and I can tell you with thorough conviction that Captain Howland would never do such a thing!"

Kaspar's timbre was suddenly shrill. "Oh, yes? Then *who* are these upstanding fellows clamoring down the tunnel toward us?"

Indeed, murky outlines of men bristled with spears, and the torch-bearers who had been hiding with Delphine pulled up stakes unceremoniously, yelling "Run, *run!*" as one of them trod on Delphine's tibia. Abou scooped Delphine into his lanky arm so that she fairly soared through the air. At a narrowing turn of the tunnel, men became jammed, their torsos squished between the slippery walls, their legs running ineffectually. It took a massive push from the people behind them, during which the air was compressed from Delphine's lungs and her face was in repellant contact with a chap's armpit, and the flood of people finally burst free.

The bursting was so violent that several men fell, and others stomped on them, and Delphine heard the dull thuds of battle in the tunnel behind her, but still she flew in the arm of Abou. The slave even hacked away with his spear at several compatriots in his fervor to put them behind him. He was a furious, murderous animal, and Delphine was convinced they might be the first to gain the exit that they had been told was outdoors at the Asasame Mikael church.

She had no breath to cry out, "Where is Kaspar?" though the query throbbed through her mind as they bounded their way down the long tunnel, men behind them falling every which way. They soon were alone in their dash toward escape.

"There is . . . light," Abou huffed.

Delphine nearly cried with relief, as she didn't think her crushed shinbone could hold her up any longer.

The flung themselves on the heavy wooden door. Abou manipulated the iron handle in every possible manner, and it didn't budge.

"Locked," Delphine panted.

"Woizero Attitegeb's men must be guarding from the other side."

Delphine fell upon the door, banging away with her fists, shrieking in English, "Let us out!"

"No!" Abou yanked her from the door.

"How else will we get out?" She was nearly blubbering with desperation now, and disregarded Abou to bang on the door some more.

Abou wrenched her shoulder with his long fingers. "What if the Emperor's men have—"

The sudden light blinded Delphine when someone flung the door open. "Oh, thank—"

Delphine was ripped bodily from Abou's steely grip and tossed face-first onto the stone walkway. Smelly men pinned her down and forced her hands into the small of her back, where she was cuffed with irons.

She heard much gibbering of "Makeda," so the men obviously knew she was the alleged Queen of the South. She was also familiar with Amharic terms denoting "assault" or "beat," as well as "steal." Perhaps some were the same men from Ravi's raiding party in Metemma, as those had also been among the elite soldiery. Perhaps they recalled her rubbing out a few of their cohorts.

She was flipped violently onto her back, her shoulders audibly cracking with the twisting of her cuffed hands. A man who straddled her pinned her shoulders down. He loomed like a malevolent hyena, his upper lip lifted in a snarl, and butter from his tresses dripped onto her chest. When captured in an impossible position, it was Delphine's strategy to lie still, and to even sink down into a sort of light sleep where she ignored all sensory input.

The soldier removed one hand from her shoulder, but it was only to lewdly fondle the crotch of his *shamma* folds. He leaned into her chest, rubbing his bulging crotch in the butter he'd dripped there, moaning wantonly. He smashed himself to her breast, wriggling and puffing as though on the verge of spending. It felt just as strange and detached as if a heated *faro* dog were massaging a taut appendage against her.

She saw more than felt men tearing her nether garments, and they were fighting among themselves with words such as "No!" "You cannot!" "You aren't allowed!" "She's a doctor!" "She's Makeda!" "You swine!" "Dog!"

The horny soldier was torn from her body, and men fell to whacking each other with their spear shafts, like newfangled religious crusaders.

A heavy body crashed on her midsection, flattening all the air from her again. She had nearly depressed herself into a state of nonexistence when many hands lifted her like a sack of *teff* flour and flung her brutally, face down, over a horse. They galloped off with excited cries of "Basha Falaka!"

The last thing she saw in her flight through the air was Ravinger Howland, riding from the Asasame Mikael Bar, the gate that let out of the road that encircled the Imperial Compound. He shot his Colt at some men before Delphine's horse charged over a viaduct bridge, and a different gate out of the city.

* * *

HE WAS OUT OF AMMUNITION.

Tewodros had oddly allowed him to leave the drawing room to ostensibly search for Kaspar's liquor. As Tewodros only credited himself with being capable of sly and sneaky perfidy, he sometimes found it incomprehensible in others. Ravinger had jumped from the second story balcony of Delphine's bedchamber. Leaping on Selpha, Walde Nebra following on the mule, he had dashed to the church where he knew the tunnel to let out.

He had shot six men, he didn't know how many of them dead.

Now he was out of bullets, and chased the thundering herd of Tewodros's men down the Royal Enclosure road armed with nothing more than a spear and his *shamshir*. He knew they were heading for the eastern road by the Adenager Bar, for that would take them to the last known royal encampment, near Debra Tabor in Begemder. Nobody shot back at him, so Ravi presumed they still respected his Likamaquas status, although he was clearly now going against the Emperor's orders.

With their unwieldy baggage of Delphine and other loot, Ravi began overtaking them as they rounded the double wall and stone stairs of the House of Espousals. Selpha crashed directly into a pair of walking men who struggled to keep upright a colossal *manbara tabot,* a heavy wooden altar chest that held the sacred ark replicas. Selpha stayed on course after stumbling sideways a bit, though the same could not be said of the two *tabot* thieves who had their ribs crushed under the hooves.

Once again gaining on them as they wheeled left widely beneath the aromatic cedars of Adenager Bar, Ravi was convinced he had won the day. He was so close he could hear one man, a former gunner of his own who had accompanied him on many missions, howl out, "Likamaquas! Go back! Go back, for we do the Emperor's bidding!"

Ravi didn't want to dissipate his power by shouting. They knew why he chased them.

And he didn't want to threaten them. They knew what he was capable of once he caught them.

"Basha Falaka! We don't want to hurt you!"

The horsemen galloped around a jog in the road that accommodated the compound of the church of Qudus Raphael. It was then that two of them threw spears at Ravi, not to wound him, but using a trick he'd shown them—to trip up his horse. The spears hurled obliquely crashed to the dirt road directly before Selpha's hooves. The horse avoided the first by dancing sideways, but the second thudded between two fetlocks, and Selpha skidded to a stop, rearing to untangle himself.

Ravi remained mounted, but he lost many valuable seconds. As his horse was a well-seasoned war gelding, within a minute he'd regained the ground lost. Now about ten of the fifteen horsemen detached themselves and circled around, allowing the soldier who carried Delphine to escape ahead.

Five came on each side. Ravi had a sinking feeling. He'd taught them well.

They came with spears gripped out at rigid right angles to their bodies. All Ravinger could do to protect himself was to clutch his own spear in both fists as a canoe paddle and protect his body. They came in pairs, flanking him expertly. He wrestled off the first pair, but the second pair lifted him bodily on their spears without harming him, sending him gliding almost gently through the air to land on his tailbone. The remaining eight men circumscribed him and closed in.

Ravi at last spoke. "Walde Nebra!" he shouted at the man he knew was shortly behind him. "Go back to Islambet!"

I am proud to say, he imagined telling Misha later, *that it took ten men to unseat me.*

PART II

CHAPTER TWELVE
THE MASTER AT LOVE

December 7, 1866
Debra Tabor

THEY HAD GIVEN DELPHINE NOTHING TO drink but the nauseating *tej*. As a result of her delicate tippler's status, she had been cronked day and night. She drifted in and out of awareness, preferring the cocoon-like entombment of dazed slumber to the painful stab of reality. She was in a fairly commodious red tent, and the first night she'd been here she'd seen muted shadows of people running carrying torches. Presumably greeting the returning triumphal Emperor, they ululated and cried "Hezekiah!"

The odd thing was, these false idolaters had strangely flat accents to their voices. She may have sworn, had she not been under the sway of the vinous influence, that she heard a couple of them speaking in what sounded like German. Who were these misguided supporters?

Surely someone's army would prevail, and would usurp this crazed despot!

God wasn't a word Delphine wished to dwell on. She agreed with the fleeing women of Gondar that there was no God in Abyssinia.

She was shackled only by the ankles, the links between her feet no wider than a hand's breadth. When they had first hammered them on, every blow had reverberated through her contused shin-bone. It took a full ten minutes to hammer on the first ring, and she was gripped by a panic the blacksmith would slip and shatter her tibia. At first she could barely take three or four steps, and her legs throbbed. But as there was no place in particular to walk to, Delphine soon gave up, and lay on the *arat*. Giant smelly Galla eunuchs guarded her tent flap, anyway, as she'd discovered the first time she'd tried to exit her harsh enclosure. They slept in the doorway at night.

In the tent there was an escritoire inlaid with mother-of-pearl, and a like delicate stool before it. Once in a fit of soused anger, she hobbled over and flung open the leaf. She snorted with approval to see stationery in a cubbyhole, and pens and wells of India ink. The previous owner of the desk had written some sheets of Amharic characters, which Delphine could not begin to make out. She was so enraged at being a prisoner again, she slammed the leaf shut, and did not investigate the desk further.

Two women occasionally brought her *hambasha* and *wot*, a sort of beastly peppery stew made from offal, and on return trips they emptied the chamber pot. Delphine condescended to eat heartily, for gaining strength and formulating a far-fetched escape plan was the only subject that occupied her mind now—now that she had convinced herself Ravinger was nothing but a lowdown traitorous turncoat.

It was now all so plain that he'd been in cahoots with Theodore for weeks! Delphine's mind reached back as far as the letter she'd received from Ravinger, instructing her to go hide at Qwesqwam. He'd planned even back then to point the Evil One in her direction! By turning her over to the Emperor, he could win even more honors, perhaps be elevated to a Dejazmach or even a Ras. After all, he'd never said anything about having any actual caring feelings for her, had he? His sole emotion—lust—merely manipulated her into relaxing, trusting him . . . So he could again point Theodore her way!

No doubt he'd known about the raid beforehand, purposely leading her into the highlands of Dembea, simply in order to lead her back again. No wonder he had ignored her idea to stay hidden for the night or for a couple of days in the highlands. Her plan just made too much sense—for anyone attempting to remain free of the Emperor's evil clutches.

She had walked right into an ambush. She had been so foolish and so mindless she had allowed her heart to soften a bit. There had even been a partial corner of her mind that imagined she might allow Ravinger to possibly seduce her—as if he could come anywhere close to replacing Eugene Quatrevaux! Eugene was a proud man, a man who prayed and wept, a man of valor and unselfish acts—a man who daily laid his life down for his fellow countrymen—to soothe and heal men *from the other side!* Whereas Ravinger Howland—oh, it pained her just to think about it! Ravinger Howland served only one God—the God of Ravinger Howland!

Was Abou dead? Was Kaspar dead, thanks to the selfish machinations of the odious Captain of War?

Delphine drank her *tej*, which did for laudanum in a pinch.

Her anger at Ravi, God, and the rest of the world had grown by the fifth day when Theodore dared to enter her red tent.

She was seated at a folding table and camp-stool at which she ate, listlessly pushing around the red oily *wot* on her dish with a hard piece of *hambasha* bread. The sheep here that passed for stringy tough mutton were barely more than Georgia cats, and the chickens were veterans of savage battles.

Delphine instantly knew it was he. He had a nimble, strapping physique, and he moved fluidly, as though imitating the royal lion. His skin, the deep brown color of melanite garnet, was very nearly black, but his fine features were more European than Negroid. He sat on Delphine's *alga*, and a valet flanked him standing.

Theodore's speech was flowery and forceful. "By the power of my creator, Makeda the Queen of the South has finally come to me," she understood him to say.

She could not tell from his tone whether he was joyful or angry, and his face betrayed neither. But his glassy eye was probing and full of flame, his preeminent air haughty and aggressive.

"Basha Falaka is my Likamaquas. Now he has brought me a Queen."

Delphine slit her eyes. "I am no one's queen," she snarled, tightening her grip on the edge of the camp-table.

Theodore continued as though she hadn't spoken. "Basha Falaka has slept in my tent door for many years. He has dined from the same table, and stays at my side for hours, telling me of the miracles of civilization and military life." Such was Delphine's general interpretation of his arrogant words. "I love you now."

"You love only yourself and bloodshed, you disgusting filthy pig!" Delphine had insisted on learning the Amharic for "love"— so she would be prepared if Ravinger Howland ever uttered this noxious word.

The valet tensed, and took slight steps toward Delphine, but Theodore lifted a calming hand. He now smiled for the first time, and even in her rage she knew it to be a dazzling smile, engaging and bewitching. "You will love me. I will keep you safe here in your tent where you will not want for anything."

Leaping to her feet, Delphine flung the camp-table aside, sending a splash of peppery *wot* against the side of the tent. "*I want my friends*, you evil monster! Where are the Deacon Nagel and my servant Abou?"

Theodore remained serene throughout her tirade. He was an exceedingly beautiful man. Perhaps that was the key to the evil that permeated men, for Ravinger Howland was so stunningly beautiful everyone, men and women alike, would stop and stare when he walked by. "The *azmary* came to the kingdom many years ago with the *debterah* Stern to preach and convince the mystical Falashas to study Christianity. Stern told everyone I was a bad man, so I imprisoned him."

Was she not asking the question properly? "Where is Kaspar Nagel? Is he imprisoned?"

" 'Let the groans of the prisoners come before you; according to your great power preserve those doomed to die'."

What was that? It sounded like a biblical quote, but it didn't bode well for Kaspar Nagel. Delphine took three hobbled steps so that she stood so close to the martial sovereign he could have reached out and grabbed her. "You're crazy! You can't just keep imprisoning people because you don't like them, or you think you love them! A new chief will rise up, and take you prisoner, and then your whole crazy kingdom will fall!"

Theodore still smiled with beatitude, and he rose. He was tall for an Abyssinian, and he looked down his aquiline Roman beak at her. "I am the son of David and Solomon, and the slave of Christ. And you are my queen."

She didn't dare spit on him, for she needed to preserve her own life.

"Give me back my medal!"

He left the tent followed by his obsequious valet.

Delphine roared with frustration, but she'd already upset the camp-table, so she hobbled to the escritoire and flung open the leaf. Jamming her behind onto the delicate painted stool, she furiously grabbed some paper and a pen and inkwell. She wrote in a blotched, hasty manner that befitted her mood.

I hate him I hate him I hate him!
By the Immaculate Conception, I hate him!

May Theodore DIE!

And may Ravinger Howland be deprived of his hands and feet and be thrown over a cliff!

* * *

Gaffat

RAVINGER HOWLAND WAS SHACKLED BOTH WRISTS and ankles in one of "the Gaffat children's" huts. He had heard the bootlicking panderers come racing out with their elated cries of "Hezekiah!" when Tewodros arrived. He knew them to be only saving their sorry hides, for to openly condemn Tewodros would have done no one any good. As missionaries, of course in their hearts they decried the Emperor's actions in razing Gondar. Still, it was particularly maddening to be chained doubly like this in the moldy hut, hands painfully cinched behind him in the small of his back, able to eat only by shoving his face into a plate of *wot*.

After a few days, when he was certain Tewodros had returned to his capital of Debra Tabor ten miles to the south down the ridgeline, Ravinger went to kick as lustily on the wooden door as he was able, with only six inches of chain between his shackled feet. In this manner he discovered he wasn't guarded by the usual Galla eunuchs, but by three or four of Tewodros's most vicious musketeers with diamond-headed spears and rusty matchlocks. The matchlocks were mostly a joke, as Ravinger well knew. If he'd been able to crash the door down and make a dash for it, it would have taken them at least five minutes to shoot at him. They measured their powder by sight before dumping it down the barrel. They fumbled about looking for their flints and steels. They had to strike the light, blow the match, prime the gun, and fix the match to the correct length and direction. Lastly, the guns were so heavy they couldn't operate them without sticking a bamboo rest into the ground. This was why Ravi had appropriated all decent Enfields taken as plunder for himself and his closest men.

Altogether it was simple to escape from such musketeers, if one wasn't chained in shackles. They opened the door, as they often did to serve him food, and kept their matchlocks fixed upon his stomach. "I demand to see a *ferenje!*" Ravi bellowed. "Waldmeier, Saalmüller, Staiger—who is around?"

He was able to raise Waldmeier, the missionary he had helped before when his wife (now recovered), a sister of Louisa Bell, had desired to see Dr. Blanc. Waldmeier was allowed to enter the hut and sit opposite Ravi, since Tewodros was safely off plundering the district. Waldmeier held the tobacco pipe for Ravi to puff from as he gave him the latest news.

Waldmeier spoke in English, at which most of the German missionaries were very accomplished, having come from the London Society for Promoting Christianity among the Jews. "The rebels' forces have increased since the sacking of Gondar. The sacrilege of the Emperor has been the last insult to many."

"Have the desertions increased? We had about fifty men deserting each day before."

"Yes. Some Begemder men have refused to plunder their own countrymen. Every day Begemder soldiers throw down their arms to join their persecuted peasant brothers. Every day more sneak off during the night."

"And what of . . ." Ravi tried to look unconcerned and prideful.

Waldmeier assisted him. "The American woman? Gar Inchael heard her screaming at the Emperor from her tent down in Debra Tabor."

Waldmeier's eyes glinted with mischief, and Ravi outright guffawed, his chest shaking with mirth. "Oh, that's good! And what was she screaming about?"

"She first screamed that she wanted her friends. She then screamed that she wanted her medal."

"Ah, yes," Ravi nodded with fondness, as though he'd expected as much. But he was secretly disappointed that she had not called for him.

It had occurred to him that Delphine might imagine he was in on the plot. But surely she must have seen him shooting at the kidnappers; indeed, he'd killed one of them on the spot, and another later died from his wounds. If she hadn't seen him, surely someone must have told her?

Waldmeier offered to feed Ravinger, but he'd rather starve than submit to that babying. He demanded his shield-bearer Walde Nebra, who was restored to him after another couple of days, and who was allowed to roam unfettered inside the hut tending to his needs. Walde Nebra had indeed returned to Delphine's house in Islambet, and he brought many valuable supplies with him. He'd brought some of Ravinger's personal effects from Delphine's laboratory, clothing, Ravi's lion's fur mantle, his silver case with tweezers for extracting thorns from the feet, leaving the weapons and manuscripts cached elsewhere.

By the time the screaming pain in Ravi's shoulders from the shackles had deadened to a dull roar, Tewodros finally visited him. His valet Paul brought a jar of the favored *tej*, and Ravi did not turn down the offer of a drink. He'd been up and down, to hell and back with The Elect of God, his master and father, Tewodros. He was convinced this was merely another of Tewodros's mercurial caprices. And above all, he was not afraid of Tewodros.

Ravi gulped the *tej* that Walde Nebra held to his lips. "Please get me out of these chains."

"Ah," Tewodros said, as though happy Ravi had mentioned it. He paced restlessly today, his perfect, lush mouth twitching with some sort of deep botheration. "Basha Falaka, you attempted to get in the way of fate. I could not allow that to happen, so I had you put into chains." He stood before Ravi now, his own hands behind his back as though in unconscious imitation of his captive. "You must know that I love you, by the death of Christ. You came to me as a son, and by Saint George, you have been more of a son to me than Alemayou or Meshesha."

Ravi was aware of the absurdity that he was Tewodros's son—he was a mere five years younger than the Emperor—but he had enjoyed that role in the past. Ravi's own father was a cold, hard, bitter man who had always been disappointed in him. It had been pleasant to have a fresh figurehead who praised him and thought he could do no wrong.

"Jan Hoy," Ravi began with as much respect as he could muster. "You say I was getting in the way. But I was trying to protect you from taking a wrong step. Doctor Chambliss is not Makeda. You wear her medal, and you can plainly see the engraving on it. I knew that if you imagined she was Makeda, you might not keep on looking for the true Makeda, and when she arrived—"

Tewodros stepped up so close that he trod on Ravinger's toes. "Stop lying to me! That is one thing I will never accept, and that is being lied to!" he shrieked, causing Walde Nebra to shrink back against the wall. "Everyone knows she is Makeda—she wore the medal! Now if you do not stop these lies, I will never take you out of those irons, and I do not want to do that, because I love you, and I mean you no harm!"

Ravi sighed. "This is clearly a *different* prophecy. Perhaps this prophecy was supposed to come *before* the Makeda prophecy. Perhaps this is a *prior* prophecy, something meant to happen *prior* to the arrival of Makeda. You see that I also wear a medal. Most logically this means that Doctor Chambliss and I are the ones meant to couple, and—"

"No more!" In one vicious motion, Tewodros had torn the

medal from Ravi's shirt.

Ravi tried to look calm, blinking like a deer up at the towering Emperor. Huffing through his elegantly flared nostrils, the Emperor secreted Ravi's medal in his *shamma*. He then perversely reached out to caress Ravi's stubbled jawbone, thoughtfully rubbing with his thumb and tickling under his chin with his fingertips. Ravi was fully aware that Tewodros had already given him a dozen more opportunities to redeem himself than he normally afforded to . . . well, to anyone else in the country.

"I love you, my son. I will hear no more of this blasphemy. Makeda wrote fondly of you in the unauthorized letter I seized from her house, so I won't punish you, and I won't send you to Magdala." It seemed that the sovereign's eyes misted over then, as Ravi had often seen happen when he thought of his dead wife. "It is clear she has affection for you, as do I." He stroked Ravi's throat now, and Ravi held his watery gaze. " 'The spirit of the Lord God is upon me, because the Lord has anointed me. He has sent me to bring good news to the oppressed, to bind up the brokenhearted, to proclaim liberty to the captives, and release the prisoners.'

"Yes . . ." Ravi encouraged him.

Now Tewodros bent over at the waist and grasped Ravi's jaw in both hands, holding it fast so that Ravi could not avoid him even if he so desired. "Now I have Makeda. As long as I have Makeda, I will never lose you. If I never lose you, I will never lose my country."

Ravi tried to return Tewodros's crooked smile, and then the Emperor left his hut.

Walde Nebra breathed several large sighs of relief, they drank Bordeaux, and Ravi's wrist fetters were struck off that very night.

Two women brought Delphine food—Yetemagnu and Alitash. Yetemagnu was a crude, bold, and ribald woman who had three children by the age of twenty. Alitash was a stunning, meek, and resentful maiden. Delphine knew them both to be concubines of the Emperor.

Every day they brought food and new items of clothing to dress Delphine in. Since she was in ankle chains, they could not fit her with the loose cotton breeches that tapered tightly at the ankle, so they draped her in a fresh solid white embroidered calico shirt that reached to her feet. They slid many silver bracelets over her wrists, and chains over her head, giving her a blue *mateb* though no one had asked whether she be Christian. They set aside some bangles that were apparently for her ankles. Rings were positioned on almost every finger, including the upper joints. They stained her hands and bare feet with *insoosilla*, and lined her eyes with kohl, as she had used to do herself.

And around her neck went a special amulet that had belonged to Tewodros's first wife. The plain leather pouch was stuffed with a long parchment scroll upon which were written mysterious ancient Ge'ez scripts.

From these women—mostly Yetemagnu, as Alitash was quiet and sullen—Delphine had learned she was near a town called Debra Tabor. The Emperor would take off her fetters once she had proven she would not try to leave. If she would just go along with everything, she'd be fine.

It was when Delphine dared to inquire after Ravinger that things went awry.

"The Basha Falaka—where is he?" There was no need to explain to them her story, that she currently loathed the Speedy Captain, though she had once imagined herself capable of loving him. They wouldn't understand.

The moment Delphine mentioned him, Alitash leaped to her

feet from where she was trying to fit a silver foot girdle that was much too small onto Delphine. She threw the jingly girdle to the carpet and cried, "Basha Falaka will never prefer you over me!" She trounced out of the tent.

Yetemagnu's laughter eased Delphine's fears somewhat. The concubine merely took the silver girdle and resumed trying to fit it on Delphine's foot. "She has a"—some more descriptive words Delphine didn't understand—"for the Basha Falaka. She thinks she is the only one who can lie with him."

Delphine frowned. "What is—" She tried to repeat the unknown words.

"That is when a woman cares so much for a man, she doesn't wish to lie with any other. That is a bad thing, for we're all required to lie with many men. If we stay only with one, we have no value."

"Hmph." Delphine tried to still her trembling lower lip. "And how many . . . women has Basha Falaka lain with?"

"Oh, hundreds," Yetemagnu said cheerfully.

"Hundreds?" Delphine mouthed, and she was now so intimidated she didn't want to again ask where Basha Falaka was.

"Oh yes. All of us, probably. He has been here a long time."

"And have you . . . ?"

"Oh yes." Yetemagnu seemed to wax reminiscent, as her fingers stilled on Delphine's foot and she gazed at a looking-glass that hung from the tent wall. "He is very famous among us for his skill and his 'Hindoo' love skills. Women often fight to be the one chosen by him. He makes women . . ." She seemed to collect her thoughts then. "Makes women happy. He is a master at love."

Delphine struggled for many long minutes to keep her face placid, but she at last had to wipe a tear from the corner of her eye. She breathed deeply. Why should this be such a surprise to her? Concubinage was a common thing in this country. Basha

Falaka—Ravinger!—was a lusty man to whom sex seemed to be everything. Of course he would sample the offerings—he was only human!

"Alitash has been upset in recent weeks past, because Basha Falaka has not called for her," Yetemagnu went on, casting Delphine dark sooty glances laden with some sort of meaning that escaped her. "He has not called for *anyone*."

Delphine pouted. "Well, tell Alitash she can call on him! I don't care! Tell her to call on him every day!"

The knowing look Yetemagnu cast her annoyed her—knowing about *what*?—and Delphine yanked her foot from Yetemagnu's hands. Standing, she hobbled to refill her red *tej barrilye*. Feeling brazen and wishing to alter the subject, Delphine finally asked, "Where is my servant Abou? And where is the Deacon Kaspar Nagel?"

"I haven't seen the *azmary* for many weeks, but I can find out about your servant. He is a very tall Takrury, right?"

Turning back to the concubine, Delphine managed a smile. "Yes. That is him. Where is he?"

Yetemagnu became guarded again. She clinked the bell girdle in her hand. "I have seen him. I will find out."

"Thank you."

Yetemagnu then inquired about a knot she had found beneath the skin under her arm, and Delphine was relieved to have something innocuous to think about.

She was a prisoner again, but the healthy highland air was vastly preferable to the hell on Earth, the piles of putrefying amputated limbs, the creek of human offal in Georgia. Hospital gangrene would start on a person, a black spot the size of a button. Soon the entire person was black, and dead. Rags of clothing were stripped from the corpses inside the dead line, sometimes even before they had breathed their last. That building Delphine had worked in was miscalled a hospital—it was a charnel house.

Here, there was food one could swallow, and it rarely returned on one. Now, in the dry season, the air was robust and the lucent sunlight lit the entirety of her tent with a rhodonite glow. All around, she could hear the bustle of women bringing back water-skins, kindling fires, grinding *teff*. Valets and messengers babbled urgent messages. She was shocked now that when she was very hungry, the peppery *wot* stew seemed to taste good.

CHAPTER THIRTEEN
THE TURKS OF CAIRO

TWO ROWS OF MUSKETEERS LINED THE road that led to the Emperor's white pavilion. This was not a good sign to Ravinger, for it denoted a formal audience, and although his ankle chains had been struck off that morning, it was the Ras Engeddeh himself who had come to escort him to the parley.

Inside, the Emperor was seated on an *alga* and was flanked, aside from the Grazmach and Kanyazmach with their American six-shooters, by some of his most beloved "Gaffat children," Waldmeier among them. They were all clad in their laudatory *kamis*, the red silk shirts given to men of rank, sometimes to give them a false sense of appeasement. Ravi knew them as well-educated and erudite men, and he didn't blame them for so obviously standing in mute judgment of him—it was their only option, and they did lower their eyes in embarrassment.

But not Kaspar Nagel. Whether he'd been brought to town trussed as a bundle, as Ravinger had, or voluntarily waving his arms, singing, and drinking *arrack*, here he was, standing in an especial position of distinction between the Emperor and his valet Paul. Kaspar had finally changed from the European suit he'd been affecting of late into the usual snow-white *shamma*, with the exception that he still wore brogans. Ravinger didn't prostrate himself, and Kaspar's eyes didn't flinch from their vacant ice-blue staring straight ahead at nothing in particular.

To the left of the Grazmach was that son of a bitch Verlaine, reveler of the "delight of the Egyptians." Ravinger cast the dilettante his most harrowing gaze, and Anatole merely twinkled his eyes and lifted the corners of his saurian mouth at Ravi.

It was Tewodros who bowed his head. "For Christ's sake, forgive me." When he looked up, Ravi was struck by his limpid cat's eyes—how easy it was for Tewodros to change characters! He gestured for Ravinger "by the death of Christ" to take another *alga*. Ravinger replied that he couldn't do so while the Ras Engeddeh, the prime minister, remained standing, so an *alga* was brought forward for him as well.

Tewodros proceeded gently. "Abyssinians are a wicked people. If I go to the south, my people rebel in the north; when I go to the west, they rebel in the east. I've pardoned the rebels over and over again; nevertheless, they persist in their disobedience and defy me. I'm now determined to follow them to every corner, and shall send their bodies to the grave and their souls to hell."

Ravi nodded, unsure where Tewodros was leading with this. "There are many rebellions to put down."

"The Mohammedans have always tried to encroach on the rights of the Christians. Before I came to the throne, the Gallas had ruled our country of the Amharas, and the Turks shamelessly took possession of Sennaar and the Soudan, which had before belonged to us. I have brought the Mohammedans under my yoke, and I hope to rid us of Turks before I die." Tewodros waited for Ravinger's reply.

"Yes." It was true Tewodros had accomplished all those things. In his ascendance, he had been a joyously unifying figurehead around which many tribes had rallied. It was exhilarating in those years to be close to him. "Turks used to infiltrate from Massawa, but now they're afraid."

"India and half the world belong to me!"

Ravi nodded. "Yes, yes. Alexander the Great. The only person who had been to Paradise in his lifetime." For Tewodros had a picture book he was fond of visiting when in his cups that depicted an Abyssinian princess going to Alexander, and begetting another son.

Just as swiftly, the Negus forged another new character for himself, this one of deep love for his de novo son Basha Falaka. "Don't look at my face, but trust to my heart, because I really love you. I wouldn't say so before my people who are standing here if I didn't mean it. It's true I behaved ill to you last week, but I have a goal in what I do. I never meant to be angry with you. I used to hear that my people called me a madman for my acts, but I never believed it. Now, after my conduct toward you, I believe I really am so. But as Christians, we really ought to be ready to forgive each other."

Ravi was cynical. "It takes a great lofty man to feel true forgiveness for another."

Tewodros's sparse moustaches twitched a little, as though a fly had alighted upon them. "I have released you from your chains, Basha Falaka. You may roam as you please, for I need you to consult with me on building roads. You would never leave me, being much too dedicated, so I am afraid no more."

Without taking his eyes from Ravi, he raised an arm in the direction of Kaspar Nagel, who stood stiffly behind him as though holding his breath. "You must realize and agree with me that the woman you call Doctor Chambliss was a hazard to my country and that she must be stopped."

Bending at the waist as though he might break, Kaspar

proffered some mangled and torn pages he had been holding behind his back. The Emperor sniffed at them as though they were horse turds, and he commanded Kaspar, "Read."

Kaspar gave one brief glance at Ravi, and Ravi plainly saw terror, manifest and simple. Ravi didn't hold it against the *azmary* that he was forced to participate in this tableau of judgment miscarriage. Kaspar began in his childish Würrtemberg patois to read. He read in Amharic, but was so fluent that he barely stumbled on the translation.

"My dearest Siobhan,"—he pronounced it "See-o-bahn"—*"How do you fare in Cairo? How I wish I would receive a letter from you! Sometimes I feel that I'm at the very edge—"* Kaspar stopped, and looked to the back of the Emperor's head for guidance.

Tewodros waved him on. "Part has been torn off," he explained genially to Ravi, as though he didn't recall it was Ravi himself who had torn it during their tussle in Gondar.

Clearing his throat as though reciting a state speech, Kaspar carried on. *"—they were only prevented by the actions of that same Captain of War I told you was such a despicable barbarian! How odd things turn out, yes? He is now living at my house, as a protector of course, and I must tell you . . ."* Kaspar's face reddened. He shifted uncomfortably, as though he'd like nothing more than to run to the water closet, but once again Tewodros waved him on. *"I do not mean to be seductive, but there has been some playing that I like, and has really put me to—"*

"Enough!" Rising imperiously, Ravi pointed a dangerous arm at the hapless deacon, who seemed altogether too gratified for a chance to stop reciting. Ravi stepped clear around the Emperor and again tore the letter from Kaspar's nervous hold. Ravi shook the pages in Tewodros's face. "It's enough that you steal personal correspondence, but to have it read in public is a . . . It's beneath someone of your regal standing, and I'm very surprised."

Now the Emperor rose too, and Ravi stuffed the pages into his filthy *shamma* to obviate another tug-of-war over them. "It was necessary in order to show you the treason that woman was committing! She writes to her allies the Turks in Cairo, committing the very same seditious act that Consul Cameron was guilty of when he traveled there rather than obtain for me an answer—"

Ravi's eyes widened incredulously. "The Turks?" *Man alive! Cairo!* He sputtered, "No, no, you don't understand. Cairo is in Illinois, which is in America, and—"

"—Even worse, she boldly writes to this See-o-bahn Turk that 'the Emperor of this benighted country sent devils to remove me by force to their wretched camp with filthy tents' and we were only prevented by the heroic actions of you, the Captain of War who is now such a hero to the Turks!"

Ravi stepped up to Tewodros so that their foreheads were only inches apart. In this manner he was able to speak relatively calmly. "Jan Hoy, 'See-o-bahn' is a *woman*, Doctor Chambliss has often mentioned her to me, it is a girlhood friend of hers in America, in Cairo Illinois, whereof the Deacon Nagel has no doubt heard. This is no letter to Turks—it's a girlish letter to her friend!"

Tewodros squeezed his eyes until they almost shut. "You cast doubt on what I say?"

"No. Yes!" Ravi turned toward the crooked poet, who was clearly delighting in this entire exchange. "Surely Monsieur Verlaine can—" Then, realizing the futility of this approach, he strode to the pavilion's doorway. He was free, was he not? He would find out soon enough, at any rate.

Tewodros called after him, "She must be stopped, Basha Falaka! And I have stopped her! She can no longer communicate with her friends the Turks!"

Ravi shouted, "I will show you a map of America, O Great One!" Then, "*Oh, man alive!*" Ravi fumed as he exited the white tent. "Turks!" He marched down the footpath that led from the hilltop pavilion without anyone intercepting him.

It wasn't until he was past the bamboo fence that he realized he didn't know where his tent was. Or, indeed, if he even *had* a tent anymore—it had perhaps been dismantled and all of his belongings distributed amongst the elite. He turned left, passing the Fitawraris' tents and those of some favored concubines, and was ecstatic to not only discover Misha's tent, but Misha himself sitting out front in the sun on an *alga*. Apparently oblivious that his partner had just had a momentous meeting in the pavilion, Misha sat before a bamboo table squeezing a gall bladder into a dish of chopped liver.

Misha's jaw dropped when he saw Ravi approaching, and he pushed away the table full of cow dross. He came to meet Ravi with outstretched fingers, as though Ravi were a sea monster walking on land.

"Gee whittaker! Rav, Rav!" He gripped him by the shoulders. "I'd heard you were—nearby."

Ravi shook off his friend's hands. "Nearby all right, in wrist and ankle chains! Surely you heard of my 'capture' in Gondar?"

Misha sheepishly looked at Ravi's feet. "Well, sure I heard about that, of course, but—you don't think there's anything I could have done about it, do you?"

Looking down, Ravi sniffed at the bloody fingerprints on his *shamma*. "At least you dropped the gall bladder before embracing me! Well, *I'sh-shi*, let's go inside and have a drink."

The neat and orderly tent, with Misha's clothing and armament hung methodically on pegs ranged along the tent posts, was a refreshing change of venue from Staiger's old fusty hut. Sitting on an *alga*, Ravi helped himself to a pipe and tobacco from an inlaid box while Misha poured two Hennessey's brandies from a cut glass decanter.

"Walde Nebra went on his mule to fetch your tent," Misha informed him, "but we're breaking down camp soon—

"Where we moving?" Ravi snapped.

"—Qorata, so why don't you just sleep in my tent until we move?"

Ravi accepted the brandy and took three hale swallows, enjoying the caustic yet smooth bite in his sinuses. "Have you heard about this new charge, that Delphine Chambliss is in complicity with Turks because she wrote a letter to a woman in Cairo, Illinois?"

Misha sat on an *alga* opposite from Ravi. He managed a tepid laugh. "Oh, is that what that was all about?"

Ravi flashed him a fiery look. "Silly, isn't it?"

"Utterly silly, Rav!" Chuckling some more, Misha wiped an imaginary laughter-tear from the edge of his eye. "Some of the things they come up with! Why, the other day, Ras Engeddeh saw Badjerund Cafty kicking a hare—"

"Mikhail Vasiliev!" Frowning, Ravi leaned forward, forearms on knees. "I don't see the fatheaded jocosity in an innocent woman—a doctor of medicine, no less—being kidnapped forcibly, bodily, bound and chained hand and foot, and thrown into a civilization she wishes no part of! Do you mean to tell me you've just been sitting here squeezing your gall bladders with no concern whatsoever for her plight?"

Misha adopted a sober face. "Ravinger. Of course I feel sadness for her. She has no wish to be in the imperial camp. But you know better than most the futility of getting in the way of the Emperor's plans. What are we to do? Our hands are tied—"

"I'll say!" Leaping to his feet, Ravi went to pour some more brandy. "My, you're an insipid dildo, Azmach Michael! I'm starting to think you're just a feeble pawn of the Emperor's! Have you no will, no spine of your own? I'm not asking you to break into the tent and grab the woman and race off on horseback to restore her to her former life—I'm asking you to simply have an opinion that perhaps on the rare occasion the Emperor's ideas are not quite *sound!*"

Shrugging, Misha sputtered wordlessly. At last he admitted, "Well, perhaps sometimes . . . he does draw an incorrect conclusion . . ."

" 'Incorrect conclusion'! It was just his *modus operandi* to snatch the woman, the woman he logically enough figures is the reincarnation of the Queen of Sheba!"

Striding to the other side of the tent, Ravi fumbled with his free hand to withdraw the torn letter from his *shamma*. He looked through the part Kaspar had been forced to read aloud, distraught yet thrilled to see the rounded script he'd previously only seen in Delphine's laboratory, when she copied down receipts for herbal cures.

Please forgive my sauciness, for he has riled me to unexpected heights and it's perfectly maddening. I'm just in a passion, and you know how I get so savage! No one could ever replace Eugene as you know so that is not the intention here—no, I just have eyes for this man.

There could not be a man as opposite from your Fred! I do not think you'd like him much—he's a veritable beast, and he's traveled the world over entering exotic forbidden cities dressed as a heathen, and he is never detected because he looks and speaks the parts so well. You would be proud to see the way I truckle at his side as though I am a schoolgirl, soaking up his flippant teachings on Free-masonry, Sufism, falconry in India, Brazilian Creoles—

There the torn letter ended.

Dropping his arm to his side, Ravi sipped his brandy and sighed. "What's that?"

Ravi was so lost in his own musings he fairly jumped when Misha spoke. Twirling to face Misha, he demanded, "Where is she?"

"Well, now, Ravi, I don't think it would behoove you to go running over there breaking down the door."

He was right. That would behoove nobody. "I won't. I just want to know where she is. She must be here; I doubt he'd send her to Magdala. Does she have her own tent? Is she near Yetemagnu, or Alitash?"

Misha must have found a scrap of humanity in his addled sacerdotal mind, for he rose and came toward Ravi holding his own brandy *barrilye*. "You . . . you're really fond of her?"

Ravi laughed, his first true laughter since the Dembea ridge searching for *michamicho*. "Ah, Misha. Isn't it obvious?" Apparently, though, it wasn't, for Misha continued staring at him with bulbous inculpable eyes. Ravi sighed. "If ever I get that woman back in my sight, I will never let go of her."

At length Misha nodded. It was plain he didn't take Ravi seriously, yet he told him, "There's a red tent between Yetemagnu's and Selamawit's tent. A big tent—the one where Woizero Tiruwerq used to live, before . . ."

Before Tewodros sent her, his second wife, to rot on Magdala, Ravi thought, as he strode toward the tent flap.

He had to walk only thirty paces up the hill to see Delphine's tent. It stood amiable and bright against the backdrop of cooking fires, distant bejeweled chlorite mountains, and three massive Gallas guarding the door. Ravi had been in the vicinity once when a desperate soldier had crept to a concubine's tent to ask a female attendant to pass him a *barrilye* of *tej*. She did so, but a eunuch had seized the fellow and he was brought immediately before Tewodros. The Emperor had asked the petrified unfortunate if he liked *tej*; he replied in the affirmative. "Well, give him two *wanchas* full to make him happy, then fifty stripes with the *girf*." One lash with the dreaded hippopotamus hide was enough to gouge a trench of muscle from a man.

Ravi squatted with arms dangling between his legs, appraising the tent. He crumpled his hand over the letter secreted beneath the chest of his *shamma*.

He's a veritable beast . . . He hadn't known her to be so eloquently bantam in her speech. Jesus H. Christ, he hadn't tumbled to the notion that she even saw much of him beyond a sizable rigid cock—for it was abundantly evident she adored select men in the physical. And yes, she'd seemed to enjoy their banter. Her acute wit had often taken him by surprise, so that he often found himself chuckling at the oddest times and places. But her individual strength—*Isgyoh*, she had undergone so much during the War, only to come to this "benighted" country and endure the tumors, boils, and catarrhs of a new race of the afflicted—had always presupposed that she could be a woman capable of softer or gentler feelings . . . to say nothing of romantic notions toward a man.

She was so insensate and tough, perhaps it was true she could survive alone in this hellish place.

But she shouldn't have to.

CHAPTER FOURTEEN
THE EMPEROR LIFTS HER HIGHER

Near Qorata, Above the Gumara River

"AND DID YOU SEE THAT BLUSTEROUS procession of *debterahs* garbed in ostentatious finery? They clogged the highway redolent of rancid grease!"

"Oh, my!" Delphine laughed gladly. "Just as I see you are finally clothed in the 'tallowy *shamma*' of the countryman!"

Kaspar drew himself up to a devotional height and proclaimed, "As you know, the King is ardently attached to the Church, but he has no sympathy with her ignorant and lazy *debterahs*. When we rode by in our Imperial cavalcade, those priests put forth their cracked and blatant throats in chanting psalms and hymns. They bawled a deafening chorus, but our royal cortege passed with an indifference that was nothing less than dissident! Even you"—meaning the godless—"would have been appalled!"

Delphine refilled Kaspar's *barrilye* with *arrack*. She was so overcome with joy to see the good deacon that she was willing to listen to his mangled tales and serve him *arrack* with utter patience. "I wouldn't know, dear Kaspar. I've been traveling at night with the women."

For she had traveled three nights in the brisk honeysuckle-scented air, sleeping three days, apparently with her own retinue of wood-cutters, cooks, and water-bearers. She had her finely caparisoned Gondar mule back, and he picked his sure-footed way down the rubble track encased in a tomb of eunuchs. She'd grown accustomed to the solitary tinkle of the mule's bells and thought there could be worse methods of traveling than to ride, eat, and speak in low tones with Yetemagnu, Selamawit, and others. More than once she caught herself thinking *These women have straddled Basha Falaka*, and before rank jealousy could flush its way up her body she stopped it dead by reminding herself that by being the only woman in the immediate countryside who had *not* ridden the Speedy Captain, she was certainly unique, and wasn't nearly as gullible and desperate as the others.

When marching, the women of Tewodros's harem left first at midnight under a strong bodyguard so that no crass eye could gaze upon their forms. Upon arrival at their destination, the arrangement of their tents was the sign for everyone else to pitch theirs, Fitawraris following soon after, drummers beating their *negarits*, and thousands of camp-followers in a frenzied bustle of donkeys laden with tents and provisions.

Delphine was still confined to her tent during the day, though unshackled now, so in many ways it was better not to know—not to know what he was doing when he was avoiding her.

Kaspar exhaled his *arrack* and pondered. An enlightened look appeared on his face, and he leaped to the tent door and beckoned.

Walde Nebra entered then. He bore items obviously saved from her house in Gondar: her portmanteau, baskets of her fragrant powders, salves, and scents, her Amharic vocabulary book, and above all, her medicine chest and surgical set. Delphine cried aloud to open the latches on the wooden surgical box and touch her bone forceps, hammers, chisels, and trephines. These were her trade tools that she'd carried with her for years—at the end of the

War she'd kept them instead of selling them back to the government—and her eyes stung with tears to see such potent reminders of a former life with such dubiously worthwhile memorials.

Holding her hand to her mouth, she looked at Walde Nebra and gasped, "Thank you." Then she remembered the Reverend Stern had been tortured for holding his hand to his mouth, so she raised it to her forehead in proper Abyssinian fashion.

Walde Nebra stood proudly, fit to bust at having accomplished such a mission. "The Likamaquas instructed me to bring your things."

Kaspar frowned and pointed stridently at the medicine chest with her brass name plaque: *D.E. Chambliss / Asst. Surgeon / 52nd Ohio Inf.* "Do not even *think* of returning these things to the Basha Falaka out of anger and ire! These belong to you, and you'll be of much more practical use to the Emperor if you can occupy yourself with medicine."

Of course, Kaspar was right. From one basket Delphine withdrew a bottle of the Bordeaux wine that had been mixed up in her belongings, and handed it to Walde Nebra. "Thank the Likamaquas for me, Walde Nebra. Tell him it is very thoughtful of him for providing me with supplies that might make the rest of my years in Abyssinia more comfortable."

Kaspar approved of that sentiment, for he said no more until Walde Nebra left the tent. He then regarded a bottle of Champagne wine. "My dear. I know this is not a popular position for me to take. But I must tell you—though it goes against all the instruction my higher soul teaches me—that I don't believe Captain Howland to be guilty of turncoat perfidy. Yes, I say this!" The cork popped, and Delphine set a *barrilye* on the folding table. "I say this because it was Walde Nebra who told me how the captain jumped from a window of your house to follow the rascals responsible for spiriting you away, how he shot his gun at them, killing one, how he then bravely chased them all, though they were a score to his one! How it finally took ten men to subdue him, after which they swathed him like a babe and lashed him to the back of a mule! Yes, I say this!"

Delphine cast her eyes toward the tent's ceiling. "If he even did one-fourth of the escapades you just enumerated, it was only to make it seem as though he didn't have a hand in it."

Kaspar sat up straight. "Walde Nebra saw all of these things with his own eyes! He is the most honorable shield-bearer in the country, my dear, you simply must believe him!"

Delphine preferred to sip her laudanum rather than continue to imbibe liquor. If she could just get enough laudanum, she would touch liquor no more. "Kaspar. You were in the tunnel with us. You were the one saying Basha Falak—Captain Howland was setting a trap for us. How else could they have instantly known exactly where we were?"

"Tewodros had men at the city gates as watchmen! When they saw us enter, they merely followed us to Qwesqwam!"

"And what of Abou? Yetemagnu has told me he is somewhere here, why have I not been allowed to see him?"

"Abou?" Kaspar looked about the tent as though Abou would be revealed to him. He sipped some more champagne. "Abou."

Delphine slit her eyes at him. "Yes, Abou. My 'tej-asale-fech'—who has also saved my life on many occasions! He carried me through the tunnel as though I were a mere bird! Where is Abou?"

"Ah. I believe Abou is in the tent of the eunuchs."

❊ ❊ ❊

LATER THAT NIGHT, DELPHINE LOUNGED IN an attitude of carefree euphoria. Walde Nebra had brought her manuscript, tentatively entitled *Being A Medical History of Abyssinia*, and she now sat at the escritoire with it laid out on the folding leaf. Now that she saw a useful purpose for the desk aside from writing tirades that could possibly get her thrown into Magdala, Delphine began to rise from the blue funk she'd been mired in that had been enhanced with large amounts of *tej*.

Theodore entered her tent.

The light cast by three country lamps, clay saucers containing rag wicks floating in beeswax, created sinister shadows on the royal visage. He was smiling, or at least trying to as well as his malevolent self would allow. He was accompanied by his valet Paul, who stood just inside the tent flap. Delphine didn't rise, merely turned on her stool to regard him placidly. He stepped toward her dangling something blue and flashy.

"My Queen of the South," he began. "I've had your belongings restored to you, by the power of Christ, and for that you are grateful. With your medicines and tools you can begin healing the people of my court and then everyone will be happy and full of love. Now I restore to you your medal of the Order of Solomon." He slipped the blue ribbon over her head, and lifted her hair to allow the ribbon to slide over her bare neck.

His fingertips grazed her neck. Delphine tingled involuntarily. She hadn't been touched with anything but violence or disdain in weeks.

"Thank you," she found herself saying.

The Emperor smiled beatifically, and she observed that he was an extremely handsome man, with unusually good teeth. "Ah, my Makeda, how it pleases me to hear you speak! Come, sit with me on the *alga*."

He held lightly onto her elbow as he steered her to the low couch. Paul approached them with a jug of *tej* that he poured for the Emperor. Delphine shook her head to the proffered spirit, causing Theodore to beam some more.

"That is good, you don't drink *tej*. Now, tell me. You are writing a sort of medical text?"

Delphine sighed. She saw that Basha Falaka's Templar medal was on a chain around his neck. How had Theodore pried that from his clutches? Or had he given it over willingly? "Yes. I am writing of the herbal remedies to be found in your country. But I need more books. Can you get me books?"

"Books? Ah." Theodore mulled this over. In this thoughtful, pondering mode, he was devilishly handsome indeed. "I would like more books myself. Perhaps I will allow you to write for more books, and have them sent up from Massawa."

His consideration surprised Delphine. *I may as well ask for more.* "Yes, and if I am to continue treating the ill, I will need more medicine. May I be allowed to write for more medicine?"

"Ah." Now came the bargaining, Delphine could see, as a fresh diabolical cast came over his face. He reached a blind arm out for Paul to hand him a bottle of some sort. Opening the stopper, Theodore breathed deeply of its aroma. Doing so incited all manner of fiendish expressions in him, none of which were beneficial, Delphine was certain. "You are Makeda," he informed her again.

She shook her head. "No. I am *Hakim* Delphine Chambliss."

Theodore shrugged. "It was told that the returned Makeda would deny it at first."

Her jaw fell open. "Well, that's certainly a cunning way of putting it!" she cried in English.

"And I am Solomon."

Spewing air from between her teeth, Delphine turned to face the center of the room. She remembered her Amharic. "You're no more Solomon than I am Makeda."

"Stop your blasphemy!" Theodore's free hand shot out and grabbed a fistful of her shirtfront. Delphine's head snapped back, and her eyes flashed with attention not inches from Theodore's face. "As royals, we must mate, and beget a new Menelik."

At the mention of mating, all Delphine's senses started the familiar process of shutting down. It had been this way when forced to "mate" in the past, when she could not fight or physically overcome a man: she simply withdrew from herself and viewed the proceedings with detachment, as though watching from the escritoire.

His fingers were nimble with the lacings to her calico shirt. He roughly yanked the fabric down over her shoulders, drawing down as well the one threadbare camisole she had retained from Gondar. Her abundant breasts nearly burst from the bodice, but Theodore's fingers held there as he panted down on her chest through his nostrils, like a stimulated stallion. He uttered some slippery Amharic words she didn't understand, his eyes so fixated on her uplifted flesh that he didn't see her raise her bland eyes to meet Paul's equally emotionless ones.

Theodore's callused hand swept like rough sand over her breastplate, her nipples instantly expanding to erection without her willing it. She understood some of his words now. "She is a flower, a picture to behold. Believe me, she is beautiful all over. Her neck is long, and her skin is like silk."

How interesting—he's a poet as well as a maniacal tyrant!

He drew himself closer so that she felt the heat emanating from his person. She was surprised that he allowed her to turn her shoulders from him. However, he now pressed his chest to her bare back, tugging the fabric of her shirtwaist even lower. She gave a small inarticulate gasp when the material scraped over the stiffness of her nipples. Her breasts bounced free, full and rounded, as though they had awaited this chance to be molested by such a baldly wicked lunatic.

"Tewodros. I want my manservant Abou to be sent to me."

"Like the expanding flowers of a mimosa—ah yes, my enchantment, I shall have your slave sent to you." His long brown fingers curled, nimbly massaging her right pectoral. His other hand snaked around with the little blue bottle of poison—*what is that stuff?* He dribbled globs of oleaginous ointment between her breasts, but the oil was warm, and heated even more when Tewodros smeared the globules in a lubricous path down the center of her sternum. His sweltering breath was on her neck. "I shall have your slave sent."

Her spine snapped erect when Tewodros's deft fingers caressed the underside of her saucy breast, delving into the sweaty cleft over her ribs. His free hand clasped her other oily breast, gripping it so tightly that the nipple poked through urgently between his greasy fingers. "I've heard he's with the eunuchs. I would be very angry and . . . displeased to hear . . . that he'd become emasculated."

"Ah, the eunuchs . . ." Tewodros groaned against her neck. He pulled her back forcefully until she sat in his lap, and he didn't let up his grip on her teats, squeezing them powerfully, and at last rubbing his thumbs over the jutting points of her nipples.

She watched his dark brown hands manhandling her plump breasts. He stimulated and kneaded her expertly, peaking her nipples between his sandy fingertips. "Please do not tell me Abou is now a eunuch."

"Tell me that you want to mate with me." He grunted with rapture, like the snuffling of a dog against her trapezius. He wedged his hips under her bottom and she felt the long narrow ridge of his stiff cock against her tailbone.

She remained confident and indifferent to his groping. "Tell me Abou is not a eunuch." *Thank Lord Iyesus Kristos he does not try to kiss me! For then one would have to actually move.*

Now he lifted both lubricous breasts high, smashed together. From his breathless gasping that left droplets of steam against her throat she thought perhaps he might climax soon inside his breeches, and would leave her alone. "The Takrury is not a eunuch, my enchantment."

"And he is not a slave. He is my servant."

"He is not a slave. Tell me you want to—" It was a word she was unfamiliar with, but she assumed it meant "mate."

"I want to be free to walk about the encampment, I want the guards taken off my door."

He snuffled so urgently and groaned, that she wasn't sure he'd heard her.

"Will you take the guards off my door, Tewodros?"

"I will take . . . guards from your door."

Speak faster. "I want more books. Then I will mate with you."

"Books," he grunted. "My Likamaquas has . . . a whole tent of books. You are free to . . . see."

"And I may walk about the camp freely? You trust me not to run away?"

"Yes, my enchantment. The woman of you sends me joy."

"Ah, I am so glad, my Emperor. For the man of you . . . lifts me higher."

It seemed as though he met his crisis, for he caught his breath, his body shuddered, and she felt the stiff elevation of him against her tailbone no longer.

"*Ah!*" he cried out, when it certainly must have been after the fact, and he smeared his hands furiously all over her greasy breasts, frantically diddling with her nipples before shoving her away from him in seeming frustration.

She almost felt offended by the sudden manner in which he stood, having no need to smooth his *shamma* about his hips. He paced with agitation for a few moments while Delphine tugged the fabric back up over her shoulders. When she turned to view him, she saw an abrupt change had turned him sour, and he now looked down at her haughtily, hands on hips. "You," he fairly stammered. "You."

"Yes, my Emperor?" she asked mildly.

He said no more—his eyes swam unfocused in his head, and he strode out the door.

Delphine sipped some laudanum, to put some insulation between her and the Emperor.

What sort of crisis annoyed a man? Even the men who had forced themselves on her had been friendly afterwards.

A crisis that . . . was not a crisis. That would annoy a man.

She still had the *merz* she'd taken from Abou in the tunnel. She'd secreted it in a flat silver case around her neck, cases that were supposed to contain talismans, but from what Delphine had seen, usually only contained scented cotton.

NOW THAT THE ENCAMPMENT WAS A somewhat permanent one with the white bamboo fence running around the royal enclosure, Ravinger kept looking at Delphine's tent. He had Walde Nebra and the artful bodyguard Wubishet spying on the tent and giving him the particulars of comings and goings. He had grilled Kaspar about his meeting with Delphine, and Kaspar had admitted what Ravi already suspected—that Delphine imagined he had plotted against them.

He saw Abou escorted from the eunuch's tent directly into Delphine's, and the tall Takrury didn't emerge again.

Foraging expeditions to surrounding districts in the plains of Foggera had yielded very little. Peasants seem to have been on the alert beforehand. Ravi spied beacon-fires on his way to "surprise" raids, and had intercepted a few runners carrying the news before them. There wasn't a soul between their camp on the Gumara

River and Qorata, just some smoldering fires, and huts emptied of all valuables, everyone having departed on Lake Tzana in bulrush *tankwa* boats. Ravinger warned Tewodros not to destroy Qorata, as the holy houses, streets, and trees had all been dedicated to God's service. Ravinger was surprised when Tewodros stayed himself at his behest.

Then Walde Nebra reported the Emperor had visited Delphine, and stayed for about an hour.

Ravinger told the shield-bearer to approach the Galla guards with a cogent bribe of a rare lynx Ravi had shot the day before, and a whole small deer. This game, together with a hefty purse of Maria Theresa dollars, induced the barbaric men to spit it out, and Walde Nebra came scurrying back to Ravi's tent when it was almost sundown.

"I'm not so sure I want to hear this story," Misha said nervously, moving the brandy decanter and *barrilyes* out of harm's way.

"Oh, garbage, Azmach Michael!" Ravi had been losing patience of late with most everything. "Sit still and hear what charming acts your beloved Emperor has committed recently." He queried the shield-bearer, forcing him to sit on an *alga* and plying him with copious amounts of *arrack*. "What did you find out?"

Walde Nebra shifted about hesitantly and seemed prepared to drink the entire *barrilye* of liquor before even starting on the story. "Tewodros told her they must mate."

"Oh, gee whittaker," Misha said with foreboding.

Of course. What had Ravi expected? So then why did he feel as though he'd been attacked by a whole slew of little *zars* whose reach only extended as high as his stomach? Closing and opening his eyes with patience, Ravi encouraged, "Go on. Then what?"

Though speaking in Amharic, Walde Nebra was suddenly stricken with the language of a six-year-old. "Then the Elect of God, he—he—he take her shirt from her shoulders."

Ravi waited, and swallowed some brandy himself.

"He—he—he put his hands on her chest." Walde Nebra demonstrated on himself.

Misha moaned, "Oh, criminy."

"Was her chest bare?" Ravi demanded.

For this, the answer was swift. "Yes! Yes, very bare!"

"He could see her breasts?"

"Yes! He was feeling her breasts!" Walde Nebra held his hands before his chest as though describing pumpkins. "The Gallas tell me her breasts very large, and white, and jiggled and shook with much bounce, and—"

"*All right!*" Ravi roared, finally giving up the aloof act and leaping to his feet. "I'm well familiar with the nature of jiggling breasts, Walde Nebra!" He shouted so loud his words could probably have been heard all the way to Ras Engeddeh's tent, if not the Emperor's. "What did the woman do?"

"She do nothing, she demand things from him, like books, medicine, her servant. The Elect pour oil onto her chest, and vigorously rub, but the *hakim*, she stay calm . . ." Walde Nebra trailed off, gazing into his empty *barrilye*.

"*Yes?*" Ravi hissed down at him. "*Then what?*"

The shield-bearer shrugged. "Then. Nothing. The Emperor got up and . . . he goes."

Ravi shook an enraged fist at the man. "*What did the Emperor say to her?*"

"That he would send her medicine and books."

Ravi roared. Mauling, ravishing his woman, it was unacceptable! He grabbed his *zenar*, shield, spear, and holstered Colt, and was at the tent door before Misha dared inquire, "Where are you going? Don't do anything rash!"

Twirling, Ravi shouted, "Tewodros should be so lucky I should do something 'rash'!"

The truth was, he had no idea what he was about to do, but he wasn't sitting lamely in his tent, and he certainly wasn't scourging the countryside for any more plunder for that deviate sovereign.

A grass-cutter Ravi knew well approached him in a friendly manner. The poor fellow barely got four words out. "Likamaquas, I was over at—"

Ravi lifted him by a handful of his *shamma* front and agitated the wretched fellow in midair. He tossed the man to the ground and continued on his way, but another naïve chap, a groom of Ras Engeddeh's, also headed for him.

"Basha Falaka! I was wondering if I could borrow—"

Ravinger jammed such a rigid arm against the fellow's chest that the man flew through the air straight up, both feet off the ground, landing ass-first in a basket of *teff* women were grinding.

No one dared shout at the Likamaquas, though most everyone else in the vicinity scattered to the four winds, and in the horse tent Ravi for good measure let loose a few horses (one he knew to belong to the Kanyazmach) and slapped them on the croups to send them fleeing through the hamlet. Swiftly packing his horse as though racing into battle, Ravi burst from the horse tent at nearly full charge. He was childishly gratified that the gelding, unaccustomed to going from dead sleep to full tilt in one breath, groggily stampeded across the coals and tools of a spear-sharpening operation.

If only Anatole Verlaine were ignorant enough to get in his way right now! But unluckily, the son of a bitch had maintained his shoddy green tent between the Emperor and the Ras, and rarely left their protective embrace.

Ravi directed his horse southwest, toward Qorata and the lakeshore.

CHAPTER FIFTEEN
THE LYRICAL DOOMFATA OF CAMP LIFE

THEY MOVED TO A NEW ENCAMPMENT alongside the River Abbai—the Blue Nile. Wherever the royal army marched, the land around them was consumed as if by a plague of locusts, so they had to keep moving.

Delphine quickened with fascination when their trail dropped from the plateau and moved toward the river. The air was moister and imbued her face, and emerald cuckoo birds darted overhead. Their camp was close enough that Delphine could hear roaring waterfalls she'd been told were called Tisissat, or "Water That Smokes."

For the first time, the appearance of the permanent camp incited Delphine's wonder. The undulating dales of the plateau were blanketed with tents of all shapes—bell-shaped, or square like an English marquee—and of all colors—the white Emperor's pavilion, or red silk like hers, and some of black goat-hide.

The Emperor as usual chose the highest eminence from which to view his servile domain. In strict order close around the Emperor were the Ras Engeddeh, Dejazmachs, Fitawraris, the Kanyazmach and Grazmach, and the attendant valets, royal bodyguards, shield-bearers, *baal negarit* drummers, stewards, wood-cutters, and dozens of other rigidly categorized ranks whose meanings were still unclear to Delphine. It was a wondrous sight to behold the milling of such an organized city, and it hearkened her back days that were something pleasant and lazy camping with the Federals in Kentucky.

It was well-known that Basha Falaka had charged off on his horse a week ago in a fit of rage. A former fellow eunuch of Abou's had come to tell them that the Likamaquas had tossed the Ras's groom so furiously that he'd soared over the horse tent and landed in the middle of a harem tent. Basha Falaka's charging gelding had stampeded four children to death along his path of escape.

"That's a mean thing to do." Delphine uttered her first words in a week regarding the savage Likamaquas. The day was lovely with a cloudless azurite sky, the brick earth warm under her bare feet as she sat out front of her tent. She was not allowed to wander about at will yet, but every day she moved her camp-table a few inches farther from the eunuchs that still maintained vigil outside her tent door. She spread out leaves of the *wanza* tree, then staked them down with *kantuffa* thorns into a plank of wood to dry.

Dead children were not a topic anyone could really argue about, anyway. Everyone would agree it was horrifying.

Abou laughed diabolically. "Did you really believe him? These Gallas are the baddest liars! They drink the warm blood of living animals. I heard that story about the children from Giyorgis Wube, who was sharpening spears when it happened. There are no dead children."

Delphine shrugged. "Oh. Well, was it true about throwing the groom over the horse tent?"

Abou didn't try to restrain his laughter this time. He laughed so raucously and for so long that Delphine was forced to take her eyes from her *kantuffa* and glance sideways at him. His stomach shook with mirth, nearly upsetting the bowl of wood ash and butter he was mixing. "How could he do such a thing? That is like them saying Basha Falaka throws his lance over the great tree and column at Axum."

"He . . . doesn't?"

"Have you seen the great column at Axum? It is as high as . . ." Sitting erect, Abou swiveled his head about to find an appropriately monstrous object. None of the towering *warkas* or sycamores were sufficiently tall, apparently, for Abou soon slumped on his stool and muttered, "It is very tall."

When they had first reunited last week, Abou had vehemently expressed the opinion that he had seen Basha Falaka shooting at the kidnappers. But then, Abou had been known to number among the "baddest liars" when it came to exaggerating proportions or actions.

"Well," Delphine sniffed. "Do you suppose he's left Abyssinia? Perhaps gone to Greenland?"

"Green lands? No!" Abou said with feeling. "He has left everything of value in his tent."

" 'Everything of value'? What on Earth could be of value? The Emperor"—and here Delphine lowered her voice—"has already stolen his Templar medal, of that I know, because I saw him wearing it when he . . . visited my tent."

"He has much of value. Chests of gold and silver, his war cape of lion, scimitars, and his gold *shamshir*. He has carpets and—what are those cups? He has his writings that Walde Nebra brought back from our house in Gondar." The former slave gave her a sly sideways look. "He has you."

Delphine spoke fast now, as though hoping to obliterate Abou's last words. "Oh, that's the *History of Weapons in Abyssinia*. He told me that, when we were picnicking in the heights of Dembea, before—" Why was she reminiscing about such a miserable period of her life? She was very relieved to see Kaspar's flaxen head among the dozens of hairless, or black, or ochre-tinged heads that moved in an eddying mass downhill from them, before the mesa dropped in a sheer cliff, as though the edge of the world of the olden days over which ships were supposed to sail.

"Kaspar!" Delphine called, flailing her arm to get his attention.

He was on his way to them anyway, not having much black-smithing or converting of Jews to do.

"Pull up a stool," Delphine offered, "or sit on the ground."

Kaspar chose a camp-stool, looking inelegantly gauche in his black Page Lapham brogans that reached to his ankles. Below the *shamma* and white breeches that barely covered his knees, the shoes stood out sorely, like duck's feet. "I am surprised by the ease with which I convinced the Emperor that I was a trustworthy entity in the vicinity of his harems," Kaspar remarked.

Delphine proffered the deacon a plate of apricots she had dried in the sun. "What do you mean?"

Kaspar poked one of the shriveled orange things into his mouth. "I have a new abode—thence and yon!" He haughtily pointed a stiff arm to a spandy new goat's skin tent a few dozen yards off, next to Yetemagnu's tent.

Delphine gasped. "Kaspar! You're my neighbor!"

Abou chuckled darkly. "He lets you, because you are a harm-less *buda*."

Kaspar's eyes sparkled. "Why must this slave of the Turks continually impugn that I am a *poltergeist* of the most heinous sort? My, what is this?"

Kaspar swiveled to observe a commotion in a nearby clearing, past what Delphine secretly called "the dead line" outside the fence she wasn't allowed to cross.

Abou stood slowly, reaching blindly to place the butter bowl on the folding table, and completely missed the table. The bowl thudded to the earth as Abou uttered, "*Doomfata*."

Delphine swiveled too. "*Isgyoh*."

Ravinger Howland had charged up on his estimable bay with white stockings. He pranced just outside the fence, attracting a rapidly growing crowd of soldiers who ran excitedly, raising their spears and shields and shouting out oaths of valor. Some shot their matchlocks into the air, and others fumbled to sprinkle powder into their flash-pans, or seat their balls with homemade ramrods while running. Delphine stood, raining leaves and thorns from her lap, and skipped to the fence to join the luminaries on her side who all dashed forward from their tents.

What was Ravinger shouting?

"*Doomfata!*" Kaspar cried, as Dejazmachs and Fitawraris around them echoed the word.

Oh, he looked splendid in his cape of lion's mane, and his buffalo hide shield emblazoned with intricately hammered silver. His admirably muscled calves flexed when he rose several inches in the saddle, the big toe of his sun-browned foot in the silver ring that passed for stirrups in these parts. She could see his very jaw tighten in his iron countenance as he drove his lance into the ground before him and bellowed, "When Selpha is hurled, Dampto is wounded!"

Ravinger brandished his favored *shamshir*, pointed to the heavens above. Delphine had never seen a more thrilling sight than this utterly virile male, his face bronzed and scarred, blazing with flamboyance and courage.

No one shot their guns now. Men crushing in around her murmured that Dampto was the Kanyazmach's horse.

"Where is the Kanyazmach?"

"Where is the Commander of the Right?"

The question spread from man to man, as a mellifluous *azmary* repeated Ravinger's challenge. The minstrel stood atop a tall tree stump suddenly materialized for the occasion, and he trilled out:

"When Selpha is hurled, Dampto is wounded!"

Ravinger now wheeled his horse this way and that, and soon a rival songster raced from the Imperial Compound, hollering out as though a gaudy performer making a great racket at "John Brown's Body." Delphine knew these singers to be dishonorably classed as women, but no one could touch them. "When Dampto treads, Selpha is broken!"

A harsh cruel grin broke through on Ravi's face as though relieved at this pugilistic response, and the crowd answered with happy shouts as many *talla wanchas* appeared lifted on high. Ravi guzzled furiously from one such horn, spitting the last mouthful onto the ground and shouting, "Unless a male is brave, his birth is no better than an abortion! I have slain three mighty lions! Who else here will agree with that?"

Apparently every last man jack agreed with this, for they all hollered a version of "Basha Falaka has killed three lions!"

"I killed one lion in Lasta with a spear! I killed one lion in Gojam with a spear! I killed one lion in Foggera with a gun!"

"*Awnat!* He killed one lion in Gojam with a spear!" everyone agreed.

The Kanyazmach was at last was sufficiently lubricated with *tej* wassails to march out of his tent, but Delphine's gaze was riveted to the lusty Likamaquas, who seemed even more pleased at the appearance of his rival.

"Why does he hate the Kanyazmach so?" Delphine asked Kaspar.

"Because it is too risky to recite your *doomfata* to the Emperor."

The Kanyazmach waited until his shield-bearer brought his horse. He mounted before shouting proudly, "I have killed three lions, one of them the man-eater who ate Bitwaddad Kidane!"

Ravi's horse brayed to hear such garbage, and indeed Ravi's lip curled back in a bitter sneer as he countered, "I have killed ten elephants, one in Begemder who trampled ten children to death . . .

on horseback . . . during the rainy season." It was a lot easier to kill most animals during the dry season when they were all tired from lack of food.

A generous ruckus ensued now as the *azmary* sang each man's boasts, and the crowd roared approval—or disapproval, in the case of one of the Kanyazmach's dead lions, where most said the victor was a local Azmach assisted by three other men.

The Emperor emerged from his tent, and watched the proceedings from a tall throne-like rock, appearing vastly amused— he smiled continuously, and even burst out laughing a few times. It was the first Delphine had seen of him since he'd visited her tent last, thanks be to Saint George.

Delphine was raised onto Abou's shoulder so she wouldn't miss a word of Ravinger's boasting story. She was awash with relief merely to see him ride up as he had, not dead or having fled in exile at all, but returning courageously to confront the feral Kanyazmach. He sat back relaxed on his haunches, his belt girded so tightly the outline of his superior penis was clearly in evidence, as if he were about to brag about that, as well.

Delphine was stimulated to hear two concubines nearby arguing over the Likamaquas's merits, unconcerned with how many men he had killed.

"His penis will not fit in my mouth," one said.

"Ha," the other rejoined. "I can suck almost all of it into my mouth."

"That is because you have a big mouth."

"I wish I were his rifle, so I could live attached to his chest."

"I wish I were his shield-bearer, so I could always follow him."

At last Delphine could stand it no longer, and she nudged one of the women with her bare foot. "Be quiet! How can you hear what the Likamaquas is saying?"

"You're jealous because you've never had him," the big-mouthed concubine sniped.

I have had him in my very hands, Delphine wanted to say, *and your talk is making me flush with excitement to swallow him now.*

Kaspar shook the slattern by the arm. "Desist, woman! Your loud complaints and praises are like the braying of wild asses!"

Their bawdy conversation instantly brought to Delphine's mind the persistent memory of her own lust for him, in particular the sight of him on the garden bench, splayed out with relaxed *savoir faire*, justly proud that it took two of her hands to frig his stupendous prick. How the moisture had trickled down her inner thigh, she was so riled by the manly ambergris scent of him, the satiny pelt of hair that covered his sturdy pectorals, the exquisitely erotic darker furrow that traveled down between the ridges of his abdomen to the steamy crotch where she gripped his phallus like a tree limb.

Every night, and often during the day in the times she hadn't been allowed out of her tent, Delphine pleasured herself with images of the fetching man, while at the same time loathing him for his treachery. She had an itch in her belly for him, as his erudite and insightful mind was so exalted and evolved.

Ravinger and his euphoric minstrel recited a litany of *geddai* reaching back ten years prior when he'd first arrived in Abyssinia. Delphine was thrilled at his bold reference to the Metemma debacle. When he shouted that he'd speared two men of the Queen Makeda's party, Delphine was one of the loudest braying "*Awnat!*" in harsh agreement.

The Kanyazmach couldn't even begin to hold a candle to Ravi's feats—his coups seemed to consist mostly of *zurruf*, which were apparently enemy prisoners taken in battle. The Kanyazmach claimed about a couple of thousand *zurruf* and everyone gasped in awe—until Ravi, with the ribbing and ridicule this pursuit required, bawled out that a man who has not even been near a battle may, by arriving at the right moment, "capture" hundreds of *zurruf*. Once a victory is obvious, Ravi cried out, all hasten to surrender to the first victor who shouts a war-cry—and a battle is often "won" if the chief flees or the *negarit* drum is surrendered.

This jesting had the effect of turning the gleefully shouting crowd into a gibbering pack of howling monkeys, some so stricken with amazement and awe that Ravinger would so boldly bait the Kanyazmach that they rolled on the ground, overcome by some arcane laughing illness. The Kanyazmach sputtered and spat in his attempts to deny or overwhelm Ravinger's claims and evidence. But again, most of the witnesses agreed with Ravi that they'd seen the Kanyazmach rushing in yowling his war-cry and tallying up the numbers of *zurruf* when he had not fired a shot in battle. The Kanyazmach waved his *shotel* a lot and came up with yet more feats of braggadocio, but Ravinger's feats were so far superior he had to eventually bend to his will, as well as the roaring of the jocose crowd. This must have frustrated him, for, still waving his *shotel* in a bellicose manner, he leaped from his horse and strode over to Ravinger.

That was when Ravinger looked at Delphine for the first time, and steely cold ichor ran through her veins.

It was impossible to not take notice of her, for she was now clad in fashionable style in impeccable white with a dozen necklaces and bangles about her toes, fingers, ankles, and wrists. Yetemagnu had finally found silver foot girdles large enough for Delphine, and her clad feet were now prominently displayed beneath the blackness of Abou's grip.

Ravi must have taken delight in the enraged advance of the Commander of the Right, so sure was he in his own fighting ability that he chose that moment to take his eyes off his opponent and look to Delphine for a reaction. She was ashamed to be thrilled to the very roots of her hair that he singled her out with such a fiery, ardent look, uncaring if the eyes of a thousand warriors as well as his Emperor saw his gaze take in her entire form, foot bells included. He saluted her with the *shamshir* as the women around her gasped.

"He was looking at me!"

"No, he was looking straight at me!"

Ravinger dismounted, tossing his lion's mane to Walde Nebra as he took several colossal steps toward the Kanyazmach. The crowd that had been pressing in on them suddenly receded to clear a circle for the combatants, but the fight was over nearly before it was begun.

Ravi thrust his Persian saber, the Kanyazmach cut with the *shotel*, and they parried a few times before Ravi casually sent the other's weapon flying with a flick of the wrist. The cheering of the multitudes was deafening, the Emperor even standing to applaud. Abou jumped up and down with joy, jostling Delphine as she joined in the general *elelta*, and Ravinger pressed the point of the glamorously curved blade into the soft pit of the Commander's throat. The Kanyazmach may not have understood the finer aspects of "giving point," but if he moved so much as a fraction of an inch, the blade would pierce his trachea.

Ravi sheathed his sword and smiled at the Kanyazmach. Delphine had once heard Ravinger say that Abyssinians were not versed in the details of swordplay, and that it was a simple thing to best them. Now his confidence may have endangered him, for after the Commander refused to shake hands, Ravi turned to approach the Emperor, who stood shouting "Wonderful!" and "Excellent!" The hateful loser scrambled to yank Ravi's lance from the ground.

Warning cries went up all around him, and the Emperor pointed with horror, for by the time the Kanyazmach had succeeded in getting the lance from the earth, Ravi was striding powerfully to him. It was as though a goliath toying with a Lilliputian when Ravi grasped the lance with both hands and lifted, leaving the Commander dangling with running feet. Ravi shook and shook, and the fellow dropped to the ground. Walde Nebra darted out to retrieve the lance as Ravi stood over the man who had been thrice-beaten now. The Commander could not surrender gracefully, however, and he once again got to his feet and charged at the larger man, encircling his throat with his bare hands.

Ravi broke the choke by jamming apart the Commander's arms with his wrists.

It was exhilarating to see the power of the Likamaquas in motion when he bent and swung his hips round under the other man, the muscular fluidity of his haunches when his *shamma* hiked up to reveal the snug breeches. He threw the Commander with an easy graceful cross-buttock, the tendons of his forearms standing out in lovely bas-relief. He had the other pinned on his back, both the Kanyazmach's hands above his head pinioned by one of Ravi's hands, the solid slab of his body enfettering the perseverant Commander, one thigh also clamped down by one of the Likamaquas's broad hands. Delphine knew she had never seen a more rousing sight.

Perhaps it was an obvious target, Ravinger's bulging member that had been so arrogantly displayed as another virile sign of his superiority. All the women clamoring around Delphine gave a collective cry of dismay when the Kanyazmach in his struggling managed to get his free knee up, and no manner of Ravi's straining thigh could prevent the odious fellow from ramming the knee into that most precious epicenter.

The women all cried foul, Delphine perhaps the loudest of all with her cries of, "Cheater! Cheater! Lousy cheating dog-pig man!"

"He will ruin him for everyone!" shrieked a concubine.

Another rejoined, "What do you care, he hasn't been to see

you in two months!"

When Ravi jumped three feet in the air, flipped, and came down on his back rolled up like a hedgehog, the Commander attacked him. Leaping upon him, he landed a shattering punch to Ravinger's scarred cheekbone. His other hand gouged at Ravi's eyes. Ravi gave a roar of rage, flipped the man off of him, and pounced to his feet.

Both men squared off now, blood dripping from Ravi's half-moon scar that had been laid open again. Shaping their hands into talons, they raced for each other. Ravi swiftly cinched a strapping arm about the other's neck and slammed several effective blows to his face.

"Kick him in the testicles, Basha Falaka!" cried an odalisque.

Ravi tossed the man away, but the Kanyazmach came at him again, though blood from his nose sent droplets spraying into the air. Two more punches to the loser's face, a few more to the stomach, and the man dropped. Ravi turned with an air of finality. He was allowed this time to approach the Emperor and bow deeply with what Delphine imagined to be a profoundly sarcastic symbolism.

Horses neighed, matchlocks fired, *negarits* pounded, and everyone without exception cheered and brayed at loud as their lungs would allow. Reedy *imbilta* flutes played in delightful harmonies as men bellowed nasal songs of victory, the Likamaquas's or their own pretended ones, and Ravinger was enveloped in the surge of bodies.

"Ah," Delphine, Abou, and Kaspar sighed as one as Abou let her down to the ground.

"That was a most rousing fight!" Kaspar was in the throes of patriotic zest. "With men like Howland on our side, how can we ever lose?"

It was a bit disappointing to trail listlessly back to her herb table as tender and boasting songs rose from the tent city. Kaspar was right, it had been rousing, though not in the dutiful manner Kaspar intended. No, she had been inflamed to the very core of her quim to watch the Likamaquas tussle and strain and display his overwhelming masculinity so passionately. The exertion of his robust gluteus, the ripple of his fine abdomen that was so powerful as to almost concave . . . In a way, it had been a most unfortunate event to witness.

Delphine's heart pounded as she resumed her seat. It irritated her when Abou casually observed, "The Likamaquas. He sings his *doomfata* to impress Curd Teeth."

Delphine snorted. "He does not. He could care less about Curd Teeth. He sings his *doomfata* to impress the Emperor."

"To impress Curd Teeth," Abou insisted.

A new voice spoke up behind Delphine. "Doctor Chambliss. Might I have a word with you?"

The skinny, grave Azmach Michael was there. Delphine had seen him about the camp, as their tents were not so far apart, but he'd never approached her before. Curious, Delphine stood and allowed the Azmach to walk with her apiece down the hill.

"Ravinger Howland is my dearest friend and partner," the dour fellow began. "And he's been most unhappy lately, which I don't like to see. He risked his life and his position in this army to try and prevent those soldiers from taking you out of Gondar."

They dodged a line of *talla*-addled revelers who were uproariously on their way to join some shindig or the like. Azmach Michael pinched her sleeve to draw her behind a tent, out of sight of the Emperor and most of his henchmen.

"Well, I just can't believe that," Delphine said stubbornly. "It was just too coincidental. He leaves us in the tunnel, and an hour later we're attacked by soldiers."

The Azmach sighed and closed his eyes as though it pained him to even ponder on this subject. "He had no hand in that. If you knew him as well as I do, you'd know he'd be incapable of a deceit like that. Doctor Chambliss. Will you please, please consider talking to him?"

Delphine arched her neck haughtily. "I haven't exactly seen him hurrying over to my tent to have a cocktail!"

But oh dear God, then Ravinger himself stepped around the corner of the tent, looking hunky dory aside from the semicircle cheekbone wound the Kanyazmach had laid open again, and which he had unsuccessfully tried to enshroud with a *shamma* about his head like a hood. Delphine staggered backward a few steps, coming up against the wall of the tent. Ravinger uncovered his head slowly, not taking his fervent eyes from her form.

"My dear," he said in a painfully beautiful Boston patois, "I would have come to your tent for a thousand cocktails, but you were a prisoner. I was too for many days, and when I was released I was told you blamed me for your capture."

Misha swiveled a patient head to view his friend. "Rav. I thought you went back to your tent."

Ravi didn't look at his partner. "I couldn't escape the well-wishers."

"I'm sure you had a dozen offers of marriage," Delphine said stiffly.

Ravi smiled warmly. "Only three."

Rolling his eyes, Misha said, "Is this all right, Doctor Chambliss? I can send this brutal warrior back to his tent, if this makes you uncomfortable."

Delphine shook her head minutely. "No. It's fine." She thought, *if looks could effect changes on physical form, we would both catch fire.*

"You can leave, Misha," said Ravi. "I've matured enough in the past week that I can be trusted alone with a woman."

Misha left.

How utterly handsome he was, with the heated lion's eyes, and the full sensual mouth. Delphine wanted to reach out and wipe the blood from his face, but she was surprised to see how well it suited him. "Yes; a week. You ran away, and everyone thought you had gone onto other adventures, in other countries." Even standing over three feet away, Delphine felt the warmth that emanated from the man.

"I went off because I was maddened at what the Emperor had done to you. The thought of him touching you sent me into a wild rage. To confront him would have been suicide for both you and I, so I left, rather than cause a conflict that could never be resolved."

"Hmm. For someone who worked so hard to bring about this very situation, you've taken a sudden dislike to it. What did you expect when you told the Emperor's men where to find me?"

"Delphine. I don't know how to get you to believe me. Maybe I *was* foolish to bring you back to the city while the Emperor was still there. Maybe I *should* have stayed with you in the highlands and waited for them to depart. But that was the only mistake I made—the Emperor had spies waiting at the city gates who reported to him that I'd arrived back with Kaspar and Abou. When I realized what he'd done, I did jump over your balcony and make a mad dash to save you."

This was the same story propagated by everyone who had been involved. Delphine couldn't give in that easily. She had come to feel in recent weeks that, as she had failed to save her brother or Eugene in Georgia, Ravi had failed utterly to save her. "I hope you're quite recovered from the wounds the Kanyazmach inflicted."

He smiled crookedly. "I assume you refer to my face. He just opened up an old javelin scar."

"Javelin?" Delphine had never asked him how he came by the gallant scar, so certain that he'd been asked that question a thousand times before, and she didn't want to appear to be like everyone else.

"Yes," he said, agreeably. "When Misha and I first came to Abyssinia we were encamped in the desert of the Danakils. Our camp was attacked, a javelin driven through my jaw—but I was the least seriously wounded of our party."

"Ah," Delphine sighed. The thought of a spear being driven through Ravi's jaw brought out her professional altruism, and she winced in sympathetic pain. "All the way through your jaw?"

"In one side"—he pointed at the weeping scar—"and out the other." A much less distinct scar was barely noticeable on the other side of his face. "Knocked out two molars, cleft the palate."

"Ah. If it had been just an inch or two higher . . ."

"I would not have gone on to annoy so many more thousands of people," Ravi agreed happily.

"Oh, poo! Ravi, please let me clean your face. As a doctor, I simply cannot stand here and watch someone drip blood on the ground."

There was nowhere to go. He couldn't very well follow her inside her tent; she couldn't pass outside the "dead line" and go inside his. "It's going to infect; if I go to my tent and get my iodine and carbolic acid, will you stay right here?"

"I'll sit here and be as good as I'm capable of."

Delphine flew back to her tent, praying that no one got in her way or tried to talk to her. Men had commenced a game of *gooks* in the clearing where Ravi had sung his *doomfata*, but Delphine barely noticed the animated galloping of horsemen to and fro in her haste to grab her medicine before Ravinger was spirited off.

For it was suddenly imperative that she be close to him. And while she perhaps wouldn't submit to believing his excuse for not saving her in the tunnel in Gondar, there was something of him that she needed. Her blood required his emanations in order to be sweet and pure, for she hadn't felt so alive in weeks as when she stood next to him.

He was still there, sitting in the shade of the tent and smoking a pipe he'd materialized from his *zenar*. He'd unbuckled his sword scabbard and leaned it against the side of the tent. His smile melted her steely heart, and she dropped to the ground beside him.

It was such a joy to be near him again! His ardent look sent shivers down her flanks, as though he were imagining loving her with his mouth. As she dabbed at the bleeding scar with her kerchief of iodine she felt his every tiny movement as a wave of heat through her shirtwaist fabric—he lifted a hand to remove the pipe from his mouth, and her breasts swelled as though stroked. He shifted on his haunches, and her quim trembled with anticipation.

"As for your other injury . . ." Delphine whispered, so intent on the gash in his face she hadn't been aware she was leading the man into even more sultry waters.

"Ah, I'll make a full recovery soon enough," Ravi said quietly.

"Yes," said Delphine, now annoyed. "I'm sure you will live to sacrifice your injured parts to the benefit of scores more women."

"No." Just one word, clipped, certain. "There is only one woman I have thoughts for, and that is you . . . my Queen of Heaven."

"Hmph." She was done applying the iodine, but kept gazing at the gash with professional interest. "You once told me you wanted to fuck me on a lion's skin . . . *in a red tent*. It would seem that even back then you had strangely prescient visions about your own red tent . . . with the lion's skin I am sure is already in there."

Ravinger drew back then. Hands on knees, he sat straight. "Only because it did create such an enticing vision! Now, what more can I do to convince you of the integrity and nobility of my intentions toward you? And by the way, I'm sure I didn't use the baser word 'fuck' when referring to you."

Delphine felt a twinge of shame. She also lowered her hands to her knees. "I'm sorry, Ravinger. I didn't mean to imply you were a heartless dog. I suppose I'm just wondering what sort of a future I have traveling with this army. Not a very long one, I'm afraid."

"Ah." Ravinger scooted closer to her to take her face in his warm large hand. "My only truth, I've been scouring my brain for ways to get you out of here. Escape isn't impossible. For now, however, I'm afraid that even being seen together might make your situation worse—we don't want to incite his jealousy."

Delphine rubbed her face against his hand, catlike. "Yes, yes! He must leave the main camp sometime!"

"He does, quite often in fact, he makes trips back to Gaffat and Debra Tabor to check on the foundry."

His fingers slid behind her neck, scratching affectionately, and Delphine was flooded with a surge of lust for him. Impetuously she leaned forward and kissed him, her tongue tasting the fullness of his lower lip, the pepper and ambergris scent of him bringing all the happy memories of him back at once, as though it were only yesterday when he first kissed her by the bonfires of Qudus Gabriel.

Instantly he gathered her to him, crushing her against his formidable torso. He kissed her languidly, as though they had all the time in the world, but one of his eager hands cradled her skull, and the other grasped her waist. Tears burned in her eyes to be this close to him again, and she was filled with joy for the first time in many weeks.

"Likamaquas." It was the sober voice of the Azmach Michael. "Bob is looking for you, he wants you to lead a team in the *gooks* game."

After a few moments, they broke the kiss, but continued panting at each other until Delphine whispered, "Bob?"

"Bob," Ravi smiled. "That's the code name for our King of Kings. I'd best go." They stood, brushing themselves off. "I'll go with Misha around the front. You wait a few minutes, then go around the back of the tent." He kissed her once more, briefly.

"We'll get you out of here, one way or another." Then he was gone.

She wanted to peek around the corner of the tent, to watch him stride off, but she didn't dare. So she sat in the tent's shade, hugging herself and allowing herself to dream about the feel of his embrace.

CHAPTER SIXTEEN
Skilled Artisans

RAVI HEADED TO A FITAWRARI'S TENT to get a final tally on the amount of arms gained after Gondar. If any were deemed excess, they could be sent up to Magdala, along with the numberless Amharic Bibles, *tabotat*, and manuscripts they'd collected there. Many donkeys had already been sent up with loads of gold, silver, and brass processional crosses, mounds of royal parchments, and scrolls.

However, a most intriguing sight stopped him in his tracks. The "wretched monster" of the French Quarter himself, who was rarely seen about the camp wandering freely, as he feared for the wholesomeness of his own person, stumbled out of the Emperor's white pavilion. His fine sun-bleached hair, never tressed well in the best of times and not lasting in plait more than a week, was mussed and blowzy about his head. He staggered a bit with a stunned absent expression.

Ravi guffawed aloud at such an unexpected sight, but the befuddled odist didn't notice him, and continued on his stumbling way. So, even though it was close on to the wintry twilight that made for especial clarity of mind at this time of the year, and

Tewodros was probably elevated on *arrack*, Ravi decided to call at his tent.

He had only to announce himself, not stand on ceremony as others would have to do. Before Paul had got his name out of his mouth, the Emperor screamed, "Show him into my presence!"

Ravinger was warmed by such a welcome. They'd met several times since his manumission from chains, and always on cordial and heartfelt grounds, as though Tewodros hadn't ordered him trussed and carried up a mountaintop to be tossed into a hut in manacles. Ravinger was cordial too, analyzing and waiting.

Tewodros paced with magisterial leonine grace, his *shamma* girded in an extremely casual manner. His eyes were alight with fraternal intimacy when he addressed Ravi with a great show of arm-sweeping. "Can you imagine the boldness of that fellow?" Impatiently he gestured to the *tej-asalefech* to pour a *barrilye* for Ravi. "He thinks that by prostrating himself like a woman, he can gain my friendship. It's no secret that I do not like that fellow, and only barely tolerate him because he amuses me with the troubles he stirs up between *frenjoch*. You know that I don't believe half the things he tells me!"

Ravi chuckled warmly as he accepted the *barrilye*. "Yes, Tewodros, I know you well enough by now. I notice when you're only pretending to tolerate someone. That traitorous fellow." He leaned against a tent pole, loosening his own *shamma* about the shoulders. "That fellow would sooner sell his own mother to the Gallas than to serve a master with conviction."

"Ah!" Tewodros agreed passionately. "You are right as usual, Basha Falaka. Now. Now that I see you handsome and fit and in the prime of male flowering, I need you to help me."

"Help you?"

"About Makeda. You knew her before I saw her. Correct?"

Ravi tensed with apprehension. "Yes," he admitted. "I knew

her in Gondar before you knew her."

"So you are familiar with her ways, with her mind."

"As much as it's possible for any man to be familiar with her," Ravi allowed.

"You have . . ." Tewodros gestured as though holding a crystal globe of the Earth in his potent hand. "Kissed her."

"I've kissed her, yes! But that's about all!"

Waving a dismissive hand, Tewodros resumed his catlike pacing. "You're familiar with the woman of her. That's what I need to know. I'm hoping that with your knowledge of the Hindoo love, that you can warm her up." Twirling to face Ravi again, Tewodros admitted heatedly, "She doesn't warm to me!"

Ravi was shocked to life in all of his senses. The idea that he might 'warm up' the sensuous American doctor had him perked in every limb and muscle. But he had to proceed cautiously. "I agree she does seem to warm to me. The only reason she doesn't warm to you is probably because she is very . . . afraid and confused. But yes, she does seem to respond to Hindoo love tactics."

"Ah." This appeared to please the Emperor. He stopped his pacing and regarded Ravi with perception. "Can you do that then, Likamaquas? I give you leave to try. Heat her up! Make her so on fire with desire for men that she jumps on me!"

Tewodros had little concept of the normal routes love might take. He was completely ignorant that it might even slightly annoy Ravi to be nothing more than a fancy man, stirring Delphine all randy for Tewodros's more supreme touch. Such preparatory training was *de rigueur* in many countries of Africa and Arabia. And obviously Tewodros had no inkling that affectionate attachments may have already formed between the two *frenjoch*. Such an idea was unprecedented. If a woman didn't love the Emperor, well she was simply incapable of love.

Ravi replied guardedly. "Yes, I can probably do that." Just

the merest mental image of stimulating the ardent woman had his penis stiffening, and he made as if to adjust his *shamma* even more casually, with the red striped edge draped between his thighs. "Do you give me leave to enter her tent?"

Of this Tewodros didn't seem concerned. "Yes, yes!" He waved a hand. "Whatever it takes. Do you think you can have her ready in, say, two weeks?"

Ravi frowned. "Oh no, it would take far longer than that. For the Hindoo love is an unhurried, quiet art. To rush it along would be to ruin it with haste. That is the whole point of its success—that it takes so long to achieve. You want to have the woman reach the"—Ravi didn't even know the Amharic for such a thing, so he said—"reach the plateau, the mesa, the uppermost *amba* of desire. *Awnat?*"

"*Awnat, awnat!*"

"To reach such a height of desire, this might take months."

"Months?" Ravi had seen that frown on many occasions, immediately before Tewodros ordered the hands and feet cut from many people. "I don't have months! Tell me three weeks, four weeks!" He assumed a confidential stance. "I would have her manservant or mine train her, but I am afraid they will leave dark dusky marks on her beautiful white skin."

Ravi nodded. "A logical assumption. All right, I'll have her ready for you, just give me time. I'll report back after, say, six weeks."

The magisterial man appeared to give this his best thought. "All right. Now Basha Falaka, just make sure you don't . . . don't impale her. I don't want seed other than my own in her."

Suddenly, Ravi wanted to whip his arm out and tear the esophagus from the sovereign's throat. How dare he restrict him, how dare he put rules upon his undying love for the esteemed woman? Ravi's eyes wobbled like his master's, but it was with a barely contained rage that ultimately only showed in the flaring of his nostrils.

"All right," he said slowly. "I'll make sure of that."

Tewodros threw up his hands gladly, crying, "Ah! Now you must read the royal letter sent me from the *Inglaise* Queen!"

The Emperor went to an inlaid desk and picked out the letter that had probably been read and agonized over a thousand times. Ravi had heard much of this letter, forwarded by Martin Flad who had now reached Massawa.

The monarch fairly chortled with glee as he handed over the letter. Ravinger glanced at the stationery with the blue royal crown emblazoned at the top. He quickly flipped through the four pages to see the large signet, and it was signed in Victoria's shaky handwriting of that year.

"Do you see? She acknowledges my letter with her own letter!"

"Yes, well, let me read it." Seating himself on an *alga* draped with fine silks, Ravi sipped his *tej* and read.

He read aloud at first, translating into rapid Amharic. " 'Victoria, by the grace of God, to Theodore, King of Abyssinia, sendeth greeting. Relying on the assurance contained in Your Majesty's letter which duly reached us, we were in daily expectation of the arrival in England of our servant Rassam, together with our servant Cameron, and the other Europeans, so long detained in your country'."

Such a simple reading sent the Emperor into ecstasies of bliss, apparently at the mere idea that the Queen had responded to him at all.

" 'When Flad arrived bringing Your Majesty's further letter of the seventeenth of April in which, while repeating that you had released and made over to our servant Rassam, our servant Cameron, and the other Europeans, in order that they might leave the country, you stated that you had kept our servant Rassam for the sake of consulting upon the extension of the friendship between us. We will not disguise from Your Majesty that we found it difficult to reconcile your assurances with the obstacles which were still opposed to the departure of our servants . . .' "

She acknowledged his quest for skilled workmen to be sent to Abyssinia, and stated that arrangements were made to send them. Flad was on the point of leaving England with the workmen when it reached her ears that Theodore still detained her servants. She wanted him to know it was the sacred duty of Sovereigns to fulfill engagements. Therefore, she could not allow Flad to be the bearer of these tokens.

Ravi continued reading as the Emperor blissfully drank his *tej*. " 'But, in full confidence that the cloud which has darkened the friendship of our relations will pass away on the return of Flad, we have given orders that these articles should be sent to Massawa, to be delivered to the officers . . . our servant Rassam, and our servant Cameron, and the other Europeans, so far on their way to our presence'."

Well. Sighing deeply, Ravi stood to replace the papers on the Emperor's desk.

"Do you hear?" Tewodros cried ebulliently. "She has said that she wishes the dark cloud of our relations to pass! It is the holy duty of all Sovereigns to do what they say!"

Ravi smiled, too. "Yes! This is great news indeed!" He clapped the Emperor on the shoulder as if they shared a moment of camaraderie. "When will you send Rassam and the others down to Massawa to meet the artisans from Victoria?"

For a moment the men held each other's shoulders. Both had fingers like claws, and both appeared to be about to pounce upon the other with malice at a moment's provocation.

"Is this not the most glorious reply?" Tewodros cried. "She says she has given orders that these 'things will be sent to me'!"

"Yes!" Ravi cried back, equally as fervent. "But first you must send the *frenjoch* down to Massawa!"

They locked eyes, each unwilling to relent on their own beliefs.

Tewodros broke the grip first. He twirled about, and Ravi was afraid he was going for the picture book of Alexander the Great. But he only approached the waiting *tej-asalefech*, holding his *barrilye* out with gusto. "Now you see, beloved son, that we will finally achieve the prophecy!"

When he turned to face Ravi, Ravi knew he'd never seen his King of Kings look more all-fired impassioned in his long career. "My countrymen have turned their backs on me, and have hated me, because I imposed tribute on them, and sought to bring them under military discipline. When these workmen come, we will pound my people into subservience."

Ravi nodded, numbly. "Yes. But first you must send the *frenjoch* down to Massawa."

Tewodros threw his head back, lost in his ebullient bliss. It used to be a wonder to see such a handsome sight as this happy Emperor, his beautiful face resplendent in its wreath of smiles. Now, however, it was just plain frightening.

"Basha Falaka. I have reformed Abyssinia, restored the Christian faith, and become master of the world."

CHAPTER SEVENTEEN
CHINESE PILLOW-BOOKS

January 7, 1867

WISHING TO AVOID THE DIVINE RUSH of the devoted making their way to Christmas morning mass, Ravi hid in his library tent. The pious always assumed there was something vaguely sacrosanct about his reading and writing. Most everyone knew he could speak twenty-three languages, and stepped back in awe whenever he was asked to translate anything. They knew that any caravan coming from the Red Sea coast might contain books, and the plunder from all such activities went speeding across the mountain ranges to Ravi. In this manner, he wound up with some entirely superfluous tomes, such as *Modern Cookery for Private Families*, instructions on how to build ice skates, and shipping logs from Malmö. The latter might have even interested him, but Swedish was one of the few languages he had little understanding of, though he had learned Icelandic to study the Sagas.

However, he came into quite a bit of prurient material that had traveled the tortuous route from Holywell Street in London. He had lately been amused by the anti-Catholic ranting of *The Confessional Unmasked, or a Nun in her Smock*, Chinese pillow-books, *carte de visites* of nude Eskimos, and adult illustrated novels that had circumvented the American Postal Act. He gladly added these volumes to the library section where he proudly displayed *Madame Bovary* alongside *The Compendium of Pleasure*. He himself had been translating volumes of scandalous Hindoo and Arabian love manuals for a few years now, but didn't know anyone who would risk publication of those.

Ravi's mind wandered back to Delphine and the license he'd been given by Tewodros, when he gazed at his most recent translation: *You see now what prevented her from acceding to your wishes; she was afraid that you would not be able to quench her flame after having fanned it.*

How could he tell Delphine he'd been commanded to seduce her? For he could think of nothing that would turn her cold faster. She was schooled in the erotic arts, most likely by that bastard in the prison camp. Her erotic education was made evident by the slick sponge of the engorged labia he'd manipulated when setting out to excite her—before he had so much as touched her body. If she knew of his instructions, she would think—and perhaps rightly so—that he was cheapening her, that he had selfish motivation for manipulating and handling her. She would imagine that there were no feelings behind it—that he only performed a service for his master!

No, this could not be allowed to happen!

Ravinger stood and paced the length of the tent. He jammed some tobacco into a pipe so he could smoke and pace unhindered. "I have very strong feelings about that woman," he muttered in English, the only language other than Lakota least likely to be overheard correctly by anyone eavesdropping. "If she finds out that I've been instructed to seduce her—though refraining from doing so would be the larger feat, commanded to or not—she'll turn from me and become an old maid cold as virgin snow. And I can't stay away from her! She's infiltrated my blood, she's sucked me up with an irresistible force! I want to kneel at her side and pleasure her in a thousand and one ways, because she's unknown, incomprehensible—whatever you want to call it!"

And he threw himself back onto his *alga*, and stared at nothing for a long time, letting the pipe go out.

This was how he successfully convinced himself that, in this matter, dishonesty was the best policy.

However, he could not turn his mind to thoughts of ice skates, or brined herring, or cold meat cookery. He had been blessed with a cock known in Arabic as *el besiss*, the impudent. When aroused, it was single-minded in its goal to knock upon the vulva's door. He had no sooner than squeezed its bursting head when a feminine voice at the front of the tent stopped him cold.

Delphine!

He had no time to formulate a scheme. He swiftly girded his *shamma* in the proper fashion—the inferior mode, with the fabric taken off the shoulders entirely and wound around the waist. He wanted to display his respect for Delphine, although it left him a shade chilly with only the skimpy European shirt covering his torso.

"Tewodros has told me I may use this library tent," Delphine told Wubishet in Amharic. They had known each other at her house in Gondar, when the touchy bodyguard had been employed mostly in leaping out of the shrubbery at odd moments. Wubishet had made the normally placid surgeon skittish, Ravi knew by the way she had nearly jumped onto his lap when the fellow bounded out from behind the colonnade to wipe a trickle of pomegranate juice from his chin.

Tewodros had told her? Then Tewodros had no doubt told her of Ravinger's newest mission!

Ravi yanked aside the tent flap and stuck his head out. "It's all right, she is the only one allowed to interrupt me," he told Wubishet.

He only had eyes for the ravishing creature he had held in his arms when they had snuck an embrace behind the tent last week. He had sung his *doomfata* for her, he had fought the Kanyazmach for her; when he directed his triumphant gaze at her he had seen her eyes moist and vulnerable, and perhaps in his imagination, she seemed to desire him.

My Queen of Heaven," Ravi said as he enfolded her in the crook of his arm and steered her inside the tent.

"I didn't expect you here. I thought you had gone to the mass."

He had to laugh aloud at that. "Me? At mass? The only mass I like is the abbreviation for Massachusetts." He held her away to regard her more fully. Although garbed as an Abyssinian lady of fashion now, the concubines hadn't tressed her hair yet, and for that Ravi was grateful, for even now he couldn't prevent himself from lifting a glossy lock of unbound hair and letting it slip between his fingers. "The Wild Boar of Ethiopia has let you out of your cage?"

She had that pleasured feline look. "Yes; Bob has allowed me to 'visit my friends' and to use your library tent, since I begged him for books."

"Ah, and what book have you come for today?"

"An English Bible!"

They both laughed at the absurdity of it. Ravi laughed brazenly. "A Bible? From me?"

"Kaspar's English version has so many pages torn from it, he usually uses his Amharic version when preaching to the Falashas. *Oh, Ravinger!*" She flung herself upon him, arms tight around his neck, her warm open mouth pressed to his Adam's apple. "How I've missed you, your warmth, your intelligence, your strength, the way you taste and smell, your affection..." When she paused, Ravi waited, for he knew it would be good. "Your sex." She gave a little hop then, and he bent at the knees to easily lift her by both thighs as she straddled his hips, her ankles interlocking behind him.

Walking backward to the *alga*, Ravi lowered her slowly, so as not to knock the woman from her most favorable position. While he admired her fervency, and the temerity with which she glued her melting pot to his cock, it had never been his intention to just take her like a raw, addled *faro* dog. "Ah, my love . . . I've been wondering if you would want me again. I'm so glad to see that you do."

She spoke against his mouth. "Ravinger, my dear Captain. I've always wanted you. You can't know how much I've missed your red-blooded ways, your reckless wild bravery! My blood has cried out for the essence of you; without you I'm just a hollow, fragile being. You're utterly irresistible, sinister, with wild lion's eyes, and every time you glance at me I'm saturated with a hot yearning over which I have no control."

She kissed him, covering his words with her mouth. She rode his hips with heated bucking movements, her sex heated against his prick. He tried to still her by holding her, but she wouldn't be stopped. She bucked more lasciviously against him, clearly taking pleasure in the friction of her pelvis against his erection. Snorting hot breaths through her nostrils, she worried and bit his lower lip and uttered keening, delicious animal sounds into his mouth.

"Ravinger . . . my blood cries out for you," she whispered.

There was nothing for it—he was going to come if he didn't detach the horny woman from his person. So, keeping her in the same attitude straddling him, he stood and carried her over to his writing desk that was blanketed with manuscripts. He lowered her backside onto a Sanskrit document, and stood looming over her.

He nibbled at her mouth and earlobes, took jewel bites from her soft throat, cradling her head to him. *"El taleb,"* he called her— the yearning one who is burning for a member. "The man that loves you truly is a lost man."

These words seemed to bring an orgasmic response to the woman, for she gasped and set to unbuttoning his European shirt. Ravi must be faster to beat her seeking hands, so he slung behind her neck all the amulets, strands of beads, *mateb*, all the blasted things the Emperor had given her. By the time he'd succeeded in undoing the lacings of her embroidered shirt, she had her hungry hands running across his naked chest. She tore the white shirt from his shoulders as she'd done with the red *kamis* the day she'd frigged him so expertly in the garden. Soon it was down around his waist with the useless *shamma*, and she sucked so on the side of his throat Misha later chided him for the red marks she left.

Her skillful fingers pinched his nipples, soon joined by her hot mouth as she worked her way down his chest. His penis was about to rupture from the glorious teasing. She was a determined minx, and he couldn't prevent her from hopping off the desk. Sucking and biting a trail down the center of his belly, she yanked the *shamma* from his hips with surprising expertise. He was clad only in the thin cotton breeches through which his erection was clearly visible, and she dove in with a voracious appetite, biting and mouthing the head of his cock through the fabric.

Although he cradled her head to him with affection, he knew he needed to toy with and animate her. "Delphine. No." He said it without much conviction.

"Yes," she murmured, her fingers slipping beneath the breeches and sliding the material over his flanks. She got ahold of the cock in both hands and swallowed it nearly whole.

"Ah!" Ravi was instantly overwhelmed with a sustained wave of rapture. He spread his thighs, leaned against the desk with one hand, and swiveled his hips into the woman's mouth. It soon became evident she had this uncanny ability to bring him to the crescendo of climax and then back off just enough to leave him hanging there, driven to distraction. She would suck, and nibble with her little teeth, and squiggle her tongue down the length of him, and just when he was gasping on the edge of an explosive orgasm, she disengaged her mouth. Sliding both hands up and down his shiny, bursting cock, she nibbled at the head until she swallowed him once more.

The sight of her small face finally did it, with eyebrows of Ethiopian blackness as she admired and slurped up his cock. Uncontrollably plunging himself deep into her throat, he erupted. Gratified that she didn't pull back—or perhaps she didn't have a choice, with his hand gripping the back of her skull to his crotch—she drained his cock without disengaging her mouth, until she was finally choking and gasping for air, Ravi realized with sudden shame.

"Oh, *Isgyoh*," he said with wonderment, reaching under her arms to drag her to her feet. "By the power of my creator! Have I hurt you?"

Her languid, dizzy smile set his mind at ease, and as she still gulped and panted, and wiped her mouth with the back of her hand, he remembered her comment. "It may be a wickedly delightful joy to taste your semen on my tongue . . ." This memory brought a renewed surge of lust up his torso, and he kissed her deeply, licking the backs of her teeth, his tongue lapping hers.

She broke away with a gasp, and touched his javelin scar with wonder. "Hurt me? Oh no, not at all. You've healed me. I feel quite sated with your delicious seed inside of me. I wonder. Does this mean I've broken my fast?"

Ravi laughed with gusto at that. He didn't feel terribly silly practically naked except for the *betoa* armband with his breeches down exposing his bare ass, while the woman remained swathed head to toe in her finery. "Why yes, *el taleb*, fasting is for avoiding all animal food, such as milk and butter. Don't tell me you're adhering to that? Why, fasts comprise about two-thirds of the year around here! They've been fasting for forty days before Christmas."

When she shrugged and pushed herself away from the desk, Ravi reluctantly drew his breeches up, stuffing away his long rubbery cock. He stopped with his hand down the front of his breeches when she said, "Yes, I've been following it. Perhaps that's why I was so hungry just now." He couldn't quite believe she'd said that, and he laughed all his anxiety away. He realized with a sad shock he hadn't been this happy in years.

"And what is *el taleb*? That's Arabic. I shall ask Abou anyway, so you may as well tell me now."

"*El taleb* is the yearning sort of vulva. It burns for a member and, having got one in its embrace, it refuses to part with it until its fire is completely extinguished."

Delphine raised one cynical eyebrow and glanced to the manuscripts that littered the table. "I suppose that's what you translate here."

Ravi nodded, utterly unembarrassed. "Some of it. Some of it is more cerebral." He finally removed his hand in order to pour himself a tumbler of Hennessey's brandy. "It's time to get some of these published, if I can find anyone willing. So my next step might be New York, actually."

"*New York?*" Delphine gasped.

"What's wrong with New York?"

"Nothing. It's just that . . . I can't picture you in New York. Your love of adventure, your iron pioneer's will . . . I think you should remain in the wilds forever."

Setting down his tumbler, Ravi caught the woman by the waist. With his thumb, he traced her lower lip, still swollen from her nursing of his cock. "You don't know me fully, Dr. Chambliss. I can tolerate a city if needs be. Maybe it's you who needs the free air of the wilds. It seems to agree with you."

Placing her mouth next to his ear and sending a chill down his spine, she whispered, "I think it's *you* who agrees with me. Now," she said in a normal tone, "I must get to mass."

✳ ✳ ✳

RAVI AND TEWODROS STOOD ON A stone bridge that spanned the River Abbai. Tewodros loved the Tisissat waterfalls that dropped in a straight plunge of about a hundred and fifty feet. He considered this his amphitheater where he might go to listen to the voice of God. At this time of the year the waters ran clear in spectacular spumes of white foam, but during the rainy season the rivers thundered like great freshets of chocolate. Here, they had to speak loudly to each other, but the roaring water prevented their servants, waiting at the end of the bridge, to hear anything.

The Emperor said, "As Solomon fell at the feet of Hiram, so I, under God, fall at the feet of the Queen and her Government and her friends. I wish you to write a letter to the *Inglaise* Queen. You have much better skills at writing than I."

Refreshing mist from the roiling water coated their faces. "And what should I write, O Great One?"

"I wish the skilled artisans to come right away that they might teach me wisdom and show me clever arts. When this is done, I will make Rassam and his friends glad, and send them back to their homes."

Ravi sighed. He had spoken to the Emperor several times about this. Ravi always tried to gently remind him he needed to free the captives first. The Emperor always pretended he hadn't heard. "Of course, I'll compose a good letter for your scribe." Today Tewodros was surly, and Ravi was weary of trying to enlighten him.

"I need you to go to Gaffat, to force the lazy Europeans to work harder, that Zander, Moritz, that lazy Staiger. We need more arms. Take the *azmary* with you to Gaffat. By the death of Christ, we will make him do something other than sit and preach! And

I need you to oversee finishing the artillery roads. From Debra Tabor we will complete the one going to Magdala. But we will also build one from Debra Tabor heading toward Gojam, to fool everyone as to our destination."

"Very wise. One thing. The *azmary* is a good friend to Makeda." He had not brought the woman up in any conversation this past week. "It might make her sad if he was sent away. Cannot Herr Zander oversee the making of the cannon?"

Tewodros's aquiline nose twitched, and his eyes narrowed slightly at Ravi. "The *azmary* must go to Gaffat!"

His ire was such that the valet Paul raced forward with an umbrella to shield the king's head, and Ravi had to ride out for a couple of weeks in Foggera and Begemder, and take a look at the pathetic state of the road-building enterprise.

CHAPTER EIGHTEEN
THE ULTIMATUM LETTER

February 1867
The Western Slopes of Mt. Guna

DELPHINE FOUND IT AGREEABLE ON THE sunny slopes of the mountains. The ancient summits of Belesa soared with stories of hundreds of thousands of warriors defending their homes against pagan Galla intrusions. To the southwest lay indistinct outlines of the coffee farms of Gojam and the dark ramparts toward Tzana. It was thrilling to be here when the wind swept a parade of cumulus clouds that cast speedily moving shadows over the patchwork watercolor of the land spread out before her. In some odd way she felt sheltered and protected here, as though no harm would come to her, though daily she heard the percussion of the seven-foot-long plaited *girf* whip. The *baal negarit* head drummer with the most dangerous job in battle was therefore allocated to mete out punishments.

Now she had a surgery tent as well, and people had come to see her as more of a *hakim* than a concubine. Here she treated ophthalmia with alum and antimony, rheumatism with visits to hot springs, and she even treated worms in horses. One day she performed the Caesarian operation on a camp-follower in a crowded tent of gaping onlookers.

Delphine received stores from Colonel Merewether in Aden, and was able to send communications down the coast through a network of messengers who sewed her letters into their *shamma* hems. Men traveled in pairs forty miles at a time to the next station, when another two men would relieve them. She sent medical supplies up to Dr. Blanc in Magdala, and they swiftly developed a correspondence. She grew very fond of the British doctor, although she did not wish to hear sorry details about their existence in the mountaintop fortress. It was enough to be a captive, but down here she could move about at will.

The farther they traveled from Gondar, the slimmer the hopes of ever making it back to the coast. The more degraded and cut off the Amhara kingdom became, the less chance of escape.

Tewodros visited her when not off on a plundering expedition, but he kept a remote respect for her. It puzzled Delphine, the sudden politeness, and he never tried to touch her anymore. She wondered if perhaps Ravinger hadn't effected some change in the Emperor. One night Tewodros showed her a curious picture book that he claimed proved that Alexander the Great was his ancestor. Another night, she told him an army of Europeans would eventually come and bring his kingdom down with the help of his enemies.

He replied with melancholy. "Never mind your Government and my enemies. Your masters have already decided upon their treatment of me; and my foes would spread evil reports about me even if I were to carry you on my head. I have only to see that you're happy, and your heart isn't vexed."

Her heart wasn't vexed at all when messages came to her from Ravi. Wubishet now found an outlet for his energies, and was employed delivering messages back and forth from Ravi—to the Emperor, but also to Delphine. One such note read:

My only truth,

Countryside around here decimated. Peasants have burned crops in anticipation of our coming, ceasing to cultivate the soil and preferring to run into the mountains and starve. Please accept this voluptuous sheepskin from my servant Wubishet, and if he claims not to be in possession of one, you may beat him with my volume of the Marquis de Sade.

Delphine had to laugh at that, because she already had so many sheepskins and blankets heaped upon her by Tewodros and Ravi both, she felt like the Princess with a pea under her mattress when she slept at night.

Our band has been twice attacked by deserters—I'm surprised they have the nerve to vent, but it appears they are so desperate they will do anything to hinder "the homicidal monomaniac of Debra Tabor." For that reason I've allowed many of them to escape unharmed. I've lost four of my own party to desertion just this week.

My love. My longing for your limbs wrapped around me is surpassed only by the desire to rain your body with kisses. When I turn over at night I get a mouth full of ashes from the fire, or a hoof in the face, and my hand is a poor substitute for your mouth. It doesn't sound very laudatory to say a vision of you is a thousand times gladder than the sight of these haggard, dripping, reeking soldiers who are my highland brethren. Last night we were nearly tossed out of bed by gigantic fleas.

Life is a ladder infinite-stepped, that hides its rungs from human eyes;

Planted its foot in chaos-gloom, its head roars high above the skies.

Your el besiss.

—I believe I will return once I'm certain these road laborers won't turn tail and run for the Wallo Gallas.

Ravi's letters gave her a feeling of contentment, a security that he'd be returning soon. It was a sound feeling of stability she hadn't felt since she was a small child, before everything went awry.

✳   ✳   ✳

Gaffat

EVERYONE WAS PAINFULLY AWARE THAT TEWODROS was extremely out of temper that morning. Ravi, Kaspar, Waldmeier, and the other European blacksmiths were standing right next to him when a supplicant for justice made the dire error of repeating his question twice. The Emperor swooped over and grabbed a piece of lumber a foot long. Smashing the fellow over the head with it, it was soon apparent he'd killed him in one blow.

Nobody dared make a move toward the corpse.

Ravi, who had lately become bolder with the air of one serving a life's sentence, broke the wicked silence. "Kaspar has an idea he wishes you to hear, a glorious idea that will display the honor of your kingdom to all of our enemies in Abyssinia."

Tewodros waited, one hand on his mule's withers. His face was as black as a thundercloud. "Yes? By the death of Christ, *azmary*, tell me this idea."

Ravi shoved Kaspar to step forward. For once, the buffoon's voice wavered weakly, but he picked up steam as the men around him murmured encouragement. His pale hands tentatively outlined something massive in the air.

"Jan Hoy! I propose that we at Gaffat cast you the most enormous mortar ever seen! Better than all of these gun carriages and small mortars that we have proven we can cast. I say we build a giant mortar with a bore as tall as a man!"

During the tense silence, Ravi smiled down at Kaspar as though at a son. The Emperor's face was unreadable. At last a corner of his mouth twitched, he took his hand off the mule, and slowly stepped up to Kaspar.

"Yes, *azmary.* Go on."

Confident now, Kaspar brayed, "When fired, it will cause an abortion to all pregnant women, and cause all old people to go deaf. All your enemies will drop their weapons and run when they hear the report from this big gun."

Ravi added, "You will then be able to run off the Turks, just like at Sebastopol in Russia."

A sly smile appeared at the corners of the Emperor's mouth, and he nodded slightly. "I thought that God had raised me up to be a blessing to my people, but I find I was wrong. So engrave on this mortar: 'Tewodros, the scourge of the perverse.' Begin at once," he said quietly. "I will go and pray upon it." And he wandered off down a ravine full of wild mint and thistle.

"Ah," sighed Waldmeier. "I'm glad he liked your idea, *Diakon* Nagel."

"Is there an aspect of it that he wouldn't like?" Kaspar was puffed with pride now. "It is a grandiloquent and superb idea in every aspect!"

Herr Moritz, the Polish army deserter, was always the first with a loud opinion. "*Ja,* the only thing wrong with this idea is that now we have to cast this giant mortar!"

The men groaned. "*Ja,* and now we have to dig and haul all that clay from the quarry."

"Basha Falaka has sent us more metals to be melted, I am sure we have enough."

Most of the metal would come from melting down brass dishes and the like that had been taken in plunder. This was accomplished in the foundry in crucibles placed in ground furnaces and stoked by hand bellows crafted by Galla slaves. The coal used was extracted from the plains of Dembea and hauled by donkey to Gaffat.

"Zander, have you finished making a new batch of *arrack?* I say we go to Zander's house and discuss this."

The men turned as one squadron, they were so accustomed to being in close quarters with one another, and began the short ascent up the hill to Zander's hut.

Ravi grabbed the enthusiastic deacon by the arm. "Nagel. Just one more item. After my visit here, I'm going to Magdala." Kaspar's eyes enlarged to the size of Maria Theresa dollars. "I have to bring money, powder, arms, and prisoners. Why don't you come with me? That way, you can have time alone with your fiancée."

Kaspar's eyes now had the frozen terror of someone who has stumbled upon his parents copulating. "Fiancée?"

"Yes, yes, Woizero Louisa Bell. You did get my missive, telling you I had cancelled my own engagement? I sent it to Gondar, along with a missive for Dr. Chambliss—"

Kaspar's new stance was serious, contemplative. "Yes, indeed! I did get that message! I just have not had a moment's worth of time to accord to giving it much thought, either way, not particularly being of the mind to go sauntering around Magdala, for fear I might never be manumitted from that bastion! Besides, I wish to visit with my countrymen, and speak our mother tongue. Saalmüller has just told me that a German inventor has made a sort of device where one can speak against a diaphragm—have you heard of that? The sound makes a pulsation that sets another diaphragm on a receiver working, and presto! A fellow down the hall can hear what is being said!"

Ravi frowned. "This is using electricity? How does he vary and control the current? Otherwise every single 'word' would sound like 'shit' and it'd be a very monotonous conversation."

Kaspar paused. His nose twitched, like an alert hare. "Well, the 'vibrating rod' is actually knitting needles."

This remark caused such an uproarious gale of laughter on Ravi's part that Frau Flad, who was waiting so patiently for her husband's return, came to the door of her hut with a quizzical expression. When she saw it was only Basha Falaka, she smiled and went back inside. In the interim, Kaspar became jittery and jumped about from foot to foot, like a boy who needed to piddle.

"*Kapitän!* May I be allowed to join my comrades at Zander's house? The *arrack* will all be gone if I tarry. Those Swiss drink like whales."

"Go, go! Remember—you're in charge of casting that huge mortar for Bob."

Still laughing, Ravi waved the missionary away and began his descent toward his horse and waiting retinue. What an odd man! For a decade Kaspar had reviled Ravi because he felt he, as a German missionary, was due the hand of the third Bell daughter, Waldmeier and Saalmüller having wed the two elder girls. Ravi had never entertained the slightest interest in the stick-thin Louisa Bell, not even when she reached maturity; he was interested only in well-seasoned women of experience. He had just gone along with the supposed engagement to please Tewodros.

Now that Kaspar was being handed the girl, he turned tail and ran!

IT WAS FIVE DAYS ON MULE to the grand African citadel of Magdala. The approach was always arduous, steep acclivities and switchbacks giving way to the Aroge Plain. Ravines were carved out by great rivers like the Bashillo, separating the Magdala *amba*

from the plateaus of the Wallo Gallas where permanent hail often covered the mesas for weeks on end. One climbed along a road precipitous enough to terrify anyone stricken with vertigo past the smaller plateau of Fahla, then past Selassie, so called The Trinity after the church that stood upon it. The next rocky crescent was Islamgie and several towns where peasants farmed the land for the soldiers of Magdala.

From Islamgie the road became more dizzying, the sheer cliffs of Magdala soaring in slick impenetrable walls, the smoky wisps of cooking fires wavering in the windless vista. Over these heights many had been flung to their death, and at some particular turnings one knew to expect the sight of human bones stacked like the detritus of a mining expedition like so many useless borax siftings.

The Magdala table-land, about half a mile wide and a mile and a half long, was the strongest fortress in the country. Tewodros made use of it as not just a fortress, but a prison, granary, and hiding spot for wives and family members of whom he'd tired. Earthworks were erected near the gates, and the summit was heavily fenced and punched with loopholes.

Ravinger's retinue passed through the second set of inner gates. A Fitawrari took the prisoners off to the prison house, where nearly seven hundred men were already jammed like sardines in a tin. Therein was a scene even the most callous Abyssinian described as something horrendous. Men were chained in couples, with great yokes of wood around their necks, and there was no demarcation between the common *shifta* and the brave warriors of past fights. Sons of kings, gubernatorial Shums of provinces, Dejazmachs alike were back-to-back with the most depraved villains, all begging from more favored companions in the name of the "Savior of Ethiopia"—Tewodros the Second.

The Emperor's nephew Bisawwir was the Commandant of Magdala, with five hundred spearmen under him. Ravi headed for the fortified enclosures of the chiefs to find Ras Bisawwir and dispose of his goods. Tewodros had been gathering all of his wealth at Magdala, and there were sheds of muskets and pistols, manuscripts, carpets, and silks.

Ravi was entering the magazine when his men murmured, and there came the sound of running bare feet.

"*Basha Falaka! Basha Falaka!*"

Men guffawed outwardly now, elbowing each other in camaraderie as Woizero Louisa Bell skipped down the road, her clean white *shamma* flowing out behind her like the wings of a graceful swan.

Walde Nebra whispered into Ravi's ear, "I will take you away on 'urgent business' if you so wish,"

"That's all right. I'm going to have to confront this sooner or later." Ravi was astounded at how he trembled in the face of the skinny waif of a girl, when he'd been accustomed for a decade to garbing himself as the Emperor to draw enemy fire in battle without so much as a rattled teacup.

Walde Nebra forcibly shoved the men down the road, for they were most interested in what transpired when the girl flung her arms about the Likamaquas's neck and, standing atop his feet, jumped to pepper his mouth with little kisses. Having never kissed her, Ravi was quite unsure who had taught her such a thing, and he lost no time in disengaging her under the pretense they would go around the corner and sit on a step of the council house.

Louisa flung herself upon his chest. "Oh, Basha Falaka! I have dreamed about you for months! I have wondered when you were going to come for me! The Emperor has told Susan"—her sister—"that it will be any day now that you will come for me, and we can be wed in the church!"

With her small, firm bosom pressed against his chest, he was surprised she was more substantial, even muscular, than he'd remembered her. Ravi took her by the shoulders. "I'm sorry,

Woizero Bell. There's been a change of plans. I won't marry you."
Good! Just say it outright like that, and be done with it!

Immediately, Louisa's eyes became brittle and hateful, but absent of an intermediate emotion of shock or dismay. Her one word was a curdled oath. *"Why?"*

Ravi looked her in the eyes, and spoke to her as an adult, with respect. "I remembered that I may not marry. I'm a Knight Templar, and cannot. But there is one who is much more deserving of you than I. A countryman to your sister's husbands, so you may be all married to the same worthy—"

Her countenance now on fire, Louisa gripped Ravi's forearms with fingers like claws. Flames seeped from the very corners of her eyes when she growled, *"Who!"*

When had this innocent young maiden become so enraged? Ravi tried to appear cool. "Why, the wonderful Deacon Kaspar Nagel, of course, who has been so long in our beautiful country, and is familiar with every—"

The maiden burst into the most horripilating round of laughter. Or *was* it laughter? Eyes closed, mouth open in a great wail of chortling as though possessed, she kept it up minute after minute until Ravi was compelled to grab her and give her a few swift shakes.

"Woizero Bell, please! Stop that right now!"

But she continued pealing gale after gale of the hyena-like laugh, until women who had been hiding behind the wall rushed forward, crying, "It's a *buda!* She's possessed by a *buda!*"

Ravinger, knowing *budas* to be the worst sort of bilgewater imaginable, released the stricken woman and turned her over to the care of her sisters. Abruptly the laughter stopped, and Louisa became stone serious, her eyes staring ahead of her, plainly unseeing. The yammering women around her hushed, and she said in a dead monotone, "I'm perfectly fine. I only want to be bled." She set to howling and flinging her arms above her head, as all the women grabbed at her and concurred, "A *buda!*"

"The *buda* is tricking us! If we bleed her, he will just attack her even more strongly!"

Some women looked to Ravi for confirmation, so he nodded dully. "Yes, yes, obviously a *buda*. I'll go see if I can find some charcoal and, er, other various filth." For people so possessed had a great craving for those items, and would sup at a bowl of shit like a *faro* dog.

"Who are you?" two women demanded of Louisa. "Who are you inside of our friend?"

When Louisa commenced to "replying" in a shrieking gibberish, Ravi backed off slowly.

"Take hold of her thumbs!" a woman cried. It was the first sign that the devil was leaving if he allowed her thumbs to be held.

Ravi rounded the corner out of sight and made directly for the prison enclosure of the Europeans. He didn't fancy spending even one night on the Magdala plateau, preferring instead to at least make it back down to the Islamgie plateau before sunset, for one never knew when a mood of the Emperor's would send a fire-footed messenger bringing news of one's surprise interment.

Ravi had a knapsack of supplies specially sent to Dr. Blanc from Delphine. He always enjoyed talking with the erudite doctor, and his companion Lieutenant Prideaux was a splendid fellow as well. It was easy enough getting inside the enclosure, and Ravi and Blanc embraced heartily. They took themselves to Rassam's house, covered now in an eighty-foot-long tomato vine that never seemed to stop producing, the poor captives mincing in the chains that had eaten deep grooves in their ankles. Consul Cameron didn't join them, being of a dysphonic mind these days, and taken greatly to lying on his *arat* staring at the ceiling. The Reverend Stern, Kaspar's boss, fell in step with them as well.

Ravi greeted the somber Rassam with remote respect, and they all sat down to imbibe the brandy Ravi had smuggled in. Rassam was most taken with Ravi's gift of a copy of *Crime and Punishment*.

Ravi waved casually, as though the book were a mere trifle. "I'll tell you though, I couldn't pry that out of Doctor Chambliss' hands, and only succeeded because she finished it in three days."

Rassam placed a hand over his heart. "Ah, I have heard many wonderful things about this woman surgeon. Is it true"—here he allowed himself to look diabolically from side to side—"that she is quite the bonny one? If I picture a surgeon I think of an old sawbones, or even worse, a crank like this fellow here—"

"Here now!" protested Blanc. "D'ye mean you're fed up with having to look at my filthy feet and ugly jib every day?"

"Oh, who would tire of *that*? So tell me, Captain—is she fetching? I've had no woman other than my far-removed cousin to look at in months." Rassam gestured to a hut pole where affixed was a much-worn photograph a relative had sent him. The guards and chiefs clamored so much for views of that woman, Rassam had finally given up, and put it up on the pole.

"Ah. She's more fetching than your cousin," Ravi said tactfully.

"Who isn't?" guffawed Prideaux. "Rassam's cousin, well—he agrees that she's pretty much a croaker."

"She's a wallflower," Rassam agreed amiably, holding out his *barrilye* for more brandy from Ravi. "But she's all we've got."

It was a source of continual wonder to Ravi how these men, in such close quarters for so long, could still get on. It was probably a British trait, for Ravi knew if he was confined with Misha for more than a few hours, he felt like tossing the old lady codger out the tent flap. "Yes, well, Dr. Chambliss is . . . a wonder. I find her incredibly ravishing. She has an air of amazing fortitude."

"She writes like a true angel of mercy," Blanc gushed, patting the breast of his *shamma* where he'd secreted Delphine's latest letter. "I'm most impressed with her winning a war medal. I should like to meet her someday."

"Don't say that!" snapped Prideaux. "That would mean she'd be up here on this desolate *amba!* Don't even think that!"

"She is a remarkable girl," agreed the Reverend Stern.

"No," said Ravi. "It means they'll both meet, down at Massawa or Aden."

Rassam agreed. "Yes, yes, that's the thinking. What have you got for me today, Captain?"

Reaching into his knapsack, Ravinger handed Rassam a letter from Lord Stanley, conveyed by courier from Massawa. Rassam wouldn't read it aloud for fear of spying ears, even after sending Prideaux out to reconnoiter the area, so Ravi told the others the upshot in a low voice.

"He's disappointed that you haven't been released, even though Victoria promised to send artisans. If British authorities at Massawa aren't satisfied within three months that you've been released, the 'presents' are going back to London. There's no further bargaining allowed on these matters."

Blanc asked, "Are the 'presents' at Massawa, then?"

"Yes, I believe they reached there a few weeks ago."

"Three months from when?"

"The date of the letter, April seventeenth."

"Well. Hallelujah and God praise the Queen," said Blanc in a hushed voice. "Perhaps there is light at the end of the tunnel after all. For you see, Howland, we will never get out unless active measures are used. Look at us, we're all getting gray, even Prideaux. Rassam's whiskers are almost white, and Stern looks like a man of seventy. Cameron is the worst of us all."

"It's this damnable beef diet," declared Stern. "The dry winter killed our lovely vegetable garden. We had cress, radishes . . ."

Blanc continued, "We're all weary, mentally and bodily, of this uncertain state of affairs. Hormuzd, what are you doing?"

Ravi imagined that Rassam was merely going to the fire in the center of the room so as to read the letter more carefully. It was now apparent that he held the flaming page between his fingers, and the act was intentional. Ravi jumped up, grabbed the charred paper, threw it on the floor, and stomped on it. There was now only a burnt corner where one could see Lord Stanley's signature: "Your sincere Friend, Stanley."

His eyes blazed accusation at Rassam. "Why are you doing this?"

The placid envoy returned the look. "I don't want to unduly upset Bob."

" 'Unduly upset'?" cried Ravi. "Man, do you realize that Bob gets 'unduly upset' whenever someone sneezes?"

"Ja, ja!" insisted Stern. "You should have consulted us before committing such a rash act!"

"It's our fate too, Hormuzd," Blanc pointed out. "At this point, I don't much care how 'unduly upset' Bob becomes. We prefer death to a continuance of this miserable existence. If he knows he has only three months to act, it can only help matters."

But Rassam was adamant. "God's will is done."

More like Rassam's will, Ravi thought angrily.

CHAPTER NINETEEN
TALKING TO BOB

POOR DOWNTRODDEN HERR FLAD, THE RELUCTANT emissary to Her Majesty, finally arrived at the imperial camp, quite near his old mission at Djenda. He was no doubt in much too big a hurry to rejoin with his wife at Gaffat, and came straight to the Emperor's white pavilion even though it was eight in the evening. This news was carried to Delphine by the Ukrainian chef Misha, who had befriended her at last, after forgetting his initial terror that some sort of harridan would suck up his beloved Elect of God's soul. Misha was a goodhearted man who had known only anguish in his life: his exodus from the Ukraine leaving behind four children, his disastrous love affair in New York with a woman who refused to leave her husband—everything in his life until he met Ravi had been a sad tale.

Now Misha reveled in his superior position in the Emperor's army. His blind worship of his master was his greatest strength, Delphine thought. He would never be disappointed or crestfallen again.

They gathered around a fire positioned outside Delphine's tent, so that they might catch Flad the moment he exited the royal pavilion. Misha had brought a hare he had shot, and had roasted it for Delphine and Abou, and they were listlessly drinking their *après diner* tea.

Delphine gulped audibly. "Mm. That red pepper sauce was enough to cause me to drink a whole liter of water."

Misha had not partaken of the hare, it being an unclean animal, but Abou had no such compunction, after making sure Misha had faced the hare toward Jerusalem and uttered the proper words before gutting it.

"I received a note from Ravinger today," Delphine said casually, expecting the way Misha stiffened with avidity at the name. He liked to pretend he was unconcerned about his partner, but Delphine had often seen the deep affection in his face. "He's finally riding to meet us here in Dembea. He should be here in two days' time."

Misha nodded soberly. "Ah. It's good he's finally returning. He needs to lead the men, not gallivant about the country delivering stores and prisoners. Anyone can do that. *I* could do that," he added, not without humor.

Delphine gasped. "There he is!"

Everyone put down their cups at the sight of Herr Flad's silhouette as he was ejected from the Emperor's pavilion. They all stood, Delphine telling Misha, "You greet him—he doesn't know me or Abou."

They went inside Delphine's tent for safety's sake, the eunuchs who loitered about being instructed not to let anyone in.

Delphine and Flad shared an *alga*, after Flad bowed low over her hand. He was a serious gangly man with sunken jaded eyes. "I had heard there was a beautiful *ferenje* woman here."

"Not just a woman," Abou noted. "A woman *doctor*."

Misha ignored him. "Tell us the news, Flad! What did you just tell the Emperor?"

Flad gratefully accepted the *tej* Delphine proffered. Drinking a deep draught, he sighed as though the weight of the world was upon him. "I told him that the Queen has said if he doesn't at once send the prisoners out of his country, he can't expect any further friendship from her. I told him if he didn't comply with her request, he's definitely involving himself in a disastrous war."

Everyone gasped, surprised that Flad was still here to tell the tale. "And his reaction?" asked Delphine.

Flad shrugged. "He said, 'I've asked from them a sign of friendship, but it is refused to me. If they wish to come and fight, let them come, and call me a woman if I do not beat them'." He shrugged again, staring into his *barrilye*.

Misha looked askance. "We will fight," he mumbled.

Abou stuck out his lower lip. "I will not fight for this crazy monster, Bob."

"And what was his attitude?" Delphine queried.

Flad thought. "He listened with calmness and indifference. He only became enraged when I presented him with a telescope— a very good one, too—sent by Her Majesty. He then raved and said it was no good, because he couldn't adjust his eyes to seeing through it. He even reminded me of the time Captain Howland first came to him, with that rug he said depicted the Lion of the tribe of Judah being slain by Egyptians. Remember that, Misha?"

Misha harrumphed. "How could one forget?"

Flad explained to Delphine. "But he liked Howland, so instead he imprisoned Howland's servant who had unfurled the rug." His face clouded. "Where is the grand chamberlain, anyway? Please don't tell me anything bad has befallen him."

Delphine said, "No, he's expected to return any—Who's that?"

For the eunuchs were arguing with someone at the tent door. The three men stood, but Delphine had the swiftest reaction, and she flew to the tent door just as Ravinger entered.

Ravi caught her up in his mighty arms and squeezing her to

him, twirling her about. He smelled of cooking fires, undressed animal skins, and the herbs of the highlands, and it was the most glorious stench to revel in. "My love," he said against Delphine's throat, uncaring that three men gaped at him as he plied her with unkempt kisses.

"My darling *el besiss*," Delphine whispered a bit more prudently as she cradled his head to her. His two-day-old beard deliciously chafed her skin, sending a torrent of shivers down her sides. How she wished the other men would leave!

Flad cleared his throat diplomatically. "I think I will repair to the Fitawrari's tent, and—"

Ravinger spun to face the missionary. "You'll do no such thing, sir! Get back down on that *alga*."

Speaking a few words at the tent flap, Ravi soon returned with a bottle of the Hennessey's brandy, the absence of which Misha had been bemoaning, and soon all were comfortably ensconced on *algas*, Ravi and Delphine sharing one now. Flad told Ravi everything that had transpired that eve, including the bit about the evil telescope.

Ravi waved an unconcerned hand as he removed his lion's mane mantle. "I'll show him how to work the telescope, don't bother about that. D'ye think he's planning on war, then?"

"*Ja*, most assuredly," said Flad. "There has not been one small indication that he plans on releasing any prisoners. Talking to Bob is a fruitless endeavor! He's got a—a—" Flad riffled his hand in the air, searching for the right term.

Ravi swiftly finished Flad's sentence. "He's got a strange obsession with keeping people close to him, and the only way he knows how is to imprison them. It's as though he can't tolerate thinking he'll be alone, abandoned, a man without a kingdom."

Flad's eyes shone. "Well he already *is* a man without a kingdom, from what I've heard from hundreds of different people on my journey up here! This madman is going on in his dishonorable way, sometimes flattering, but then abusing and imprisoning those who he used to call his friends. There is no advantage to sending him the artisans. He would just go on demanding things from the British government. This I told them in London. They must use stronger force."

"Yes, yes," Ravi said thoughtfully. "And everyone in Magdala would agree."

"*Tewodros yemut!*" Flad agreed heatedly. *May Tewodros die (if we are not speaking the truth)!*

Ravi said, "The question is, what role do we play? Misha, you're in a very awkward position."

Misha spoke for the first time since Ravi had made his appearance. "Rav. You know what I would do." Misha stood, placing his *barrilye* onto a low table. He made a funny little bow, and left the tent.

Abou exhaled mightily.

"Yes, well." Ravi seemed to agree with Abou. "Bob has three months to respond to Lord Stanley's ultimatum letter, starting April the seventeenth."

"He will do nothing!" Flad spat. "I suggested to Whitehall restoring Bob his convent at Jerusalem. I thought it would help ease Bob's approach to the captives. Samuel Baker recommended a joint action with British and Egyptian forces."

"Spare the thought!" cried Ravi. "Sam must have a brick in his hat! If the British plan to come in, to even make it to the highlands through Tigré, they'll have to placate first Dejazmach Kassa and then Wagshum Gobaze in Lasta, gain their assistance, and assure them that they don't mean to occupy the land, that they're just passing through to get to Bob. Kassa and Gobaze aren't going to take kindly to a force of Turks! No one will!"

"And what shall *we* do, Ravi?" Delphine asked mildly.

Looking down, Ravi smiled and put his arm around her. "My Queen of Heaven," he purred, stroking her throat, as though they were alone in the tent. "I have a plan. I won't let you suffer a moment longer."

At this, Flad and Abou stood. Flad rearranged his *shamma* nervously and said, "Captain Howland. If you're planning on leaving, I'd appreciate foreknowledge. You don't know how it might affect the way Bob treats the other prisoners, if one was to . . . leave."

Ravi stood too. "My dear sir. That has been the only thing preventing me from leaving up until now. I won't do anything to jeopardize anyone's safety."

The two men were nearly filed out the door like pallbearers. Flad paused. In the dim light of the country lamp, Delphine imagined she saw his face twinkle with impishness. He placed his fingertips on her arm, and said, "Be careful of this one." He pointed at Ravi. "He looks like Othello, and he lives like the Three Musketeers squashed together as one. But you will never fear with him, for he has earned Bob's trust by his habit of splitting a sheep from head to tail with one blow from his sword."

The men left.

Ravinger stretched with false ease, yawning toward the ceiling. He casually bent to retrieve his brandy.

"Split sheep?" Delphine teased. She curved her torso around the delectable muscles of his back, so that when he stood up straight, she clung to him like a baby sloth.

Ravi smiled over his shoulder at her. He sipped his brandy and looked at her escritoire. "He enjoyed watching me do that. Sort of an amusement, to pass the time. Who gave you that desk? I've never been in your tent—where did you get that black sheepskin?"

"The escritoire was in my tent when I first came here."

Delphine slid her hand inside his *shamma* and the European shirt that was so threadbare it was like tissue. Ah, the feel of his solid fleshy pectoral was enough to send her fingers squiggling into the depths of his armpit. The thought that she would get a handful of a week's worth of dust only raised her blood's temperature, and soon she was fairly crawling up the back of the man, her knees cinched around his scabbard on one side, and his belt of armor on the other.

"I've missed you so. Your beautiful letters only heightened my ardor for you. There is something so incredibly erotic about a brilliant mind such as yours." She pulled the *shamma* down over the massive shoulders darkened by the sun.

He sipped the brandy and didn't touch her, just allowed her to cling to him. "My only truth. I would have left this country long ago if you weren't here." His voice was strange, strangled perhaps by her dangling from him. "I've heard we're to go to Lake Tzana next—"

She bit his neck. "What you wrote about your *Pleasures of Women* book, Ravi, it drove me crazy as a bedbug." When her fingers pinched his erect nipple, he uttered a small gasp. "I excited myself dreaming about your words, it was perfectly maddening." Hiking higher up his muscular trunk—was this the 'climbing the tree' he'd referred to ages ago?—she breathed in his ear, sultry. "No number of solitary pleasures could bring me nearly to the satisfaction that your nimble fingers gave me."

He caved in then, like a great wall bowing under a tidal wave. Bending at the knees and dropping several feet, he sent her suspended into the air, hovering for a fraction of a moment. But he was so fast in his turning that before she could fall, he'd caught her, their chests pressed together. He launched her directly back onto the black sheepskin of the *arat*, lowering her athletically yet gently. He struck like a python's tail it was all so fast, but she floated delicately onto the *arat* as he sat on the carpet between her thighs, one hand on each of her knees.

"How often do we hear women in modern society lamenting they have absolutely no knowledge of their own physiology...? The mock virtue, the most immodest modesty of society, pronounces the subject foul and fulsome."

He was quoting from his own letter. Leaning back on her elbows, Delphine easily recalled his written words. " 'Shall we ever understand that ignorance is not innocence'?"

Lifting her foot, he pressed it into his crotch, so she could massage his splendid erection with her toes. "She is allowed to have feet but no toes ... ankles but no calves ..." He got to his knees and clamped her ankle between his powerful thighs, and he began a slow ascent, humping his way up her leg. "Knees but no thighs ..."

Delphine suddenly could recall no more of the letter. The heated length of his penis through the flimsy breeches sent her into a frenzy of desire that allowed no logical thought to break though its haze. He was so hot and real, it was unthinkable that he would ever go away from her. As he hefted his erection over her pleasured kneecap, the sight of his undulating hips when he tossed his *shamma* aside the most excruciating delight she'd ever known, his sly fingers hitched under the waist of her breeches. Gently but firmly he tugged them down.

"Hips and no haunches ..." he recited.

Her tongue found itself. "Oh, no! You mustn't—I can't allow you." Her fingers tried to still his wrist, but he was having none of it.

His voice was rough, demanding. "Oh *yes*, Delphine. You can allow me. You say you can't allow yourself to feel pleasure by a man, and I'm here to prove you wrong. I'm as filthy as a *buda's* breakfast, so there's only one option—for me to pleasure you."

Her breeches were soon down around her feet, then tossed somewhere in the tent, but Delphine didn't clap her knees together. Instead, she flung her torso onto the black sheepskin, her hands over her face, so she wouldn't have to look. His sweltering chest covered her thighs as he plastered large lubricious kisses to her lap—"she has a stomach, but no belly"—winding his lithe tongue around the silver chain girdle she'd been forced to wear.

She made a final attempt. "You must leave, Ravi." It came out barely a whisper. "While Bob has relaxed his restrictions on me somewhat, I don't think in his present mood he'd see the brighter aspect to—"

He growled something against her pubic crest. His fat, searing tongue slurped up her bulging clitoris, and she cried aloud, a note higher than she thought she could reach.

She was so loud she set nearby dogs to barking, causing men to shout at some boys watching over sheep, but Ravi didn't pause one beat in his fervid guzzling at her honeypot. He sank in deeper, with an apparent goal to swiftly getting her off.

Sliding both hands around the crevasse of her behind, suddenly eight snaking fingers were limning glorious artistic motifs along her labia. When he added his thumbs to the smoldering onslaught, Delphine's entire upper body jerked upright, and she grabbed a handful of his thick black braids—whether to yank him away, or press him to her, she didn't stop to wonder.

The most achingly exquisite sight Ravi was at that moment, slathering at her trough, his brawny shoulders hoisting her hips. He lay spread out gloriously on the carpet, his hips rasping the beefy penis against the lion's fur he had tossed there. Gulping for air, she stretched a trembling leg out, sneaking her foot down over the edge of the *arat*. Phosphenes swam in her blood-starved brain as she wedged her foot between his penis and the lion's fur.

He bore down on her clitoris, and she exploded in his mouth.

She was gripped with convulsions that rocketed her more forcefully against his dexterous mouth. He wolfed the very core of her, and she didn't realize until much later she was probably strangling him with her other thigh coiled so tightly about his neck. He humped her thoroughly pleasured foot, and she was gratified to feel the heat of his own discharge spreading over her arch.

Her spasms went on and on, and he licked as though he regulated her by his very lapping. He backed off, and gave her respite enough to catch a breath of painful air, then he set to once more, his tongue slowing like a fat oyster petting her core with long, sure stokes.

It seemed that she fainted—the French *petit mort?*—because later she had no recollection of the next few minutes. She knew she squirmed and tossed on the *arat* like a beached dolphin, cried out, and moaned. She hugged a silk pillow to her stomach, and bore into it against the *arat*, and it never occurred to her to be shy, or embarrassed at the crescendo he had just caused in her.

When she came to, she was still twitching, and she slid her palm between her legs to stop it. With her behind end-up in the air like that, he could have easily taken her like a mule, but instead she heard him rustling about, on his feet, arranging things, pouring brandy. It took more long moments for her to gather the sentience to flip over and smear her tousled hair from her face.

"*El besiss,*" she whispered weakly.

He stood in profile, the warm radiance of the country lamp showing his glorious muscular form to its best advantage. His European shirt was down around his hips, and he absently stroked the exquisite ridges of his abdomen, the other hand holding the brandy *barrilye*. He turned his head and smiled at her with a fierceness of eye that was devilish and alluring. A lick of flame was caught in the ruby glass, a semaphore of a very incubus himself.

Putting down the glass, Ravi came to squat next to the *arat*. He stroked her hair with an air of dominion, then moved his hand to outline the concave sweep of her bare waist as she lay on her side, warmly fondling the summit of her hip.

"I see that when the tool is honed sharply enough, you're capable of great summits of ecstasy, my Queen of Heaven."

She wasn't ashamed. Instead, she was imbued with a sated, relaxed blood, as if she had downed an entire bottle of laudanum, though she hadn't a chance to drink any all day. Still, she was spry enough to raise herself on her elbow. "I see that when the arrogance is swollen enough, you're capable of taking credit for it."

Ravi shrugged modestly. "How can I help show such prowess, when sucking on a mango of such appetizing taste."

Delphine wrinkled her nose. "That's your Hindoo love."

"Yes. They say the 'mouth congress' should never be done by a learned Brahman, that there's no reason why it should be carried on. So a man should pay attention to whether or not it's agreeable to his nature and to himself."

Delphine's finger touched his full lower lip. "It seems to agree with you."

"I always liked the last line. 'But after all, these things being done secretly, and the mind of man being fickle, how can it be known what any person will do at any particular time and for any particular purpose'?"

Delphine laughed freely then. "I see there is a justification for everything. Good." She kissed him then, reasoning that the brandy had burned any trace of her taste in his mouth. "Ravi, is that . . . 'mouth congress' . . . isn't that a French thing?"

"As much as any other nationality. Perhaps more so than the Icelandic or Finnish, who believed that masturbation led to blindness, epilepsy, and premature, miserable death. So yes, probably more French than Finnish. Why do you ask?"

"My . . . lover in Georgia never did . . . that. And he was of French extraction, a Creole."

"Ah. But there's your answer right there. You said 'Georgia'."

Before Delphine comprehended Ravinger's meaning, he stood and stuck his arms through the sleeves of his European shirt. What an infuriating man! Casually buttoning his shirt as though he performed mouth congress on women every day! And of course he would be a snobbish boor, being from Newport-on-the-River, Massachusetts. "I've told Wubishet to heat my bath, and it's probably cold as July in San Francisco by now."

Standing, Delphine pulled her embroidered shirt down so that it resembled a nightdress. "Are you here to stay? I mean . . . you're not going on any more excursions?"

"I think my activities from now on will be concentrated on road-building, if what I hear is correct." His hands stilling on his wrapped belt, he regarded her soberly. "Which will be one and the same thing with the movement of the imperial camp."

"What do you mean?"

"I mean Bob wants a road built from Debra Tabor to Magdala."

"Whatever for?"

"To transport all his artillery. He plans on making his stand on Magdala."

CHAPTER TWENTY
AN ISLAND BANQUET

Lake Tzana, Near Qorata

TEWODROS REMEMBERED A PLACE HE HADN'T yet plundered.

The holy island of Mesraha rose from Lake Tzana about twenty miles north of Qorata. *Mankuse* monks had peopled the island in tranquility for hundreds of years since the dawn of Christianity in the black highlands. As told in the Kebra Negast, the glorious chronicle of Abyssinia, this was where the Imam Ahmed Gragn, the pugilistic Somali warlord who had murdered Christopher de Gama, was blown out in 1543 by patriotic Abyssinian troops. Here also on Mesraha were buried the remains of the Emperor Yohannes in 1682, and Iyasu the First, being killed there on orders of his son.

Decimating his way with the army through Begemder, Tewodros had proclaimed to the huddled peasantry, "You have no more homes, grain, or cattle. I have not done it. God did it. Come with me, and I'll take you where you will find plenty to eat, cattle in abundance, and punish those who are the cause of God's anger upon you." In this manner they gained several thousand more bodies, as the bedraggled countrymen had no other choice open to them but to follow.

Encamped just north of Qorata, the Emperor ordered Ravi to go before him with a hundred troops to build *tankwas*, the flimsy canoes made from papyrus.

The island was luxuriantly wooded and peopled with various monasteries. One of them Ravi knew to boast an ancient stone banquet hall. The roof of this part of the monastery was partially collapsed, but this was no worry until the rainy season next month. This knowledge had fomented in his brain since the moment he'd been given orders to Mesraha.

Ravi decided to hold the most glorious banquet his soldiers had ever seen.

Putting Misha in charge the *tankwas*, Ravi sent some Fit-awraris and soldiers into Qorata to seize whatever food stores they could. He sent more men out hunting, loaning them a few of his personal Enfield rifles in lieu of the patched muskets they were normally armed with. He then paddled out to the island to make arrangements with the friendly *mankuse*, who turned out in full canonical ochre dress to greet him in the belief he was bringing them a message to surrender or die. Becoming truly merry when they found out the Likamaquas's real mission was to fete his soldiers and the islanders with a banquet honoring some vague saint, they eagerly showed him to the banquet hall attached to the round church with a conical roof.

The hall was as Ravi recalled it, a long narrow building with a sturdy wooden table that could seat maybe forty men at a time. After handing the head *mankuse* a pocketful of Maria Theresas, Ravi gave instructions for the floor to be swept, carpets to be laid, and a goodly quantity of *tej, arrack, hambasha,* and *wot* to be served. On his way out, he selected three oxen to stand as the main course, and they were driven into a slaughter enclosure.

He paddled furiously back to where the men were building *tankwas*, singing a jolly song he'd first heard played in Deseret

Territory back home. He imagined it was called "Vilikins and His Dinah," and he belted it out lustily as he paddled. "It is of a rich merchant I am going to tell, who had for a daughter an uncommon nice young gal; her name it is Dinah, just sixteen years old, with a very large fortune in silver and gold."

Back ashore he hastily composed a message to Tewodros and, as he had no seal with him, entrusted it to an illiterate man.

By The Power of Saint Michael the Archangel—Ravi preferred swearing by the saints, with whom he felt a bit more friendly than the avenging trio of the Father, Son, and Holy Ghost—

O Great One. How have you spent the morning? I trust your health is fine. I am writing you to request that the Empress Makeda be allowed to join me for a feast on the island of Mesraha. You are invited to join us as well, but I feel she will be more relaxed and not worried about her appearance if you are not there. If you agree, by the power of your Creator send her with her valet Abou at once.

I am your servant,
Basha Falaka

❋　❋　❋

IT WAS AN UNPRECEDENTED THRILL, THE message from Tewodros. Delphine was allowed to leave the encampment to go to church on a nearby island! She could scarcely contain her excitement as she flew about her tent making arrangements. She carefully dressed from the skin out, first in the naughty *choli* and *sari* Ravi had given her all those months ago, covering these carefully with the usual white embroidered shirt and breeches. She even wore the almost untouched pair of awkward red leather slippers with the turned-back toes given her by Tewodros. They made her feel like an Arabian princess, or an elf.

She carefully applied kohl to her eyes, and refreshed the *insoosilla* on her hands and feet. She had not yet dared tattoo herself as she had seen Yetemagnu and Alitash do, their necks, arms, and feet adorned with the blue *fleur-de-lis* and concentric circles imitative of rings and bracelets.

Once on the beach, Misha arranged for the *tankwa* boats. Delphine went first, deserving an entire boat to herself with a boatman, as an additional body would have sunk her up to her loins in the placid waters of Lake Tzana. Misha then sent Abou, other men with *teff* flour, and a fellow who had rounded up giant jars presumably of *tej*. It was a serene smooth ride, once Delphine learned to sit up high and think like a cloud, and not to make sudden movements, for the slightest tilt would toss everyone into the drink. By paddling with poles that looked ineffective but propelled them quite fast, they cleaved the water through gaggles of pelicans that squawked with disinterest. But when they came within sight of a few hippopotami frolicking in the bulrushes, the men commenced shouting in excited profusion, waving their arms while standing up in the boats, and this terrified Delphine more than anything. But the hippopotami had no plan of attack, and soon she was gliding to the beach of Mesraha, where smiling monks in orange robes awaited them.

At the top of a winding stone trail, men insisted upon washing Delphine's feet (but not the feet of Abou, whom they termed a slave), and their insistence on calling her Makeda was a little unnerving. They proceeded down a wide, quiet path under trees where great birds with black legs nested, past a church with a thatched roof. It was a peaceful, cloistered feeling riding through the coppice with the *mankuse*. But when Delphine asked to go inside the church, the monks looked apprehensive, explaining that in these island monasteries, no women were allowed at all. On the mainland they were allowed in their part of the church, but not here.

"I do not want to go inside their god-damned church anyway," Abou growled from where he walked next to Delphine, not having been given a mule.

A most extraordinary thing then happened. Ravinger himself stepped out of the darkness of the church's doorway, leaning irreverently against the wooden doorjamb. Delphine gasped to see him, smiling directly at her with a sensual and devilish look, so freshly handsome even his silver *betoa* armband seemed to have been polished. It was one thing to see him so archly virile with his hands folded before his crotch, but the idea that he'd been waiting for her inside a church confounded her even further.

Delphine knew then that she loved Ravi irrevocably. She knew that her love for Ravi equaled the sublime passion of her heart for Eugene, only in a different manner—one not bound by four prison walls, one set free to relax in her enjoyment of him.

Ravi sprang down the steps like an idealistic youth. He was so confident, so carefree! Delphine had never been like that. Her life had been serious, one travail after the other to be endured. She had always expected disaster around every corner, and perhaps as a result, she had always found it there.

Ravi beckoned for her to dismount, his arms spread open to her. She slid off the mule as he lifted her effortlessly.

Ravinger stood so close he nearly stepped on the curled-up toes of her leather slippers. "It's right around the corner. Come."

He took her hand, and they walked up a tranquil lane. Ravi said, "You told me you were an orphan. How did that come about?"

Delphine wrapped her free hand around his massive forearm, excited by the ridges of the stony veins that enlaced it. "I was ten. My father, who was a very great teacher of Transcendentalist thought, and corresponded with Thoreau and Emerson—ah, there were always people and fascinating conversation around our house!—my father died of drink because he couldn't save my mother from expiring of consumption, both within the same year."

Ravi lifted a hand and cradled her head to his shoulder as they walked. "My only truth. I see now why you're so temperate. Stick with me, and you will always have family."

"What are you then, a brother? Or an uncle, for you are far older than I," she teased. Ravi was probably only about eight years older than her.

"Mm. Call me a devoted servant."

Around the corner of the church was a long stone building. Men and women bustled about in attached pens, shouting orders to each other as they milled around cooking fires. A pen held two oxen awaiting slaughter, Abyssinians desirous of waiting until the last moment to ensure the absolute quivering freshness of their meat.

The hall was lit by torches and country lamps of rags soaked in butter, and colorful frescoes such as were painted inside mainland churches adorned the ceiling of this room. In painting these saints and angels, the artist had been perfectly apathetic to perspective or anatomy: the eyes were bigger than the mouths, thumbs were portrayed as longer than middle fingers, and emaciated legs supported elephantine feet. Another cartoon showed a crowd of smugly satisfied nobles watching Saint George crushing a dragon under his horse's feet. All Abyssinian saints were depicted as white, with Satan painted such a deep black he had no features at all.

"It's a shame these are fading," said Delphine.

"They're painted with animal blood and flour from natural dyes. They're beautiful in a naïve basic way." Ravi steered her to the head of a long wooden table, where a retinue of enthusiastic *mankuse* were already quaffing *arrack*. "There's my favorite Saint George, slaying the dragon."

Walde Nebra and the energetic Wubishet stood at attention by the head of the table, while other servants spread fresh grass over the carpets to impart a fresh smell, and yet others stood sentry over large wicker baskets covered with red cloths. Most people would be seated on the grass spread beneath the low table, but Ravinger had provided Delphine with some queenly cushions upon which to sit, Indian style, Abou at her left elbow. Ravi sat beside her, arranging his limbs with an ease borne of a decade of practice under low tables.

"Please," said Delphine. "Don't let me stop you from having *arrack*. I don't want you thinking I'm a tub-thumping teetotaler—"

"Which you are." Ravi smiled as a *tej-asalefech* poured from his jug a hollow palm of *arrack*, from which the servant drank first, to Ravi's approval.

"—which I *am*, and . . . *Oh!*" Flustered, Delphine had to laugh. "Do you think the friars have any herbal tea?"

The *tej-asalefech* then poured Ravi a more moderate sized *wancha* than the gigantic steer's horns the monks were drinking from. An assistant tapped the cloth covering the jar's mouth so the liquor flowed freely, and a bowl underneath caught the excess that was then the property of the pourers. "I don't know, let me ask. Do you have any herbal tea?" he asked the *tej-asalefech*.

"No, *Tewodros yemut!*" The fellow wailed as though protesting the murder of his firstborn son.

Ravi turned back to Delphine. "I'm sorry, my truth. It's completely understandable after what happened to your father that you should choose to remain abstinent. What happened to you after you were orphaned? You were just a child."

"I . . ." Next to Delphine, Abou rudely thrust his own colossal *wancha* under her nose to demand some liquor. She would have to thank him later for his feeble attempt at changing the subject. "We, that is my brother and I . . . We were able to keep our parent's house by taking on chores such as laundry. We were well-known and popular in the community, and eventually . . ."

She pretended to be absorbed in the sight of a fresh crowd of men entering the banquet hall, almost all of them calling jovially to Ravi. "Basha Falaka! How have you passed the time since I saw you last?" She recognized a couple of Rases, Dejazmachs, and Bitwaddads.

"*Egzaiair yemesgen!*" Ravi hollered back to the men. *Thanks to the Lord.*

They came forward in strict rank order so that Abou was crowded by a Bitwaddad, Ravi was jostled by the buttery arm of Dejazmach Deris, and the *mankuse* were hustled down to their proper grade at the end of the table, where they capered with a frivolity Kaspar would have found repulsive. To the accompaniment of clanking *shotels*, more palms of liquor were poured and tasted, more giant horns were filled and lifted, and soon there was the signal for the house-steward to come forward and inspect the baskets of bread, more of which were being brought in on servants' heads.

"The breads are arranged," Ravi fairly shouted over the din of the clamoring men, "in precise order of type. The *hambasha* and barley bread is laid at the bottom, then the average sort of *teff*, and at the top you'll find the very best white bread. When this has met his approval—see?"

Men who were apparently designated bread-handlers were placing prodigious piles of spongy bread before each diner, Delphine's half of the table deserving of the fluffy white bread Ravi had mentioned, the ranking soldiers farther down receiving the ordinary *teff* and heavy *hambasha*. But nobody touched the bread until two other servants came down the line, starting with Ravi, proffering brass ewers of water for the washing of hands, the dirty water then pouring onto the carpets and grass below.

That was when Delphine was pinched in the leg by something

that crawled under the table. *"Ooh!"* she gasped. Ravi was busy in a jolly shouting match with a Ras. "What is that?" Leaning back, she could see nothing beneath the darkened, low table. "A dog?"

Nobody listened to her, for great iron stands were now brought, followed by women with pots of what Delphine knew were minced mutton, swimming in the usual red pepper buttery gravy. One such pot being jammed down between her and Ravi, a servant reached rudely over, tore a piece of bread from Ravi's pile, dipped it into the pot with relish, and pressed this mixture to Ravi's mouth. He swallowed it in one bite to great acclaim from the entire table of starved banqueters.

Abyssinians had a great zest for hot condiments. It peppered their meats, and was mixed into bread, milk, and even drinking water. Soon all were gulping their first bites of fire, Delphine nearly being stifled by an overly large dumpling of bread dripping mutton and pepper. She almost choked and bit the tip of the man's finger, but soon the demonstrative servants stepped back to allow the diners to fall to with energy.

Never had Delphine seen such a gross display of wolfing than at the trough of this Abyssinian monastery. It was normally considered rude to eat without making sounds that would shame a hog, but everyone appeared to be attempting to outdo one another in the arena of gustatory sounds. Delphine had heard the Abyssinian proverb: "Only beggars and thieves eat small pieces, or without making a noise." Thank goodness Ravi didn't adhere to this practice. Using only his right hand as was proper, he would tear off a bit of bread, roll it into a ball, dip it into the sauce, and pop it into his mouth. Delphine followed suit, though her eyes watered from the surfeit of pepper—there were additional dishes of the sauce on the table, for those who had not quite scoured their entire digestive tract yet.

Squeaking when another beast under the table pawed at her

ankle, she turned to Ravi and was silenced when he poked a handful of the mush into her mouth. As shocking as it was, she couldn't protest, and as she gulped to swallow the large ball, she saw other men thrusting the same mouthfuls of muck into each other's mouths. It seemed one didn't need to feed one's self at all—one's neighbors did it for you, sometimes so swiftly they could hardly have swallowed the first ball, and must be squirreling them away in their cheeks for future use.

"Abou, I've never seen—

Abou shut her up by pressing a peppery pill to her lips, laughing so maliciously that she swiftly set to preparing her own spicy revenge for him. But now he was beset with mouthfuls from his left side, and Dejazmach Deris to Ravi's right leaned forward, clean over Ravi, coming toward Delphine with another handful.

"Ravi, I can't eat as fast as—" *Gulp.*

Ravi seemed to think it was just a merry time, for he leaned back to allow the fellow access, all the while laughing fully, as no one was currently smashing puddings down his mouth. "My *el taleb*, you've never been to a formal banquet before! And imagine, this is just the first course!"

When the Bitwaddad to Abou's left grabbed her by the arm and attacked her with another lump of offal, Delphine quickly turned to Ravi and spit the thing into her hand. This caused untold mirth on his part, as she slyly disposed of the gob in the darkness beneath her feet.

"Now you're learning. Believe it or not, it's a sign of honor to be fed." He put his hand on her thigh.

The inside of her larynx was on fire. "My mother used to tell us not to talk with our mouths full of food. Just look at these masticating swine! Why, it's enough to make one heave!" For some of the men were eating and talking at the same time, and red globules rolled down their stained *shammas* and onto the table. "May I have some water?"

"Water? Why, I don't think I've seen any—" Ravi craned his neck around his neighbor, and was stuffed with more morsels of esteem.

The next time Dejazmach Deris tried to feed her, Delphine protested. "It is too good for a mere *hakim* as me—" She took it into her mouth, again depositing it beneath the table, where she felt the scramblings of the beasts one more. "Ravi, what's crawling around down there?"

"Down there? Why . . ." Leaning over so far he was folded nearly in two and his head was in her lap, Ravi soon emerged with a grinning ragamuffin of a naked boy who was simply coated with crumbs, grass, and red pepper. The urchin even smeared a fingerful off his own face, smiling at Delphine the whole while, and popped the finger into his mouth.

Stuffing the boy back down, Ravi said, "So you see, Doctor, nothing goes to waste in Abyssinia."

It was enough to make Delphine reach for the *arrack wancha*, but she was able to desist. Over the raucous confabulation of the men, she had heard the braying death knell of at least one of the three oxen outside in the pen. "What of the jugs of water they're using for washing hands? They must have water somewhere." Following Ravi's example, Delphine wiped her dripping fingers on one of the spongy breads as a napkin, slapping it back onto the table.

"Oh, my truth, you don't want to drink that water. The wells this time of year are nasty. *Kantiba Hailo! Bring it on!*"

Had Ravi gone completely raving mad? For he was ignoring her in order to wildly wave his arm at a fellow who stood in the hall's doorway holding what looked like an entire ox's shoulder. As the fellow came forward to the accompaniment of encouraging cries from the men, Ravi spun facing outward, brandishing a *shotel* he must have borrowed for the occasion, as Delphine knew he scorned them as weapons. His eyes shone with excitement like a child playing at Blind Man's Wand. Other men unsheathed their *shotels* with the seeming intent of whacking off portions of the bloody hump as the chosen waiter brought it forward to Ravi.

Nobody paid much attention to their fiery missiles anymore as the waiter presented the meat to Ravi. He studied the meat with a virtuoso eye, touching it here and there with the blade, and turning it about while the fellow held it. At last he made his choice, and deftly sliced a section of the *brundo* about fifteen inches long. The room was now so quiet one could hear from the outer enclosure the hacking away at the ox carcass as less choice sections of animal were carved.

Placing a large dollop of the red pepper sauce onto a round of white bread, Ravi laid one end of the meat onto it, the other end going into his mouth. With the *shotel*, he cut a mouthful so close to his nose it was a wonder he didn't take off her nostril and, proclaiming it good, chomped away with carnivorous intent.

As everyone cheered encouragement, to Delphine's horror the next choice was up to her. Not having a blade of any sort, Abou eagerly did the honors with a voracity that bordered on the murderous. His turn wasn't next, as the waiter then went in order of rank, so Delphine gratefully slid her portion of quivering purplish meat in front of Abou and bade him masticate at the dead animal.

Now that the room roared with the guttural tumult of forty rapacious beasts, Delphine felt safe enough to lean into Ravi. "This is the most hideously disgusting thing I've ever seen."

At least Ravinger swallowed his mouthful of raw meat before answering. "Have you never eaten *brundo*?"

"No, I've only eaten the cooked *wot* stews, and the roasted *tibs*."

"Ah, well then! You're in for a real treat."

"Oh, no, Ravi, please! Do you know how beastly that is?"

"It's as fresh as it's ever going to be, no need to fear for diseases." Ravi touched the end of the dripping meat to her lips. "Come, my Queen of Heaven, trust me. Just don't move."

She had no choice but to grip the detestable meat with her teeth, though she did shut her eyes as Ravi swiftly slashed the strip off so close to her nose she felt the breeze from the blade. Opening her eyes, she regarded him dolefully as she chewed, while he looked as proud as a mother hen.

"There. See? There's good nutrition in this raw meat. Think of all the blood combining with yours, the strength of the ox seeping into you."

It was a lucky thing she'd managed to swallow before he mentioned the ox again. In the frenzy of the moment, with all others occupied with the flesh on their *shotels*, Ravi leaned forward and kissed Delphine squarely on the mouth. It was a wonderful kiss, full of affection and lust, and she found she didn't mind the raw taste so much in Ravi's mouth, mingled as it was with the pepper and *arrack*.

Delphine was stupefied when a fresh round of diners was ushered in. The sated and elevated first round were expelled vigorously, some of the more fired-up monks conking their heads on the doorjamb. Misha led this new party, taking his seat to Ravi's right, and Delphine was further mortified to see some of the newcomers pick up the bloody "napkins" left by the first party and bite into them as though they were apple fritters.

"Ravi! We don't have to sit through another dinner party, do we? I don't think I can fit one more speck into my stomach."

"Ah, relax, my Queen. These hungry soldiers will whistle through this meal, and then we shall be done."

Misha leaned forward to address Delphine. "So? What do you think of our outstanding banquets? We sure know how to eat, wouldn't you say?"

Delphine couldn't believe that the refined Mikhail Vasiliev would find solace at a table such as this, but he killed off an even greater quantity, it seemed, than Basha Falaka himself.

She had to sit through three more rounds of diners, the Ras Engeddeh himself even attending the last meal. By that time she had gone to the backhouse four times, her legs were numb from being crushed under the table, and even Ravi was showing signs of tapering off. She knew from having been outside that the sun had been down for at least two hours, and she wondered how they would get back to the mainland. She supposed the paddlers could take them, as the moon was very nearly full, as long as they didn't hit any sleeping hippopotami.

"BUT THIS ISN'T THE WAY TO the beach," the woman protested.

Ravi held her forearm close to his chest as he walked. "No, it isn't. We're not going back to the mainland tonight, it's too late for that."

"So we're just taking a constitutional?" Her face, lit from the side by the torch Ravi carried, was young and smoothed free of all worry. They passed a gaggle of *mankuse* who were probably still navigating home from the first meal hours ago, from the way they stumbled into ditches and clutched each other's arms for support.

"Basha Falaka!" they cried. One called out, "You have melded the bond we had thought broken with the church!"

Ravi laughed. "Ah, you're just happy because your belly is full."

Another protested, "No, tomorrow we will honor the Emperor's request, and pay him tribute. Come see us, and we will pay you many dollars."

"Then you will leave us in peace again!"

They were already well past the oiled monks then, and Ravi

finally answered Delphine's question. "For now. But I have a welcoming lodge for us to sleep in. Don't worry," he said quickly, anticipating her distress. "There are separate apartments for us."

"But I wasn't—"

"Please finish telling me your story."

"Story?"

"You left off telling me how you and your brother fared after your parents' death. You said you were popular in the community, and eventually . . . There you broke off." He remembered exactly how she was sitting when she had started telling him the story, and how Abou had attempted to intrude with his giant *wancha* horn.

"Oh! Eventually there was an older man, a successful merchant, who took an interest in us, and he was the one who paid for me to enroll at Syracuse."

"Ah, that's nice," Ravi said automatically. Something about it seemed wrong, perhaps her nonchalant manner. "And how old were you when this fellow 'took an interest'?"

She answered just as breezily. "Oh, let's see. Zachary was thirteen, so that would have made me twelve."

Ravi threw away her arm. "He only waited two years!" he bellowed.

Delphine stopped walking and stared at him with round eyes. "Ravi? What's wrong?"

Wiping his face with his hand, Ravi realized he was acting rashly. The *arrack* did that to a man, made him draw the wrong conclusions, conclusions that were almost always sordid. He exhaled, and took her arm to walk once more. "Forgive me, my truth. It just seemed for a moment that—let's never mind. I'll tell you about my brother Edward."

The idea that he had a brother seemed to please her, for she fairly skipped next to him now. "Oh, you have a brother? Older or younger? How perfectly delicious!"

"Edward is two years younger. He looked up to me, but he couldn't escape our father's iron will, so instead of being booted from West Point like his genius older brother, he excelled, and went on to make Colonel in the Confederate Army of the Mississippi. Ah, just around this bend is our lodge."

"And Edward. Is he as splendidly handsome as you?"

Ravi thought. "It depends on what you see as handsome."

Delphine stopped walking, but Ravi continued, allowing her arm to slip away. He soon had to pivot on one bare heel to regard her.

He held the torch aloft. He'd never seen such a trusting, ingenuous woman whose heart was so wide open.

"I see *you*," she cried. "I see nothing but adoration in you, the quest for knowledge, the pithy wonder. I see a savagery in you that's only a mask for the pain you find no matter where you go, in all quarters of the world. I see a man of lofty bearing who is so exquisitely handsome his truth shatters the leaves and crickets into ten thousand bits of glass when we walk by, and you're so involved in your own thoughts you don't even notice."

Ravi found he was panting, though they hadn't been walking briskly. He lifted his free hand to her. "Come, my only truth. The lodge is right here."

She came with head down, as though sorry she'd made such an outburst.

❋ ❋ ❋

THE LODGE WAS AN INFIRM STONE building of larger dimensions than the banquet hall. There were turrets, and castellated battlements Delphine could see in the argent moonlight, as though the *mankuse* had imagined Vikings would attack them with flaming arrows from big canoes.

Ravi led her through knee-high dead grass to the open archway through which rain would have flooded in the rainy season.

Weeds grew between the cobblestones that lined a roofless inner atrium. Delphine couldn't imagine there were any sorts of beds here, but when Ravi strode to use his torch to light others that were placed in crannies in the stone walls, the courtyard lit up with a grandiose illumination, like a New York opera house. Plants grew from the walls, tumbling over the stones with finesse. Ravi placed his torch into a rut in the floor, and he looked at her from thirty feet away.

The courtyard matched the monumental bearing of such a man. Delphine felt life flooding through every vein in her body. She rose on her toes, and without willing it, she ran toward him. Lightly, as though her body were a fluttering *shamma*, and her fingers had feathers.

But when she reached him, she saw he was withdrawn, collected. So she stopped short.

"Ravi?"

Why was he breathing so heavily? "Your room is there," he said, pointing vaguely to the left.

"Yes, all right."

He took three strides close to her. "I only ask one thing, my Queen of Heaven."

Her voice was a squeak. "Yes?"

"I agree to sleep here with you tonight in separate rooms. You have to only promise me one thing. Take nothing without asking my permission, and I'll take nothing from you by force."

Delphine looked from side to side. What was there to take? "Certainly. Shall I show myself to my room?"

This seemed to confuse Ravi, for he stepped up to her. He regarded her with head slightly cocked, at last bending down to press his sensual mouth to hers.

She chewed languidly at his mouth. Her hands wound around

the back of his muscular neck, and she pulled herself close to his strapping frame. Among all of the banqueters, they alone had emerged unsullied from the carnage and, although there were some bloodstains adorning the front of Ravi's *shamma*, Delphine had no hesitation in plastering her bosom to his chest. When she lifted a foot and snuck it around his Achilles' tendon, she felt the swelling span of his erection against her belly, and an intense wave of lust washed over her, weakening her legs.

He bent at the knees and swung his hips into her, lifting her a bit and making her weightless as an angel. But he broke the kiss, and withdrew to look quizzically at her.

"Delphine. I've got an insane thirst for you. But we have to retire now."

Delphine frowned. "I was hoping you'd demonstrate to me why I am called Queen of Heaven."

His eyes sliding shut, Ravi groaned, a deep shudder that vibrated through his chest. Was it such a repellant idea? Delphine began to worry. Surely they were well acquainted with each other, and surely they had already committed several such indecent acts upon each other.

He released her, and took several steps back. "There are candles in your apartment—take this torch."

That was it, then! Delphine's face warmed with shame, and she couldn't face him as she accepted the torch.

Her chamber was a large breezy stone room with an *alga* heaped with clean dry counterpanes and pillows, as she was accustomed to at home.

"Home!" She scoffed at the word her brain had utilized. Placing the torch in a niche in the wall, she whispered furiously to herself. "Why do I call that place a home? I have no home! My last home vanished when I was ten. To think! He almost succeeded in getting me to tell him about Mr. Oliver!" She fussed about as she removed her outer calico shirt, disgusted to remember that underneath she wore the *choli* and *sari*. "Jonathan Oliver, intellectual Transcendentalist, and wealthy man of means! I need never tell Ravi about my humiliation—why, he has no desire to take me now, think how much more undesirable I'd be if he knew about that."

Furiously kicking off the slippers, Delphine collapsed onto the *alga*. She'd decided to sleep in the Hindoo outfit, just in case someone set fire to the building and she needed to run out.

She continued muttering to herself. "He has no desire for me. Perhaps he's afraid of pregnancy. Perhaps I should have told him that I'm barren. Oh, he probably *wants* a passel of brats running about!"

But at last, due to the exertions of the day, she did drift away into a light slumber, lulled by the snorting of the river cows, and a lovely orchestra of cicadas outside the window.

Awakening Saint Michael only knew how many hours later, Delphine was wracked with a gripping thirst. All of that pepper sauce had finally taken its ultimate toll; her throat was so dry she couldn't even swallow. She tossed about for awhile, unwilling to accept this torture, and hoping she'd return to sleep, but at length she bolted upright and flung back the covers.

Sliding on the elf's shoes, Delphine used the torch to light a candle, and she went into the atrium in search of water. She purposely avoided Ravinger's apartment, but she knew if this building had been set up as a lodge, there must at least be water for washing somewhere.

One room was another unoccupied bed chamber. Another looked to be a prayer room. In the third room off the courtyard, Delphine struck the mother lode. Here, on a high shelf to keep it away from wild creatures, was a plate of *teff* bread, a pot of butter, and a gloriously cool jug of water. Conveniently, a couple of *wanchas* were on the shelf. Eagerly lifting the heavy urn and one of the horns, with difficulty she bent at the waist and poured the water.

"Hmm." Now she was standing with two delicately balanced vessels. She couldn't leap high enough to replace the jug on the shelf, so she again struggled, bending at the knees, to let the heavy clay container slide to the floor with a dull thud, sloshing the water around.

She had just straightened her spine and was lifting the delicious horn of water to her lips when she heard movement behind her, as though distantly rustled curtains moved by a passing lion.

Spinning, she jerked the horn of water so suddenly that half of it spilled onto the ground. "*Ravi*."

His mouth betrayed no shadow of a smile. He stood almost entirely in buff, draped only in the loose, slightly bloodstained *shamma*. It lay over one shoulder, the other shoulder bare to the torch and moonlight, the deltoid furrow so muscular it stood out in sharp relief. Delphine was uneasily aware that his gloriously shaped legs were bare, and she didn't dare lower her eyes. "I told you not to take anything."

Delphine attempted a giggle. "Well. I hardly think you'd deny me a *wancha* of water, Ravi." She started lifting the horn to her mouth, but her arm was trembling so, she dropped it to her side. "Like water to a thirsty woman . . ."

As he stepped forward, the cotton material of the *shamma* slid lower to reveal the heavenly plane of his pectoral. Delphine's eyes and hand holding the horn dropped accordingly. "I wouldn't take anything of yours by force, but you took something of mine. Drink," he commanded her, lifting up a graceful arm.

He held her by the elbow to enable her shaking arm to bring the horn to her mouth. The water tasted good, and at first she swallowed timidly, then finally, lustily, with closed eyes.

He seemed pleased she'd drained the horn. He took it from

her and, without looking, replaced it on the high shelf. "Solomon gave to Sheba all her desires, whatever she asked."

"Whatever I ask? I don't think you're capable of giving me all that I ask, Ravi."

He circled around her, sleek and refined like the vigorous lion. "And how do you know that?"

She lifted her chin. "Because I ask so much."

Delphine had to pivot on one foot to keep her eyes on him. The cotton slipped farther down his chest, until it hung about his wrists and hips, the lambent firelight playing across the panoply of his torso. "I think you don't ask enough." He recited with his eyes afire. " 'A woman of such splendid beauty has come to me from the ends of the Earth'."

Delphine felt the play of a smile across her mouth, and she lifted a beseeching hand to him. She knew the story of Makeda and Solomon, read to her by Tewodros from the Kebra Negast, the Glory of Kings. " 'It's a true report I heard in my land of your acts and your wisdom. I didn't believe it until I came and my eyes saw it'."

Standing still at last, Ravi held a hand out to her. "Come."

Delphine hesitated. "If you will give me all my desires? I desire only *you*, Ravi. That's too much to ask, in this benighted land."

"What do I know?" he asked in a hushed voice.

She felt on the verge of a cliff—to fling herself over, or not? Her hand lifted, afraid to touch him. He was "a bad, bold bandit," as children in camp called him, possessed of a sinister face, a grand dimension to his bearing—when he stood beside other men, he dwarfed them with his brave, original character.

Her fingers touched his, and at once he grasped her hand, pulling her into the atrium still lit with torches. They spun about, watching each other intently. They twirled into a heavenly kiss that had Ravi pressing Delphine into a stone wall, cradling her jaw in his broad hand.

He seemed to be muttering in an ancient language as he gulped at her mouth, a guttural locution deep inside of his massive chest. She scrabbled her fingertips against the sleek hair of his chest, her fingers slipping over the lustrous surface of his pectorals. He bore her into the wall with his hips so that the head of his penis smeared against her hipbone, barely covered with the thin silk of the *sari*. He humped her dry in this manner, his costume all in folds about his naked hips, his snorting against the side of her face like a slathering animal she knew in her heart was a tame, purring lion.

She opened herself to him completely, allowing her thighs to part and be lifted, her feet leaving the flagstones, her slippers tottering from the tips of her toes.

His mouth traced a sucking path down the side of her bared throat. She thought she could understand some of his language, and it sounded distinctly Arabic.

This enflamed her further, and she clutched at his silken shoulders, warm from the torch fire. "Ah," she gasped. " 'Your wisdom and prosperity surpassed the fame which I heard. Happy are your men—' "

Her words were wrenched from her mouth by his forceful hauling of her from the wall. With his hands clasping her behind and cradling her to him, he lowered her slowly to the floor. A lion's fur slipped beneath her back as her fingers crept into the mass of braids behind his neck.

He kneeled tall before her. All her limbs were flung out like a wide river, willing to accept all. Panting with a ferocity that made every muscle in his formidable torso shiver, with a minute movement of his wrist the *shamma* fell. His impressive penis lunged, and Ravi tamed it, slithering his fingers around the magnificent elongation of it.

His voice was a deep mixture of Bostonian and Arabic

flavoring. "Ah, *el taleb*, forgive me."

Delphine lifted both ankles and entwined them around the back of his iliac crest, his hips so firmly cushioned with muscle one could almost do a dance on them.

He slid into her with a roaring, low groan that resonated throughout the stone chamber. At once, she was so alert that she could hear gleeful hyenas calling from another hillside monastery. All senses melded into one: his slick gluteus under her fingers, the rocking of his hips into her, how he abraded her insides—drenched as she was, as she hadn't been used in several years—the greenish hue of his forearm veins, like the sky before a storm, the pepper smell of his throat.

How she never wanted it to end. So glorious, being taken on a silky animal's fur like this! She urged him on with her hips in the air, the imposing bulk of his penis filling her to her navel. He caved down over her, covering her with his splendid torso, and he came at once, growling a strangled lexicon into the pit of her throat, creating humid drips of moisture that rolled over her shoulder.

How did I ever forget how this was, she thought, gripping him fast to her.

Her quim clutched at his thick penis. She bucked at him, wanting every atom of him. She admired the way he heaved and panted, yet kept his torso above her by leaning on his elbows.

He breathed, "Forgive me, for coming so fast."

So glorious, a man of his bearing and substance, turned into such a quivering mass of jelly between her thighs. She placed sucking kisses on the corners of his mouth. "Happy are your men, who stand continually before you, and hear your wisdom."

He laughed, and with his hand smeared her hair back from her forehead. He lowered his mouth to her brow and breathed. "If you think it wise, then it's wise, my Queen . . . of Heaven." He whispered again, "*Alokom*. What do I know?"

She pinched his nipple between her fingertips, and he lurched inside of her with a gasp. She sucked noisily on his ear, like the pigs at the banquet trough. "If you rest," she whispered, "can you demonstrate the position of my namesake?"

Ravi smiled against her forehead. "We just did."

Delphine stilled. "That . . . that was it? That was the Queen of Heaven for men who are tremendously endowed?"

Ravi laughed harder. "I'm sorry if you were expecting something involving saddles or stirrups."

Raising herself on her elbows and shouldering the man's torso off her, Delphine frowned. "Well if you were thinking to spare my delicate constitution, I pray bid you not to bother!" Pushing him off her completely, she got to her knees, smoothing the *sari* down over her thighs. "I know Diana was the Queen of Heaven." She pointed to the open sky above without looking at it, as Ravi was a most heartwarming sight nearly nude as he was, leaning back on one elbow and regarding her with amusement. Without the silver *betoa* cuff, and of course he'd never worn a *mateb*, there was nothing to distract from his fine, sun-browned form. The merest shred of a *shamma* lay across his loins, the strapping legs so nicely molded. "I know she was the goddess of the hunt—"

"Come." Ravi lifted his chin. "Don't break the loving congress."

"—and she led people hunting through the night skies, so she was strong and powerful and can certainly take a man of such . . . such . . ."

"Solomonic proportions?"

Delphine exhaled. "Precisely." Turning, she crawled on all fours across the lion's fur, in the hopes that by the time she returned from getting her drink of water, Ravinger would have renewed zest, but before she could reach the paw of the lion and could rise, he leaped upon her from behind.

With both his sturdy arms about her, she couldn't move an inch, and she quickly relaxed into his touch. Hastily yanking down the bodice of her *choli* that had remained undisturbed until now, Delphine gasped to feel her breasts sway in the air. Barely grazing the tip of her hardened nipple with a fingernail he kept curiously long, he placed a necklace of jewel kisses to her shoulder and neck. "Follow me, and I'll complete your instruction, for you have loved wisdom, and you will dwell with me until the end, and forever."

Delphine knew that Sheba didn't stay with Solomon—she had to return to Abyssinia to be delivered of Menelik—but she wasn't much concerned about that aspect of the story, for his other hand trailed downward to gather her *sari* as he slid his erect penis between her thighs. She leaned back into him, sighing a delighted purr, locking her thighs tightly about his erection. "I would love to dwell *here* . . . until the end." Sliding her hand lower, she captured the head of his penis and pressed it to her slick labia, exciting him with a gently swinging motion of her hand and hips.

But he'd have none of that, for he tore her hand away, and pressed the delicious tip of his phallus deeper between her thighs. With a slight arch of her spine, she lifted her behind to him, and was impaled on the admirable length of him.

"Oh!" she gasped. "By the power of my creator!" Flinging her arms up behind her, she grasped him around the back of the neck, bowing into an impossible flexure.

Ravi wedged himself up against the mound of her womb, seemingly content to hold himself there as he rubbed her engorged clitoris between his skilful forefinger and thumb. She clutched his penis with her inner muscles, enraptured that she could draw out a tortured "*Isgyoh!*" from him before he bore down with ferocity on her clitoris, rubbing her into a lather that had her uttering high, mousy squeaks in the pit of her throat. He gently swiveled his hips so she felt the twitching of his fat penis inside her. If only there were a looking-glass on the wall! She would have delighted to see the muscular ripple of his haunches as he humped her like such a potent satyr.

Oh Lord, I should not have bragged to him about my huntress' prowess . . . He is going to completely split me from stem to stern.

But as his fingers jounced her so precisely, her pelvis was flooded with a tense relaxation, as though he stimulated her very blood and it all went rushing to her hips, consuming all keenness from her brain. She hung from his neck like a vine from a tree, her inner muscles sucking on his member as he tremulously rocked her back and forth.

Ah, his strength, his virility. I'll be washed completely from the face of the planet with the might of his love. I can't be released!

Then, all at once, she was released.

Overwhelming contractions raced down the length of her channel at the moment Ravi's penis erupted. In one of the first mighty spasms, she dove forward onto all fours and remained there.

It must have been many minutes later when she managed to gulp enough air to resuscitate her blood-starved brain. Ravi covered her like a stallion, embedded deep inside her, twitching and gasping, but he held her off the ground with his free arm, as though saving a drowning goat from a swollen river.

It was too much. She had never been so swept away by the spirit of a man, by the primitive hunger of his masculinity. Without thought to form or manners, she crawled forward on all fours until she was free of his clutches, panting and gasping.

The cold flagstones on her palms and knees woke her a little. She collapsed to one side, flattening her flank against the chilly stone, her bedraggled hair falling like creepers about her numb face. Raising one trembling arm, she felt her breastbone, flushed and sweaty, hot as though an oven burned within. What was happening to her? She was falling apart at a fundamental cellular level. She shook her other arm, and drips of sweat sprayed from her fingertips into the moonlight like a hundred falling stars. Where was her soul going?

He panted behind her. It took her more long moments to look over her shoulder.

He sat back, hands on knees like a proper schoolboy awaiting instruction. His lovely fleshy chest heaved with ripples; the sight warmed her heart and made her feel of this world again. And he had that devilish cast to his eyes.

"A woman never disregards a man kneeling."

The laughter that burbled out of her gut was refreshing, bringing her down to the ground again. She regarded him with affectionate eyes. "How is it, Ravi . . . Every word from your mouth . . . is something completely original."

When he laughed heartily, it was too much for her wrenched heart to take, and she had to stare at the flagstones. She was too weak to stand.

"When the heart overflows, it comes out through the mouth." He got to his feet. His lovely long, sun-browned fingers dallied on her shoulder. "Come," he said.

She allowed him to raise her up, and they went to the storeroom where the jug of water was on the shelf. He poured her a *wancha* of water, tossing the jug back onto the shelf effortlessly.

She drank deeply from the horn, then they walked back into the moonlit atrium. Scooping up the lion's skin, Ravi went about snuffing out torches until he held just a candle, and led Delphine into his chamber. The *alga* was too narrow for two people, so he heaped all of the bedclothes on the stone floor atop the lion's skin, and they slipped between them, Delphine's backside bundled to Ravi's crotch.

He murmured, ". . . finds a solace for his weary round in gentle ripples that are but a warm caress . . ."

She knew it was happening—she was a goner in her desire for him. It wouldn't stop, or abate, and no amount of reasoning with herself could talk her out of it.

CHAPTER TWENTY-ONE
THE SHELTERING CRADLE

Mesraha Island, Near Qorata

WHEN RAVINGER HEARD THAT TEWODROS WAS onshore by the boat-building enterprise, he immediately paddled out from Mesraha, Delphine and Abou going before him. He landed the little canoe at the same time as an important *mankuse*, one who had helped him the day before with the banquet, and who probably still had a brick in his *timkin* from all the imbibing.

Tewodros seemed in a jovial mood, Misha standing by monitoring the scene. The Emperor paced with hands behind his back, and was ecstatic when he saw Ravi.

"Likamaquas! How was your banquet?" he asked slyly in a low voice. "I trust the Empress Makeda was shown a happy time?"

Ravi managed to smile. "I'd like to think so. I think it all went very well. Here, this is the *mankuse* who helped me yesterday with the finest banquet Mesraha has ever seen." He bade the monk step forward, noting the instant distasteful curl to Tewodros's upper lip. "He wishes to pay half of all Maria Theresa dollars in their treasury, as tribute to our empire."

Regarding the monk with narrowed eyes, Tewodros nodded minutely. "Yes. But sometimes I cannot obtain grain for the love of God. We must have all of your grain."

Ravi could see the monk was shaking, so he answered for him. "I'm sure he'd be willing to give what little grain remains after our joyous feast yesterday."

The monk nodded his head. "Yes, grain . . ."

"All right. Go back to your island and get all the grain and tribute ready for us. We will not bother your men if you just bring those things. Go, go!" The Emperor waved the trembling fellow away. "Now who is left on the island? The Kanyazmach?"

"Yes, he's got a company of men still stumbling about looking for their *shotels*."

"Fine, that will be enough men."

Dismissed, Ravi walked rapidly to where Walde Nebra tended his mule. He yanked a field-glass from the saddlebag and observed the island as Misha approached him.

"Likamaquas," Misha said formally. "I hope you adhered to Bob's rules regarding the surgeon."

Ravi walked around the other side of the mule so no one would see him looking through the field-glass. "Of course," Ravi breathed. Something disturbed him. "He's my master, why would I not adhere to his rules?"

"And if you did not, I certainly don't wish to hear about it. But Dejazmach Deris said you took her to the old meeting hall last night after the banquet, and someone else saw you both leaving it this morning."

From a westerly spit of land on Mesraha, Ravi saw a group of men in ochre robes scrambling for *tankwas*. "Yes, that's quite true, Misha. It's sometimes advisable to sleep, if one wishes to be refreshed, and to continue one's master's work the next day." When the monks shoved off from land, it was clear they were heading directly toward the Zage Peninsula. They should have departed from the other side of the island, where no one could spy them. Sighing, Ravi lowered his glass.

"Well, I certainly don't wish to hear about it," Misha repeated. Ravi looked down at him. Perhaps Misha was trying to tell him he really *did* wish to hear about it? "I have no wish—"

"Likamaquas!" Tewodros roared, in a terrible rage.

Ravi emerged from behind the mule, and saw Tewodros storming toward him, his feet soundless on the sandy beach, all men around them frozen in strange comical attitudes of boat-building, bodies twisted at bizarre angles. "Do you see those sons of Mohammedan mothers attempting to escape? Fire!"

Ravi remained placid. "None of my rifles has a range that far."

In times like this, Tewodros's eyes spewed fire. One could see the air before them shimmer in the heat that was pouring forth. "No, you *dadab!* You have the mortars—use them!"

Dadab? Ravi stepped so close to the Emperor he could breathe down on his forehead from his superior height. Curling his upper lip in imitation of his master's, he whispered malevolently, *"Dadab?"*

For an instant, Tewodros pressed his eyes together, perhaps in the only version of apology he was able to muster. "Fire the mortars," he shouted, much quieter.

Ravi walked over to the men who guarded the valuable artillery and gave them half-hearted orders to fire. The shells fell far short of their mark, and as the mortar hadn't been fastened, it kicked a few feet out of its carriage.

"Ravi!" It was that ineradicable pest Misha. "You've got to come, Tewodros is sending men to the island and I don't think it bodes very well!"

Ravi turned to see a retinue of wide-eyed men behind Misha, anxiously awaiting an order, so he waved a relaxed arm at them. "Go. Go. Why don't you go too, Misha? It'll give you a chance to distinguish yourself."

As expected, Misha's face crumpled. "I'm not so sure."

"Why not?"

"Aw, you know I'm not a very good aim, Rav! I'm a chef! Those . . . those . . ."

"Those *mankuse*? Will beat you to a jelly, jam you into a cocked hat, and fling you into the middle of next week?"

Misha laughed thinly. "Of course not, Rav! Why, they're just . . ."

"Monks?" Ravi motioned for Walde Nebra. "Did those men bring back my Enfields? Good, bring one of them." To prove it was loaded, he ran the ramrod down the barrel, then shoved the gun at Misha. "Here, my good Azmach. With this, you're safe from those marauding monks!"

Misha set off uncertainly.

Ravi watched the island drama with awed detachment, as though at a spiritualist séance watching disembodied trumpets and accordions floating about the room playing. More shots were fired, and puffs of smoke appeared spouting through the heavy tree canopy. Perhaps he was just too weary, or knew he could do nothing, but he barely breathed for a long while. It was only when the puffs billowed into clouds and it became apparent some structures were on fire that Ravi moved.

"I should get over there," he told Walde Nebra indifferently. "I know I can no longer stop this bloodshed, but maybe I can prevent a few men from drilling everyone in sight."

He paddled off in a *tankwa*. He was so fatigued by the ceaseless murder, he felt as though he could sleep for two weeks.

Nearing Mesraha, *tankwas* laden with bags of grain, gold crosses, and gilt manuscripts were passing him heading back. He had barely touched land when two fellows laboring with a cumbersome *manbara tabot* nearly pasted him flat in their efforts to steal his boat. He didn't bother telling them that the boat would sink if they tried to take the *manbara tabot*.

The church where he'd reposed yesterday awaiting Delphine was afire. Ravi knew why he didn't see any monks rushing about. They had all been crushed inside the church, where soldiers leaned against the smoldering doors, as though crusty blackened skeletons might be trying to make a break for the lake. Ravi knew well the stench of burnt flesh. It was Tewodros's favorite method of eliminating a lot of people fast without wasting bullets, and the crisp, sulfurous stink seeped into Ravi's sinuses.

Some of the men who had forced the monks into that unholy inferno had been the same who had supped with them at the banquet last night. Now the soldiers grinned and waved at Ravi, standing atop hacked-off hands and feet, as though expecting a dessert course to follow their performance. Ravi wanted to breathe, for he needed air in his exhausted brain, so he walked swiftly past the church.

The lodge where he'd slept with Delphine hadn't been molested much. There wasn't a thatched roof, and the hall was made of stone, so it was no good for the army's pillaging purposes, though Ravi saw that someone had taken the remaining *teff* bread from the shelf on the wall.

He stepped back inside the inner courtyard and put his hands on his hips. Looking toward the heavens, he tried to remember how brilliant the night sky had looked the night before, how sheltering and benign its cradle. How many thousands of nights he'd spent navigating by the stars that he'd come to rely on their direction. He was by far a man not to curse *budas*, heavens, or gods, but in this moment Ravi wished there were a power greater than the tangible cosmos to rail against. Perhaps this Father, Son, and Holy Ghost might suffice.

He was turning to leave the courtyard when a rickety and smoke-stained monk sprang from one of the outer rooms—the room where Ravi had slept with Delphine.

"*You!*" the benighted fellow pointed. "You told us that we'd be safe! Look what's happened! I would get my brothers to kill you, if only I had any brothers left!"

Ravi raised two calming hands. "Look, father. I was fooled just as you were. I had no knowledge beforehand this would happen."

"Oh yes you did! You're the Likamaquas! You're the one who rides into battle dressed as that devil from hell to spare him from the bullets of his enemies! He calls himself the Slave of Christ, yet he banishes us all into perdition! You're the one who shelters him from the spears of his enemies!"

Ravi didn't know what to say, and it was a good thing, for the elderly monk was already running out of steam. He staggered toward Ravi, and the closer he got, the more his accusatory hand wavered and fell, as though Ravi were sucking out all of his blood's force.

They finally looked at each other like two combatants with no more ammunition, prepared to throw their empty weapons at each other.

At last, just as the man collapsed forward like a sack of clothing, Ravi croaked out "Father."

Ravi easily caught the bony man and set him back against the wall. Taking everything from his own *zenar*, which at the moment wasn't much, he dropped the dollars into the man's lap and backed away slowly. He wanted nothing more than to be rid of this place.

He found himself running from the lodge. He ran like greased lightning until he reached the burned-out church. He slowed down to a jog, for he didn't wish to appear to be running away from anything.

CHAPTER TWENTY-TWO
THE WONDERFUL MARCH

September 22, 1867

RAVI WAS PROUD TO LEAD A raid in which they gained eighty thousand head of cattle. As the entire camp gorged on *brundo* and *tibs*, the joy of this rare moment of satiety was ruined when Tewodros began the slaughter of all the beeves. There was a prophecy, he shouted at the soldiers as they leaped over the cliff to execute his wishes. "A king will seize a large amount of cattle, peasants will come and beg him to return them. The king will agree, and afterwards die." It was the blond-eyed Frankish bird who had informed Tewodros of this insane prophecy.

Ravi was at Gaffat the day Tewodros decreed that Kaspar's mortar Sebastopol was fit for travel. The Europeans were nervous, trembling in their bare feet, as the last test at casting the behemoth mortar had failed. Ravi had seen that the failure was due to rainwater in the mould, so he'd commanded a trench dug for the rain to be conveyed to a drain down the hill, and the mould stayed tight and dry. The Emperor was delighted, and gave more red silk *kamis* shirts to all the Europeans, and had Ravi make preparations for hauling the great mortar up to Magdala.

As Ravi had invited Kaspar down to Debra Tabor for dinner, they chose to walk before their mules, preferring to savor the triumph of the moment. Waldmeier, Zander, and Flad had indicated they also wished to be invited, but Ravi wanted to talk alone with the good deacon. Kaspar swilled from a *wancha* of *arrack* the entire while, reminding Ravi pleasantly of the old days.

"Do you remember that time," Ravi said, already laughing at the memory, "in Gojam when that female boar chased you through the bush?"

"*Ach!*" cried Kaspar, smiting his forehead with the back of his hand. "I killed her husband—or her brother, as may be the case—and I clubbed her with the butt of my rifle!"

"Yes, she didn't want to ruin your rifle, so she ran within two feet of you and dashed her nose into the sand . . ."

"*Ach!* She dashed her snout to such an extent that I was covered head to toe with dust—just like one of those Coptic mummies! Captain Howland . . ." Kaspar appeared to drift off into reverie. "We have had a good time here in the black highlands, have we not?"

"So you chose to run, and with her tusks she speared you in—"

Kaspar held up a warning forefinger. "Never a good part where it is respectable to show a scar!" Swigging from the horn, he meandered silently down the worn footpath, his threadbare brogans clopping against his bare feet, his socks having been given to a woman who unraveled the silk to embroider shirts with.

At length Ravi's chuckles faded away, and he cleared his throat. "Kaspar. I need to approach you about leaving this place."

He had hoped the missionary would not cry aloud in alarm. He was heartened when Kaspar merely looked about the landscape in alert surprise, as though a hare whispered his name. "You know, Captain, I cannot escape while the Reverend Stern is in prison."

"Is that still your definite standpoint, then?"

They were almost to Ravi's tent now, the red silk of his pavilion positioned upon a prominent hillock so he could observe most of the doings of the encampment. Walde Nebra was there, ordering about the horse groom, the wood-cutter, and grass-cutters, taking charge as he paced on the great carpet rolled out before the tent.

Kaspar paused, his mule stopping too, as they'd been melded together for the better part of twelve years and did everything in tandem. For the first time that Ravi could recall, the deacon's impudent face turned to Ravi, and he looked the taller man in the eye. "I'd have to say yes, it is, Captain." He sighed deeply. "I have no family, no one to await my homecoming—unless you took me to America with you! But alas, I do not believe you wish me dragging along on your braces everywhere you go. Abyssinia, and Reverend Stern, is my home. I cannot leave while he still molders in his fetters in Magdala. He is a great man, Captain. I would never rest had I abandoned him. He saved me from the street, when I had no home, in Stuttgart."

Ravi nodded. "And you're to wed Louisa Bell soon. You should join her in Magdala, and marry her in the church."

Kaspar turned his head away. "*Ach!* We will be in Magdala soon enough, Howland! There is no rush to embalm our spirits in the barbarian climate of that bastion. I have heard that Woizero Bell is still stricken with the *buda*, or now it appears it may be more of a *zar* . . ."

The two men continued down the hill. Ravi settled the deacon in front of the tent with one of the larger *barrilyes* of *arrack*, and he caught ahold of Misha's arm as the Azmach showed the wood-cutter how to stack wood in the Ukraine. Such were the topics of vast interest in Abyssinia.

"No! You see, if you do not slightly turn the logs, then the rain—"

"Mikhail, I need to speak with you. Let's go smoke our pipes over by the big rock."

Misha followed, huffing and puffing with dismay that the wood-cutter had insisted upon stacking his wood in the incorrect, unscientific manner. They settled themselves down on the mossy rocks, and Misha said, "Rav. Delphine came over, wanting to know if we had enough chickens for the stew, because her cook found one. Well, it was sort of buried underneath a—"

"Misha." Ravi knew that when he used this resonating tone, everyone around him shut up. "I'm here to discuss escape." He put out a calming hand. "I know this isn't your favorite topic. But the King of Kings has just approved Sebastopol for movement onto the road tomorrow morning, and I see a great stretch of desolation in front of us if someone doesn't make a move."

Misha's reaction was almost as prompt as Kaspar's. "No. No, Rav, no."

"No?"

"No," Misha shouted quietly. "There is no way of escape from this place! You know as well as anyone all the roads are cut off by the rebels, and just *think* if they caught ahold of the Likamaquas of Tewodros, why, the torture would never end! No, Rav, no!" He seemed to become more heated the more he thought upon the subject. "Do you want to wind up with one ear cut off one night, the other ear the other night, then the next day one thumb, the next day—"

"Well, if presented with the option, *no!*" Ravi yelled. "But that wasn't exactly what I had in mind, my cowardly yellow buddy! Torture and dismemberment aren't in the plan, pal!"

Misha flung his arms about with abandon. "Oh, I suppose then you're planning on a certain 'magic rug' like in your Hindoo stories to come and carry you off so you can sail up the Red Sea, and—"

That was enough. Ravi could see where this was heading, and his disgust knew no bounds. He, too, stood, angrily tamping out his pipe against the palm of his hand. "*No!* That is not the plan at all, Mikhail Vasiliev!" Having finally succeeded in getting the thin man to button up, Ravi stood so that he loomed over him. "Don't worry. I can see you're happy in your complacent existence, toiling for the Wild Boar of Ethiopia. If I decide to carry off my plan, I won't compromise you by letting you know."

Misha's face crumbled. "Ah, now, Rav, you don't have to be like that!"

Having seen Delphine greeting Kaspar before the entrance to his tent, Ravi went down the rise.

"Queen of Heaven, I heard you found a chicken underneath a rock? Come inside."

"It wasn't quite under a rock . . ." Delphine ducked inside the flap Ravi held open for her. "It was more like huddled inside a small cavern. Rather bony and beastly, but the best offering I could bring to your stewpot today—Oh!"

Delphine squealed when, without preliminaries, Ravi enwrapped her in his arms and walked backward with her toward his *alga*. "Now. I've promised you I'd get you out of this place, and I've got a plan." He allowed himself to fall onto the couch slowly, so as not to muss the woman, and they lay side by side.

He pressed an importuning finger to her lips as he quietly spoke. "I make sure our friend Bob is good and elevated one night. Walde Nebra has a friend with a wife he wishes to dispose of—we dress her as you, and put her in your bed, to delay the realization that you're gone. We make our escape with you clad as a Galla slave I'm trading to some Mussulmen in Gondar. We ride hard and fast all the way to Gondar, where of course we have many friends. It's no secret that I'm the second most hated man in Abyssinia after the Emperor, but I do have friends I've done favors for in the past, say refrained from murdering them when I was supposed to, and—" Why was she laughing? Ravi raised himself on one elbow and looked down at her. "We have many supporters in Gondar, after it was seen by many that I was against what Bob did, and indeed tried to spare the women who were being blown out in the streets, and chased after Bob's men, and—My truth! Why are you laughing?"

Now Delphine got up on her elbow. She wasn't laughing exactly, but had a mildly condescending grin on her face that annoyed him all to pieces. When she reached her graceful hand to his face and caressed him, it felt as though she berated a child. "My *el besiss*. It isn't your plan that I doubt! I have the utmost faith in any plan that you might concoct."

She preferred to be silent then, as though her warm, amused gaze would answer all of Ravi's questions. He snorted. "What is it, then? I have the strangely foreboding feeling that you aren't in agreement with the plan."

She sat upright, with legs crossed in the Plains Indian style. "You're right; I can't go along with the plan, Captain. The most important reason is the other captives. Why, just think of how ill-treated they would be when Bob retaliates, and uses them as his whipping post! Think of poor Mr. and Mrs. Flad, Mr. and Mrs. Rosenthal, not to speak of that poor Cameron, who after all is a servant to his Queen, and Rassam, and my dear Doctor Blanc! I couldn't bear the thought that they were bring tortured just because you and I decided to go 'purser rigged and parish damned'!"

In a cloud of anger, Ravi got to his feet and headed straight for the brandy. He kept his back to the woman as he poured his *barrilye* of liquor. He held the bottle out at arm's length and huffed at the tent wall. "Doctor Chambliss!" Twirling, he faced her. "I have just offered you the only opportunity you're going to get before we dump that monstrous lump of metal that Kaspar pretended to design onto a carriage and brutally haul it a hundred miles up the sheer cliffs to Magdala! Every single damned Gaffat person is coming with us; there won't be a free *ferenje* in the entire country!

And you tell me you're more concerned with the welfare of a lot of simpering missionaries who grumble the livelong night about not having enough *vegetables* to eat?"

She rose sinuously from the bed. The strength in her fiery gaze cowed him, and he shrank back a few inches from her body. "Ravi. Those people are more your friends than mine. You've been with them for ten years. Yet I find it within myself to feel anxious for them, to wonder what might happen were we to leave! Dare I say that I think you're more upset because I scoffed at your plan?"

Ravi snorted down at her, but she was too close to him, and this made him nervous, so he broke away and paced the length of the tent, from his desk back to his wardrobe of hanging *shammas* and lions' skins. He had to breathe many large breaths before he was able to say to a shield hanging on the wall, "Perhaps I am callous, after ten years of living with murder and death as my close neighbor. Living in this festering sewer where at every turn your friends are being popped off, that's bound to happen. You're right; I'm a ruthless savage, exactly like my mentor."

"Captain." Ravi saw that her eyes were misted; he knew she didn't cry for him. "You're not ruthless, and neither is the Tewodros. I've seen aspects of him full of love and consideration, when he takes a child on his knee—"

"After he's murdered the father!"

She only shouted louder. "—aspects that make me understand how you loved him years ago! He's not a thorough tyrant, he's a human with shortcomings and flaws—"

Ravi snarled down at her. "*Shortcomings? Flaws?* I can't believe what I'm hearing! 'Oh, so sorry to have thrown your grandparents over that cliff, I was just in a foul frame because I was constipated; let's go have a horn of *arrack*'?" Ravi strode to the far end of the tent, burning with rage. "You're starting to sound like Azmach Michael."

"No, no, Ravi, it's not like that. Of course I deplore the murder! I'm saying that he—Bob—isn't so thoroughly evil, just as you aren't so heartless and cold, and I've seen—"

"You're sweet on him, then."

There was a silence. "Excuse me?"

Ravi walked forward to face her down. "You're sweet on him. You can't leave him. That's why you dropped to your knees begging him not to slaughter the cows." He shook his head as though he pitied her. "See how much good it did."

"*What?* Sweet on . . . ? Why, I've never heard anything so absurd! I begged him not to slaughter the cows because I thought I might have some power over him, and given my druthers I'd prefer not to see eighty thousand beeves gone to waste, that's why!"

Ravi sat on the camp chair before his desk, his forehead pressed to his palm. He had just been denied three times—Kaspar, Misha, and now Delphine—when he was only trying to save their lives. Something was forebodingly biblical about this, but Ravi didn't care what it was, he just wanted to get drunk. He jumped when Delphine put her warm hand on his shoulder.

"*El besiss.*" She bent to kiss the shoulder she had always seemed to love so much. "There is only one man I'm sweet on. I would follow you to the ends of the Earth."

Ravi sighed, still staring at his manuscript on the desk. "But you won't go to Gondar with me."

Wrapping her arms around his chest, she rubbed her face against his neck. "I can't be the cause of our friends being tortured or killed."

Raising his hands, Ravi took her arms from about his person. He turned and looked up at her. "Delphine. We're going to Magdala. We're leaving when the carpenters build the wagons for Sebastopol. And everyone who is too timid, complacent, or cowardly to escape is going to die anyway."

She shrugged. "There's a chance the British will come. I've heard that Merewether has been reconnoitering the Red Sea for a landing place, and they're using troops from India. Why, orders have been given in London for war."

"And you're pinning your life on that."

She nodded, a barely perceptible motion of her head. "It's our only hope."

Sighing deeply, Ravi threaded his fingers together at the back of his neck and looked up at the woman. All that she had accomplished—the medical degree, the Congressional Medal, thousands of lives saved in America and Abyssinia—she was tossing to a certain doom because she didn't want to risk her friends being beaten! "You don't know what Magdala is like. You look around and see only sky, because you're up above the world. No mountains, no scenery, no beauty—the fortress walls block all that out."

Delphine sat on his lap and pressed his stubbled face with the back of her calming hand. "I've been in worse places. 'This hell on Earth, where it takes seven of its occupants to make one shadow'."

Ravi risked asking her a question he'd wanted to know for months. "You were so terribly in love with your lover, the surgeon who died down the hallway from you and became a ghost?"

Her look became wistful. "Oh, terribly. It was the terrible sort of love where one thinks of the other at every possible second of the day, where one is so consumed by passion that all else takes on a dull unimportant cast, which in this case was a good thing. I couldn't face the death and disease that I had to wade through every day. Without Eugene by my side at the operating table— well, the operating *plank* I should say, we had boards stretched out on barrels—I could not have withstood the stench, the muck, the screams. But knowing Eugene was there and was suffering the same fate as I brought out a sort of integrity I never knew I had . . ."

"So. A 'terrible' sort of love that you would never want to repeat."

"Well, who knows if it would have been the same had we met across a ballroom? Anyway, I think one loves another . . . differently in every case, don't you? My love for Eugene could never be repeated. I clung to him so desperately that when he died, I . . . I died too, and I can never repeat that, Ravi, I cannot. I need to remain strong for all of my patients—for *you*, if you were to catch ill! I can't have the grumps, I have to stay festive, and what if Doctor Blanc were to fall ill, who would doctor the doctor?"

With that, she raised herself off his lap, and left the tent. *One loves another differently in every case . . .* Shaking himself as if to rid himself of his sudden blue funk, Ravi went to pour himself another brandy. *I can never repeat that.* Here he was, acting like a blushing youth, dying from want of a beautiful surgeon telling him she loved him!

"Doesn't she know," he whispered aloud, "that by consigning herself to this rathole . . . she's also dooming me?"

So they began the Wonderful March to the Magdala plateau.

CHAPTER TWENTY-THREE
RED SAILS

He had a dream that a wet warm mouth was sucking his cock.

It was such an arousing and erotic dream, almost better than waking life, he willed it to continue. The talented mouth teased the head of his cock with little calf's licks. Ravi groaned and wriggled his hips, and the mouth obliged by pressing licking kisses to his balls, delighted loving strokes that had his cock pulsating, straining with craving. Spreading his thighs, Ravi stretched and unfurled his spine, delighting in the midmorning silence of his tent dark as the storied realm of Pluto, and the exhaustion of incessant road-building that led to such rapturous and vivid dreams.

He'd had a dream that he and Delphine floated smoothly in an Arab *baggala*, a fantastic craft with a five-windowed stern, carved like a Portuguese caravel with lateen sails. They ate white radishes, and Ravi breathed in the crisp aroma of cloves, and he felt they were heading for the port of Sur in Muscat. The Suri on board made a distant racket, as though shut out by a gaseous wall—he could see them clearly clapping their huge hands and drumming, but their din was muted. Ravi showed Delphine the onshore coolies slaving beneath sacks of salt, stolidly brutish with dripping muscles against the ice-white membrane of sand.

They skimmed toward liberation, and his heart was as airy as sky when the dream shifted to this insouciant sucking, the hot, loving ministrations of an ardent mouth. The mouth drew on the entire length of his cock, urging the sperm up its length to spurt forth, and he was on the verge of erupting when a resonating moan vibrated the core of his prick, and he opened his eyes to the tent ceiling.

Isgyoh. *This was no dream. This was real.*

"My only truth, how did you get out?" He slipped his fingers into a halo of satiny curls. Not Delphine. There was no possibility of Delphine escaping her tent, with the eunuchs that still sat guard at night. An incubus? Ravi was confused. "Alitash?" Alitash had been grabbed by rebels as they traveled one night, not thirty feet behind Delphine.

The tongue laved him now in a frenzy, and for a brief moment he relaxed back onto the *alga* and the wooden pillow that kept his coiffure tidy. He allowed the mouth to sweep him into a lather of exquisite transport as he laid his thighs wide, exulting in the rapture that had him rotating his hips with lewd abandon. *Ah hell, who cares who it is? It's obviously a concubine or other who misses me terribly, and—*

No! He couldn't allow a concubine into his *arat!* What would Delphine think when she inevitably found out?

As much as it pained him—and it did hurt when he forcibly disengaged by shoving the concubine back from the shoulder, and his rigid phallus slapped up against his belly—Ravi could not do this. In Amharic he shouted quietly with what he hoped was disgust, though that was hard to muster in the situation. "You come to me while I sleep, hoping in my dreams I'll mistake you for my queen!"

"I . . ." the concubine whispered. "I . . ."

A strange foreign inflection to just that one syllable. As a student of two dozen languages, Ravi's ear was alert to such things, and he became uneasy. Shoving harder against the bare shoulder, he leaned on an elbow to fumble for the match safe with which to light the country lamp. "I must tell you," he muttered, hoping to regain his former regal bearing, "I'll have none of this being taken advantage of, and if I hear this story repeated anywhere near my queen, I'll have you wrapped in cowhide and thrown over—hey now, where do you think you're—"

Sprinting from the *arat* like a deer, Ravi stood between the concubine and the front tent flap. In a flash of the most grotesque and sickening realization of Ravi's robust life, Anatole Verlaine wept pitifully, soundlessly, as he extended his hands toward Ravi in supplication. Clad in a silk *shamma* of androgynous origin, he quietly cried in his stunted English, "Master Howland! You must forgive me! All the sins of my childhood and the stark puritanical ravings of my religious mother have—"

It was frightening how the rage took control of Ravi, like a gargantuan hand that impelled him. He closed the distance of ten feet between them with one giant stride, and had the perverse rat by the throat. He could have easily crushed the larynx with just one hand, that's how thin and sickly the poet had become, but for some reason he needed to hear what he said, so he eased off on the windpipe.

"I love you, Master Howland. You're a Knight Templar, so I knew you were like me. I know what the Knights were really about . . . You wanted me to come to you . . . I can see it in your eyes, the way they flash when you look at me—"

"*You god-damned sack of shit!*" Ravi wrenched the bag of bones down upon the floor, and in a flash had snatched his trusty *shamshir* from its hooks on the tent wall. With a foot firmly planted on each side of the evil poet, he wielded the saber up to the quaking pit of the sniveling thing's throat. "My eyes flash with hatred pure and simple, and it's not for your anus beating pathological love because

I could care less, you cretin! It's for the traitorous scheming and plotting, the lives and cows you've destroyed—"

Oh, why was he explaining? He had plenty of reasons to kill the catamite, so practically rolling his eyes with the ease of target with which the poet presented him, he skewered him with the shamshir through the throat.

But the blade only went through the carpet and several inches of soil. The sickly man had rolled, and now Walde Nebra was there with several other henchmen, yelling blue murder, but before they could assess the situation, Ravi targeted the pathetic scribbler as he cowered against a display of shields, knocking them all into a mish-mash on the ground. Ravi draw-cut the *shamshir* at the belly of the squealing worm, but a soldier yanked Anatole aside in time to prevent any mortality, and Ravi screwed the point into a band of flesh at his side, the blood and plasma spurting out of all proportion to how terminal was the wound.

"Likamaquas!"

This time, it took about six men to wrestle Ravi off the quarry, and he still retained his sword when they raised him to his feet.

"You cannot kill him; he's a favorite scribe of the Emperor!"

Ravi flicked the sword so that stripes of blood appeared across the poet's horrified face.

"You will die," Ravi roared, "the most vicious, putrid, tormenting death, and there will be *no one there to comfort you,* you worthless traitorous bastard, God may damn your soul!"

The remaining soldiers whisked Anatole from the tent so rapidly the blood pouring from his side splashed the tent walls.

"Likamaquas," panted the men about him, tentatively releasing their hold on him. "Likamaquas."

Ravi snorted with rage. When the last soldier had removed his fingers from his person, Ravi shook like a great polar bear, waving his *shamshir* so stridently the men scattered to the far walls of the tent. He didn't care that his *shamma* hung from his hips like a loincloth.

"The next person who prevents me from killing that lousy dog is going to have their head as the main course on the banquet table!" he roared.

CHAPTER TWENTY-FOUR
"HEART AND REASON"

October 30, 1867
Mekan Iyesus, Begemder Province

RAVI THUNDERED UP THE PASS ON Selpha, who was agitated and full of energy after not running for so many long days. Ravi eschewed the reins and gripped the mane at the crest as the Dakotas did in the Black Hills of the American West.

Claiming an urgent mission of a nebulous nature, he had thrust the surveyor's compass into Misha's clammy hand and leaped upon his mount to beat a retreat back up the pass where the imperial camp awaited a road to travel on. He had sent a fire-footed messenger before him to make arrangements, and he now halted at the ridgeline, admiring the magnificent sight of the five-mile-long valley cloaked in the thousands of black, red, and white tents. It was still such a stirring sight for Ravi, though he now quailed to see the Emperor's white marquee, a gift from the Pasha of Egypt, on its usual eminence. Once he'd sighted his goal, he galloped down the road, a surging cloud of dust churned up by Selpha's hooves.

Sprinting past the well-wishing raised spears of soldiers, Ravi attained his library tent, dismounting before the horse had even halted. Pressing some dollars into Wubishet's palm for distribution to the other men, Ravi flung aside the tent flap and ducked inside.

Delphine burbled out an unintelligible cry and flung herself onto him. He crushed her with equal fervency, immediately lifting her and placing her bottom onto his desk. He was funky with fresh sweat, he knew, but her fingers already yanked the fabric from his slick shoulders as he leaned into her powerfully as though he wished to press her through the desk and onto the carpet. Phosphenes wafted before his eyes and at last he remembered to breathe, gasping out like an injured ox.

"*Isgyoh!*"

"Oh! How I've missed you!" Her sharp cry hurt his ear, and he set to taking great sucking bites from the exposed side of her neck, slipping his tongue beneath the cords of her *mateb* and amulets. Her fast surgeon's hands already stripped him to the waist. "How I need you," she purred, sucking upon his ear. Her hands glided over his moist haunches, beneath the cinch of the armor belt, heaving him toward her so that his pulsing phallus was firmly glued to her mons veneris. She set to furiously working free his voluminous belt, while gripping him between her tenacious thighs. "Forgive me, forgive me," she whispered.

"Forgive you for what, my Queen of Heaven?" Ravi untied the front laces of her shirt and laid bare her proud, wide shoulders.

She tugged the loosened belt down about his feet. "For being too eager, for not being able to wait for you to take me."

That was all the encouragement Ravi needed. "Ah, no, my only truth. It is *I* who cannot wait." Kneeling for a brief moment, he peeled her cotton breeches from her and rose up only to be clamped by her thighs, her hand massaging and fondling his straining cock and balls. Sliding into her, he laid her back atop the slippery manuscripts of the desk, the desk relatively clear as he had not been able to work there in over a week, and free of the herbs and medical test tubes the woman had set up on another table.

He loved her furiously, swiveling his hips with great bursting lunges, each stroke sending him deeper into the core of her, to the realm where one loses one's thought completely and the mind becomes a blank void. He felt her open wide to him, her sex as relaxed as her importuning eyes that latched onto his, and she didn't blink one atom when she wedged a hand between them and slathered her palm to his aching full balls. Her agile fingers described lubricious feathery swoops; and in his forceful ejaculation he pinned her to the table as she murmured encouraging steamy words against his throat.

Gasping and wriggling with exquisite pleasure, Ravi held himself over the woman. When his head cleared, he noted the manuscript that lay beneath her quivering shoulder was the story of the savant Abou Nouass, and he laughed.

She frowned, and in her panting said, "What do you laugh at? Please, sir, I am not that humorous, I hope!"

Ravi smiled. "This manuscript underneath you. 'For God! What of buffoonery I've got, should it be that no other member is like mine? Here! See it, measure it! What woman tastes it falls in love with me, in violent love'."

"Oh! You arrogant ass!" Delphine shoved at him, and he was willing to disengage and allow her to stand, to gather her breeches up about her waist again. He didn't bother clothing himself; he merely went to the wooden liquor cupboard where he hoped some brandy was still secreted.

But when he turned with the *barrilye* in his hand, he saw her standing with a listless arm, fingers trailing over the Arabic characters of the papers, her shoulders twitching in a sad attitude. Putting down the flask, Ravi stood behind her and enveloped her in his arms. When he gently rubbed the side of his face against hers, he felt her hot tears.

"Do I make you that melancholy?" he asked her.

"No," she suddenly sobbed. "It's just that . . ."

She heaved so with inner tears, Ravi gathered her and took her upon his lap on the *alga*. She wouldn't look him in the face, but preferred to gaze fuzzily at the carpet.

"What, my only truth?"

"It's just . . . it's just . . ." She finally looked at him, great streams of tears rolling down her cheeks. *"I'm barren."*

She looked away again.

"Oh, *Isgyoh*," Ravi whispered.

When she struggled to rise, Ravi held her fast, shaking her a little, trying to force her to look at him again.

"And how do you know this?"

"I've never . . . I've never been with child, and—It's caused by excessive coitus! In Georgia, we did it forty-six ways to Sunday, and nothing ever happened—we did it at night, which causes infertility, and—now with you! Absolutely nobody wants a woman who cannot conceive! I'm a worthless excuse for a—"

"Stop it!" shouted Ravi, truly shaking her this time. "I will *not* have you belittling yourself! *Isgyoh*, woman, you are the most accomplished, ravishing, intelligent, strong-willed woman I've ever had the honor to know, how can you tie up your entire life's worth in the happenstance of a biological function? My God—"

He was so overcome with violent emotion he was compelled to lift her off his lap, and set her aside while he slid onto the carpet on his knees. He held her forearms in his stern grip. "My God, you don't know how much power you hold over me. You have the power to tame this brutal, heartless, murdering beast into a purring—well, a purring lion—and you have the power to completely transform me from head to toe, to throw our lives on the line for the sake of your high and noble ideals. *No!*"

"Ravi, there—"

"Don't you see that I'm willing to throw my life into the

bonfire because I'm inspired by your lofty nonesuch, and your higher ideals make my selfish yearnings look like the dog shit of a *buda*'s breakfast, that I'm not going to stop loving you because you cannot conceive a child!"

"Ravi! There is no man in the four quarters of the world who will stay with a woman who is barren! That's what men are about, their heirs, their progeny! They will gladly cast aside a wife who has borne them at least one healthy child, throw her onto the dump heap and then kneel at the shrine of the infant who is merely gurgling air bubbles, that is how important children are to men!"

Ravi shook her forearms. "*Isgyoh*, where did you get these insane ideas, woman? In the first god-damned place, you're a surgeon, by Saint George! You should know better than these Paleolithic fallacies about sex at night turning you barren, or too much lovemaking ruins the chemical electricity of your womb! What next, my dear doctor—cold baths? Amputation of the clitoris?"

"No, Ravi! That's not it at all!" When she turned her face back to him, fulsome tears spilled from her eyes. Her fists jolted his hands in her attempt to break free of his grip. "Don't you see that you're eventually going to want a child? As much of a Knight Templar as you are, and marriage being denied to you, and as exalted a Likamaquas as you are, you're going to want a god-damned child, and I *can't give it to you!* Don't you think if it were going to happen, it would've happened by now? You're going to turn to others, to concubines—to your fiancée, Louisa Bell!"

With that she wrenched her arms from his grasp, got to her feet, and stormed to the opposite side of the tent. Ravi was left shocked, staring at the rumpled place in the sheepskin where she had sat.

She erupted now into full-fledged sobbing, the echoes of which were enough to rip the very heart from Tewodros and stomp it into mush on the carpet.

Slowly, Ravi rose to his feet and turned. He put his hands on her shoulders that now felt so small and birdlike, the shuddering of her shoulder like an earthquake. "My only truth," he whispered. "This false betrothal to Woizero Bell was something the Emperor thought up ten years ago, and it's pleased him to think that it might happen. She's the daughter of his first Likamaquas, the Englishman John Bell. I've never even kissed that fine woman, who is currently laboring under the delusion she's beset by a *buda* in order to avoid marrying Kaspar Nagel. For that I can't blame her. I'm sorry that someone upset you by giving you this false information." She shuddered greatly then, and seemed to still beneath his hands.

"My dear. *You* are the only woman I've wanted in my entire grand lifespan of forty years. I never wanted to marry another, and I was content to pretend that it was the Templar way of life that prevented me from doing so. Now?"

He turned her forcefully to face him, and he lowered himself onto his knees once more, gathering the folds of her shirt into his fists. "Now? I see a woman who has utterly torn from me that which I thought was noble, and made it seem like dirt. A woman with the strength to withstand the Emperor, to saw bones and patch together vast intestines of the most heinous quality, even when people are keeling over around her. This is the woman I want to marry. Will you give me the honor of marrying me in Magdala, in the church? For you are the only truth I've ever known, and the only truth I know is you."

Her trembling hand tried to hide her mouth, and her wide eyes stilled. It seemed that she didn't breathe. At length, all in a rustle of fabric and limbs, she dropped to her knees before him. "My darling *el besiss*. I don't think you know what you're saying. Even if the Emperor were to allow us to wed . . ." She touched his half-moon scar. "You would soon loathe me, not being able to give you an heir. What would be the point of such a coupling?"

He cradled her jaw in his palms. "I don't care," he whispered ardently. "If we're in need of children, there are thousands of orphans looking for parents. *Will you?*"

Her eyes shivered. It seemed that her pupils expanded with warmth when she looked at him, then contracted into sandy grains when perhaps she thought of the Emperor. "The Emperor will never—"

"*I don't care.* We'll wed in secret, then, but with the blessings of the sanctified church. The church in Magdala—the Savior of the World—is one of the most sacred in Abyssinia. *Will you?*"

She brushed his lips with hers. "I love you more than I ever thought was humanly possible to love and still breathe at the same time. Of course I'll marry you."

Covering her mouth with his, he swept her into his arms and laid her onto the carpet.

✴   ✴   ✴

DELPHINE LAY PLACID, SATED AND PROTECTED by the strapping man, He bared her breasts and tentatively licked them sweetly like a small cat. As she felt his penis stiffen again against her hip, she ran her rapacious hands over his finely molded flanks.

He had utterly taken her by surprise by his proposal of marriage. She had thought he could never wed, or had to wed Woizero Bell, or preferred to marry no one. There was plenty of time later for stark realizations that this would be a completely doomed coupling, for in the extreme event that they were both alive a year from now, would she wish to traverse Greenland—which, after all, was ice? *Hmm, perhaps.* Or maybe better Iceland, which after all was green. He had mentioned New York, to arrange for publication of his manuscripts . . .

She knew he'd stayed in Abyssinia for her. He could have easily escaped and at least saved himself. Perhaps she had made an error in wanting to stay. After all, the prisoners would die or be tortured regardless of who else escaped. Perhaps—if she could just convince Kaspar, for Abou needed no convincing—if the four of them could escape—*Ah.*

His persuasive nibbling at her nipple wiped all cohesive thoughts from her mind. All at once she remembered *he wants to wed me*, and such a rush of love imbued her she grasped him to her and squirmed fitfully.

"Ravi," she whispered hoarsely. "Perhaps it was a bit precipitous of me to turn down your offer to leave."

Immediately his head came up. He dragged himself over her, his eyes shining. "You've changed your mind?"

"Well, perhaps," she said, all in a rush. "How much more murderous will it make him that four *frenjoch* escaped? He's already so brutal—"

"Yes, and not liable to become more heartwarming by the minute—"

"—that perhaps if we can convince dear Kaspar to come with us—"

"No, no, leave dear Kaspar behind, he has no interest in escaping—"

"—but we must, *el besiss*, he did save my life when I first came to this country, and if we left him behind I could never live with the idea he was tortured—"

"All right, bring Kaspar with us, ah, my Queen of Heaven, you don't know how happy you've made me!" Gripping her jaws in his hands, he laid his mouth atop hers and kissed her, a greedy and sloppy suckling that had her spreading her thighs to enwrap his massive flanks to her. Ah, the delicious slope of his thoracic vertebrae beneath her hand, the achingly exquisite incline of his gluteus, he was a solid man who made one feel substantial and alive.

Indeed, she had clamped her thighs about his penis and he now reamed her salaciously, the long donkey-like length of him slipping between her muscles with a lubricious friction.

"Woman," he gasped against her mouth. "It has been an honor to be allowed to feast at your body—"

"Get your filthy donkey's penis off of her!"

That seething Amharic command could have only come from one, and Ravi and Delphine reacted like shots, having both been trained by different harsh lives to leap for defense at the slightest provocation.

Delphine didn't know where to look first—Anatole cowering against the tent wall, several brutish musketeers crowding the doorway along with several hulking Galla bodyguards, the roaring Emperor who seemed blown up beyond all reasonable proportion as he waved his favorite *talwar* over his head, or to Ravi, inflated to nearly twice that size with his terrifying *shamshir* in the same attitude. Their glaring, bulging eyes seemed set to incinerate the other. Delphine jumped between the two and pivoted on one foot, unsure who needed protection from whom.

"Just calm down," she beseeched them.

"You have betrayed me!" Tewodros roared over her head, looking through her as though she were invisible. He stepped to his right. She stepped to her left, protecting Ravi. "You have ruined her with your donkey's penis, and by the death of Christ if she bears your child I will have both your heads cut off!"

"It's all right!" Delphine cried. "Tewodros, you see there's been a misunderstanding. I'm barren—you see, I can't have children anyway, which would have made it impossible for me to beget—"

Ravi shoved her bodily several feet so he could pass her by and confront the Emperor, his saber lowered now. "My King of Kings!" he shouted. A few of the gargantuan Gallas were insinuating themselves along the inner walls of the tent and were slowly flanking them. "It will please you to leave my tent. As I do not come rushing into your tent when you are making love to a woman, I will only ask the same courtesy of you." He faced the smaller man who appeared to be shrinking from the sheer power confronting him, daring to shout down at him with his face not three feet away, though the Emperor still hefted his *talwar*. "I will forget you ever did this, if you will kindly leave this very moment."

Tewodros's guttural growl was so saturated with hatred, Delphine could barely discern his words. "You have done the unthinkable," she thought he uttered. "Makeda came to my kingdom to partake of *my* wisdom, and instead she has been at your side daily!"

" 'She was in the greatest admiration imaginable, insomuch that she was not able to contain the surprise she was in, but openly confessed how wonderfully she was affected'," Ravi snarled down at the Emperor.

"She visits you and is gratified, and you visit her and are gratified." Tewodros's eyes were but slits of venom. " 'Solomon marveled concerning the Queen, for she was vigorous in strength, and beautiful of form, and *undefiled in virginity*; and regardless of her gracious attraction and her splendid form, *had preserved her body pure*'."

To the sheer shock of everyone present, Tewodros did not strike with his sword arm, but swung out his weaker left hand and gave a cracking slap to Ravi's face.

Though the slap had affected Ravi not at all, as though a fly had alighted upon his face, Delphine leapt between them, only to be knocked aside by Ravi's powerful arm when he unstintingly belted the Emperor into the middle of next week. Just one immense blow sent the thinner man sailing across the tent, punching a dent into the tent wall where he sprawled like a squashed bug. Immediately Ravi was beset with the hulking men who grabbed ahold of his limbs, and he only had time to carve a gory flap from a Galla's pectoral with his *shamshir* before he was rendered immobile.

"Stop! Leave him alone!" Delphine shrieked ineffectually, her punches and kicks to their marbled legs hurting her far more than them. She grabbed Ravi's spear from the carpet and clouted men across the shoulders until one of them released Ravi and turned to choke her by the throat.

"Don't touch her!" Tewodros shrieked.

Even through her terror, the repellant odor of butter that sprayed from the ugly Amhara's skin sounded an atavistic note in Delphine's brain, and it came to her: this was the same odiferous gargoyle who had mauled her in Metemma, and who had later been so eager to receive her when she'd burst out of the tunnel at Qwesqwam!

Suddenly the greasy fingers relaxed their hold around her throat, as the head had only just now been detached from the body with a silent slice of a Galla's enormous scimitar, and the body had not quite decided to collapse and die just yet. Delphine was left staring in horror at the clean, ice-white cross-section of hyoid bone where the head had separated from the throat, splashed with the pulses of blood the heart pumped up the severed carotid artery. As Delphine was saturated with copious buckets of the raw, carmine slop, the head hit the ground and rolled, and all men scrambled away from its trajectory. Ravi, suddenly released and sprawled like a tarantula on the ground, gave a direct path for the head to undulate in a clear target for his crotch, where it rolled to a stop to regard Ravi's naked phallus with an amazed snarl.

Groaning as all air left his lungs, Ravi's eyes spun up into their sockets, and he fell back onto the carpet.

"Ah!" the soldiers sighed in wonder.

Delphine tore the deceased man's hands from her throat and flung herself on top of Ravi, heedlessly lifting the heavy, oozing head by its queue of braids and hefting it out of his lap. "Ravi,

Ravi," she called in English, gently slapping his face. "Ravi, it's all right, wake up, it's me, Delphine, Queen of Heaven!" Her voice became more urgent with every word. "Wake up, Ravi! *It's me, Delphine, your only truth! God-damn it!*"

She was ripped from his warm body and carried kicking and thrashing to the tent door, where the Emperor pressed himself among the crowd of bodyguards who entombed her. Pushing his repellant face near hers, he crushed her to him with a vicious arm, as though the gouts of warm blood that glued them together were as pleasant as fresh butter. "There is nothing that you desire that I will deny you—"

"Basha Falaka," she whispered.

"—as I am generous and liberal in my temper, and will show you the greatness of my soul in bestowing on you that which you desire—"

"The Likamaquas," she hissed with hatred.

He squeezed her face with his other hand. "Remember the covenant that existed between us, and give yourself to me willingly."

"I don't love you as a man, and I never will. I love you as an Emperor and nothing more. Swear that you won't take me by force." For she remembered what Makeda had said to Solomon the night he prepared a spicy meal for her and gave her nothing to drink.

Luckily, this perplexed the Emperor, for he knew he had to play by the story. "Then take nothing from my house."

"I'sh-shi."

Tewodros shoved her, and nodded to the men to indicate they should haul her away.

✳   ✳   ✳

RAVI DRIFTED IN AND OUT OF wakefulness. They had been giving him water, which told him they wished him to live, so he spent his time in the throes of Sufi meditation, sending his spirit into another realm as Delphine had told him she did when being accosted by the Emperor, or other men she didn't wish to be near.

During one of these mindful lulls, Kaspar Nagel came to his tent. He squatted silently next to Ravi, and lifted a horn of water to his mouth. At last he said, "They've taken Delphine and Abou to Magdala on a mule."

Ravi said nothing. He was surprised Kaspar had the sensitivity to try to cheer him by saying, "The British have started coming from Zulla. They're building a road toward Senafé, up the spine of Ethiopia. They're bringing elephants, Howland! Forty-four trained elephants to carry the artillery!"

In his desperation, Ravi had to chuckle at that. He had known Field-Marshal Robert Napier, the conqueror of Sind, in India. As a visiting American Captain and a soldier-of-fortune, Ravi had trained many of Napier's regiments in the use of the sword, languages, falconry, and surveying. He'd been given the secret detail of investigating Karachi male brothels where British soldiers were alleged to visit, a mission that had nearly destroyed Napier's career when he'd forgotten to burn Ravi's report. Now Napier's Bombay army was being redirected to Abyssinia.

"They're laying railroad tracks from Zulla, and telegraph line! I tell you, Howland, I think the Indian Army will be the salvation of all of us, although I don't see how they plan on getting all that heavy equipment up the passes and through the chasms. Elephants, *unglaublich!* Perhaps with the help of a great engineer such as you . . ."

Ravinger finally spoke. "Napier is a great engineer. He's worked up and down the length of India building canals, bridges, and roads."

"*Ach!* Well, we need you here, Howland. Those bumbling *Dummköpfe* have completely deviated from the road that you laid out! They are already about two hundred yards up the canyon where waterfalls from the Beshema River come pouring in the rainy season. When they excavate rocks, they just throw them down on the heads of the men below so they tumble about like *Bowlingspiel* players! And I have tried to understand that instrument you explained to me—"

"It's a telescopic alidade."

"Whatever that confounded contraption is, I cannot get the horizon to sit level with the road! It keeps swimming about like you are on a boat in the English Channel just waiting to puke up your breakfast! I tell you, Howland, it's of the prime importance that they release you from these chains, that's all I've been telling the Emperor!"

"Well, good, Kaspar. Thank you for all your hard work on my behalf. Keep working at it. And I need you to promise me something else."

Kaspar looked askance at Ravi, as though he would ask him to donate his favorite pet fish to science. "Yes?"

"I need you to care for everything in my library tent. I need you to personally escort everything up the mountains to Magdala, now that Delphine isn't here."

"And why is this?"

"Because once I get out of these irons, I'm leaving. I'm not going up to Magdala. I need you to take care of all my possessions, my manuscripts mainly, my books, Delphine's laboratory and medicine. Once you get up there, put everything into the Treasury under the care of Bitwaddad Damash. Give Delphine her medical supplies of course, but put all of my manuscripts into safekeeping with Damash."

"Leaving?" Kaspar whispered. "But you cannot! Not without Miss Chambliss! She has told me you are betrothed to wed, and would wed in secret on Magdala, and . . . *You are betraying her!*"

"No, no, listen to me, Kaspar. We *are* betrothed, and we *will* wed. Just not this way. The longer I stay with Tewodros, the more often he throws me into chains, the worse everything becomes, and the less help I can be of to Delphine, or you, or anyone. Tewodros has become so desperate, and so besotted with his dwindling power, that it wouldn't surprise me if he chopped off the head of General Gebraye or Ras Engeddeh next. No one is safe around him, Kaspar. And I'm hardly liable to be of any use when I'm minus a head now, am I?"

"What is your plan? No, don't tell me! I don't want to be accused of knowing your plan!"

"Then I shan't tell you. Can you grab that sheepskin, and slide it under my ass? Ah, much better. I'll just tell you this, Deacon Nagel. I'm not sneaking out of here under cover of the night. There is no devious plan for you to be party to."

"Not escaping?" gasped Kaspar, *sotto voce*. When Ravi didn't answer, Kaspar sighed deeply with resignation. "Then I cannot imagine what your plan is, unless you will build some wings and fly off the edge of a cliff."

※ ※ ※

WHEN RAVI'S CHAINS WERE REMOVED, HE was escorted onto a promontory where Tewodros awaited him. It was nearly sundown, the sky above the plateaus like the violaceous slate of an opera backdrop, the Emperor's fine profile a study in magisterial righteousness gone wrong. He leaned on his spear on one leg in his favorite stork-like attitude, and though he must have heard Ravi padding up in his bare feet, he didn't turn to face him.

Ravi folded his hands and waited. The musketeers stood twenty paces behind him, as though they feared going for an impromptu journey into the lowlands below.

"I know I have lost your love." Tewodros's well-modulated rich voice didn't seem confounded by *arrack* this evening. "I knew I lost your love when I saw how deeply you love Makeda. When the blond-eyed bird brought me to your tent, I saw how you paid your respects to her with your body, and a man who didn't love a woman would be incapable of pretending that."

Ravi spoke calmly. "You are wise in some respects, and that is one of them. I could never pretend to love a woman I didn't love. When I first saw Makeda, and saw the medal she wore, I knew she was meant for me, for I used to wear the medal of Solomon until it was torn from my breast."

Tewodros turned. Ravi could see nothing in the potentate's dusky face other than the eerily gleaming whites of his eyes. "You just had that medal to keep safe until it was time for me to reclaim it."

"I've finished your business well and faithfully; I now ask for my discharge from your service."

"No." The Emperor spoke mildly. "I can't lose my best soldier and engineer."

"Azmach Michael and the *azmary* can finish the road-building. You've got Waldmeier, Saalmüller, the other artisans. Jan Hoy! You may be a great man, you may have a heart and reason, but though I'm not a king, I have a heart and reason also. When I first came here, you requested my service, promising me good pay and promotion. I agreed to serve you, and I've served you faithfully for ten years. I've been on the battlefield, and with your own eyes you saw my conduct, and promoted me now and then. While on the road I've built to do your bidding, you chose to believe lies told in your ears by worthless traitors who deserve to be rolled in cowhide and thrown off a cliff. I've served you until I can serve you no more, and I demand my discharge."

Tewodros's voice was almost soft, as though Ravi merely

recited him another tale of Burnt Njal. "And where will you go?"

"I will go home."

"Suppose I choose that you won't leave the country?"

"Then somebody will get killed, for I will fight, and you know I'm not an infant."

Tewodros's eyes shimmered. He was sentimental, and was equally as adept at displaying love for his men as he was at maiming and murder. "Will nothing persuade you to remain with me? I will give you more gold, more manuscripts—you can have half of all that we were given in Gondar and Mesraha."

"Nothing will persuade me. I'm tired of the treachery and lies that I've seen around me."

A trace of his usual malice crept into Tewodros's voice. "You will leave Makeda without a lover, without a warm hand, without your strength to guide her?"

Ravi had prepared himself for the Emperor's particular brand of warfare of the mind. He had crafted a painfully artificial lie for such an eventuality. "I trust that she'll be safe under your guidance, for I know how much you love her. Can you promise me your royal word that no harm will come to her, that she'll be taken good care of on Magdala?"

Tewodros stepped even closer then, as though he needed to impress Ravi in the darkening night with the ferocity of his brimming eyes. "I cannot promise that, Basha Falaka. You know how cruel I can be when someone displeases me."

Ravi should never have shown the Emperor his vulnerability. He told himself Tewodros only sliced those malicious words at him in a desperate attempt to get him to stay. The Emperor would never harm Delphine. *Isgyoh*, he had just commanded a Galla chop off the head of an elite musketeer because the man had dared put his hands on Delphine. "Then I shall have to leave without your assurances." Bowing slightly, for the last time Ravi looked into the eyes of the man who had caused him more pain than his own father ever had. And he had loved him more than he had loved his own father. "In the name of the Father, the Son, and the Holy Ghost."

Turning, Ravi marched back to the waiting group of men who now hovered expectantly like a tremulous rock formation.

Tewodros could have easily speared him through the back, or shot him with his revolver, or attacked him bodily. With a motion of his hand he could have ordered the thugs to grab him and throw him back into chains; there wouldn't have been a peep out of any man if he ordered his limbs struck from him.

Tewodros's voice sailed over the promontory, wavering and plaintive. "My only son! Why have you forsaken me?"

Ravi strode past the quaking musketeers, only Walde Nebra among them detaching himself from the mass of highland men. Ravi felt solid, safe, strong, a man without a country, a man without a king.

PART III

CHAPTER TWENTY-FIVE
"THE BLESSINGS OF CHRISTIAN MORALITY"

January 4, 1868
Magdala

DELPHINE SKIPPED TO RASSAM'S HUT AS fast as her fettered feet would carry her. The surly doorkeepers had allowed Wubishet and other messengers through with the first messages from the royal camp in weeks. The captive's quarters were a flurry of sudden activity of hobbling *frenjoch* galvanized into life by the prospect of any news, whether good or bad, anything to liven up the monotony of life on the plateau. Even Consul Cameron staggered over, his crazed eyes wide and blind. He had fared the worst of all the captives.

"Henry," Delphine cried, taking Dr. Blanc by the arm. "Dare we hope?"

Dr. Blanc ignored etiquette today. He clasped her hands in his and jabbered, "I've already heard the Wagshum Gobaze is lying in wait to attack Bob—there's also some news about Captain Howland, but it's all verbal, as Bob has been afraid to commit anything to paper."

"Miss *El Taleb!*" Wubishet called from the door of Rassam's hut. "Miss *El Taleb!* Come!"

Without ceremony, Dr. Blanc bundled Delphine into the

packed hut where she staggered to take Wubishet's hands. "Wubishet, what is the news?"

His flashing eyes were full of import. As all voices in the hut had now hushed to hear Wubishet speak, he couldn't very well give Delphine the intimate message first, so he stood tall and hollered in a plaintive tone. "The Emperor's camp has reached Bet Hor. He has issued a proclamation to the people of Dalanta that they will have full amnesty if they stop rebelling and return to their former allegiance to him. But the Wagshum Gobaze has announced his intention to attack Tewodros as soon as he descends into the valley of Chetta. He has thirty thousand men under two Dejazmachs and he will prevent the Emperor from reaching Magdala."

"Salvation!" gasped the Reverend Stern.

Lieutenant Prideaux added, "I'll believe it when I see it."

"He will liberate the fortress, allow all Europeans to leave, and take his place as rightful Emperor of Abyssinia!"

"My eye!" said Mr. Rosenthal.

"My ass," agreed Dr. Blanc. "The fighting force of the Emperor is still the strongest in the nation, the most brutal and best-equipped."

"Don't forget," pointed out Prideaux, "all the arms that French traitor has been funneling to Dejazmach Kassa."

There were general exclamations as the men crowding the room descended into eager bickering, debating the merits of each leader's forces, as men were wont to do. Delphine nearly had to sit down, she was so weakly debilitated and anxious to hear news of Ravi. Perhaps the yammering men were sucking all the oxygen from the room. She was just able to grab Wubishet's arm before he lowered her onto an *alga* and told her quietly: "The Likamaquas has left the Emperor's camp."

"Left? How? Escaped?"

"He walked away after being released from his fetters. He told the Emperor he did not wish to work for him anymore, and he walked away, taking only Walde Nebra with him."

"The Emperor allowed this to happen? He didn't try to harm him?"

Wubishet spoke faster now, as men were pointing at him, demanding the next part of the story. "No. I think the Emperor is now so crazy he completely forgot to kill the Likamaquas. And he loves the Likamaquas, no matter what he does to hurt him."

"And where did the Likamaquas go?"

Wubishet paused. "No one knows."

"Oh!" Delphine sobbed into her hand, the tears truly dripping now from her eyes, uncaring that all the men in the hut stared at her, unblinking.

In the time she had been confined to Magdala, she had grown to love and cherish her fellow captives. She was like a mother confessor figure to them all, though young enough to be the daughter of some of them. They all felt relaxed around her surgeon's practical demeanor and, as she was the only white female on the entire blessed Amba as long as their wives toiled below in the royal encampment, she gave a feminine charge to their lives. She felt loved and adored by them—with the exception of that inscrutable Rassam, who preferred sending laudatory letters to the Emperor at the expense of finding out any real news or accomplishing anything that might help their situation—and she was sure they had seen worse than her crying into her hand with relief that, at last report, their hallowed Basha Falaka was still alive.

Abou's head towered above even the lofty heights of Stern and Rosenthal. "My Curd Teeth! What has happened?"

"It's all right, Abou," she blubbered. "Ravi has escaped from the Emperor's foul path of destruction, unharmed!"

A general hubbub of hallelujahs and huzzahs ensued, Delphine's friends wrenching her arms in their effusive congratulations.

She left the hut and went to her own, situated by the *amba's* wall on the edge of a four thousand foot sheer drop to the profound abyss below. She lived in between Rassam's hut and the hut shared by Blanc and Prideaux. She had her vegetable patch, with green peas that trailed over her hut's walls. A small plot of potatoes, beets, and radishes were interspersed with a dozen forms of herbs and lettuces. Thanks to "Rassam's children," tiny birds of all descriptions he encouraged by spreading *teff* grain and then building a water trough for them to bathe in, she was never alone, the beautiful critters including the plumed honey-bird flitting in and out of her arbor, and chirping in their cheerful manner.

She went now to sit on a bench in her garden under a *kosso* tree. She knew that Ravi's last imprisonment had been the breaking point for him, and that he'd been unable to serve the Emperor for a long time before that, and only stayed because of her. Now he'd abandoned her and the rest of the European population, no doubt to go publish his manuscripts in New York before setting out for the wilds of Greenland. She couldn't blame him. A man could only suffer so many travails before he must put his own existence foremost. And although the other captives were erudite and scintillating company, she passionately missed Ravi's absolute originality of character, his prodigious curiosity, and his authority on all that was bestial in man. He was unique among men and, because it pained her too greatly to imagine conversing with him, she called upon Eugene's spirit to comfort her.

"Eugene, *ma première passion*. Why has he forsaken me? Am I so loathsome that all men must either leave, or die to get away from me?"

Eugene stood by the bench, clad not in a blood-drenched surgeon's smock but in his regimental uniform the color of fog, his fingers resting on his gun holster. "He hasn't left you, Delphine. He's an honorable man."

"He's left me because I'm barren! And I'm barren because I

had—too much—too much—"

Eugene became very angry at this. He squatted down before her and shouted in a whisper, "You're barren due to those aborted fetuses in your girlhood, Delphine! That monster Oliver forced you through the torture of the douching syringe how many times? Forty, fifty?"

"What are you talking about?" Delphine asked him in horror. Aborted fetus? She remembered no such thing!

"Can you imagine how many times you were douched and cleaned out, and scar tissue built back up over the womb? At last you could conceive no more—Delphine! It's not a flaw worse than murder to be infertile, and your beloved Captain isn't concerned by it. He left because he's lost faith in the Emperor, not in you."

"Yes, but Eugene—"

"Curd Teeth." Abou's soft voice called from the edge of the vegetable plot.

Eugene abruptly vanished. The last thing she could see was the rims of his intense turquoise eyes.

✳   ✳   ✳

February 25, 1868
Near Ad-Abaga

TEWODROS HAD OFTEN SAID HE LONGED for the day he would see a disciplined European army.

Ravi sat astride Selpha. Though Selpha deserved every medal they could pin on him, it had been necessary for intelligence purposes to strip him of his gay headstall of white and red leather. His jingly shiny brass *benaika* was the most sorrowful loss, as Selpha now tossed his head to no avail, and flashed no one's admiring eye. Ravi had only retained his tiny metal toe stirrups, as he could still not bear to wear boots, and argued that he couldn't maneuver in the clunky army stirrups after a decade in Abyssinian saddles. He had even been forced to send his glorious silver-studded saddle back to his brother Edward in Charleston, and was now seated in the dull and extremely impracticable Otago saddle with no streaming black and white monkey tippets, so completely unadorned Ravi felt a sniper must surely shoot him for being so egregiously boring.

He was mounted beside Dejazmach Kassa, the prince of Tigré through whose lands the British Bombay Army now crawled their cumbersome way up the backbone of Ethiopia. Walde Nebra was mounted upon his left hand. Ravi had traveled with the Major James Grant to Kassa's capital of Adowa earlier that month, bringing Napier's message of friendship that was so necessary to procure safe passage through the country. The two armies now met by Ad-Abaga, in Mai-Debar, the valley chosen for the durbar.

"The *frenjoch* must be good Christians," remarked Kassa, a refined man of high angular cheekbones and sharp chin. "God would not grant them the intelligence to mould such wondrous weapons."

Ravi snorted. He didn't want to admit that after not viewing a disciplined European army himself in ten years, it was a thoroughly wondrous sight to him, too. "The greatest blessings that can be given to Christian morality are fire-arms and gunpowder."

Kassa, perhaps even despite understanding Ravi's sarcasm, nodded and smiled beatifically.

Though the detachment was only a column of five hundred infantry, three hundred cavalry, some tiny knot of the Royal Engineers, and four twelve-pounder guns, absurdly less than the astonishing figures Ravi had given the Dejazmach at Adowa, it was a thrilling sight. Down the malachite Mai-Debar valley came the brigade, backed with the purple eminences of mountains that dove into low puffy cumulus clouds. Their Snider rifles on the present, the infantry in their gray khaki marched sharply behind the military band with the blaring trumpets announcing the grandest sight to which Abyssinia had ever laid witness—ponderous, trained Indian elephants, with the boxy, shimmering howdahs on their backs, bowing and snaking their trunks beneath the skilled ridership of their mahout drivers.

"Truly, Basha Falaka," said Kassa. "The *ferenje* Negus must be a man almost as great as the Chief of the Chiefs of Ethiopia." For that was what Kassa termed himself.

From his green knoll, Ravi saw the Commander-in-Chief leading on his gorgeous charger, cantering ahead of the column, coming to stop beside the burbling stream that bisected the round valley. At an order, rifles were piled up, and infantry and dismounted cavalry strolled to drink deeply from the fresh stream.

Kassa chortled. "They cannot see my men."

An uncommon cloud of what seemed to be heavenly ether enshrouded the Dejazmach's four thousand soldiers who stood at attention on the other side of the rivulet. When a tempest of wind dispersed the dust, Kassa clapped his hands with glee. To the beat of drums, revealed to *frenjoch* eyes were the neat rows of his motley army, long white *shammas* edged with scarlet, proud chestnut faces sporting elaborately plaited coiffures. Almost all had matchlocks or double-barreled rifles, many gripped pistols, funneled through the graces of Anatole Verlaine no doubt. And all brandished the absurd curved *shotel* that, as far as Ravi was concerned, was much better suited for supping on *brundo* than cutting an enemy. The field of men was spiked with shields and spears, hefted in such a manner that Ravi had to smile widely, knowing the fear of God that the sight struck into the Bombay troops, though many were veterans of the Crimean campaign.

"If Tewodros's army was as well-armed as yours," Ravi told Kassa, "and as attached to their sovereign, the *ferenje* Negus would never make it even close to Magdala."

Kassa was obviously torn between descending the gentle slope, and admiring the alacrity with which the British and Indian troops sprang into action when Napier shouted at them.

"Everyone to his place, clap your knapsacks upon your backs, grab your rifles! Fall in, dress up, and look your best!"

Kassa pointed like a young boy. "Hoo, look at the gunners, those tall fellows by the field-guns!"

Ravi affectionately slapped Kassa on the arm with his *shamshir* blade, one of the few barbarous items he'd been allowed to retain as Interpreter-in-Chief attached to Napier's Headquarters staff. "Come, Chief of the Chiefs of Ethiopia. I'd better rejoin the *ferenje* Negus, and you'd best get into your tent to receive him."

"Stay with me, and we can greet the *frenjoch* together!"

They charged down the knoll toward Kassa's red tent, as Napier rushed into his own hurriedly erected tent to make his toilette.

The Dejazmach Kassa had been hanging onto the British right flank with ten thousand men. As his domain covered 150 miles through which they had to traverse even to attain Lasta, the stronghold of the Wagshum Gobaze, it was imperative to gain his friendship—though once that was secured, the next task was to attain the assurance of Kassa's mortal enemy Gobaze, a tricky dual position to maneuver. Ravi had been galloping about the countryside bearing messages and treaties for weeks, with additional theoretical duties to advise the 10th Company Royal Engineers on the geology of Abyssinia for a trigonometrical survey, if ever allowed a break from tearing about being called upon to translate every shred of paper found stuck to the bottom of anyone's boot in Amharic, Tigriyna, and Arabic. When in camp, there were nightly durbars in Officers' Quarters with Napier, Grant, and Merewether, during which Ravi held court, giving haranguing dissertations on Amharic ethnology, economics, and mating habits—the latter subject upon which there was the most intense discussion.

When the two chiefs emerged from their tents on opposite sides of the stream, Ravi walked before Kassa and his Rases, as Grant, Staveley, Merewether, and Gough walked before Napier, who was borne in a beribboned howdah on the back of an elephant. Flanked by his musketeers and covered with a maroon velvet umbrella, Kassa dismounted his steed when Napier dismounted by a rope ladder down the side of the kneeling elephant. Backed by their legions of bristling, snorting soldiers, neither chief was certain who was to cross the stream first. Ravi reached a hand out to the skeptical Napier.

"Come. Meet us on the other side."

Napier looked at Ravi as though a lifeline to hell led through that small rivulet, but he stepped through it in his sturdy boots and embraced the savage Prince like a Tammany leader. At once there was a roaring outburst of good cheer, and the men of the 3rd Bombay Light Cavalry in their silver and blue uniforms were beset by buttered Tigréan limbs. The mood was buoyant, and the British were fairly raised and bound over to the Prince's red tent, lifted by happy drums.

"Strange days are afoot," Jim Grant mentioned to Ravi, his red face wreathed in giddy smiles.

Ravi agreed. "Beats sitting in a drawing room playing whist."

Kassa and Napier entered the durbar tent first, and as Kassa's shield-bearer and other chiefs ducked into the flap after them, an artillery salute roared from the British side of the stream. A commotion was raised among the Tigréan warriors as they regarded the *frenjoch* with cynically raised lances, but the tense scene was no matter when Ravi entered the warm cinnabar glow of the tent.

The men arranged themselves in the appropriate order on carpets, Ravi as interpreter between the black and white parties, and Kassa declared, "Greet the *ferenje* Negus for me."

Sir Robert Napier replied that he was happy to see Kassa, and that it was with great pleasure a Christian nation like the English beheld another nation adhering to the same creed.

Kassa returned that while he didn't like strangers in his country, if they must come, he preferred they be Christians.

Napier remained cool and collected. "Captain Howland. Tell him we only came here because bad men held our countrymen in captivity. When we have released them, we shall go back to our own country without disturbing their dominion in the least."

"That's right," Ravi interpreted back from Kassa. "Theodore is a bad man; I hope sincerely you will punish him as he deserves."

It was agreed that though they had nothing whatsoever in common aside from a love of the Father, the Son, and the Holy Ghost, everyone thoroughly detested Tewodros and would band together to achieve his ouster. Kassa would allow them free passage through his country and assist them with supplies of food, and wished the British to give him aid after defeating Tewodros. Napier regretted he could only follow his orders to secure the release of the prisoners, and could take no sides behind any of the various princes. Kassa seemed content that if the British could not aid him, neither could they aid Gobaze or Menelik of Shoa.

Major General Staveley then put the crowning touch on this moment of glory by beckoning outside the tent for the presents to be brought forward. Ravi handed over a double-barreled rifle by Purdy of London and Bohemian glass vases, and Kassa had to be led outdoors to see the magnificent Arab charger from Sir Robert's own excellent stud. In return, Kassa presented Napier with an enormous new lion's fur mantle, and Ravi showed him how to arrange it upon his shoulders in the correctly fashionable manner.

The interview was over, and the troops were paraded and drilled for the benefit of the Tigréan army. Ravi knew by Napier's brisk stride back over the creek that he was hustling to get to Antalo, their next station where the advance column awaited, and

Napier didn't dare remove the lion's fur until out of sight of Kassa. He knew Napier would feel awkward so attired before his army, but Napier didn't look nearly so ridiculous as the strange effeminate sight of some in their party, namely the eccentric lordling who always rode with kid gloves and a green veil.

They spoke stiffly, out of the corners of their mouths, and had to press their shoulders together intimately to preclude the need for shouting as they wended their way through the milling crowd. Staveley and Merewether yelled orders for the Sindh Horse to saddle up, and the 4th King's Own to furl their regimental flag that had been shredded by rivers of fire in the Crimea.

"I'd advise you, sir, to remain armed at all times," Ravi said. "Petty chiefs who haven't heard Kassa's new edict or are covetous of plunder might continue to raid."

"Yes; I'll keep strong sepoy posts guarding the convoys—"

"—the telegraph line constantly patrolled, vedettes ordered along the front and flanks—"

"—and strong and frequent garrisons, and what's the latest news from this Wagshum Gobaze fellow? Your next move will be to make a treaty with him, for we're into his land once we pass . . . what's the defining border?"

"It seems to be Lake Ashangi. Gobaze was supposed to have been within spitting distance of Magdala, but he withdrew without ever confronting Tewodros, probably back up to his stronghold at the lake. Unfortunate, as last I heard, he had thirty thousand armed men. It also doesn't stand us in good stead to be incapable of offering protection—anyone who throws in their lot with us will be wide open for reprisals by whatever little of Tewodros's men are left in the dust after the fact."

"Yes; the moment we meet with success, we desert them."

"And if we suffer any reversal of fortune at all, absolutely everyone will unite against the *ferenje* enemy, to avert the expected wrath of Tewodros."

"Nobody wants to be seen as confabbing with the enemy." It was time for Napier to mount the elephant again so as to make the properly regal departure, and he turned crisply to Ravi. "Thank you, Howland. I knew you were a likely candidate for the British Army when you returned from my Karachi mission with a full..." A smile flickered at the edges of his mouth. "... a rather complete and thorough report on the brothels."

Ravi smiled crookedly. "Too bad the report wasn't merely verbal." The detailed handwritten report had been shipped directly into the hands of Queen Victoria, with such expedience and momentum one might have imagined it were her breakfast eggs. Nothing moved as swiftly in the army as the infamous American engineer's descriptions of the scrotums of boys who had been castrated being utilized as bridles for directing the movements of lecherous debauchees.

Napier grinned. "I'm sorry about that, Howland. You were the only man in the vicinity of the cantonment who spoke Sindhi and had the basest inquisitive nature necessary for the job. I should have destroyed the report immediately upon reading it." Leaning in closer, he confided, "I can't promote you as you have the unfortunate experience of being an American, but I can see to it that your delicate translation work is seen favorably in ... New York, is it?"

Ravi saluted. "New York."

They parted, and began the withdrawal to Ad-Abaga.

Uncomfortable clothing aside, it was oddly exhilarating to be on "the other side" once more with the stiff and humorous British troops Ravi had come to love in India when he was a soldier-of-fortune. To avoid anybody mistaking him for the dreaded Basha Falaka, or the jumpy and edgy Bombay troops mistaking him for an Amhara, to evade surprise beheadings he forbore to wear the scarlet tunic and the blue trousers of the Royal Engineers. He found the trousers terribly tight and uncomfortable about the thighs, but he was grateful for the military frocks of tartan and duck, the civilized material warm and soft against his chest. He remained shoeless, as the soles of his feet were tough enough to withstand tramping across any sort of chain- or grape-shot he might happen to stumble on. With his toes through the small Amhara stirrups, his new ace breech-loading Snider rifle (he'd given his favorite old Enfield to Walde Nebra), and trusty *shamshir*, he felt a strange new hybrid of man.

Jim Grant, a stalwart fellow recently distinguished as the co-discoverer of the source of the White Nile along with the cranky, annoying John Speke, had prevailed upon Ravi to shear off the mass of gathered architectonic braids gathered that had reached nearly to the lumbar of his back. Ravi came close during this horrifying operation to nearly breaking down with sobbing at the loss of his former self and status. His now close-cut poll felt light as air, and his hand kept moving to his head to pat his coiffure, shocked at finding almost nothing.

Later that evening at the camp in Ad-Abaga, Ravi sat before Grant's tent around the long camp-table laden with decanters, plates, and cruets. Walde Nebra, for lack of anything better to do—what with the Indian *khansamah* butlers, cooks, syce grass-cutters, and other under-butlers attached to the expedition—had gone out shooting, and had brought back wild geese and guinea-fowl. The lantern cast sinister lights on Jim's face, and their talk was muffled by the sound of bass drums booming and fifes skirling on the outskirts of camp.

Jim drawled with the effects of "Old Tom" gin. "It's probably entirely possible for you to get a message through to Magdala, Ravi, to that woman doctor of yours. We've received a few messages from Rassam, he's got a regular station in Sakota, though his messages be mealy-mouthed and beg for leniency for his Emperor."

Other officers chomped on their ragouts, potato cakes, mulligatawny soup, and fowl cooked *à l'Anglaise*. "Not worth the risk, Jim. Tewodros finds out I'm with the British, no telling what sort of mayhem he might wreak upon the hapless citizens of Magdala."

"Ah, Ravi. Don't you think the poor woman deserves at least a note that the savage Lickomenquos of the Black Highlands is alive and well? After even half of what I've heard she's been through I'm sure she's a half-addled wreck—besides!" He pounded his palm on the tabletop, causing wineglasses and cruets to spring up down the line, and men to lean forward over the table with accusatory glares. "You've told me yourself she's your bloody *intended*, Howland. How do you think she's faring, up there on that bloody table-land with those murderous hellions surrounding her? Why, I've heard that thirty thousand natives have been murdered up there by the whip, stabbing, or decapitation, within three months! Seems she could use a—"

"Major." Ravi drew himself up in his camp chair. "What the Abyssinians are today, not many centuries ago the warlike British barons were, or the Highlanders who used to make wild forays upon the peaceful burghers of the Lowlands, or the robber counts and barons of the Rhine."

They stared at each other. Finally the Major broke, leaning back in his chair and flinging his white scarf across one shoulder. "Ah, I see. I shall bother you no more, Captain Howland. It just seemed to me what with your bloody blubbering about the queen of your heaven—"

"Jim!" Ravi stood. "I've composed a thousand messages in my journals, and nothing can come close to assuring her that I haven't heinously abandoned her, as every male figure that's come before me has done to her."

"By my word, Captain Howland! Has it occurred to you that

your intended won't be safe if we ever lay siege to Magdala? What're the chances of that demon slitting her throat before we ever storm the Bastille? From what you've told me, he's not likely to release her into the adoring bosom of her family once we come to—"

"Jim. Did you love that man as though he were your own father? No, you did not, so I don't want to hear your half-baked ideas about what might be going through the Emperor's mind right now. I'm telling you," Ravi growled, "he wouldn't harm a hair on that woman's head." He kicked at a tin of essence of beef someone had dropped, and pointed down at the seasoned Nile explorer. "But if it'll make you feel like a pig in clover, I'll dispatch that message before the light of first morning."

Grant stood too, and spread his hands out. "Ravi. I'm just leery. Napier should have made a great show today of shooting off rockets and shells to put the fear of God into Kassa's savages. We still don't know what sort of force Theodore will have at Magdala, or what he's capable of."

Ravi shook his head. "They know that we've got weapons that throw whizzing balls of fire through the air and can set fire to houses three miles away. I'm telling you, Jim, we have nothing to fear. The Wagshum Gobaze has thirty thousand men, Kassa forty thousand. How can we go wrong?"

"We can go wrong if they turn against us, like you just informed Napier."

Ravi was left feeling empty and bedraggled. "I wanted to cover all of the possible outcomes. Hate to be able to say later that I missed something." He swallowed brandy. "But thanks, Jim."

He walked to his tent. He was allowed his own American wall-tent as a member of the Intelligence Department, along with a *tente d'abri* for Walde Nebra, the most luxurious the shield-bearer had ever had to himself. In addition, as the army's chief raider—no, now he could rightfully call himself *provisioner*, as he paid the fixed amount of Maria Theresa dollars for everything obtained—he was well-stocked himself with camp kettles, dishes, curry powder, gherkins, figs, and brandies. He'd even managed to attract at least four native Indian servants whom he could speak to in Marathi.

After tossing the unwieldy scarlet tunic onto a chair, Ravi reclined on the camp-bed. He felt strange, with no wooden pillow to lay his head upon, his head light and airy without five pound's worth of hair dragging it down. Outside the tent, Walde Nebra, proud in his stiff Punjabi attire of green uniform with red facings, kicked dirt around in his ceaseless quest to convince servants to move freshly laundered clothing out of the line of cooking fire smoke.

"My *el taleb*," Ravi said aloud, as though dictating to a scribe. "By the power of my creator, I am coming to you."

He just didn't know how to phrase it, in a missive that might well be intercepted by Tewodros's men.

He flipped and turned on the lumpy camp-bed. He sat upright to unbutton the duck frock work shirt, and he threw it atop the tunic. When he lay on his stomach it brought to mind the many languid nights in the breezy warm highlands, air feathering his bare shoulder blades, with his *shamma* draped lightly over his hindquarters.

In particular there were those few days in Gondar when, protecting the gentle surgeon from the potential ravages of the Emperor, he'd lain atop an *arat* thus attired. He'd been aware, in one of those half-asleep states when one isn't really sure whether those gnomes who appear to be leaning against the windowsill are really there or in some memory of an Icelandic fairy tale, that she stood at the door watching him heatedly. It was the first time he'd ever felt someone's gaze literally boring into the small of his back, but he'd willed himself to remain still until he felt her walk back down the gallery. Then he'd breathed, and turned face-up to the cracked ceiling, relieved she hadn't taken a peek at his heaving erection.

He turned now, and only viewed the tent's ceiling lined with yellow cotton.

But a meandering tune brought him forth from the cot, some sort of lilting Irish violin playing on the fringes of camp now that the drums and fifes had all gone to the sack.

Ravi rubbed his grizzled face. Since he was supposed to be a member of an official army regiment, he didn't shave nearly as often. "It's probably those fellows of the Crimea," he told himself, getting up to take his glass of brandy to the table. There was an Irish detachment that had received praise from Wellington himself for their treks through Himalayan snows and the heat of Sindh. They had many good musicians among them, and one played now as Ravi sat and gazed at his mess of dispatches and translations.

The violinist bounced his staccato bow in his repetitious, circular song that told of lost love, passionate exchanges, arguments. As Ravi opened the inkwell and dragged out a fresh sheet of paper from underneath a pile, the fiddler sauntered about the camp, unheeding of the bustle of clanging pots, and men sloshing water, swearing at each other.

Ravi was accustomed to the noise of a camp. It was the penning of a letter to a woman on a mountaintop he wasn't certain of.

My Queen.

The ink made a blob on the comma.

CHAPTER TWENTY-SIX
THE THIN BLUE SKY

March 18, 1868
Magdala

SHE WAS IN THE HANDS OF the good Deacon Kaspar Nagel.

She wrapped her arms around him and clutched him to her heart, allowing the surge of men to pass them, and leave them alone in the dusty street. She steered him back to her leafy arbor under the *kosso* trees.

"Have you come with Flad?"

Kaspar strolled along arm in arm with Delphine, relaxed as though about to board a punt on the Thames. "*Ach*, yes, we've been allowed out of our artillery hauling for just one day, Miss Chambliss! We've come with messages, Mrs. Rosenthal and her tiny baby, transporting prisoners, some of whom are the unfortunates that our dear friend—or should I term him 'fiend'!—Anatole betrayed to Tewodros's evil henchmen!" For another shenanigan concocted by the French poet had been to pretend to complicity in an escape plan along with Staiger and some others, only to betray them to Tewodros at the last moment. "We're here to remove Rassam's fetters, and quite possibly yours, if these purblind fainéants give us a moment to breathe!"

With shining eyes, Delphine sat her dear deacon onto the

garden bench. She held his hands fast in a steely grip. She couldn't resist touching his cloud-white hair that was still moist after so many years in the sun. "Kaspar. I hate to ask this of you, but . . ."

Kaspar sat upright. "About the beloved Likamaquas, of course, my dear. I have a note that Flad has kindly given me." Casually, he shuffled around in the folds of his most hated *shamma*.

She clutched the front of his robes. *"He's alive?"*

Kaspar cleared his throat, and almost seemed to draw out the drama, just for the sake of drama. His hand stilled against his chest. His nostrils even trilled with the theatrics of the moment. *"He's alive."*

"Oh! *Where* is he alive?"

Kaspar gazed out at the vines of Rassam's hut, as though so unconcerned he may as well be delivering a message to someone's herd of sheep. His hand finally unveiled the letter, stamped and sealed with the wax insignia of the British Army. "He's with the British."

Delphine swept the letter away into the arbor. Gray and yellow blobs of sunlight danced across the surprisingly pristine paper. She breathed the aroma of the letter, though by now it had certainly lost any vestiges of its original ambergris and chocolate rum and had been overlaid by the less tasty odor of Kaspar's chest. But when she drew the letter back, she saw Ravi's beloved handwriting on the envelope that clearly stated the missive was for Hormuzd Rassam, the much-favored envoy and "friend" of Tewodros's many effusive messages.

"But . . ." Delphine held the letter out with a trembling arm, her eyes already stinging with tears. "Kaspar, this is the wrong letter!"

Kaspar waved her on with an encouraging arm. "Open it."

"I can't! It's sealed, and if Rassam finds out I've read his letter, I'll become the much-less-favored one, and by the power of my creator, I can't be of much use in hand chains!"

Sidling over to her with the surreptitious air of a spy, Kaspar spoke from the side of his mouth. "He just wrote Rassam's name on the outside, knowing the reverence in which everyone holds him, and that nobody would dare to open anything destined for Rassam. Go ahead." But even Kaspar could not tolerate the suspense, and he cried, "Do you want me to do it for you, woman?"

"No, no, no!" Delphine spirited the letter away even farther into her vegetable garden, safe from Kaspar's marauding claws. She slowly sank down atop a plot of dead radishes as she read:

My Only Queen of Heaven,

I've refrained from writing up until now, out of fear the message would be intercepted and you punished, and that's the last thing I'd ever want. So I'm praying that this "Rassam" idea will work out for the best. I want you to know first and above all that my powerful love for you has never wavered . . .

You wouldn't recognize me now in my British uniform, shorn of all semaphores of my prowess, and stripped of my brave betoa medal, practically a naked, simpering bore. This most sturdy and stalwart disguise is necessary to strike the proper respect and fear into the hearts of the good people of Tigré and Lasta as I go about the districts. I find I am gaining many more supporters as the turncoat Likamaquas of Tewodros, especially as it is not a very hard task to find enemies of the Wild Boar of Ethiopia, and we come well-stocked with the requisite vintage Maria Theresa dollars.

I can't give you any more specifics in case this letter falls into depraved hands. Suffice to say I know we (though who "we" are at the moment is a question of much concern to me, so I should say "the British crusaders") will prevail in any battle, and so far have been unmolested. We are a wild and kaleidoscopic bunch of reassuring types that hearken me back to lazy days in Sindh. There are Poles from the Bastarnic Alps, bold Arabs breathing the smoke of a sweet pinch of latakia, a Jew remarkable for his wondrous limpid eyes stalking at the head of his string of mules. Hungry Persians looking for a chance to turn an honest rupee into two walk onward with purpose next to well-greased Sikhs from the Mahrattas, ferocious Somali, and athletic Nubians. In short, the entire column has a piebald and martial look. When we face Tewodros's men on the field, most will decidedly keel over from shock—or perhaps I should say from laughter.

My only Queen of Heaven, it pains me too much to be separated from you. So I work ceaselessly keeping this motley column moving, and ensuring its protection. By the power of my creator, I am coming to you. Stay alive until I—

Here on the letter the inky words were obscured by watery splotches. Delphine allowed a tear to join it on the paper.

✳︎　✳︎　✳︎

"I RECEIVED A COMMUNICATION FROM RAVINGER this morning," Delphine told Henry Blanc. "He's now in Dalanta, only a few hours' journey from here."

From their perch on Blanc's roof, they could see over the *amba*'s ramparts to the tents of the imperial camp down on the plain of Islamgie. Over the past week, with the aid of the fieldglass, they had picked out the tents of Herrs Nagel and Flad, Misha Vasiliev, Waldmeier, and the Kanyazmach, Grazmach, and General Gebraye—in addition to the white pavilion of the

Emperor himself. The filthy green tent of Anatole Verlaine was still protected on the lee side of the white pavilion.

Magdala was situated about ten thousand feet above sea level amid gigantic mountains, piled atop each other like immense building blocks, encircled by profound abysses a mile deep. It was an ancient, extraordinary wilderness bristling with boulders and crags, soaring spires and vaulted rock domes. In recent weeks, it had been Delphine's greatest joy to climb a ladder to Blanc's roof where they could scan the surrounding countryside with the field-glass, and with the new addition of Ravi's zenith telescope Kaspar had sent on ahead to the "Magdala Treasury," the scientific-minded residents of the Amba could view the trajectories of meteors.

Delphine handed the field-glass to Henry. "They decreed that twelve soldiers should club together in one tent, and every man must reduce his kit to seventy-five pounds. Everyone is thoroughly angry about it, but most are finding a way around the order."

Henry chuckled. "Oh, such dainty heaven-born children! By the time they write to the War Office to complain, the expedition will be over."

"Bitwaddad Hailo will be seeing Basha Falaka before any of us." Abou sat behind them, as he was tallest and could see over their heads.

Delphine and Henry cranked their necks to view the sober Takrury. "Excuse me?"

"Last night he went over a cliff using a ladder. He went to seek refuge with the British."

Delphine and Henry gazed at each other. It was no big surprise. Hailo, a top member of the Magdala Council, had lived in fear of the Emperor's wrath for a long time.

"You know," said Henry. "He approached Rassam about escaping a year ago. The same way, too! He told him they could escape down a ladder, down the south wall, where they could go and join up with Menelik of Shoa. Rassam said he couldn't abandon his fellows, so Hailo agreed to include Prideaux and I in that offer."

"And what happened?" Delphine whispered.

"Ultimately, we didn't want to leave the others to the Emperor's rage. I can't see those messengers anymore."

They had been following the approach up the Islamgie plain of four mounted messengers from the imperial camp. "Bitwaddad Hailo always gave me the lightest fetters. I hope they bring food," said Delphine.

"They have no food," said Henry. "Did you see those scrawny sheep that Bob sent to Rassam? They all died before we could give them away."

Abou intoned, "I hope they bring saws to take off these chains." For contrary to Kaspar's ostensible mission, only Rassam's fetters had been struck from him.

"What are you doing when you get back to America?" Henry asked Delphine.

"I'm not going back to America."

"Not . . . ?" Henry gasped. "Where are you going, then?"

"Zanzibar, maybe. Or possibly Winterhoek in southwest Africa. Somewhere they need medical help."

"Zanzibar? There's a fantastic medical man there, a Doctor John Kirk. You must go see him!"

"Oh, there's already a *ferenje hakim* there? Then I must go to Madagascar."

"There's my Doctor Chambliss. Always has to be the first."

"The only," Delphine agreed.

It scared her to be "up above the world" like this looking down at such dizzying crevasses. Sometimes she still felt light-headed and tiny, terrified of her high spot beneath the great lowering bowl of sky. Often she had to stop moving and put her hands out into the thin blue sky to steady herself when a wave of vertigo would lift her up out of her body. It had been a particularly fearsome feat to overcome this, climbing up the rickety ladder onto Blanc's roof.

"Dr. Blanc," she ventured. She only called Henry that when she had a medical concern.

Henry smiled. "Yes, Dr. Chambliss?"

"Is it possible . . . That the application of a womb syringe too often, and in too zealous of a manner, perhaps combined with the ingestion of Portuguese Female Pills . . . could cause permanent barrenness?" Because the question was so delicate, Delphine hastened to add, "Someone recently suggested that to me, that there might be a causative effect of such activities."

Henry nodded, politely gazing off at a butte. "If you mean the womb syringe used for relief, for removing obstacles, I'd definitely have to say yes, if used too often. I've seen it happen myself. But not around here, my dear. I've not seen too many womb syringes in Abyssinia. Not a one. What sort of device, exactly?" He finally looked at her, smiling indulgently.

"Ah. I seem to recall it, the syringe in question, as a crude contraption of brass and pewter; you know the sort, with a long hose one inflated by mouth to provide suction onto the womb opening. The syringe would inject the medicated solutions into the womb."

"Yes, I used to see that type. And how many times did . . . you use it for your 'suffering parts'?"

Delphine was relieved Henry had guessed at her intent, without her having to spell it out. "Oh, my. It was forced upon me many times in my youth, habitually, almost as a preventive measure, not always even to correct a condition that we knew to be true. Perhaps forty, fifty times before I turned sixteen."

She heard Henry's intake of breath. "Forty, fifty?" he whispered. "My dear! That's—barbaric! Were you—were you a—Ah! Under what condition was this allowed to happen, if I may enquire?"

"An old man pervert, a Mister Ja Oliver!" Unable to contain

himself any longer, Abou's rage boiled over.

Turning around, Delphine slapped Abou lightly on the forearm. "Oh, shoo, Abou. He wasn't all bad." She explained to Henry, "He took me in when I was an orphan with no prospects, and he did pay for my medical college."

"As well he *should* have!" sputtered Henry. "For inflicting that upon you, I hope he provided you with an ample dowry as well!"

Delphine brushed aside Henry's indignation. She had concluded it did no one any good to seethe with rage. It merely created a sort of black pall over one's head that seemed to color the way one looked at everything. "But since then, my menses have come irregularly, one month twice, then not again for three months. Yet I never conceive. And as we know, Dr. Blanc, if the flow is obstructed and denied its normal egress, it floods the brain and leads to, well, shall we say, imbalances of the mind!"

"Yes." The doctor nodded in sober agreement. "And you fear you have mind imbalances?"

"Well." Delphine wasn't sure how to put this. She knew Henry to be a stolid Calvinist and not at all inclined to view her Spiritualist bents favorably. "Perhaps not 'mind imbalances,' perhaps that isn't the correct term. It's just that sometimes, perhaps from loneliness, I . . ."

"She talks to her dead friend!" Abou assisted heatedly.

"Abou, really now! I'm perfectly capable of explaining my condition to the doctor myself without your help!"

But the damage was done, and Henry was interested now. "A dead friend? Do you see her when you talk to her, or do you just talk into the air?"

Delphine spoke to the valley below. "I see him." She pouted. "I've been seeing him since the night he died. It's quite soothing, not irritating in the slightest, I'm just wondering, perhaps if my menses weren't so irregular and the blood wasn't flooding my brain—I know that to use the brain to think too much will cause the blood to cease to flow downward, and that one should attempt to dull the mind to allow the process to proceed unimpeded, and— Well, it is my job to think when I examine patients, and I simply can't afford the time to sit in my hut for a week trying to make my mind a blank, or playing whist with myself, reading stories about Constant Azarian!"

"Oh, my, no!" Henry laughed, rocking back with his arms locked around his knees. "That wouldn't do at *all*, my dear! Besides, how much stock do you really put in that 'dulling the mind' business? How can the thoughts of the mind affect the processes and flows of the body? That's a theory that needs to be examined again, I believe. Anyway, if seeing this dead friend isn't bothering you, perhaps there's no harm in it. I'd say the real harm lies with that Mister Ja Oliver who put you through such needless medieval torture!"

"He should be tortured in the same manner," Abou grumped.

"Wubishet!" Delphine twisted to see around Henry, and indeed Wubishet and two more royal couriers approached down the main street of the *frenjoch* compound.

Abou didn't seem to notice, or care. "Nail *him* to a table and shove a burning rod into his belly. Watch him cry then!"

Delphine stood on the roof with difficulty, holding her arms out to the sides to maintain her balance. "Wubishet!" she called.

The eager bodyguard jogged over to stand beneath them, trailed by the other two henchmen.

"To whom do you bring a message today?" she inquired.

"To you, Miss El Taleb!"

"To me? Let me come down, so you don't have to shout."

She laboriously clambered down the ladder and stood off to the side so that Blanc and Abou wouldn't descend on her head.

Tewodros was returned to the old method of having his scribe write out his messages for him, and Delphine took the missive with suddenly trembling hands.

Reading swiftly, Delphine let the letter in her hand drop to her side, and she looked up balefully at her companions.

"What," breathed Henry.

"Bob's coming," Delphine whispered back.

Henry and Abou sucked in their breath.

"Tomorrow morning. He enters the walled fortress, and he sends for me. He says now there's only a span between us, and our meeting can take place. He's conveying all of Magdala's artillery and ammunition and sending it down to Islamgie—"

"He intends to meet the enemy on the field down there!" Henry deduced.

"—and he is coming to me, by the power of God, may God realize his good wish."

The little knot of people seemed to shiver collectively then, and all cast their gaze in the direction of the main double gates.

Only Abou dared be irreverent. "May God be deaf to you, *Yabn el Wiskha.*"

Delphine knew only a few curse Arabic terms. *You son of a dirty woman.*

CHAPTER TWENTY-SEVEN
THE HIGHWAY OF HORRORS

Magdala

THE FIBRILLATING ELELTA, THE UBIQUITOUS CRY of Amharas on occasions joyous and bloodthirsty alike, had a notably different quality this morning. A universal tremor ran through the ululation, a strain of foreboding, or outright fear. Summoned to the Emperor encamped just outside the *frenjoch* compound, Delphine dressed in her finest copper silk gown with the dainty pine branch and cone embroidery about the oversleeves and bodice. She was overjoyed that the elliptical hoop of the expansive skirts was intact and serviceable, for the wider her skirts, the farther the Emperor would have to sit from her.

She wanted to resemble the Queen of the South as little as possible, so she coiled her hair into a chignon and stuffed it under a snood.

The guards allowed her through the gates, and Delphine stepped into the world she had only been allowed to hear for the past four months. Fully two hundred carpets must have been laid over the plain before the captive's compound, capped by the Emperor's white pavilion and red flannel tent. Her route was clearly marked, flanked by scores of the *elelta* singing women and men, and Delphine looked with dread down the avenue that bristled with outthrust lances and spears, a particularly harrowing gauntlet to run.

Approaching the pavilion, Delphine breathed so rapidly her head began to spin, but she couldn't will herself to slow it down. The last time she'd seen Tewodros, he'd commanded his Galla swordsman to decapitate the man who had been choking her. He evoked very powerful emotions in her and it confused her, this willy-nilly mélange of feelings, especially when the Emperor was liable to go off half-cocked at the slightest imaginary provocation.

However, Tewodros stood before his personal red tent, and she was dismayed that he waved her toward it, away from the white marquee. Tewodros didn't look in good health. He seemed to have aged about ten years. His handsome vibrant face was now carved with worry, and the gray hairs in his plaited coiffure seemed to have doubled in number.

He snatched her by the arm so forcefully her skull banged against her spine. "My Queen of the South, my Makeda. I have heard that you have broken your promise not to take anything from me."

"*What?*" Delphine whispered. "I've taken nothing! How is it that I've taken something of yours, when many miles have separated our camps these last months?"

"You do not need to be in my tent to have taken something of mine!"

"Perhaps Your Majesty is in error, or was given wrong information, because I have been in chains night and day in Magdala!"

Tewodros angrily yanked the tent flap away from the guard who held it open. He gestured impatiently for her to enter the tent.

"Tewodros, please see reason. You are much too intelligent to believe I possibly could have taken anything from you."

Tewodros looked briefly to the heavens for assistance. His

tenuous patience snapped then, and he shouted, "Then how do you explain why *this* is around your neck?" He pulled at one of the several necklaces she still wore with her *ferenje* dress, a simple leather pouch that contained a nine-inch-long strip of parchment written upon in ancient Ge'ez. "This amulet belonged to my first beloved wife! The only explanation of how it came to be around your neck is that you stole it!" Tewodros firmly grasped her about the arms and propelled her bodily inside.

Delphine was aghast, and confronted the addled Emperor face on. "But it was you who gave it to me, Tewodros! Do you not remember? You had Yetemagnu put it over my head. You told me never to remove it from my person because like the blue silk *mateb* cord it was the sign of our entwined souls." He had told her the amulet would protect her from death, her main reason for wearing it—otherwise, she should have removed it a long time ago. She couldn't be sure if Tewodros was truly so depraved or addled he couldn't remember giving her the amulet, or if he was showing his sly and foxy wits and simply making the entire thing up as an excuse to maul her.

"Why would I give you the amulet of my dear Tewabech? You are nothing to me. You are just a foolish ignorant *ferenje* woman who has been teasing and tantalizing me. You show nothing but disrespect—"

"Aha!" Delphine cried as Tewodros dragged her across the tent. She dared to point in his face as he collapsed back onto an *alga* and tried to wrestle her into position, sitting properly on his lap. "You just said it yourself! I'm nothing but a stupid foolish *ferenje* woman, so how can I be the reincarnated Queen of Sheba? You said I am nothing to you! Do you want your amulet back?"

Tewodros's long agile fingers closed around her wrist to still her. "No, keep it! I cannot be with a woman who isn't wearing the amulet!"

He had not addressed her question as to her identity, so Delphine started afresh. "Just now you called me a stupid *ferenje* woman. Tewodros! You must admit that I am not Sheba, or Makeda, or anything other than a *ferenje hakim* just as it's engraved upon the brass plate of my medical chest—and this war medal around my neck!"

Tewodros's gaze suddenly turned distant. "I hope that when the English soldiers arrive, they will not despise me because I am black . . . God has given us all the same faculties and heart."

Gripping fistfuls of the front of his *shamma*, Delphine leaned forward, and said almost kindly, "Tewodros. You must know, for you've seen the color of my skin. You of all men know the color of my most intimate places."

"Ah, yes, your breasts so full and big," Tewodros agreed before sinking his face into her bosom.

Perhaps that had not been the best approach, after all. "The color of my skin is *white*, Tewodros, *white!*" Cradling his skull in both hands, she tried to wiggle and worry him free of her breasts, but he was burrowed in like a gopher. "I cannot be Makeda, nor can I bear you an heir, because *I am barren!*"

She succeeded in shoving him free of her chest, and he had an astonished face of enlightenment. Delphine took this opportunity to jump off his lap, storm to the opposite side of the large tent, and straighten her bodice. When Tewodros next spoke behind her, his voice was gentle and devoid of all rage. "How do you know this?"

Turning to face him squarely, she replied in a dead voice, "Because. I've mated hundreds of times and never been with child. When I was young, a . . . man who was supposed to act as a father forced me to mate hundreds of times, and then he would . . . clean out my insides, my female parts, with a rude mechanical device that rendered me barren." She said no more, just observed the smoldering blaze of Tewodros's sharp eyes, trying to read him.

At last he stepped forward and raised his hand to her face. He stroked her face lightly with the back of his hand. "Ah, Makeda," he whispered, and just the sound of the name was enough to stoke Delphine's ire again, but he was soon soothing her once more. "There is no worse abuse of power than someone who is supposed to be as a father to take such liberties—no, to torture you! If I could kill him now, I would strangle that white bastard ass with just my hands! You have suffered much, my enchantment. Perhaps your pretend father was afraid of you leaving him. I would then know how he feels, because the closer your people come to Magdala, the sooner the time they take you away from me. Yesterday we held a trial—"

He stopped then, the pupils of his eyes dilating and contracting, his look uncertain. Delphine held him by the arms to steady him when he wavered, and she gently walked him back to sit on the *alga*. "What's wrong? You're weak."

He panted, though he kept his mouth firmly closed and seemed to try to focus his eyes on a specific point on the carpet. "Nothing," he said at length. "Just a bit of *tej metall*."

She pressed her hand to his forehead and nearly got burned. "Tewodros, allow me to go back to my hut and get my medicine."

"No." He weakly shoved her hand away from him. "I don't have time. I must address my subjects. I've lost all of Abyssinia but this rock. I may not be weak now!" He looked at her, and it was with the old gentle deer's eyes. "A warrior who has dandled strong men in his arms like infants will never be dandled in the arms of others."

Delphine frowned. "What are you trying to—"

"We held a trial yesterday," he continued, with more power in his voice. "Ras Bisawwir and Bitwaddad Damash, members of the Magdala Council as you may know, were accused of inviting Wagshum Gobaze to seize Magdala. Many witnesses came forward to accuse them, but it was evident to me that many of the witnesses themselves were men who have been passing treasonable messages back and forth to Gobaze. I am certain that the blond-eyed Frankish bird has been talking out of both sides of his mouth, but once he realized what I suspected, he feigned illness like a lousy swine, so he's been under guard. I want you to go to him and examine him, and report to me what you find."

"Of course."

He remained staring intently at her, leaning with his forearms on his knees, and he seemed shaky. Delphine placed both cool palms on either side of his face. "I shall forever love Tewodros, the greatest Emperor Abyssinia has ever seen."

He then smiled beatifically, as in days of old. How mercurial he could be! "One day you may see me dead. While you stand by my corpse, it may be that you will curse me for my bad conduct toward you. You may say, 'This wicked man ought not to be buried; let his remains rot above ground." He silenced her protests with a dry hand on her lips. "I trust to your generosity."

While Tewodros went back to the white levee pavilion, Paul accompanied Delphine to where temporary tents had been set up. These were perhaps the tents of Bisawwir and Damash, and other political prisoners, and Paul opened the flap to another tent, where Delphine ducked inside.

She hadn't seen Anatole since he'd spied on her and Ravi making love, and she was unprepared for the sight of him. He reclined back on an *arat* with a limp head propped up on many pillows. His hair was patchy and indeed had fallen out in places, and she spied a few oozing tumors on his cheekbone and neck.

All of her former anger fell from her. "Ah, awful," she murmured, and hobbled to kneel at his side.

"Who is that?" Anatole whispered in Amharic.

His eyes were open, yet he stared at a spot somewhere to the left of her, to the light from the tent flap. In English Delphine said, "It's me. Delphine. May I examine you?"

"Delphine?" Her presence seemed to horrify him, and he drew his blanket higher up his neck, but his vacant aquamarine eyes still didn't focus on her. "Why are you here? Have you come to poison me?"

Gently she tugged at the blanket he clutched in his steely talons. "Poison? No, why would I do that? I'm a doctor, Anatole. As ruinous and muddled as you are, I could never intentionally harm anyone. Well, anyone who wasn't directly coming to kill me at the moment, anyway. May I see your chest? I'd like to see your back." She moved a hand in front of his face, and his eyes didn't seem to catch it.

His wasted and trembling hands allowed her to slide the blanket down over his sunken, pitted chest. Rank, seeping furuncles littered his chest and stomach, and Delphine moved the infirm man forward by touching his shoulder as lightly as possible with her fingertips. His entire back was a mass of the gelatinous tumors, and she suspected many more lay deeper—muscle tumors, bone tumors, brain tumors.

She laid him back gently on the grimy pillows, and just in time, for an unaccountable rush of tears ruptured from her eyes, and she barely had time to hobble to the other side of the small tent, in the hopes Anatole wouldn't hear.

After five minutes, Anatole said, "It's bad, I know."

Though she had made sure not to touch any of the open sores, Delphine nevertheless wiped her hands on a scrap of cloth. She approached Anatole. "*Qitegn*. Tertiary syphilis."

Anatole exhaled mightily. "That's what I thought. What is tertiary?"

"Third stage."

"The . . . last stage?"

Delphine nodded, then remembered he couldn't see. "Yes. I have some mercury in my hut, I could cauterize your tumors and give you mercury vapor baths. I can send someone out for the *top-pya* plant, and mix it with pus and barley flour—"

Anatole raised his upper body from the slimy bedstead and shouted in his thick argot, "But nothing will do any good!" His body trembled, and his vacant gaze fell to the carpet. "I am scared . . ."

All in a rush Delphine dropped to the ground next to him. She soothed him in her best surgeon's voice. "Anatole, I have some *merz*. I'm sure you know what that is. Just tell me the word, and I'll give it to you. I have it right here around my neck. It's in this amulet for scented cotton. It's enough to . . . to stop your pain, now and forever."

His entire body was fraught with tremors, as though he were gripped by a sudden virulent fever. "What exhaustion, what despair, what sadness to think of all my past journeying! How active I was only six months ago! Where are the treks across the mountains, the riding and the walking, the deserts, the rivers, and the seas? And now just this cripple's life! *C'est de la torture. Je veux faire ceci et cela, aller ici et la-bas, pour voir, pour vivre, pour partir . . .*"

"Anatole, Anatole," Delphine called distantly, tears rolling down her face. She was glad he could not see her. "But you have nothing to fear. Remember? We know that death isn't the end. A beautiful spiritual realm awaits you on the other side. You should rejoice! You can be born again—"

"*Bah!*" spat Anatole. "There is nothing awaiting me but a mighty, endless void!"

"You told me you believed!" cried Delphine. "Don't you remember, we'd sit and talk—"

"It was an affectation, Delphine, something I thought sounded lofty and holy, not something I could ever truly believe in myself! *Bah!* Remember how you would accuse me of moving the planchette around the talking board!" He was shaking so horrifically he flung himself back onto the bedstead, his staring eyes now sunken deep in his skull. He muttered, and Delphine had to draw closer to hear what he said. "Try to tell you the story of my sleep and my fall ..."

Trembling herself, Delphine withdrew the *merz* amulet from about her neck, gingerly placing it over Anatole's head. "There is the *merz*."

At the tent's doorway, just as she thought a sob would be wrenched from her throat, she managed to gasp, "If you need any more *afyuni*, any *soporifiques* ..."

"The first dog in the street will greet me ..."

The sob roiled up from her chest, and she staggered from the tent.

April 8, 1868
Southern Edge of the Dalanta Plateau

THERE SHE WAS, THE "FROWNING *AMBA*" as Kaspar so persuasively called the towering Magdala summit that rose beyond the daunting plateaus of Fahla and Selassie, where Tewodros was now encamped. Ravi was glad to see the strategy he'd proposed to Napier was now eminently workable: If they could take Fahla and the Aroge plain below it, they could proceed up the saddle that connected it to the Islamgie plain. Ravi could clearly see the regiment of tents encamped on Islamgie, the silver gyres of cooking fires rotating in the still air, and he reckoned the number of fighting men he'd already assumed, about five thousand.

Dismounting from Selpha in one continuous motion without

removing the field-glass from his face, Ravi walked to the lip of the steep couloir. Walde Nebra moved silently in tandem with him.

Walde Nebra spoke in a whisper, as if afraid of causing an avalanche into the Bashillo Ravine below. "Whether he fights on Aroge or Islamgie, we still have to reach Magdala."

Ravi handed the field-glass to Walde Nebra, who took great pleasure in looking through it, as well as all other surveying instruments. "Delphine is still confined in Magdala, though her chains have been removed," he reported to the shield-bearer.

"Then we must find a way up the walls, perhaps around the eastern side of the Kâfir Bar."

"Yes, with the help of scaling ladders and torpedoes—oh, for Christ's sake!"

At the very moment a pewter anvil cloud above them erupted and poured forth a hail of frozen globules, Napier and Munzinger galloped up the rise. Ravi had gone ahead of the Pioneer Force with Napier, the French Consul at Massawa named Munzinger, a few sappers, miners, and a wing of the Sindh Horse. Ravi waved his arm wildly, and Napier and Munzinger veered, Ravi and Walde Nebra leaping on their horses and joining them under a stand of *warka* trees.

The trees didn't completely obliterate the pelting balls of ice, so the two older men held their waterproof sheets above their heads while stuffing various papers and instruments into their saddlebags. Ravi and Walde Nebra, however, sat upright, impervious, merely blinking now and again whenever blinded by an errant hailstone.

"It's a very strong place," Napier shouted, "stronger than any *amba* we've yet seen, which confirms your impression that the Emperor would have never neglected any of the other fortresses we passed along the road, had he not held a much more impregnable position."

Ravi yelled, "Sir, I recommend each man carry in addition to his rifle and ammunition four pounds of rations and a water bottle, which they can fill when we cross the Bashillo below. Let sappers and infantry lead the way with guns coming up behind—"

Napier cut him off. "Yes, yes, and we'll hold the cavalry in reserve. I'll set the Engineers to work making escalading ladders for the assault up the cliffs. Howland, can you lead the 33rd Irish? You know those nooks and crannies like the back of your hand."

"Certainly. To prevent Tewodros—Theodore from clearing out at the last minute, I can ask the Gallas to keep picket at the Kâfir Bar gate. I'm certain they're eager to undertake that mission."

"Yes." Napier laughed with jollity, though the pellets of ice were now nearly the size of billiard balls. "Just an hour ago you should have seen the people streaming out of the ravines, bringing us grain, flour, bread, honey—"

"Ah!" cried Ravi. "Did they bring goats and oxen, as he promised?"

"Yes, yes!" Munzinger answered for Napier. "And chickens, and chopped straw! Now, may I say, General—"

"Let's get to camp," Napier agreed, and turned his horse back down the rise.

They drew within sight of the Engineers and Sindh Horse camp. It was at once a warming and a repellant vision to Ravi. He slowed to accommodate Napier's skittish steed who was unaccustomed to salvoes of ice. Ravi could tell the hailstorm would soon pass, the worst of the anvil clouds sweeping so low over their heads he felt he could touch them with his spear, being up above the world as he was.

"Likamaquas," said Walde Nebra. "The Irish? Are they the ones who play the strange stringed instruments at night in worship to their divinity?"

✳ ✳ ✳

"Tell me, my friend," said the Emperor magnanimously. Attired in a clean *shamma* and sporting two double-barreled pistols at his waist, he sat atop a pyramidal stack of rocks on the edge of a precipice, and he had invited Delphine, Rassam, Blanc, and Prideaux to sit immediately behind him. This was a vast sign of trust, as with one feeble push, they could have sent him tumbling head over heels into the gorge below. He looked at Rassam now. "What do you think of Sebastopol?"

For below them on the royal road that Delphine secretly called the Highway of Horrors, the European artisans oversaw the grueling work of hundreds of soldiers dragging the various mortars and guns cast at Gaffat lashed to wagons up the steep acclivity.

"It is a splendid piece of artillery, and I hope that soon the British army will be viewing it with the same amicable feelings that are filling me right now."

"I hope so too," said Tewodros.

The four *frenjoch* sat back to enjoy the novel tableau unfolding beneath them. Without a field-glass Delphine could still make out Kaspar's form, as his corn-bright hair in its flowing pigtail reflected sun from miles away, and he still wore his brogans with his *shamma* ensemble. With Flad, Waldmeier, Saalmüller, and every other possible chief of note, Kaspar directed the activities of perhaps five hundred men working on just the mammoth Sebastopol, men who affixed long leather ropes to the chains around the gun carriage wheels in preparation for the big pull up the cliff face from the royal road to Islamgie. Delphine recalled Ravi calculating a cliff of this forty-five-degree gradient as a "one to one slope," which meant that for every foot one advanced, the slope rose in height by a foot.

"Kaspar has told me," Delphine called conversationally to Tewodros, "that the mortar weighs seventy tons. That's as though eight elephants were sitting in that wagon!"

Tewodros looked over his shoulder at Delphine, and she thought she'd never seen him look more handsome, his face smooth and serene, as at the moment one could pretend things were going well for him. "It is a beautiful gun," he said warmly.

The other *frenjoch* scrambled to the edge to follow the progress of Sebastopol up the cliff face, and Delphine's curiosity getting the better of her, she crawled on hands and knees to cling to Dr. Blanc's shoulders and peer down. As the men grunted and strained, their animal keening coming like the collective drone of a plague of locusts sweeping up the mountain, the chiefs scrambled behind the gun carriage, in rotation placing large stones beneath the wheels so it wouldn't roll back down the hill should one of the five hundred haulers take it into his mind to faint.

The *frenjoch* on the plateau gasped and sighed in unison whenever one of the leather cowhide strips snapped and broke, threatening to send the mortar plummeting to the valley below, blowing out anyone who had the misfortune to get in the way. The first time this happened, Tewodros shot to his feet, crying "wait!" to the *frenjoch*, and dashed down the road toward the soldiers, a fine and wiry form of a man leaping nimbly from boulder to boulder. Positioning himself on a projecting rock and leaning on his spear, he took over the direction of the mortar.

It was a grand sight, Tewodros raising one hand and silencing five hundred groaning men with a gesture, and his voice rang clear in the silence this one movement had produced.

At last the great mortar was hauled onto level ground on Islamgie, and the *frenjoch* were ordered to come forward to inspect it. Awash with relief the mortar hadn't tumbled, and that

Tewodros's rage hadn't sent any further human forms tumbling after it, they dashed across the plain eagerly. The three Englishmen were intent on serving their Emperor, but Delphine made a beeline for the strutting and preening form of Kaspar.

She didn't wish to impinge upon his glory, but she couldn't resist clinging to his arm as he continued with his harangue that was not made any less florid by his Amharic rendering. "Then, you see, if we had not put the boulders under the wheels at the proper angle when we were turning that most terrifying sharp edge by that *quolquol* tree, it was only a matter of displacing the boulders a mere fraction of a finger's length before lo! The wagon would have plunged to the valley below, squashing hundreds of men as though they were bugs!"

The assemblage sighed deeply at each wondrous word, this being the most amazing event that had yet to happen on Magdala.

CHAPTER TWENTY-EIGHT
THE GHOUL KING OF A MILLION DEAD SOULS

TEWODROS SUMMONED DELPHINE TO LOOK IN on Anatole.

She met him down on Islamgie. He gestured at the stables on the cliff's edge, where mules and servants had been turned out to make room for the native prisoners.

"Do you see? To demonstrate how much I love you and want you to be happy, I have released some of the prisoners."

And indeed there were several dozen women and children wobbling freely away from the stables, their shackles having been newly struck off. In the warm distance that gave the place almost the look of an Eden garden, many of the heartier refugees made relatively robust dashes for the road that led to the canyon below. Delphine in her felicity quite forgot herself, and grabbed the Emperor's arm.

"Oh, Tewodros! You *have* made me so happy! How many will be released? Only women and children?"

He held her hand fast to his arm and shrugged magnanimously. "Oh, perhaps . . . *all* of them?"

She had not seen that sparkle in his eyes in a long time. She jumped up and down in her excitement, and pressed her free hand to his chest. "You *are* the kind benevolent Emperor! I know that part of you, and some people don't! And the imprisoned chiefs?"

Shrugging again, Tewodros seemed to enjoy playing the part of one who could care less. "If you look close enough, I believe they are next in line to have their fetters struck off."

"Oh, yes!" The chief Kantiba Hailo looked serenely into the sky with his foot atop a rock as a soldier allocated to the task worked at hammering his chains. "May I go tend to him? The last time I saw him he was complaining of stomach ulcers."

Tewodros's face clouded then. "I think it's best if you go see the blond-eyed bird first. It's more important to see the ones who are suffering the most."

Delphine removed her hand from the kingly arm. "Yes, but Tewodros, the Frankish scribbler is dying, dying of *qitegn*, if not already dead. There is nothing I can do, but give him more *afyuni*, which I don't have any of. I've given him *merz*, and he may have taken that. Why can I not go tend to the living, or those who may still live if given the chance?"

Smiling indulgently, Tewodros was firm. "No, my enchantment. Perhaps later. Go see your former *fiancé*"—he used the English word here—"and ease his suffering. There is plenty of time to help the living later."

"Ease his suffering?" Did he mean her to force Anatole to take *merz*? Tewodros turned and walked toward the stables, so she couldn't ask the meaning behind his words.

She didn't want to see Anatole. It was a strange facet to a surgeon's life, she who normally rushed to the deathbed of hopelessly terminal patients, but when they were friends, or she knew them as friends from a former existence, she couldn't bear being near them.

As she strode toward Anatole's tent, a tantalizing revelation overcame her. Perhaps her fear was due to nursing Eugene through the typhus that eventually claimed his dear, sweet life. To sit by, wringing one's hands while the only man one had ever loved thrashed about in mad convulsions, his brain eaten away by virulent germs for which there was no medicine, was the worst sort of infuriating insanity, and Delphine hoped to never sit still for that torture again. Perhaps the predicament maddened her even further, for she had been down the hall sleeping when Eugene's spirit had finally fled his body for good, not at his side as she should have been.

"Maybe it's better if I do . . ." Delphine whispered to herself as she ducked inside the tent flap.

Immediately she cringed back almost against the tent's wall when she perceived that Anatole was muttering incoherently to himself. The rank, fetid aroma of oozing tumors permeated the very air, and she grabbed the nearest cloth she saw to hold to her mouth and nose. The cloth unfortunately turned out to be a *shamma* of nearly as saturated putrescence.

"I may as well be back in Andersonville!" she sobbed quietly.

It sounded as though Anatole said, "I promise to be good . . . Please come back, and I promise to be good . . ."

Curiosity overcame her revulsion then, and Delphine crept closer to Anatole's *arat*. It was strange that in his death throes, he would not be speaking in his native French.

"Come back, come back, dear friend . . ."

Who was his "dear friend?" Antoine, or Arthur, or George from the Latin Quarter? She knew he'd been particularly attached to Antoine, and there was something about one of them shooting the other during a drunken argument.

"Come back and all is forgotten . . . O Nature! O my mother! Mother is responsible for putting me into this grim pit!" Perhaps the thought of his mother caused him then to relapse into French. *"Ma mère est une sorcière sinistre responsable pour tous les maux qui s'abattent sur moi . . . que de souffrances elle m'a données!"* My mother is a sinister witch responsible for everything wrong in my life . . . What a terrible pain she's given me!

Slowly lowering herself to the floor in an Indian position, Delphine again felt the pity, the sorrow for a life so wasted. Anatole had been a lauded poet in Paris, the equal of Theodore de Banville, albeit a much-maligned writer who delighted in horrifying the narrow-minded mundane bourgeois with silly antics such as pissing into their absinthe glasses. To give it up, to come to Abyssinia to "discover himself," it all seemed so ludicrous now! All he'd discovered was misery and despair.

Abruptly he spat out more sentences in English, his blind open eyes staring at the tent ceiling, as though images of the transitory realm where he now resided would be etched upon his corneas. "It's unbearable to think that you took my joke seriously. I have been crying for two months straight. You need only to come back . . . We will live here once again, bravely, patiently, I'm begging you. Tell me you haven't forgotten me; you couldn't! If you won't come to me, I'll come to you . . ."

It must be Antoine to whom he was speaking. Gingerly, Delphine inched her hand closer to his chest to open the scented cotton amulet and find out if the *merz* was still there.

"That awful moment when I crept inside your—" As swift as a flung spear, Anatole's hand grasped Delphine's, and he shot to a halfway sitting position. She gasped loudly, almost as frightened by the sudden motion as by his continued staring at someone who apparently sat next to her. "Basha Falaka! You've come back! I knew you would!"

Basha Falaka! He was the one Anatole lamented!

Delphine's shock was usurped by sorrow. "Anatole, it's only me, Delphine." She could not bring herself to touch his ulcerated cheek.

She instantly knew she'd committed the worst, most grave

error. His face fell in encompassing chagrin, and he flung her hand away in disgust, jerking his torso back onto the pus-stained pillows. *"Je l'ai su! Ah! Les haillons pourris, le pain trempé de pluie, l'ivresse, les mille amours qui m'ont crucifié!"* I knew it! Ah, the putrid rags, the rain-soaked bread, drunkenness, the thousand loves that have crucified me!

Perhaps she'd become inured to death and suffering, but at that moment Delphine's attention was drawn away from Anatole's torment by a sudden roar of people racing past the tent. The collective rumble of the crowd was like a tsunami wave washing over the tent, carrying it out to the ocean with the din.

Anatole appeared not to hear. "Ah!" he continued now in English, perhaps still seeing the Basha Falaka sitting next to Delphine. "Will you never have done, then, you ghoul king of a million dead souls . . . *you will be judged!* My skin is rotten with mud and pest, and in my heart much bigger worms!"

"Anatole!" Delphine cried, nearly frantic now, as sharp *elelta* from the prisoner's stables pierced the shoddy tent. What was happening? "Basha Falaka is on his way up here! As God is my witness, I just had a letter from him yesterday, and he says they are two days from crossing the Bashillo River and—ow, let go, you're hurting me!" For his claw-like hand had once again grasped hers, in joy upon hearing that his dearest "friend" was drawing near. "Anatole, Anatole, I have to go. There's something happening over by the stables. I'll—*ow!*—I'll bring the Basha Falaka over to you the moment he arrives here on the Amba, I promise you that!"

For the moment, Anatole seemed placid. A smile even played at the corners of his mouth. "Ah, I might have died among strangers, then. I might have died alone . . . unbearable evocation! How I loathe death."

Delphine patted Anatole's hand, the only part of his body that wasn't diseased. "Stay right here, dear friend! That commotion you hear outside, perhaps it's the Basha Falaka arriving! Let me go see, and—"

She didn't bother finishing the sentence, for when she flung back the tent flap, she knew it wasn't the British Army causing such a tumult.

Tearing over to the prisoner's stables so swiftly the folds of her long shirt and breeches became enwrapped in her legs, the knowledge that she was a prisoner completely evaporated from her mind. Swiftly she reached a knot of people all snuggled together like dumb oxen, staring with spittle dripping from their lower lips.

"What's happening?" she demanded.

Most observers were so stupefied they couldn't answer, but one helpful soldier pointed and said, "Tewodros. He's trying prisoners."

"What?" Delphine clawed her way through the throng of stolid, numb men. Each arm she gripped was like a slippery hunk of recently killed beef, the way they slid from her hands and made dull, insensate way for her.

She was soon in a horrifying clearing. The prison stables stood to her left, and a sheer drop of some three thousand feet occupied the entire right. Tewodros stood over a youth of about thirteen, his *talwar* already lubricious with blood, his face disfigured by rage. Delphine raced forward, her garments tripping her. She landed on her knees next to the squirming body of a man who had been hacked apart by Tewodros's sword.

"Tewodros! Why do you do this? Why do you try him? You told me you were benevolent, and would let them go!"

"Do these people think they can oblige me to strike off their chains? Now they cry and moan for food, when I do not even have enough food to give my devoted soldiers!"

He evidently recognized her, but he was so distorted with anger, he was in an entirely different sphere altogether.

Delphine's hands slapped together in prayer. "What has this boy done? How could he have possibly—"

"He is the son of a man who took liberties with a concubine!" Tewodros shrieked, his hair in unseemly disarray.

"But then you must kill the man who did that, not the son!"

She saw only sky then, for she was wrenched from her kneeling in the mud, her limbs were jerked about, and she was hauled back into a buttery cocoon of men's limbs. She shook her head to clear it of phosphenes, and she was staring into the bug-eyed visage of Kaspar Nagel, who agitated her rudely.

"*Mein Gott*, woman, will you never cease your unhelpful ravings? Leave the Emperor be! He is the only one who can pass judgment and carry out the sentencing!"

"But that poor boy is only the son of a man who had eyes for one of—" She turned to gesture where Tewodros had stood, only to view the enraged monarch toss the flailing boy over the edge of the cliff. The boy hovered for a moment suspended on the breeze, a black figure cut from a block of wood with no features or defining marks. Then he was gone.

General pandemonium broke out now, the prisoners yet waiting in the queue to have their fetters struck suddenly changing their minds and trying to flee back inside the stables. The inmates still inside prevented their access by pushing to get out, as they had not witnessed Tewodros's acts of murder. Soldiers in the audience who thus far had numbered among the perfectly free, innocent, and liberated also turned and made tracks in a disorderly fashion toward the peaks of Selassie and Fahla, as though in his mania Tewodros might select random victims from among the general populace.

"Do you see? See what he's doing, Kaspar? Not an hour ago, he promised me he was freeing *everyone*! Now he's throwing little boys over the—there's another one! What has that man done?"

Kaspar wrestled with her arms as though determined to throw her to the ground and sit on her, so she beseeched a nearby man, "What has that man done?"

"He loaded a musket for the Emperor, and it misfired."

"Misfired!" That fellow went sailing over the cliff's edge.

The crime of the next man, who had been a valet to the Emperor, was of daring to laugh with a royal bodyguard. He was swiftly dispatched. And because the water wells were situated at the base of that cliff and some of the victims fell into the water, thus not arriving in the properly deceased mode, Tewodros sent musketeers to finish them off, blasting away ruthlessly in a neat line on the cliff like so many architectural crenellations.

"Misha! Misha!" Delphine spied the placid Azmach standing aloof and leaning on a spear, the lion's mane mantle about his shoulders. His eyes flickered when he heard his *ferenje* name being called, but no muscle on his face twitched at all. "Misha! Why don't you tell him to stop? This is barbaric!"

Kaspar grappled more severely with her now, his natural masculine strength at last overpowering her, and he twirled her to face him. *"Mein Gott, schließen Sie gerecht oben?* If you keep up that hollering and shrieking we are *all* taking a journey over that cliff, and it will be one from which no one will return!"

"He's right, Delphine." Suddenly Herr Flad was there, his calming hands on her shoulders entombing her even further. "Please, please! Do not intervene in matters you know little of!"

"But—what is there to know? You don't have to *know* anything to *know* it is wrong to throw men off a cliff for the offense of laughing! Not an hour ago he told me—*ach*, what are you doing, Kaspar?"

"We must leave here!" Kaspar yanked her by the arm so stridently she felt her elbow would dislocate. "Flad, help me! Let us get her back to our tent! That's the only safe place!"

"Yes, yes!" Flad flanked her other side, and between the two

Germans Delphine was fairly lifted in the air, and ran without her toes touching the ground.

Kaspar growled, "Believe me, Miss Chambliss! You do not want to be directing attention to yourself at this moment, and it is best if we all remain as quiet as cockroaches, for that is in our best interest—"

"What's that?" Delphine yelled.

A new voice carried high above their heads. A voice of lazy, happy, opium-infused afternoons. "That's Anatole! Who has him? Why do they have him? Kaspar, he's dying in his tent! Tewodros asked me to look in on him!"

Kaspar hissed heatedly, "He's not in his tent anymore, he's been the worst sort of traitor, and he's no concern of ours!"

"Yes, yes, Doctor Chambliss," Flad tried to soothe. "Let us not interfere . . ."

Anatole's wailing voice carried over the Abyssinians, a wail not of desperation, but almost pleased, jubilant. As she couldn't move side to side, Delphine jumped up and down, and saw over buttered heads Anatole's jerking ulcerated limbs as he was borne aloft by a group of eight men. "Anatole! Anatole!" she shrieked.

"Shut up, woman!" cried Kaspar.

Jumping down upon Kaspar's foot with the heel of her elf's shoe, he at last released her, uttering choking sounds of pain. It was easy to escape Flad, and Delphine shot forward. "Anatole!"

"Ah! Basha Falaka! I promise to be good!" he cried. He didn't thrash in desperation to escape. Rather he flailed atop the men's hands in some sort of seraphic transport where he apparently believed that anyone who spoke English was the beloved Likamaquas.

"I know you will be good!" she called to him. "You're always good, you're a good man, and a great poet, the greatest poet the world has ever seen! And you're brave—"

"I'll be brave!" Anatole cried, and she saw the glimmer of one tear on his cheek before Kaspar and Flad grabbed ahold of her once more, and the crowd of soldiers bore away with him. "I'll be on my best behavior . . . I'm waiting . . ."

They didn't need to grip her very sternly anymore, for she staggered like a fluttering flag. The wobbly blond head was carried off to the cliff's edge, and there was no ceremony of even trying him. The Emperor merely waved a disgusted hand, and Anatole sailed, almost billowing with lightness like a filthy feather mattress, and where he'd been there were only two hawks wheeling against a void of pale sky.

✸　✸　✸

April 10, Good Friday

UNDER A LOWERING, OPPRESSIVE SKY, THEY climbed the Royal Road Tewodros had caused to be built. With straight backs and bare feet Ravi, Walde Nebra, and the Magdala refugee Bitwaddad Hailo alertly marched their horses up the Aroge Ravine, along with the men of Lieutenant-Colonel Penn's Battery and the Naval Rocket Brigade who joined them, after having unintentionally taken an impromptu baptism crossing the waters of the Bashillo. There were no enemy sentries or pickets situated upon the flanking ranges, so it appeared the army *à l'Anglaise* had no cause to shake in their boots at those looming bluffs. If all continued as now, calmly sweating and toiling up the slope with nary a sniper to harass their progress, they would meet the other brigade of the Bombay and Madras Sappers and Miners and Punjab Pioneers at the juncture below Selassie and Fahla.

There were abundant opportunities for ambuscade, chances for men with fire feet to torment the lumbering column with enfilade, slant, and reverse fires. A modern force defended with civilized engineering could have easily lurked behind any promontory and turned the defile into a bloodbath like the Afghan passes. But there came nary a peep from the *quolquol* trees—suspicious, almost. Ravi's cotton drawers swarmed about his crotch like a hill of biting ants, his lined blue serge trousers engulfed his thighs like the broiling sun itself, and he longed for the freedom and cool of his former breeches and *shamma*. But he'd promised Napier he would throw on his uniform tunic at the first sign of enemy movement.

They spurred up a rounded abutment of hill, and Selassie at last towered in their view, many threads of smoke the only indication that anyone lived on the great heights.

Ravi espied Colonel Phayre lounging with other young officers on a green sward, so galloped over. Dismounting, he chose not to loll, but took two frugal swallows from his canteen before searching for his pipe. His guard, being Abyssinian, also stood at attention, as was more comfortable for them.

"I don't believe there's anyone in Magdala," said an officer, chewing on a long piece of grass.

"By George, neither do I!"

"Nor I."

Colonel Phayre stood, serving as a hearty example to the other men. "Oh, pshaw! Just last night there was a messenger from Rassam reiterating his warning, telling that Theodore intended to fight. 'Be careful, Theodore is on the move,' he said."

A lieutenant got to his feet. "I've ridden up that road that you see within pistol-shot of this summit, and don't you think if people were there, they would've fired on us?"

"That proves nothing," said Ravi, his voice hoarse from not having vented in several hours. "Tewodros is cautious and sly as a fox. He's not going to sacrifice any good chance he has for the sake of bagging a few men. He may have decided upon giving up his prisoners, and in that event he wouldn't fire, and—ah, Napier!"

Conspicuous in his snowy sun-jacket, Napier surveyed the heights of Selassie and Fahla through his field-glass, at the head of Penn's Battery column, clambering panting up the slope behind him to occupy and hold the head. This position, connected by the undulating dales of the Royal Road, was on the same level ridge as that of the Naval Rocket Brigade. Napier surveyed on a slim saddle that connected with the base of the Aroge Plain, and Fahla could be reached from the Plain by a series of eroded termite hills. This was a fortuitous choice of positions, protected by lofty slopes in the rear, and commanding all approaches while remaining out of sight of any artillery the Emperor may have upon Fahla. Tewodros had long ago chosen the most inviolate heights for his aerie.

Ravi rode over to Napier while looking at his pocket chronometer and taking up his own field-glass.

"I wonder if Theodore intends to fight at all," said a lieutenant.

"Not he," said Colonel Penn.

Napier lowered his field-glass and cocked his head in Ravi's direction. "I can understand, Captain Howland, if you choose not to fight," he said bluntly.

Ravi snorted. "As I stated last night. There's only one *ferenje* on that *amba* who doesn't desperately want to be remanded out of that despot's clutches. I've chosen which side to fight on."

With firmness, Napier phrased his statement differently. "I can certainly understand not wanting your brother's blood on your hands."

Ravi sighed gruffly. It wasn't his most highfalutin reverie either, the notion of having to face a man he'd soldiered beside for a decade, and blow him out. But it was exactly that notion—that he'd been a soldier his entire life—that wiped his guilty slate clean and gave him the certitude that he was on the irreproachable side of this war. In Abyssinia, factions and armies changed loyalties as frequently as refreshing their buttery coiffures. It was always a matter of who had the most food, the most armament, the most friends. The most loved ones on which side.

"There will be only one brother's blood on my hands, Colonel," said Ravi. "Of that I'm satisfied."

A sergeant dashed over on his horse. "There are men on top of the hill, sir!"

Colonel Penn hollered, "What? Aye, by Jove! I see them!"

On the instant, a perfect line of horses moved forward on the knoll, and the row of officers lifted their glasses to their faces.

"Ah," uttered Ravi. The hazy horizon of Fahla's pinnacle came into focus, familiar rocks and battlements, with red-shirted *kamis* men scrambling to maneuver the unwieldy guns of Gaffat into position.

"Egad, they line the whole summit from one end to the other!"

Someone cried out, "Theodore has opened the ball! D'ye hear the sound of the chain-shot?"

A tremendous boom imbued the entire valley, large "O"s of smoke rising to mark its origin upon Fahla. The formation of horses backed up slowly as there came a loud harp-song winging like greased lightning toward the battalion. Instantly Ravi calculated the acceleration and trajectory of the missile, and his bellows and arms indicated to his men to stand still. Their horses skittered in a variety of caracoles, unsure of which way to run, unfamiliar with the blaring tremor that rocked the world between the plateaus.

Bearing toward his company, Colonel Penn hollered, "Bring up those guns, boys! Get ready for action!"

A huge whirring chain-shot of cannonballs and links went lickety-split above their heads. As men crouched, kneeled, and covered their skulls, Ravi saw the sixty-eight-pound Sebastopol chain-shot bury itself about fifty yards behind them, digging up a huge circular trough of dirt before it flew harmlessly over the edge of the bluff.

"Look smart, boys! Keep your eyes open, lads!"

As Selpha stumbled, Ravi slid around his flanks and righted himself quickly along his withers, grabbing handfuls of his mane, with no help from the slippery and stiff Otago saddle. There was one quick view of a terrified Walde Nebra's face in a frozen mask of horror, but he was all right, he had the Enfield Ravi had given him at the ready, prepared to shoot the devils from the sky.

"Down with those guns from the carriages," commanded Penn as he stroked his sword above some loafers' heads. "Lead the mules to the rear, man guns! Keep your wits bright, or by Jove I'll spur you to it!"

Ravi hollered at Napier, "They have ten guns at work!"

Napier sat calmly astride his charger as though observing an exhilarating cricket match, unruly spectators swirling around him in frenetic activity and thrill to finally sight the enemy. "No point in firing; the First Brigade's still climbing up that damned slope. Away, sir," he shouted at an aide-de-camp. "Bring up the King's Own on the double-quick—and you! Order the Naval Brigade here instantly. Sir Staveley, let the Punjab Pioneers deploy across that narrow plateau in front, but don't fire until the enemy are within two hundred yards of you. Colonel Phayre, have you examined those ravines?"

Ravi yanked his ridiculous uniform tunic from his bedroll, and before he could shove one arm into a sleeve, *boom boom boom* came three concussions from Fahla, echoes of the deafening charge bouncing in turn off all cliff faces in the valley. Once again the enemy's shot, though at a distance of almost two miles and aimed expertly into their position, plunged harmlessly over their heads due to excessive powder charge.

Walde Nebra shrieked with an uncharacteristic fear. "Are those the *ferenje* guns from Gaffat? The *azmary* promised the whole world would fall on its face when they set it off!"

"It's all right, Walde Nebra, I believe the *ferenje azmary* was either very faithful to the British when he made that mortar, or very incompetent. *Ho*, what is that?"

For pouring from the slopes of Fahla, the summit of which rose straight up a thousand feet above Ravi and Napier's position, came a seething, spreading flow of men like a bloodstain oozing down the giant anthills of the butte. Ravi estimated about five hundred ululating chiefs were mounted upon their war-horses, their scarlet shirts a remarkable resemblance to the red coats of the Royal Engineers and Sappers, and three thousand footmen with only muskets and *shotels* racing on foot to fill the Aroge Plain. Motioning Walde Nebra and Bitwaddad Hailo to the rear of the rumbling Naval Brigade, he shouted at them, "You've done enough to help; I don't expect to turn you against your brothers. I order you to the top of that knoll along the Aroge Ravine, the one with the rock face shaped like Bitwaddad Hailo's mother-in-law."

"Action, front!" bawled the naval captain, and the command was echoed down the line.

"Action, front!" from the lieutenant and boatswain.

Appearing not a moment to soon, the band of sailors of the Naval Rocket Brigade, quick as lightning and prompt as powder, unstrapped the rocket tubes from the carriages. Ravi wished to join the flood of sappers and miners being ordered down onto the Aroge Plain where, armed only with the ancient muzzle-loading Brown Bess, they seemed prepared to be annihilated. He gave his stubborn servants the salute of a great Likamaquas and wheeled Selpha about, only to be nearly speared in the shin by a rocket man wielding a pry pole.

"A soldier can never leave his master's side!" cried Walde Nebra through the confusion, but Ravi was already halfway through the rear of the brigade, threading his way through rocket carriers and muleteers.

Ravi reached the naval captain just as the frenzied command to "Fire!" was issued, so he paused to appreciate the spectacle that had a beauty he had once enjoyed in bygone days. Rivers of rocket fire shot down the graciously undulating slope, even appearing to rise to seek out the dusky targets, vaporized at once even in the action of lifting their spears. Through his field-glass Ravi saw petrified horror on the faces of the men who still stood in one piece, glancing at each other with outstretched hands and agape jaws. He almost broke into a cheer as the sailors were, but he saw how rapidly Tewodros's men regained their masks of ghastly determination, and surged forward once more down Aroge.

Again a barrage of flaming rockets shook the ground on Ravi's ridge, and again the brave warriors rallied in a desperate essay, as Ravi knew they would, having trained and ridden with these tough highland soldiers for so many years. He kicked Selpha into a run down the knoll to join the flow of the King's Own who were heading to the hollow on Aroge, forming line all the while, to join the Sappers and Miners who were already in position under *wanza* trees and brush.

Leaving Selpha safe with a Punjabi muleteer who acted as a horse holder, Ravi fell in with the men ascending the small slope that separated them from the Aroge Plain, jogging with their Snider rifles at the ready and sharing untrammeled faces of joy to at last be confronting the bloodcurdling *elelta* of savage warriors. In the short second before cresting the rise, Ravi took a deep, chilling breath with a prayer he wouldn't face any friends on the other side.

A few Abyssinian soldiers on horseback had already neared the rise of the slope, charging up ferociously hefting their spears and matchlocks. Almost before the Colonel had called out, "Commence firing from both flanks," Ravi and the men of the King's Own opened fire with their Sniders to devastating effect. Without exception, every Amhara on the slope was cut down by the volley of leaden downpour, some men shot by the missiles of more than one *ferenje*. Ravi recognized one he had blasted in the chest as a former grass-cutter, a sign that Tewodros was desperate for warriors.

The footmen of the wave behind them again became paralyzed in the very act of lobbing the spears that fairly oscillated in their hands. When they came to life and looked around amazed at the sudden extermination, Ravi knew that they were perplexed because they'd been ever-victorious on the battlefield prior to this day. They hadn't even been able to fire upon the *frenjoch*, as their corroded matchlocks only had a range of a hundred yards, as compared to the Snider's nine hundred.

"Retreat!" hollered their Fitawrari as another two rapid volleys of hail tore through them, and they attempted to take advantage of any possible hiding spot of a boulder or a bush. But the whizzing bullets ricocheted off each mound and rock, and hurled the men behind dead upon the ground. Some withdrew up the anthills of Fahla to hide behind thickets of *quolquol* trees, from which hiding spots they opened up a sneaky fire on the right, wounding several soldiers.

Still another wave came at them, and as Ravi picked off an older man he knew as an intensely religious fellow who carved elaborate altar crosses, some one of the King's Own yelled out, "There's the Emperor!"

Ravi knew it was not the Emperor, but for a moment he was shaken with a sudden panic that it might be Misha, whom he had heard was fancying himself Likamaquas and wearing a lion's fur mantle, so perhaps dressed as him in battle, although Ravi could not imagine such a bold thing from his old partner. It was a dashing form wrapped in a leopard's skin cape and a velvet mantle embroidered with silver stars and crosses charging up the rise on a gorgeous bay gelding, waving one of the fine rifles they'd looted from Gondar.

"That's not the Emperor!" Ravi bellowed, making an energetic dash behind the skirmish line. "Hold your fire! That's not the Emperor!"

"Eh?" bawled a private. "Well, if it's not the Emperor, then isn't that even *more* bloody reason to shoot him?"

Ravi hollered, *"Don't shoot that man in the leopard's skin!"*

"Here now, Howland!" Colonel Evans trotted over. "What's this bloody business about not shooting that fellow? He's roaring toward us with a perfectly deadly rifle."

"It's the Emperor's General, sir. If we can capture him we've got a much better chance of leaving behind someone who's fairly competent in this country. I know this man well, and—" He twirled, and there was only the briefest blur of Fitawrari Gebraye's spotted fur as he was ejected sideways from his saddle. The horse, instantly aware he was riderless, and wishing to be with his master, caracoled about to go nuzzle the inert body in the grass.

"I say," Colonel Evans uttered dispiritedly, "it looks he's a bit of a croaker."

"Send someone out when the field's clear to recover the body," said Ravi, returning without fanfare to his former position.

The Amharas were sprinting on the double-quick, one Basha in the process of dashing for a copse leaping into the air and falling to his face, grasping the earth as though it promised life. Another Azmach tearing for a hollow had a sudden hole where his nose had been, and went whirring down the rise like an iron drill. The large leaden Snider bullets left yawning chasms wherever they struck a limb, the wounds like volcanoes of churning alluvium through which one could sometimes see the earth or sky beyond.

A low cloud of the putrid egg creamy smoke from the black powder engulfed them now, as the fight was a battue of ceaseless British volley firing. Ravi could empty and reload the Snider ten

times in a minute and continued to do so, but it became questionable what exactly he was shooting at in the thick pall of nauseating
smoke. Too, he heard fewer Amhara horsemen, and since he was
backed up admirably by Baluchi forces on the knoll behind him, as
well as the Bombay Sappers on his right flank, he chose this lull to
decamp up a ravine to find how Penn's Steel Battery were faring,
dropping a few more Amharas on his way. One was a man he'd led
in battle many times, and whose shocked look of utter recognition
at seeing the ghost of Basha Falaka stayed fixed in Ravi's mind as
he clambered up the ravine.

His ravine intersected with another, larger and more cavernous, which the rains in prior years turned into a raging river. Now
it was awash with a flood of Abyssinian footmen racing full blast
down from Fahla, Dejazmach Deris apparently at their head, bellowing a full-lunged "Forward!" They bounced and jumped and
fairly ricocheted off the rocks that dotted the canyon choked with
tamarisk and wild olive trees. Deris had last been seen on Mesraha
forcing morsels of *wot* down Ravi's throat. This thought gave Ravi
pause for only a fraction of a second, and he took an abandoned
leap off a boulder as a springboard, giving him the momentum to
clutch the opposing cliff face and scramble up the sheer wall like a
spirited tarantula. He was a sitting duck had any of the Amharas
chosen to look up, but soon he was outside of their range.

He topped the rise just in time to be swept away by a rushing detachment of the Punjab Pioneers, hale and eager fellows who
welcomed Ravi into their advance.

"They're going after the baggage train, sir!" a soldier told him.

"They seem armed only with spears, maybe a few matchlocks,"
Ravi assured him.

Arranged in a semicircle were the six guns of Penn's Mountain
Battery, and when the Punjabis dipped beneath the lip of the knoll
and dropped packs on the ground, Penn's order to "commence

firing" sent flaming discharges of cannon shot booming over their heads. The Amharas' ravine had turned a serpentine course into dense brake and jungle, but the shells met their mark in a maelstrom of wails, explosions, and flying tribesmen. Ravi again thought of the musketeer's face when he'd shot him nearly point-blank, and his instinct conflicted with his actions. Instinct told him to dash into the ravine and lead the Amharas in this pitiful battle that was surely "death in the front, and certain destruction in the rear." Yet now he, too, lifted his rifle in a bold cheer at the rubbing out of those whom he'd slept next to by campfires for so many years.

There was nothing for it—he was a soldier first and foremost and he'd chosen his side.

He dashed around the right flank to approach Major Chamberlain, still mounted upon his horse. "They're going to rally again."

"By Jove. Don't you think we've got them all by now?"

"I know their commander. They're very good at climbing these canyons. If I could venture a guess, I'd say they might have traversed obliquely up—there's a ravine you can't see from here"—Ravi pointed—"and may be preparing to issue out of that gully—"

"By Jove!" shrieked Chamberlain, as all at once a rush of flailing warriors erupted from the gully Ravi had indicated, closer to their enemy than had been seen all day, and Ravi took flight toward them as Chamberlain ordered his men, "Right about! Left oblique! Forward march!"

As rocket men on the bluffs above worked to adjust their sights, on Ravi's knoll the soldiers kneeled to the accompaniment of a heated clicking of triggers. Punjabis with faces almost as dark as the Ethiopians' roared their Sniders directly into the wall of approaching warriors, the explosive sound deep and thunderous like a train through a tunnel. Ravi didn't see a single Amhara musket fired.

Again the enemy seemed too astonished by the show of fire to even bother shooting back. It was a rout, a shooting match at a carnival. With shattered limbs ravaged by the Minié balls, the enemy collapsed to the ground all across the killing field, and where there had been perhaps a thousand swarming from the gully, only about six hundred were left to dart back into the jungly ravine.

Stamping through the field carpeted by bodies, Ravi followed the retreating army, potting them mercilessly, then rejoined the other Punjabis who were sweeping up the glacis back to the battery, perhaps in expectance that the Amharas would be disgorged from another arm of the canyon. Just so, the dark warriors were vomited forth and engaged once again with cataclysmic fire. Fixing bayonets, Ravi and the sepoys rushed down the slope to at last meet the brutal ululating enemy hand to hand. Now that Ravi knew it was possible he could be recognized, he'd be the ultimate target of their savage rage, but he knew from the clash of past heated battle that one did not take the time to memorize one's enemy's visage, and merely saw him as an obstacle to be mowed down.

Spears hurtled at the regiment, one whizzing so close to his face Ravi felt its wind and heard its passage, like a mosquito tearing by one's ear. Dropping the Snider to its sling behind him, Ravi drew his *shamshir*, instantly parrying several murderous *shotel* swipes, and knocking the swordsmen almost comically to the mud. Slicing one fellow across the stomach, he delivered a resounding backhand across the throat to the next man who leaped at him, and Ravi ducked away from the ensuing gout of blood. Here he was in his milieu and he knew well his superior swordsman's capabilities over that of the swarthy enemy, and as bold Sikhs stabbed at dark bodies with their bayonets, Ravi remembered the odd thrill of chopping off limbs with one muscular stroke. The steely slicing tingle in his sword arm, the power he wielded over another man's life in battle, it had been months since he had known this delight, and once this engagement was finished, he may very well never know it again.

He still had no fascination for blood per se, and it was abhorrent when a sepoy next to him, in drawing his own *talwar* and hacking off an Amhara arm, rudely splashed the dusty scarlet shoulder of Ravi's coat. His disgust propelled him to throw the weight of his entire body into an uncustomary thrust between the ribs of the next opponent—the curved *shamshir* blade sank in easily, as was attested to by the dumb shocked look on the warrior's face as his snarl turned to stupefaction. Ravi was just able to yank the blade and shove the disgusting body from him before it fell, seemingly determined to pin him to the ground with its ghoulish weight. As inky thunderheads above opened up and poured loose a torrential spout of water onto the battlefield, Ravi spun to vent his adrenaline on the next victim who was soon to be limbless.

"Likamaquas!" cried Walde Nebra just as Ravi was about to slice him.

"*Isgyoh!*" Ravi flung his sword arm to his side and gave Walde Nebra a hefty shove with his left hand. "By the power of my creator, get the hell out of this mess before these Sikhs mistake you for—for an Amhara!"

Walde Nebra, already drenched by the life forces from the recently deceased, jutted out his lower lip. "I am here because I fight alongside my master, to protect you—" His attention whipping to a spot just over Ravi's shoulder, Walde Nebra fairly soared over Ravi's head in a swirl of *shamma* to slice his *shotel* into the waist of an oncoming warrior who probably had no idea that the shield-bearer was an enemy.

Ravi had no more chance to lecture his servant, for he was suddenly elevated off his feet and was twirling like a top in the air, spinning fountains of water as the tempest above unleashed its most vigorously cleansing downpour. But he held to his sword, and he landed on his tailbone in an elegant glissade through the mud and blood, only coming to a stop against the riddled corpse of a dusky former comrade.

Was he shot? Ravi knew enough to get to his feet, as sprawling on the ground he made an even more inviting target. He discerned that a spear had grazed him from the rip in his uniform tunic at his left side and the viscous gore when he plunged his hand into the muck. As Tewodros's cannons, that had lain dormant for so many long minutes now, stormed into life on Fahla lighting up the ridge with a veritable rim of fire and smoke, Ravi faced down the charging, screaming Kanyazmach, the nemesis of his former life. It must have been the Kanyazmach who had flung the spear, for he advanced now waving only a *shotel*, and that he clearly recognized Ravi was evident in the manner in which he shrieked, "*Yet abat!* Where is your father, you blasphemous traitor to the King of Kings?"

Hefting his saber and twirling it like a sling full of shot, Ravi jovially returned the compliment. "Eat earth, Kanyazmach!"

Overhead, channels of jagged streak lightning intertwined with trailers from Penn's rocket guns now trained on the summit of Fahla. Ravi skillfully ducked beneath the upper cutting arc of the Kanyazmach's *shotel* blade as it whooshed in the air where Ravi's neck had been. As fast as the lightning that illuminated the seething mass of limbs and bodies at his feet, Ravi sprang up with a sweeping backhand of the *shamshir*, all the rage and power in his brawny arm bearing down upon his foe, the blade cleanly slicing a few inches off the Kanyazmach's bicep. The momentum of the blow sent Ravi into a graceful pirouette where, with feet off the mud at the same time like a jack-in-the-box, he cleaved the Kanyazmach obliquely at the shoulder, as he had used to split sheep for the Emperor's amusement.

Ravi couldn't bear the gruesome spectacle of the inside of

the Kanyazmach's torso, opalescent lungs the color of chalcedony intermingling with permanganate sludge like a lunatic's oil painting, so he kicked the mess of organs to withdraw his sword, and quickly turned.

The odor of murder was so pungent that no forceful deluge could wash it from the field. Listless now, he sought out Walde Nebra, trailing the *shamshir* in the bloody grass to clean it of residual gore as phosphorescent rocket trails outlined supernatural arcs above, hitting their marks on Fahla. He didn't even bother looking out for other adversaries—the smoke was beaten down to the mud beneath his feet, and he could clearly see almost all foes still mobile had vacated the field.

Warriors lay in thickets, their white and red *shammas* splotches like blooming poppies. Men writhed and flopped like beached fish in the gelatinous mud, Ethiopians the color of earth, entrails spilling out from between clutched fingers, and Ravi thought *we could use a good doctor like Delphine down here*. But she was, he hoped, safely stowed in the mountaintop fortress, from where she'd never have to witness another battle.

Ravi now knew he never wanted to see another one again.

CHAPTER TWENTY-NINE
THE SUN UPON THE ENEMY

DELPHINE WAS AFRAID TO SLEEP.

Sitting on Blanc's roof under an umbrella, they had listened to continual firing for two hours, unsure if Tewodros had engaged the British, or if he was "fakering" it. The gates of the fortress were closed with no communication between Magdala and Islamgie, so at dusk they'd all retired to their crowded huts, a heavy ball of doom sitting in Delphine's stomach. She was now housed in her hut with Mrs. Flad, a weak and sickly woman, and her children, as well as the expectant Frau Moritz, so she couldn't even get up to light a candle, and had to lie abed for hours listening to the unusually loud baying and crying of jackals and hyenas from the plains below.

She feared if she slept, she would miss Ravi's spirit if he came to her. It was a painfully agonizing knowledge that once again she would not be allowed to be present at her lover's deathbed—once again in a prison herself, but this time she would not sleep!

She was fully prepared to leap from her bed when she heard Kaspar and Flad come from Islamgie to Rassam's hut. They had a letter from Tewodros to Rassam. For the first time they heard of the battle of Fahla, and everyone wept with joyful relief to hear it had been a complete rout. Delphine read the note in the scribe's handwriting, which said:

I, being an Emperor, could not allow people to come and fight me without attacking them first. I have done so, and my troops have been beaten. I thought your people were women, but I find they are men. They fought very bravely. Seeing that I am unable to cope with them, I must ask you to reconcile me to them.

"I know the question foremost in your spry brain, my dear," Kaspar told Delphine in confidence, the other men clustered around the letter trying to make out the hidden implications behind it. Kaspar's waist-length bleached hair straggled from its queue in disarray, smudges of cannon powder on his face and neck. "I'm happy to say that several men who made it back into camp had their heads still attached to their necks, and so were able to report they saw someone who resembled your beloved dashing hither and yon about the Aroge Plain, and a soldier saw one of Howland's bullets go through three men at once."

"Yes? And how many British did your favorite Sebastopol mow down?" She said this louder than propriety demanded, in order that many of the *frenjoch* might turn around and frown at Kaspar.

But he seemed pleased someone had asked, for already his hand was going to his chest, and he looked around impudently. "It behooves me to report on the complete and utter disaster of Sebastopol! Yes, some dunderheads took it into their mind to cram two cannonballs in at once, and in a big shower of leaden flame, it burst!" While he was rained with the gratified laughter of all men in the hut, despite that Kaspar told them many of the Emperor's men had been killed by the explosion, Kaspar continued, "We were left with only the smaller cannon, most of which were clearly not designed for accurate propulsion in any way whatever, and most overshot their mark."

"And which dunderhead," asked Blanc, "might it have been who crammed two balls into Sebastopol?"

Kaspar's nostrils flared. "Having been momentarily distracted by some *azmary* who kept pulling on my sleeve to show me the might of the British battery, I will never be able to ascertain that. Us *frenjoch* were only to load the guns, but Amharas fired the mortar. Let us just say it was most unfortunate for the King of Kings."

Come the next morning, Kaspar and Flad returned to Tewodros with Lieutenant Prideaux as an envoy, hoping to effect some manner of understanding. Later in the day, the captives heard that the Emperor had sent Flad and Prideaux back to Napier with an angry letter refusing any terms. Delphine and Dr. Blanc were allowed out of their compound under heavy guard to tend to the hundreds of wounded that were carried up to the plateau. Rambling reports from the dazed soldiers still able to talk were horrific tales of exploding planets, shooting stars, heaven and earth opening before the might of the *frenjoch*.

Abyssinians were so rabidly curious as to her operational procedures they pressed in on all sides with their choking stench to watch, as though it were a puppet theater and not a surgery, and Delphine had to employ a dozen youths to keep them at bay.

She was swiftly swept back to her battlefield days of three years prior, but what might have frightened her only a year ago she now viewed with a stolid resolve, and she worked with Abou by her side, him being vastly unafraid of anything to do with a human body, detailing and explaining to Blanc the advances in amputation that had been made in battlefield surgery since he'd last been called upon to perform. Delphine had more experience than Blanc digging out the .58-caliber Snider balls from bodies.

In the afternoon the repatriated Commandant of Magdala,

Ras Bisawwir, came to tell the captives the Emperor wished them to proceed to the British camp. Delphine was bodily hauled off her surgery detail and hustled back to the *frenjoch* compound, where all was a stew of frantically racing folk and contradictory rumors. The general opinion was the Emperor meant to have them massacred on the road to the British, or to keep them close at hand until he could bargain with Napier. But the moment was at hand, and Delphine barely had time to wash the worst of the blood from her limbs in a tub of water from yesterday's rains before Abou arrived, frantically stuffing what little clothing and belongings she owned into her battered portmanteau, the idea being someone would carry their baggage after them.

Mounted upon their mules, the *frenjoch* passed through the northwestern Kôbet Bar, a pagoda-like tower with a heavy wooden door.

"If the idea ever occurs to Bob he might need to surrender himself to Napier as a prisoner, he'll surely have us cut to pieces before he gives us up," Blanc opined lightly. Along with Rassam, he'd put on his dusty and rat-eaten uniform, and Delphine was in her threadbare copper gown.

Nobody took offense at this glum outlook. All were too glad that the end of captivity had arrived—the results seemed to matter little now.

Delphine said, "Abou thinks we should say goodbye to the Emperor before proceeding to the British camp." The implication was obvious—all of them had been arrested and rearrested at different times merely for having had the gall to proceed where the Emperor had told them to go, without paying their respects to him first.

Rassam waved a dismissive hand. "I've never taken the initiative before, and His Majesty would surely have sent for me had he so wanted. I shall not defy his direct instructions."

"We're going to certain death, either way," said Cameron.

Across the Islamgie Plain they rode without incident, past the stables that had been the site of such heinous abominations, and were nearly to the juncture with the Royal Road when a runner came huffing up the road.

The message was that Rassam and Delphine were to proceed to the Emperor. No one else. They were all to continue to the British camp.

There was a brief parley. Cameron and Rosenthal advocated the fastest direct route to the British, and Abou, Blanc, and Stern argued they should not leave their fellow captives behind. At last, Blanc's head prevailed, and Delphine and Rassam continued down the Royal Road while the others waited.

The heights of Selassie and Fahla were choked with the last vestiges of the imperial host. Menacing, angry men who had just lost many of their comrades lined the basalt walls of rock like so many bristly gewgaws on an ochre silk drapery. The mules even seemed to sense danger, and proceeded more hesitantly than before.

"He likes us," Rassam said, spy-like from the corner of his mouth.

"Yes," replied Delphine in the same surreptitious manner. "Note he didn't send for those he dislikes."

They found Tewodros standing on a precarious outcrop of rock surrounded by about twenty musketeers and the remaining European artisans of Gaffat—Kaspar, Waldmeier, Saalmüller, Moritz, Zander. Beckoning Rassam to stay with the artisans, Tewodros drew Delphine away, close to a headlong drop where one shove would have meant instant annihilation.

Delphine was pleased the Emperor was in apparent health, and she told him so. "But," she added, "You know I don't like these heights. Can we walk a bit, over here?"

However, he drew her close to him just inches from the edge of the sheer cliff, and her gaze didn't flinch from his, the pupils so dilated they seemed to suck up the eyeballs in their blackness. Stroking her under the chin with his coarse thumb, he said intently, "When I saw the discipline of your army, and when my people failed to execute my orders, I was consumed with sorrow to think that although I killed and punished my soldiers, they would not return to the battle. While the fire of jealousy burned within me last night, *Saytan* came to me in the night, and tempted me to kill myself with my own pistol."

Delphine shook her head. "No," she said vaguely.

"But I reflected that God would be angry with me if I went in this manner, so I sent for you in a hurry, lest I might die . . ."

"Don't say that. May we step away from this cliff, O Great One?"

He didn't appear to have heard her, and in fact his thumbs slipped beneath her jawbone and jabbed at her soft throat. Her mouth went dry as a fistful of sand as she clutched at the folds of his *shamma*, about the only thing keeping her from collapsing altogether. All she could see was Tewodros's intense, almost crazed eyes, and the gray bowl of squally sky above. "Do you hear this wailing? There is not a soldier who has not lost a friend or a brother. What will it be when the whole *Inglaise* army comes? What shall I do?"

"Your Majesty," rasped Delphine. "Peace is the best." She felt his thumbs tremble against her throat.

He released her with such a sudden toss that she stumbled and looked down, the cavernous gorge a mile below the only thing in her sights, so dizzying she at once collapsed in a pile of limbs. She heard gasps coming from all sides, top, bottom, left and right, she didn't know which side was up, and then she felt hands lift her.

She felt as though she'd drunk an entire bottle of laudanum—yet she hadn't had any in weeks now. She was dragged away from the ledge and soon was leaning against Tewodros's chest as he stroked her hair. Weak as a new lamb, she felt strange solace in his moonstruck touch.

He continued speaking as though nothing had happened. "Do you not think it is late for you to go to your camp? Would you rather spend the night with me, and in the morning I will send you straight to your people?"

"I wish whatever Your Majesty wishes."

Tewodros sighed, and smiled wistfully. "I've always had a sincere regard for you. It's true I have behaved ill to you, but that was due to the conduct of my enemies. I can only say God's will be done. But I want you to bear this in mind—unless you befriend me, I shall either kill myself or become a monk. Now," he said, almost seraphic with gentleness, lifting her limp form from his chest. "You had better go."

Touching her dry lips to his equally dry and immobile ones, Delphine staggered across the narrow saddle that led to the royal road. She looked back, and he seemed such a forlorn figure, his ratty *shamma* billowing about his frame, so much gaunter than in months past. Surrounded by his musketeers who had closed in, he now gripped a six-shooting pistol, and Delphine willed her knees to stiffen, to carry her on. She proceeded a few steps further, and when she looked back again, Tewodros motioned her to proceed. Although there was no security that Tewodros would not order her to be shot down, she stumbled on, past Kaspar, Waldmeier, Saalmüller, the beloved artisans still captives of the mercurial despot. Rassam broke away from them and joined her.

Around the bend came her fellow inmates on their mules, and she roused herself to a slight jog, her arms outstretched to them, Rassam now taking her arm and urging her on.

"Abou," she moaned, when that worthy came into view.

But again, she was yanked. Her head snapped back, and she saw only the roiling black clouds above. Her face was thrust into the snarling countenance of her most demented sovereign. He shoved Rassam to continue, and he growled at the pack of mules. It was lucky in that instant that only Abou and Blanc, whom he liked, had come into view, for the growl abated from the face, and he dragged Delphine back to his throne on the ledge.

"Go, Abou, go! I will be along soon! Go, Henry!" was all she dared to cry, before being remanded into the most frightening prison yet.

✳   ✳   ✳

April 12, 1868

RAVI PACED THE ENTIRE LENGTH OF the bell tent. "By Saint Michael, prince of angels!"

Napier sipped his scotch. "He sent me cows *and* sheep, is that what you're saying, Howland?"

"Yes, but you can't accept those critters, Robert; to do so means you accept that not only hasn't he surrendered himself to us, he still holds European prisoners!"

Flad inserted, "The least of whom are my wife and children. She's too ill to be moved, so of course I'll return to the devil's den with any message, and I understand if Prideaux doesn't wish to return."

"He just grabbed her!" Henry Blanc cried from where he sat on the camp chair wrapped in a blanket. "He let her go, and she started to come to us, then a diabolical sheen came over his face, and he grabbed her!"

Ravi rubbed his weary face with his hand. "Dr. Blanc is right; the Emperor just keeps getting worse, and he's very clearly gone insane. Can we believe the word of a man like that?"

"I'm willing to go back up," Prideaux said. "Theodore is

demanding us to deliver the body of his friend General Gebraye, and I'll look in on Dr. Chambliss."

Flad clapped his hands together. "Good, good. We'll arrange it with the interpreter Samuel. Now where has he gotten to?"

"I'll go find him," Rassam volunteered.

"General Gebraye's body is in the tent next to the Assistant Quartermaster General," Ravi instructed Rassam as the older man ducked out the tent flap.

Napier spoke in his soft manner. "Yes, yes, there is no possibility of accepting those beeves from Theodore. How many did you say there were, Howland?"

"About a thousand cows and five hundred sheep. I've kept them held at the pickets so he wouldn't get the erroneous idea that we were accepting them."

"Very well. Can you get back to manufacturing those escalading ladders, Howland? I'll draft up another surrender demand; I know it wouldn't do to use your script, why risk his further wrath?"

"Yes, if it's all right, we're using *dhoolie* poles for the ladders, and pickaxe handles for rungs."

"Abyssinian invention!" Stern observed happily.

Ravi patted the venerable churchman on the shoulder. "Good to see you made it," he said warmly before exiting the tent.

He checked in on the ladder-making enterprise where the engineers were also at work making powder charges. He didn't see the interpreter Samuel, who had been such a useful scribe and messenger while also imprisoned on Magdala. At length he found Rassam heading back to Napier's tent.

"Rassam. Where's Samuel got to?"

Rassam cheerfully told him, "Oh, he decided to start back up to Magdala immediately. Once I told him the Emperor's gift of cows and sheep would be accepted, he was most eager to dispatch this glad news—"

"What?" Ravi grabbed the envoy by the front of his ratty uniform. "Why on earth would you tell him that? It's not true, man!"

"It isn't? Why, I can even now recall Napier telling me 'I accept them.' He must have changed his mind." He sneered down at the hammy first that gripped his tunic. "Please, Howland, unhand me."

Ravi only shook him harder. "I never heard Napier use those words, and we were all sitting in the same tent the entire time! Do you know what an irresponsible and flat-headed pile of garbage this is?"

"Please. If anything, the news will make Theodore so happy that he releases the remaining prisoners."

Ravi threw the man away with the utmost disgust. "Yes, and also lead him to believe he has no need for surrender!"

"I was merely the channel through which the Commander-in-Chief's message was delivered to the Emperor."

"Yes, well, we'll see about that. Now I hate to send Flad and Prideaux back up there without any rest, but there's a chance they can catch Samuel and set him straight."

Ravi stormed back to Napier's tent. What was wrong with Rassam? The kind of weak, effeminate, and nonsensical correspondence the envoy had enjoyed for years with Tewodros had garnered the captives nothing but continual imprisonment! It was time for action, not flowery words of conciliation!

✺ ✺ ✺

Islamgie

"WHAT DOES 'HONORABLE TREATMENT' MEAN?"

Flad hesitated before answering, "It would appear to mean . . .

that you and your family will not be harmed—"

"Or imprisoned?" Tewodros demanded.

"About imprisonment, I can't be certain," replied Flad. "But now that you've done the right thing—you've released my wife and children, and the Deacon Nagel, Mr. Waldmeier, Zander, Staiger and Saalmüller—"

"And Doctor Chambliss—" Prideaux gestured at the woman, who reposed on a rock in her copper gown, her only item of attire since her baggage had gone down the mountain with the others. She felt in a sort of nether world, her head light without laudanum to bring her down to earth, her stomach empty, especially now without even starved sheep to sustain them.

Tewodros cut him off. "Only because my offer of cows was accepted! But now I hear that my enemy Basha Falaka has been seen counting the cows, and he has refused to let them inside the picket lines!"

"Are you a woman to cry?" snapped the Ras Engeddeh.

"*Dadab!* And you're nothing but a stupid fool!" Tewodros shouted at him.

Flad wrung his hands. He must have been to that desperate point where one no longer cared, to interrupt Tewodros at such a time. "Excuse me, O Defender of Christendom. May I proceed to my wife and children? And Prideaux would like to gather Herr and Frau Moritz—"

"Yes," Delphine called weakly. "Frau Moritz is preparing to bring forth a baby any moment now. She told me she shall name her Theodora."

Tewodros waved an uncaring hand at the *frenjoch*. "Go, go!"

Flad made one last admirable crack, made all the more poignant in that it might have meant the murder and mutilation of his entire family. "And Doctor Chambliss—"

"Doctor Chambliss stays with me!" Tewodros roared,

fingering the grip of his *talwar* so that both white men backed off with upraised hands.

Delphine shoved herself off the rock and came forward a few paces. "Go, Martin and Bill, please go, and see to your people."

Prideaux yanked on Flad's arm, but Flad still took a risk to say, "Doctor Chambliss can attend to Frau Moritz—"

This time Tewodros really did unsheathe his *talwar*, and the two men stumbled off down the rise, salaaming and praising him the whole way.

Covering her eyes with her trembling hands, Delphine incanted quietly in English, "I shall forever remember that man who smashed his violin over his instructor's head ..." It was strange that in his discombobulated mania, Tewodros had forgotten to call her Makeda, and had finally acknowledged her as Doctor Chambliss.

Tewodros shook her by the shoulders, his eyes suddenly large and limpid like a beseeching dog's. "These people, having got what they want, now seek to kill me!"

"Tewodros, they just ask that you surrender—"

But Tewodros rushed down the knoll, his *shamma* flapping behind him, calling out to all chiefs who remained to be ready to march with him during the night. For an hour they parleyed, many chiefs waving guns and insisting they could not bring their families anywhere, as they had no more pack mules or carriers, and many retreated to remoter parts of Islamgie to avoid Tewodros. Some counseled the Emperor to come to terms with the *frenjoch*, as not all of Abyssinia united could extinguish the fire of the invaders.

The Emperor then raved that they were cowards, and it was their fault he'd surrendered all the *frenjoch* before getting better terms from the British.

An eminent Ras stepped forward and bawled up at him, "If the European captives were still with Your Majesty, you would have just revenged upon them the refusal of their brothers to accept your peace offer, and thereby have made their hearts hurt; as it is, you have everything to lose. We're Your Majesty's children unto death, if you will only listen to our advice, and come to terms with the *frenjoch*."

Tewodros withdrew to Kôbet Bar and said nothing for two hours, trembling and praying. He then ordered Damash and other chiefs to find four hundred men to place Gaffat mortars on the road leading to Magdala, evidently planning on making a show of defense, but Ras Bisawwir told him every petty Chief said they would not lift a finger to fight the *Inglaise*. However, if Tewodros were ready to make peace, they'd all go before the great *Inglaise* Negus with stones around their necks and beg for pardon.

While Tewodros was engaged in prayer, Delphine heard Ras Engeddeh and others taking a solemn vow that if they were ordered to fire upon any of their own people, even if against a native prisoner, they would disobey. She had already heard the plans of a great number of them that once Tewodros was out of sight, they would all hurry to the British camp and surrender.

It was a nerve-wracking night, shivering in the little tent with none of the creature comforts of her former home inside the fortress—fire, pillows, *arat*.

In the morning, undeterred by his much reduced force, Tewodros set again to placing mortars below Kôbet Bar, until he saw British cavalry on the heights of Selassie. He commenced dashing about like a maniac on his white steed across the Islamgie plain, calling upon his meager force to die fighting like a man, and shrieking at the British, firing into the air and shouting out boasts of his own conquests. "Come on, are you women, that you hesitate to attack a few warriors?" Only Ras Engeddeh, Azmach Michael, the valet Paul, and a few other Fitawraris and Dejazmachs stayed down on the plain with him, and upon one such Fitawrari being shot in the arm, they finally retreated beyond the ramparts of

Magdala, where they piled huge stones behind the gates.

"This is lunacy," Delphine said to Misha, when he wasn't other-wise engaged in ordering men about and sauntering in his mantle of lion's fur. He seemed to be affecting the role of a Likamaquas, though he had not nearly the skill or training, knowing more about sautéing pheasants than ordering men about the field. However, as there weren't too many men left to order about, it probably was all the same. "Thinking boulders can hold back the British!"

Misha sighed, leaning wearily on his spear. "I'm sure you're right, and Ravi's laughing at our feeble tactics as we speak, Delphine."

"I certainly hope we live to see Ravi laugh, Misha! But I don't think their rockets will selectively avoid the *frenjoch* they may not even know are still up here!"

Misha's features seemed to have matured by about ten years in one year's time. Dusty creases lined his countenance, and the muddy smudges beneath his eyes were from lack of food. He shook his head sadly. "Ravi will never forget you're here. I cannot leave my Emperor."

"He is *not* your Emperor, Misha!" she hissed. "He is no more your Emperor than Andrew Johnson is your President! Listen to me, you and I could decamp to the British tonight. I heard Ras Engeddeh, Bisawwir, Damash agreeing that they would shoot no one who attempted to surrender; all we have to do is—"

"I'm not abandoning him, Delphine!"

Misha's outburst was so forceful as to draw attention from several masons, who glanced at him curiously. "Hush, Misha, please don't make a scene—"

His eyes remained fiery. "The Emperor has been the father I never had, our men the family I never had!"

"I never had much of a family, either, but really, Misha, what sort of a father would—"

A shrieking whistle pierced the sky, and Delphine only had

time to look up at the fortress wall before a rocket skirled into the compound, the explosion knocking her off her feet and throwing her onto a pile of boulders. Though the air was struck from her lungs, she still knew to cover her face with her arms, and clods of earth pelted her upturned body. She jumped to her feet immediately, took a breath, and dashed for the old European captive's compound, the closest shelter, men racing for their lives overtaking her, as her cumbersome copper skirts shortened her stride.

She later learned three Chiefs were killed by the explosion of the shell that stabbed them with singing, shooting pieces of metal; another chief by a rocket. She never made it to her old compound, as she was yanked from her mad dash by the powerful arm of the Emperor, who bellowed at everyone, "Leave if you like! Go seek shelter, or run like cowardly dogs over to the enemy!"

"Tewodros!" Delphine shrieked. "We must find shelter as well! There is no winning this battle!"

"No!" he roared, his fingers nearly crushing her humerus bone into tiny shards.

And he dragged her into a passage cut between two rocks that buttressed the Kôbet Bar gate.

❋   ❋   ❋

REFUGEES POURED DOWN THE SIDES OF the Magdala tableland as the storming party began their ascent. A two-hour bombardment of Howitzer shells sang their piping tones as they gyred and hurled through the sky. Ravi was to lead the 33rd Irish, the "Duke of Wellington's Own," at the head of the assault column, before the Royal Engineers and the 4th King's Own. The Dragoon Guards were commanded around the eastern Kâfir Bar to back up the vicious Gallas who were already posted to prevent Tewodros from absconding in that direction.

Leaving Selpha down on Islamgie, it was on foot from here on up, the infantry marching four abreast through narrow gorges to the martial tunes of "Yankee Doodle" and the equally bellicose notes of artillery bombardment upon the heights of Magdala. They soon had to wend their way through the rivers of émigrés hotfooting it out of there, some of them grandees in their silken bodices and brocaded gowns, glistering with neck pendants and silver ornamentation. Ravi hoped no one recognized him, but their faces were all downcast, and in their race to skedaddle from the plateau, and the infantry's haste to march through them, only a couple of Amharas had faces of shock at Ravi's apparition.

Behind them were the King's Own who had distinguished themselves so well on the Aroge Plain, and the Royal Engineers who seized the mortars Tewodros's men had planted, many human rivers converged and Ravi heard the thrilling *elelta* of his former countrymen along the crags of Selassie as they hailed the conquerors. Above him, elephants laden with the Armstrong battery lumbered up the ridgeline, black crenellations against the lazulite lune of sky. The Union Jack already fluttered from the ramparts of Selassie and Fahla, the two lower fortresses having been surrendered to them last night by a retinue of deserting Abyssinian nobles.

Captain Hewson briefly touched his arm. "Eh, Cap'n Howland, whaddye make o' that rubbish heap?"

Ravi stopped in shock. Not shock at the sight of the entire ravine below the water wells utterly chockablock with hundreds of mangled and bloated corpses, some still manacled together by hands and feet. But shock that he'd been prepared to saunter past the sight without even flinching. He wasn't so distantly removed from this rustic existence himself that such vistas jammed him into a cocked hat and flung him into the middle of next week. It was fortuitous that in his lack of a reaction, he was probably being viewed as a great, brave leader. He merely adjusted his Indian helmet and wiped away the sweat that had already pooled in his eye sockets.

"Yes, we heard about that," he remarked casually. "Just Tewodros's last handiwork, and just one more reason to know that you're doing God's will." Religious prattle went over well with these fellows, Ravi had noted.

"Aye, I'll say," nodded Captain Hewson, holding his kerchief over his nose.

"Let's pick up the pace, get everyone past this garbage," Ravi suggested.

Within fifty yards of the base of Magdala, Ravi drew his men into battalions at quarter distance with the Engineers under Pritchard deployed in front as skirmishers. The signs for rapid firing being given to the artillery upon the heights, he marched his men forward underneath the rampageous onslaught against the fortress walls, boulders booming down onto the hapless stragglers who had not cut out in time.

Converging missiles exploded on the plateau now—conical shells from the Armstrong battery upon the captured heights of Selassie rotating with a painfully shrill song burst directly over the fortress. Mortar shells with funereal tones that felt capable of rupturing the eardrum sailed in high arcs, then dropped abruptly into the Emperor's compound, and the ground shuddered as though Ravi walked on pudding.

"If we proceed at this pace," Ravi shouted to Hewson, "we can make it to the lip of the canyon and the first revetment in about ten minutes."

Abruptly the cannonade silenced, and the echoing waterfalls of tumbling rubble and slag resounded throughout the buttes, one tinny distant cry of "cease fire!" still reverberating in the quietude. When the Engineering skirmishers opened fire with their Sniders upon the battlements of Magdala, Ravi ordered his men to follow suit, plying their breech-loaders with a zeal borne of months of eager waiting. Tewodros's soldiers leapt to the loopholes along the wall surmounted by fabrications of twigs and withes and began shooting, spitting out smoke rings of powder and wounding several soldiers below.

"Fire at the revetment!" Ravi shouted. They leapfrogged upward in alternate ranks, some men falling back to drag and shelter the wounded, as the sky above opened on them and poured forth lakes of rain, nature's thunderous roars and flashes washed out by man's own explosions. They banged away at every suspicious rock embrasure and every wild recess or opening that looked to possibly contain a savage hell-bent on a suicidal stand.

At an abrupt dogleg in the path, the last stretch before one reached the perpendicular barbican tower at the Kôbet Bar, Ravi was hit in the bicep by a matchlock bullet, no doubt made from melted ore of stolen loot from Gondar. The shot twirled him about and he nearly knocked over another fellow.

"Son of a bitch!" he cussed, because he was hit in his right shooting arm. He saw Major Pritchard, only ten feet ahead, slam into a rock wall when a bullet grazed his thigh, and at once Ravi's ire was raised. He roared, and the battalion around him rained a hellfire of bullets upon the barbican above.

He made a mad dash through the men to the gate, which of course he found solidly blocked by what he reasoned were boulders stacked against the other side to a depth of about ten feet. "Hurry up with the powder!" he bellowed, his order repeated by men down the slope.

Ravi paced, looking for an opening in the hurdles of the barbican. Captain Hewson was at his side now, and Ravi grabbed a handful of the bloke's tunic.

"Where are the canvas bags with fuses? Where are the scaling ladders, the hammers and wedges, pickaxes, the handsaws?"

"I believe, sir, that the pack mules were deterred for a few moments by a hail of a rock shower—"

"*Isgyoh!*" Ravi paced, raging like wild to find a way up the cliff face, and then—

"*By the power of my creator,*" he breathed, taking a few powerful steps back and leaping upon the wall like a swatted fly.

He'd never seen a man scale this wall—no one had ever had the reason or the gumption to—but all at once there were footholds and handholds looking him smack in the face, and if he just followed his nose—

A rousing cheer rose from the canyon below, and another fellow, a Sapper, scrambled after him in his gamy crawl up the wall. He cleared the first revetment, seeing a couple of *shamma* flashes of his old countrymen scurrying away, and he opened fire on the top revetment at a few dark heads. Glancing down and seeing more soldiers following his pathway up the cliff face, he leaped to scale the next seventy feet above, stepping on the shoulders of a dead Abyssinian. He stopped only to insert his Snider into cracks in the loopholes and pick off those who may have once been his fellow cavaliers, his spear injury from the Aroge battle at last coming to sink its stinging tentacles into his side.

Below, shirty Irishmen crashed gigantic boulders against the city gate. Men bawled as one their resonant "huzzahs" and "hoorahs" as they banged away at, pounded, and bayoneted the gate. The gate was laid flat as Ravi crested the wall, clawing his way through the twigs and sticks that stood for hurdles. He caught a fleeting glimpse of the city he had thought he knew so well, the narrow streets hedged by the houses and storehouses with thatched conical roofs. This gorgeous spectacle was ruined by the vision of twelve matchlocks trained at his head, so Ravi popped off a couple of them with his Colt before making a hurtling Icarian leap onto a pile of corpses below the inner wall.

It was unfortunate he landed with his face smack into the ghastly torn chest of an expired compatriot, and the resulting nausea slowed him down long enough to hear a few bullets slogging into the sprawled limbs about him. Simultaneously someone yelled in Amharic, "Cease firing! Cease firing, you godless swine!"

Sprinting to his feet, blood and who wanted to know what sort of gore filming his eyes, Ravi lunged to the right, toward the Kôbet Bar, then froze.

"*Misha.*"

The former Azmach stood about five paces away apparently dumbfounded, his eyes frozen into a sort of mad stare at the sight of his partner in a British Major's uniform, hairless, with his face dripping entrails. Misha had gained about ten years of age since Ravi had last laid eyes on him, and his bloody *shamma* hung in folds over his sunken chest. Misha too had lost an inordinate amount of hair from the top of his head, and he seemed to be compensating for it with the moldy lion's pelt he had draped about his shoulders.

"Misha." His voice hoarse from shouting, Ravi started a few inches toward his friend. From the corner of his eye, he could see a flood of red- and gray-coated soldiers surging through the gate, as the men under Misha's command faded into the background. He raised his damaged arm, forgetting he still held the Colt, but Misha didn't budge at all. "Misha, come with us." He beckoned. "Come, and all will be forgiven, I guarantee you that. Come. Take off that lion's fur, and come."

Misha finally spoke in Amharic. "Rav. I can't. I've done this too long. It's all I know."

"You'll remember civilized ways fast enough. *I* did. If *I* did it, *you* can."

Sadly, with a ghoulish empty tinge to his eyes, Misha shook his head. "Rav, I—"

There appeared a little hole right between those empty eyes, and what light there had been in them instantly dissipated, as though sucked up straight like a tornado into the pouring clouds above. Misha dropped his musket and collapsed into a pile, like so many corpses that already littered the clearing.

"Misha!" Ravi jerked forward and fell to his knees to shake his friend, as though rousing him to go play *gooks*.

"Bloody heathen!" A Sapper by the name of Bailey, the one who'd followed him up the wall, had just murdered Ravi's best friend. Tearing off his Indian helmet and pouncing upon the sapper, Ravi grabbed a handful of his stupid red coat and rattled him mercilessly.

"You damned white-livered son of a bitch! By Jesus Christ, you just shot a white man!"

"A . . . ? Damn it, sir, he were threatening you, about to kill you! And I just saw the Emperor showing his phiz over there by that haystack, tossing around a white lady!"

"God may damn your soul, I've cut a better man's throat than yours, you son of a—"

Stunned with the realization of what Bailey said, Ravi twirled to face the haystack with the zealous dolt still in his hand. Throwing him down next to Misha's body, he roared, "Stay here and protect that corpse, you red-headed arse-sucker, or you're going to be eating earth, by the power of my creator."

Indeed, by a haystack about fifty yards off down the parade-ground, unseen by any of the surging and roiling soldiers that now filled the plain mowing down anything Ethiopian that appeared to be running away instead of surrendering, Tewodros flailed his enraged limbs about in an effort to capture a shrieking Delphine, who tried to dash toward the troops.

Ravi was a charging leopard. He had raced this fast once before, when bathing alone in a pool and a band of thirty bloodthirsty Gallas had taken him unaware. Now he charged for Delphine's life, driving oblivious soldiers away from him as though they were made of lead. They tumbled over one another like toys as Ravi sprinted, ducking their limbs and weapons, all soundless now with a roar filling his ears.

He saw, but didn't hear, the woman shriek and beg for her life as Tewodros battled her, in one hand a silver-plated pistol Queen Victoria had sent to him as a token of friendship. As Ravi bounded and tossed men from his path, he saw, almost as though the roar in his head had slowed down his vision, the Emperor's claw tear the bronze gown from Delphine's shoulder.

From the corner of his eye he noted a wayward Amhara roaring free of two Irishmen's crossed bayonets, slashed across both cheeks with the blades like a feral Red Indian. Untrammeled, he surged in an arc through the air, his mouth wide open in mad ululation as though the vibrations of his war-song propelled him into a straight trajectory toward Ravi's head, his *shotel* flashing like a meteor in the sky.

Ravi ducked and withdrew his *shamshir*, and as the Fitawrari flew above his head, he sliced a clean fissure through the back of his legs, effectively hamstringing him from future activity.

Did Delphine see Ravi coming, or did she just cry out for any soldier to save her? Tewodros must have driven his knee into her tailbone, for she went crashing to the ground, her lovely chestnut hair all in disarray about her bared shoulder, the light of her eyes almost as murky as Misha's.

When he charges, it is not a man but a sun bearing down upon the enemy . . .

Ravi hurtled over the last dead Abyssinian just as Tewodros, who spied him now, roared at him with especial hatred as though a hundred *budas* and *zars* had taken control of his limbs. He dragged Delphine behind the haystack, the little elf's shoe flying from her foot as her dainty ankle disappeared from view. Charging so swiftly he had to skid around the corner of the hay, his Colt cocked and ready to unleash at the Emperor's head, the explosion of a bullet ruptured the drumming in his ears.

Delphine sprawled over the prostrate Emperor, a little powder cloud drifting over their forms. In one great leap, Ravi took her by the shoulders and shook her gently until she opened her eyes.

She looked at him slowly, starting with his throat, then raising her gaze over his chin and mouth. She gulped, and gasped, as one who had just been pulled from a deep lake, and he crushed her in his arms, muttering words of thanksgiving in Amharic he couldn't later recall, cradling her skull to his neck. She shook like a mosquito skittering across the water's surface, and he breathed hot, calming Amharic words onto her forehead as he smashed her thin form to his chest. He rubbed his face against her dusty, sunbrowned one, realizing he was probably mashing her with unnecessary gore, but he didn't care.

He squeezed her through her soundless sobs, as though hoping to press all the sorrow from her, and he found that he was speaking in Arabic, and calling her *el taleb*. He had always found Arabic the most romantic language, and he was able to express deep sentiments more floridly in that language than any other.

"Ravi," she gasped, and squirmed until her arms were around his neck. She was on her knees cradling him to her, and he pulled her onto his lap, drawing away so he could make sure she was all right. More tentatively now, Ravi stroked her face to reassure himself, moving the hand that still gripped the pistol down over her skinny hip, feeling for anything broken. He saw no flinches, only a deeply engraved sadness that would perhaps never be erased. She touched her nose to his.

"*Isgyoh*, I love you. I love you more than the power of my creator."

At that, he lost control of his senses. Through all the murder, misery, torture, and crackpot activity he'd been witness to in his forty years, the last time he'd shed a tear was the day his pet New-found-land dog had died, and his father had thoroughly whipped him for his weakness. But all he could do now was stare at her beauty with wonderment as a decidedly unmanly tear dripped down his face. He could only hope that all the grime decorating his face hid it, but it must have cleaned a track straight down his cheek, for with a tiny smile the woman reached out and wiped it off with her thumb.

"Tewodros." She inclined her head toward the man who was now, presumably, dead.

"Yes," Ravi said stupidly. "Who shot him?"

Her smile evaporated, and she looked gravely over at the Emperor's form. He saw her beauty had matured, become deeper and more fluid, more heavily burdened with suffering. "He shot himself." She crawled the few paces to his body, and Ravi followed.

Tewodros still clutched the Queen's pistol in his crooked arm, and he had an eerie smile on his lips, the smile from days of old when he'd sit on his *alga* regaling those around him with his Shakespeare stories, and Ravi in turn would tell the tales of Burnt Njal. The smile lent a mask of regal beauty to the face of the cruelest master Ravi had ever known. His elegant, beautiful feet were crossed one over the other, as though he had just lain back for a brief nap, and had died for no apparent reason.

"I thought he was going to shoot me, rather than let me return to you," Delphine whispered. "He held the gun to my forehead, and I closed my eyes and prayed. I heard a shot, and thought I was probably dead, and that you'd come tearing around the corner to be shot too, and then we could at last be together in the spirit realm. I was calm, and had something happy to think about. When I opened my eyes, he was lying here."

As much as Ravi dreaded touching the corpse for fear Tewodros played one of his mercurial gags and would jump up and shoot him, he inched his hand over and first removed the Queen's pistol from the fingers that still gripped it like a trap. Sliding the gun on the mud behind him, Ravi reached behind the Emperor's neck to lift his Templar cross, queasy with revulsion when he was forced to slide the chain around the back of Tewodros's exploded skull, for he had shot himself in the mouth.

But the medal came off with a minimum of plasma fluids, and Ravi gratefully slid it over his own head. He was further overjoyed when Delphine lifted the plain leather amulet Tewodros had given her from her neck. "He said this would protect me from death," she said, and returned it in a stolid surgeon's manner over Tewodros's head, fussing with its placement in the hollow of his clavicle.

Ravi drew Delphine onto his lap, turning his back on the Son of David and Solomon, the Ruler of the Universe, that Incarnation of the Evil One. "My *el taleb*," he murmured against her cheek, prepared to speak in English now. "Who fought for female as for food when Mays awoke to warm desire; and such the Lust that grew to Love when Fancy lent a purer fire."

To Ravi's utter shock, a smile played across Delphine's face, and she finished the verse for him. " 'Where then the Eternal nature-law by God engraved on human heart? Behold his simian sconce, and own the Thing could play no higher part'."

"What in . . . ?" Ravi breathed.

Delphine tormented him a few moments longer with a delightfully seductive smile that seemed to have developed a depth since he'd last seen her; it pricked his male pride to wonder how. "I used to read your writing. After you left. Sometimes I'd even just look at your Arabic scrawls or your 'pornographic' translations, just to feel closer to you."

"My writing?" Ravi was awed that she would even bother to look at his writing, but she took this to mean that he was concerned about its safety, for she said, "Yes, it's been stored in the

Treasury; if you like, I can show you where I believe it is. Let's secure it before your men take a torch to the place."

Since that was an entirely likely event, Ravi agreed, and helped her to her feet. They turned and paid a quiet respect to their fallen master.

"He's finally gained some peace. I've never seen him looking so at rest," she remarked.

Ravi pulled a handkerchief from his trouser pocket and tried to wipe his face free from grime. "I have."

As they turned to go around the haystack, a detachment of soldiers came by, excitedly gibbering. One was that Sapper Bailey Ravi had ordered to stay put, but Ravi didn't want to display any rage before Delphine, who had endured her share of it.

"What d'ye think, Henry?" A private of the 33rd Irish spoke, pointing at the Emperor. "Can this be that unblessed devil of a Theodorus, the 'No-goose,' as they call him?" They appeared not to see Ravi and Delphine, who pressed back into the haystack.

Sapper Bailey replied, "Mebbe, Mac, can't say, but we'd better stay near him until the Sergeant shows his phiz inside Magdala. Och, what's this now?" He bent to pick up the pistol. " 'Presented by Victoria, Queen of Great Britain and Ireland, to Theodorus, Emperor of Abyssinia, as a slight token of her gratitude for his kindness in 1854'!" If this don't beat . . . This must be him, then!"

Ravi gripped Delphine tighter about the shoulders, trying to cover her with her torn gown, as the jackass sauntered over to the body and squatted down. "Eh, look at this!" And without ceremony he tore the amulet necklace from the body, without bothering to lift it over the head. "A dear bauble, the spoils of war."

Delphine shivered beneath Ravi's hands. "Tewodros told me once. 'One day you may see me dead . . . I trust in your generosity'."

Ravi strode forward. "Look here, Sapper Bailey. I ordered you to stand guard over *that body*, and here you are, already ruthlessly looting. I'm going to run you in for this."

"Perhaps we should find Ras Engeddeh to stand guard over the Emperor," Delphine suggested cheerily.

Ravi turned to her, his mouth moving, but no sound coming out. In his dash across the parade-ground, the inert body of the Ras was one he had callously leaped over.

"Oh," said Delphine. "Then perhaps . . . Where is Azmach Michael? He'll be devastated."

Again, no words came from Ravi's mouth, and all he could do was embrace the woman, who looked quizzically up at him. Fortunately, just then a rolling clamor like a tidal wave reverberated across the plateau, and with an odd thrill Ravi realized it was the battalion cheering. Escorting Delphine onto the open plain, he saw the Wavy Cross ensign streaming from the roof of the Emperor's House, and the soldiers who had doffed their helmets cheered so enthusiastically that the universal "hurrah" was taken up by those still down on Islamgie, Selassie, and Fahla. As the martial band struck up "God Save the Queen," Delphine buried her face in Ravi's besmirched uniform.

"Everything will be all right now, my Queen of Heaven," he whispered loudly in her ear, petting her head. "I'll make sure of that. No one will harm you."

Above the military din of the table-land fortress, a hearty tenor soared with the healthy lungs of a hyena.

"Thy choicest gifts in store, on her be pleased to pour! Long may she reign!"

Delphine disengaged her bleary face from Ravi's armpit, and Ravi beheld the strangest sight of the entire day. The Deacon Nagel, clad in a whimsical hodgepodge of attire, marched from the direction of the native prison at the head of the most motley stew of Abyssinians ever assembled under the blue sky. These must have been some of the native prisoners not yet emancipated, sprinkled with a healthy dose of surrendering chiefs, and Kaspar led them proudly as he stepped high in his white breeches topped with a blue serge waistcoat the British had apparently clothed him with. This ensemble was made all the more dashing with the addition of the white cummerbund "cholera belt" and cotton braces. And above all, he still retained the *ferenje* brogans that had never marched so proudly across such victorious ground.

"May she defend our laws, and give us ever cause, to sing with heart and voice, God Save the Queen!"

"Kaspar!" cried Delphine, and dashed forward to greet her friend. The hundred or so men behind Kaspar all apathetically stopped moving, like cows that had eaten too much grass.

She showered Kaspar's ruddy face with kisses, and he couldn't hide his abashment, even going so far as to take her by one hand. "I'm so very glad you're well, my dear. Many a night I have lain awake, pierced clean through to the heart with grief and anguish not knowing the fate—"

"Where's Abou?"

Kaspar saluted Ravi. "Safe and sound, but down below, my dear."

"Down below?"

Ravi stepped in. "He means he's down on Islamgie, isn't that right, Deacon?"

Kaspar frowned as though Ravi had just told him he had shreds of *chat* clinging to his teeth. "On Islamgie, yes, of course! What else did you think? He wanted to come up and help, but he was afraid he'd be enslaved again. Now, to be quite open and frank with you, I'd much rather be singing something more uplifting and patriotic, such as—"

There was nothing Ravi could do to prevent Kaspar from filling his lungs with bracing air and belting forth as though surrounded by a beaming throng of admirers, and not a bedraggled troop of the defeated, some of who had begun to collapse unnoticed on the ground behind him.

"Yes, we'll rally round the flag, boys, we'll rally once again, shouting the battle cry of Freedom! We will rally from the hillside, we'll gather from the plain, shouting the battle cry of Freedom!"

To Ravi's further astonishment, Delphine took Kaspar's free arm and joined him lustily in this ignominious display of fervor. "We will welcome to our numbers the loyal, true and brave, shouting the battle cry of Freedom! And although they may be poor, not a man shall be a slave, shouting the battle cry of Freedom!"

At this point, Ravi had to wipe his eyes again with the filthy handkerchief.

In his musical zeal, Kaspar shook Delphine warmly. "You see? While I'm perfectly willing to sing along with whomever is the conqueror of the day, it must have been so inspirational to have been in the midst of the exciting and picturesque sights of your War Between the States, and not in this squalid and polluted hovel that passes for a country!"

An Abyssinian who wasn't occupied in expiring on the ground rushed forward. Ravi's hand went for his *shamshir*, but the fellow stumbled right past him followed by a few of the more intrepid survivors.

Kaspar cried, "Now, what is this?" but Ravi stayed Kaspar's arm, seeing the men had spied Tewodros's body, and they had every right to wail and rend their ragged garments. Kaspar's eyes went round and glassy and he staggered toward the body as if in imitation of the wraiths around him, so Ravi grabbed a passing Lieutenant and ordered him to take Kaspar's prisoners away.

"Let's get to the Treasury," Ravi advised Delphine, particularly as now privates, sappers, and miners were like jackals occupied in stripping the Emperor's body of its shoddy garments, and the bereaved wails of "Tewodros! Tewodros!" were drawing quite the crowd.

"But we must get someone to protect the Emperor!" protested the woman. "I don't care if he was a tyrant in life, he deserves better than this!"

Kaspar was surprisingly calm and lofty. "I say the perfect man for this job is the Azmach Michael!"

Ravi at last had to tell them. "Misha's dead. Over by the Kôbet Bar."

They were now fairly bowled over by the rush of people trying to glimpse the body, where several Irish soldiers dragged it by its feet. "Sic semper tyrannis!" shouted one, and the cry was taken up.

Jim Grant approached as the band's song turned to "See the Conquering Hero Comes" as they welcomed Napier to the plateau. Without losing his grip on Delphine, Ravi approached the Major eagerly.

"Ravi," Jim said warmly. "I presume this is your lovely intended?"

Ravi was fit to bust with pride, though the situation certainly didn't call for it, his "intended" a filthy sylph in a torn gown that was much too large for her, her having lost much weight from starvation. But she curtsied charmingly as he presented her, and he knew he'd never loved a woman more. "May I present Doctor Delphine Chambliss."

Grant crinkled his eyes at the woman with a smile, and pressed his lips to her dirt-streaked hand. "It's a great honor, Doctor. I know that Ravinger Howland would only cross twenty mountain ranges for the most exemplary of women."

"Oh, but indeed, Major," protested Delphine just as politely. "It is our incredible and utmost honor to have the best army in the four quarters of the world move heaven and earth to come and unchain us. May I ask you just one small favor? Can you please not allow anyone to molest the Emperor's body? I've promised him—"

Grant frowned. "Yes, yes, the body, where is it?"

"Delphine was with him when he shot himself," Ravi explained as they led the way toward the knot of men surrounded the body. He stopped short when he saw soldiers waving shreds of grimy *shamma* in the air like trophies. "Can you assign someone—"

"—they can take him into the former prison compound, lay him in one of our huts," Delphine suggested.

"Yes, yes," agreed Grant. "This is unconscionable." He ordered an aide-de-camp to clear the field, dress the body, and have it ready for interment tomorrow.

Ravi mentioned, "Oh, and will you have that Sapper Bailey put in the stockade immediately? He's guilty of murdering a white man. And on their way, have Bailey point out the body by the gate, and place it near the Emperor's in the *frenjoch* compound." Ravi attempted to firmly steer Delphine toward the Treasury, knowing she would balk.

"Major Grant," Delphine ventured, "I would like to be allowed to attend the wounded Amharas."

"My dear," said Jim kindly. "We have enough doctors. You just take care of this one savage Lickomenquos, yes?"

Ravi nodded. "Thank you, Jim." Saluting, he pulled Delphine away.

"But," she called back over her shoulder at Grant, "there are many Amharas wounded! Some still lie on the ground crying and groaning while your men trample them, and many more from the Fahla battle a few days ago hide in their huts crying out; it is cruel and brutal to—"

"Enough, Doctor Chambliss! I will not allow it! Napier would never hear of it!"

"Did you hear, my Queen of Heaven?" Ravi stroked her face as he dragged her away. "Napier won't hear of it! My only truth, don't you know there will always be wounded no matter where you go, and you can't possibly tend to all of them without killing yourself in the process? Look, see my arm? I am wounded. Why don't you occupy yourself tending me for, say, the next six hours? For I'm sure it'll take that long, probably a nice long surgery involving lots of boiling water and opium."

"Oh, that? That's nothing more than a little scrape. What, did a mosquito bite you?"

He'd succeeded in getting her to smile, and she hugged his injured arm to her breast as they threaded their way through the enthusiastic troops, some already plundering and weaving about brandishing crosses, censers, richly chased goblets, jars of *arrack* and *tej*—two Sappers even reeled by wearing war capes of lion's and leopard's skin.

"We'd best hasten to the Treasury," said Ravi, upon seeing the expedition archeologist taking off with a sixteenth-century painting of Christ.

"Ravi, the Empress!"

The Empress Tiruwerq, Tewodros's second wife and so unbeloved by him he hadn't even seen her when he'd triumphantly returned to Magdala last month, huddled surrounded by other harem women in the center of the parade-ground, stood guard over by a few Irishmen. Ravi recalled Tiruwerq had been ill, and the Imperial relict now looked downright consumptive almost entirely shrouded in her raiment, tended to by her small son Alemayou.

Delphine shuddered beneath his touch. "Oh, that woman hates me. She's always putting the evil eye on me."

"Yes, yes, let's get out—"

Delphine was full of a new mission. "There's Louisa Bell! Ravi, where did Kaspar go?"

"Oh, *no* you don't, my little minx! Have you forgotten about her *buda* possession? Why, Louisa is so strong she's capable of throwing both you and me over the roof of that church!"

"Ravi! He's fixed to marry her! He can't just let her be led away as a prisoner!"

He couldn't stop her. She dashed back in the direction of the Emperor's body where they'd last seen Kaspar, and Ravi had to follow.

He met them halfway. It was apparent Delphine had wisely not told Kaspar the reason she eagerly dragged him across the parade-ground by the way they laughed and joined in camaraderie, their arms linked. Kaspar held an *arrack* horn in his free hand, and he had to bend awkwardly at the waist to sip from it as he expounded forth.

". . . and when we blasted a cannon over the great gate, there was an ill-fated cow who came sailing over the wall and impetuously squashed the very fellow who had ordered the fire! Ah, Howland, this has been the most glorious day of my illuminated life, and I must confess I partially have you to thank for it, for who knows where this army would be stumbling about without you? Perhaps wandering around Nubia, looking for the sacred grapevine that is said to—"

His sharp gasping intake of breath was so loud it overpowered the revels of celebrating soldiers, and when he tried to make a break for it, dropping the *arrack* horn to the mud, he slammed right into two looters who reproached with ire.

"Eh, watch it there, Father!"

"Ay, there's plenty enough to go around for everyone!"

"But . . . but . . . !" Kaspar whispered in a shout, pointing a tremulous arm to the group of concubines. Woizero Bell, ensured of having spied him now by his blustery behavior, slowly got to her feet, her eyes narrowing in proportion to how tall and distended she could make herself appear. "That woman's trying to kill me!"

Ravi tried to stay the shuddering deacon by gripping his shoulders. "Now, now, Kaspar. I wouldn't go that far. She's merely, ah, how would you term it, Delphine?"

"Nervous?"

"Yes, that's it, nervous and shy around suitors, because, as you know, she's entirely—"

Delphine filled in. "Innocent, and . . ."

Ravi glanced over his shoulder. Louisa Bell was about twice her normal size by now, and the blaze in her eyes was that of a medieval dragon. "Inexperienced! You must give her time to—"

But Kaspar was having none of it. Uttering a last piercing "*Aaahhhh!*" he broke free from his circle of jailors and scampered off in a bowlegged dash like a terrified crayfish.

The two looters chuckled. "Odd thing, that. Why's he afraid of a native girl?"

The soldiers had their answer when a roaring dervish burst into their midst, snarling and growling like a carnivorous jackal. The privates were immediately bowled over, the manuscripts and bibles they held flying like so many colorful autumn leaves, but they weren't the intended prey, and Louisa pivoted on one foot with out-stretched claws, spitting and darting her murderous eyes around. Stuffing Delphine protectively behind him, Ravi cocked his Colt and leveled it at Louisa's head, but when Louisa's eyes alit on him she stilled, even sucking some of the drool back into her mouth.

It was an amazing transformation, chilling in its suddenness, to see that a *buda* could be so easily tamed, and could be so un-aware of the lethal potential of a Colt. Her back straightened, the fangs were retracted into the jawbone—she even smoothed her hair down.

"Basha Falaka," she smiled, fairly toeing the soil in modesty.

"Crikey!" squeaked the private, who hadn't bothered getting to his feet.

"Basha Falaka! By the power of Saint Michael, you've come for me! Please take me away from this awful place! I—"

Delphine writhed her way free from the protection of Ravi's shadow. "He hasn't come for you, you crazy witch!" she bellowed in Amharic. "Why can't you accept the real love of a man who truly loves you, and stop sobbing about—"

The talons came out again, the spittle flew, and Louisa Bell charged. Ravi lunged to the right with Delphine under his arm, making a heroic leap over the bodies of the fallen looters, just as three Irishmen guarding the harem finally realized something was going on, and tackled Woizero Bell to the mud like felling a great tree. Ravi and Delphine dashed off toward the Treasury, not wishing to look back.

"You have the power to tame a *buda!*" cried Delphine as they ran.

"Ah, that's not my power, just some lovesick schoolgirl's imagination!"

"Yes, but did you see how the *buda* completely left her when she spied you?" Delphine was already panting, weak from so many months of captivity, but she didn't slow her pace. "I wonder, will it always be this way with you?"

"What way?" Ravi feigned diffidence.

"Hussies throwing themselves at you, hopelessly mired by your manly presence, completely stupefied by your courageous daring and your ability to make them weak in the knees?"

She was laughing, her face open and aglow from inside. It was a sight Ravi had thought to never see again, and he was perfectly happy to chase her all the way to the Treasury. "Yes, I'm afraid that's something you'll just have to learn to tolerate."

"And women killing other men just to get their hands on you?"

"A hazard of the job, my dear! Any potential wife of Captain Ravinger Howland knows . . ."

Scrambling through the open gates of the Treasury fence where there were no guards, they elbowed aside a few drunken marauders who tottered under their armloads of booty. Ravi captured the breathless woman against the rounded stone wall, loosely propping his arms above her shoulders, and breathed down at her.

Delphine caressed his half-moon scar with light, infinitely tender fingertips. "Knows what, Captain Howland?"

"Knows that I will love her through all hardships, and Emperors can hack my fingers away from the doorknob, men can throw me from a roof, famines and eighty thousand dead cows can stand in my way, and I will traverse twenty mountain ranges to find her again."

She flung her arms about his neck and plastered her mouth to his. Snorting hotly, she pulled him to her. Groaning, he blindly tried to holster the pistol he'd sheathed so many thousands of times, and could not find the damned thing at his hip, so just lodged it in the waistband of his trousers and backed her up against the wall.

He swept her away in a kiss that spoke of all the unfulfilled longing of the past several months, the hundreds of nights he'd lain awake with his hand around his cock, embroiled in the crazy emotional desire that threatened to engulf him. Yet even as his hips lifted her higher and higher up the stone wall, he withheld displaying outright lust, and crushed her to him humanely, and with dignity, as he didn't want to harm the distressed woman with the terrifying totality of his passion.

When they pulled away slightly, they panted into each other's mouths, touching the sweat of their noses together, and a delicious smile lifted the corners of Delphine's mouth.

"I do believe you, Ravi," she breathed. "I do believe you."

Ah, she drove him insane! Disregarding the stumbling shouting buffoons at their backs, he was about to dive in for another divine kiss when a shaky voice hard by his right elbow caused him to stop.

"*Is she gone yet?*"

The sudden words were a shock that nearly stopped Ravi's heart, and he clutched at Delphine protectively, but relaxed when he viewed the stunned visage of Kaspar Nagel, his eyes awash with horror.

Ravi threw his head back and laughed, an all-encompassing laugh that drained the nerves from his skull, and made his blood flow freely once again. Delphine collapsed against his chest with a bubbling happiness, and he clapped a hand on the deacon's shoulder.

"It's time to go home, Kaspar."

EPILOGUE
THEODORE'S LAST ASYLUM

The Southern End of Selassie

ON THE FOURTH MORNING AFTER THE fall of Magdala, they rode up to see the demise of the fortress.

The Royal Engineers blew up the Kôbet Bar first, then the eastern towers and magazines. Sappers and miners set torches to each house in quick succession. With the wind coming from the east, soon the entire tabletop was a crimson igneous lake of fire. Loaded pistols and muskets and shells from the batteries were thrown into the conflagration. From the southern end of Selassie, they felt the heat.

Ravi got down on a bended knee. His face seemed to have been battered by the wind, his half-moon scar nearly vanished. Age had made him handsomer, as though the black highlands had graced him with its peculiar rough, reflective hand. Delphine knew now that her heart wouldn't burst from love, the more she cared for a man. She knew now that the more one loved, the more happiness was returned to one, so she wasn't afraid to look at him fully any longer.

"Misha Vasiliev." His voice was drenched with the warm tones of a linguist who had spent decades outdoors. "Buy your mules, get

497

ready your provision, and pay your servants. For after such a day, they that seek me here shall not find me."

Abou Bekr knelt on one knee also. "Cut down the kantuffa in the four quarters of the world, for I know not where I am going."

She was still afraid of cliffs. Nevertheless Delphine edged forward a few steps to join the men on the rim of the escarpment. Gratefully, she slowly genuflected, too. "I'm encamped upon the Bashillo. He who doesn't join me there, I will chastise him for seven years."

Ravi turned to face her, the distant dilated cast to his eyes slowly vanishing. The corners of his mouth turned up.

She couldn't help but touch his face then, even though the beautiful scar had been eroded from its exquisitely made planes. All at once, she fell into his arms, pressing her mouth to the lemon and pepper taste of his neck. She knew she was safe.

Kaspar now stepped up. "May the only Christian nation in Africa become famous for whatsoever is honest, lovely, and of good report."

Lifting a hand, Delphine dragged Kaspar down to the unfamiliar position of sitting like a Red Indian. His legs fairly creaked with unaccustomed vigor, but he bestowed her with a small smile before gazing back out at the flames of Magdala.

Delphine inclined her head toward Ravi. "Many people have been disappointed the British are leaving."

Abou piped up. "Yes, they said 'we were born in bondage and must die slaves'."

Ravi nodded. " 'You mean we must cut each other's throats'."

They were on the very edge of the world.

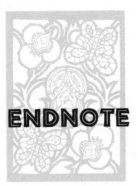

ENDNOTE

IN A DISCUSSION IN THE BRITISH House of Commons, on June 30, 1871, the great British statesman, William Gladstone, commenting on loot taken from Magdala, observed: "He deeply regretted that those articles were ever brought from Abyssinia, and could not conceive why they were so brought. They [the British people] were never at war with Abyssinia . . . he [Gladstone] deeply lamented, for the sake of all concerned, that those articles, to us insignificant, though to the Abyssinians probably sacred and imposing symbols, or at least hallowed by association, were thought fit to be brought away by the British army."

Ravinger Howland and Delphine Chambliss were wed in Zulla on May 28, 1868. In New York, they formed the Lazzat Un Nisa Society, a small and highly secretive organization that privately published his translated Arabic and "Hindoo love manuals," although Captain Howland used the pseudonymous moniker A.G. Grundy to avoid prosecution. Mrs. Howland attended to the business affairs of the society, and started a medical practice serving Ukrainians on the Lower East Side, with a tall and frightening scarified African as her assistant, but who was nevertheless well-mannered and kindly with patients. Eventually it was said even pregnant women overcame their fear of him.

The income from the private editions was sufficient in 1872 for the couple to purchase a town-house in Hyde Park, where the stables bred exotic Wallo Galla horses, and Mrs. Howland shocked society by wearing men's trousers under her skirts. Abroad starting in 1876, they traveled first through Greenland and Iceland, then to St. Petersburg where they spent a year and made fast friends with Fyodor Dostoevsky. They studied aborigines in inner Australia, and sailed down the west coast of Africa to live with the cannibal Fan tribe and observe gorillas.

During their two years in Count de Brazza's Congo, Mrs. Howland set up a native hospital that served thousands of Africans, but her medical books never earned as much as her husband's folk tale and erotic translations. While the Captain and their companions, the Deacon Kaspar Nagel and the tall Takrury Abou Bekr, continued to achieve athletic feats such as scaling Mt. Cameroon and rafting down the Lualaba, it was said Mrs. Howland was already ailing when they set off in 1882 to sail down the Niger to Timbuktu and Gao, but valiantly hid her condition from the Captain.

"She had always been beset by certain female ailments after many scurrilous and gratuitous surgeries in her youth," Deacon Nagel explained in his popular biography of the couple, *Wanderings among the Cannibals*. "Eventually the viperous tentacles of such nefarious operations sank morbidly into her womanly center, and strangled the very life from that most noble and divine of all creatures."

Nowadays, of course we would interpret this to mean that she died of ovarian cancer. According to Herr Nagel, she persevered until they reached Timbuktu, where in a mud house at the age of forty-nine, she expired in her husband's arms, her last cryptic words being, "I shall never forget that man who smashed the violin over the head of his instructor."

Captain Howland traveled for another ten years, through Arabia, Patagonia, and Alaska, not returning to Hyde Park until

1893 with his weary retinue, which by that time included the four children of Abou Bekr and his Congolese wife. He never wed again, though Deacon Nagel's book alludes to some "unsavory nautch girls" who appear to have lived in the town-house. Lecturing widely, he published more translations in his seventies than he had in all the preceding years, and was so robust that as a fellow "champion of the strenuous life," in 1898 he accompanied his friend Theodore Roosevelt to Cuba, where he was considered an invaluable military advisor.

The "Bad Bold Bandit of Hyde Park" finally passed in 1915, much to the relief and grief of his neighbors who had always suspected he was really A.G. Grundy, mainly owing to monogrammed towels in his bathroom.

The Lazzat Un Nisa Society also published a slim volume by Anatole Verlaine, *Hiver Désolé*, but it failed to find a following until 1923, when he was compared favorably to the legendary poet Arthur Rimbaud.

The Deacon Kaspar Nagel never wed, although in a 1934 interview one of Abou Bekr's sons claimed that on more than one occasion he heard a man singing "Follow the Drinking Gourd" in the apartments of the "questionable ladies," after which Kaspar Nagel would emerge in an ebullient mood, shreds of what was called "chat" clinging to his teeth, clutching a large cow horn.

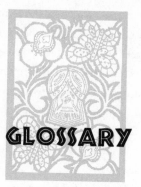

GLOSSARY

abiet: master, lord. Expression used by beggars when asking for alms

afyuni: opium

alga: couch constructed of poles lashed together with thongs of cowhides

alokom: "I don't know"

amba: mountain

arat: wooden frame laced with rawhide strips and covered with blankets for a bed

arrack: colorless liquor made from honey

awnat: true

azmary: minstrel who entertains with song

bar: gate

barrilye: Venetian flasks used for drinking liquor

benaika: flashy gold plates that adorn a horse's headstall

betoa: silver cuff enclosing the forearm indicating that a solider has killed ten men

brundo: raw beef

buda: evil spirit who inhabits one

chat: astringent spinach-like leaves chewed for amphetamine effect

dadab: idiot

damera: bonfires lit during Maskal celebration

debterah: lay priest

doomfata: boasting recital of a soldier's exploits

elelta: ululating cry upon joyous or warlike occasions

endod: *Phytolacca dodecandra.* The pulverized seeds are used for washing clothes

ensete: *Ensete maurelli.* Red Abyssinian banana palm

faro: dog of hyena family, yet differing greatly

ferenje (pl.: frenjoch)**:** Europeans, white men

geddai: killing

girf: long whip made of plaited hippo hide

gooks: mock warfare played at festivals with wands instead of spears

gwassa: tufts of grass on mounds of earth. Used for ropes and covering houses

hadji (*Arabic*)**:** one who has made the pilgrimage to Mecca

hakim: doctor

hambasha: heavy, thick cakes

imbilta: wooden flute

insoosilla: root similar to henna used to stain hands and feet

isgyoh: expression of amazement or alarm

I'sh-shi: very well; OK

kamis: Red silk shirt conferred upon people of distinguished merit

kantuffa: long thorns that molest one when one travels abroad

kosso: *Hagenia abyssinica.* Medicinal tree used to expel tapeworm

limoot: brass chains hung around a horse's necks for show

mankuse: monks

mateb: necklace cord of blue silk that distinguishes Christians

medhanit: medicine

merz: *Acokanthera schimperi.* Small shrub widely used in preparation of poison arrows

michamicho: *Oxalis semiloba.* Purgative bulb superior to kosso

narguileh: hookah water-pipe

negarit: drums beaten whenever army marches; *baal negarit* is the head drummer

qitegn: syphilis

quolquol: *Euphorbia abyssinica.* Spiny arborescent succulent

shamma: toga-like covering worn over clothing

shamshir: Persian saber

shifta: bandit

shotel: Abyssinian sword shaped like a sickle

tabot (pl. tabotat): replica of the Ark of the Covenant, the original of which is said to be in a chapel in Axum; *manbara tabot* is an altar chest to hold the *tabot*

talla: beer

talwar: Indian sword with Damascus blade

tankwa: papyrus boat

teff: cereal crop grain

tej: fermented drink, an amber mead, made from honey and hops, restricted to the aristocracy

tej-asalefech: butler or server of mead

tej metall: cold in the head

tenesu: get up!

Tewodros yemut: May Tewodros die if I am not telling the truth

tibs: roasted meat

timkin: turban

tukul: round thatched hut with conical roof

wancha: very large horn cup

wanza: *Brucea antidysenterica mill.* Tree with white, delicate flowers like snow

warka: *Ficus vasta.* Huge, majestic, spreading fig tree

wot: peppery stew

yet abat?: Where is your father?

zar: evil spirit that possesses one

zenar: men's leather case for holding necessaries

zurruf: prisoners taken in battle

AUTHOR'S NOTE

I COULD (AND PROBABLY WILL, ON my website) write an entire bibliography of all the wonderfully vivid Abyssinian travelers and scholars who enlightened me about this grand, dramatic epic. But among those still living, I must give the utmost thanks to Dr. Richard Pankhurst of Addis Ababa, Ethiopia. I first wrote him as a sycophant. "Esteemed Professor, is there any way possible you could assign one of your students to proof my manuscript?" This grand scholarly gentleman, a giant among giants of Ethiopian history, replied back to me, "I'd be honored to do it myself." I was blown away. I kept expecting him to tell me, "You've got to be kidding. Go back to grade school now, Karen, and play with your dollhouses." His *The Medical History of Ethiopia* was the inspiration for Delphine's manuscript.

I've combined the two Napiers: Sir Charles "The Conqueror of Sindh," and Sir Robert, "Lord Napier of Magdala." I thought it would add gusto and verve to the relationship between Ravi and Napier if they had a paternal background together, as Burton did with Napier in India. I suppose I just really wanted to add the story of Burton's infamous "homosexual brothel" report to Napier that put Richard under such a cloud of Victorian disgrace that it haunted the rest of his life and career.

As the character of Ravinger Howland is obviously based

almost entirely upon Sir Richard Burton (as well as elements of John Bell and Captain Tristram Speedy), I felt free to attribute stanzas of Burton's most gorgeous poem, *The Kasidah*, to Ravi Howland.

For the character of Anatole Verlaine, he's almost entirely my favorite poet Arthur Rimbaud, mixed with a bit of Bardel, a sleazy soldier-of-fortune and artist whom all "the Gaffat people" loathed. Rimbaud never made it up into the highlands of Abyssinia (as Burton did not, having had enough of the Somali area after having a spear thrust through his jaw). In Anatole's gorgeous death scene, I took almost the entirety of his ravings from a letter Rimbaud wrote to Paul Verlaine when they were temporarily at odds, and from some from his deathbed letters to his mother. "I promise to be good . . ." What a beautiful, ravaged, tortured spirit!

The character of the Deacon Kaspar Nagel spoke quite a bit in the language of the real Reverend Henry Stern. It's a joy to read Stern's *Wanderings among the Falasha* for its bombastic, bloviated flavor that contributed so much to the terribly fun and unpredictable character of Kaspar.

Almost all of the words of Tewodros are actual words he spoke. I merely mixed and matched them, and put them into his mouth at different times. I started out loathing this evil despot, and I think you can tell that at the end, I had a lot of love and compassion for this enigmatic man of vision who was one of the most confoundedly complex sovereigns of all time.

Regarding Delphine Chambliss, I gleaned much of her history from the biographies of Dr. Mary Edwards Walker. Most of the details of her life in the States are true: she was the first female graduate of Syracuse Medical College in 1855. When she went to enlist with the Federals at the start of the Civil War, she was denied a commission, and was only allowed to volunteer as an Acting Assistant Surgeon. She was in the front lines in the battles of Bull Run, Chickamauga, and Atlanta, and often went behind enemy lines to treat civilians. In 1864, she was captured by Confederates and sent to prison for four months—in Richmond, not in Andersonville, as Delphine was.

She was an early proponent of women's dress reform, appearing often in tails and top hat, and during the war in "Turkish pantaloons" under her uniform, always carrying two pistols at her side. She remains the first and only woman to earn the Congressional Medal of Honor. In 1917, her medal was rescinded along with 910 others (864 from the 27th Maine, who received it merely for reenlisting) when standards were revised to dictate only "actual combat with an enemy." She refused to give back her medal, wearing it every day until her death, and in 1977 President Jimmy Carter reinstated her honor posthumously for her "distinguished gallantry, self-sacrifice, [and] patriotism . . . despite the apparent discrimination because of her sex."

Sapper Bailey did not climb up the cliff at Magdala, nor did he shoot a *ferenje*, but he did steal an amulet from the Emperor's neck consisting of a leather pouch containing a nine-inch-long parchment written in Ge'ez. In 2002, an anonymous donor contacted Professor Pankhurst saying he was in possession of this item, and it was repatriated to Ethiopia.

Regarding spellings: as English spellings of Amharic words were all phonetically transcribed, and as a result you have about ten different versions of a single word, I've chosen to go with the spellings mostly used by the *frenjoch* writers of the time. Dr. Pankhurst took exception to some versions of place names such as Lake Tzana and Djenda, but this is how primary source journalists such as Blanc, Rassam, Stanley, Parkyns, and Plowden spelled them.

Also available by Karen Mercury from Medallion Press:

CHAPTER

1

September 2, 1896
Old Calabar, Niger Coast Protectorate

Perhaps she shouldn't have said it quite that way. She should
have been more circumspect.

"I'm here to study clitoridectomy."

Ralph Moor stared as if Elle were wearing her drawers on the
outside of her skirt. The nose on his marsupial face twitched. "I . . .
see. Well, Mrs. Bowie. I am sure that to a young anthropologist this
godforsaken coast seems an inviting opportunity. I feel compelled
to tell you, however, that these people are extremely barbaric and
vicious in their dealings."

Elle leaned forward in the chair. "I had heard something to
that effect, Consul. And it only served to incite my curiosity even
more. I wish to learn about the most far-flung aboriginal peoples
of the world. Why, last year, I was in Australia studying the bush
people." That was an exaggeration. The closest she had come to
bush people in Australia was a harried one-hour stop in Sydney
rushing from steamer to steamer on the docks. "Did you know, sir,
that they believe a kangaroo can turn into a rock?"

Moor barked a small laugh. "Oh, my, my. If you think that is
exciting, the people of Benin City will keep you occupied for years."

"Years?" Rip McCulloch jumped in his chair. He was a
handsome man, with tendrils of white-blond hair clinging to his
shirt collar, and a dimple in his chin. After ten years as Elle's
partner, it was still a pleasure for her to gaze upon him. He fanned

his face with his Stetson hat. "We don't have years, do we, Elle?"

Elle laughed charmingly. "Rip is in a big hurry to take his photographs. He gets very edgy when he cannot be around native peoples."

Ralph Moor turned suddenly sober. "Well, surely you've heard of the saying . . . 'The Bight of Benin! The Bight of Benin! One comes out where three goes in.' "

Elle and Rip looked at each other knowingly, chortling with camaraderie, as if they had just been singing that very song. Elle ventured to say, "Well, then. We had better be three people in our party, hadn't we?"

The Consul General was too stodgy to understand Elle was joking. "Yes, and I have just the man for you. Mateus Barbosa. He speaks the corrupt Portuguese dialect spoken by the older inhabitants of Benin City."

Becoming sober herself, Elle said, "That is a good idea, sir. Where can I find this fellow?"

"He lives in Sapele. I'll write you a note of introduction. Just be sure to not look . . . agape at him or his surroundings. He can be very touchy. He lives aboard the old hulk Hindustan, and I daresay he's most sensitive about it. And be certain not to drink any palm wine when you're near him." He was already scribbling a note for Elle. She looked on eagerly, but could not read the spiky, upside-down handwriting. "While you're in Sapele, look in on another man for me, would you, my dear? This chap has been known to trade with the Benin people, which is something the rest of us cannot say." He handed the note to a waiting servant for the man to seal, then looked at Elle with a sudden flashing of his dark eyes. "The place is a fortress, my dear. They refuse to trade with us and have cut themselves off from all contact. Many valuable trade products are lying in storage in this dusky king's territories due to the fetish rule of that unfortunate land."

"Oh, they won't refuse to deal with me, sir. I have methods for cajoling and coercing men into . . . dealing."

Rip nodded. "Yes, Elle . . . er, my wife has the power of persuasion, as they say."

"Well, then. Perhaps you can cajole Brendan Donivan into

opening up the trade routes. We need the hinterlands trade, the palm oil, the ivory." An idealistic sheen came to Moor's eyes when he said, "Palm oil is the life blood of the Delta, flowing down the main artery, the River Niger!" When he got no reaction from the Yankees, he added gravely, "You'll find Mr. Donivan along the Ethiope River, in the house on stilts. He's an American also, so you should have a lot to discuss."

Elle was sweltering inside her hunting costume. She swore to hang her corset from the branch of the next tree she saw. And the boater hat was the height of absurdity. "I am not one for trade or politics, being strictly an anthropologist, but if you say Mr. Donivan has knowledge of Benin City, then I shall look in on him."

Moor accepted the note from the servant. He seemed about to proffer it to Elle, but he had something more to say. "If you can convince Mr. Donivan to speak with the king of Benin City on our behalf, the whole of Britannia would honor you. As you know, it helps everyone when the needs of three continents are met. Just think! Your country may have never fought the War of Independence, if such was the case."

"Yes . . . " Elle said vaguely.

"Yes . . . " agreed Rip.

Moor inhaled and exhaled. "Well, then! Good cheer to you." He held the note out as a tribute, and stood. "Now, be certain to hire the best canoe boys. These rivers are most treacherous." Moor turned his angry eyes onto Rip's innocent form. Rip stood, adjusting his corduroy vest. "Doesn't your husband have to attend to the bags outside? I cannot guarantee they will still be there. These natives are most—"

"Yes, sir!"

It made Elle jump when Rip saluted, his body all coiled like a rattlesnake. She wished he wouldn't do that. She followed Rip out of the room, a drip of moisture rolling down into her cleavage. The hunting costume with its tight belt of shotgun cartridges was smothering her, and she longed to be out of doors.

In front of the stone Government House, Rip guarded their baggage with his Colt in one hand, taking assiduous swigs from a flask with the other. Elle rattled him by the arm. "No palm wine!"

Rip exhaled happily. "I tell you . . . I'm still tickled to death whenever someone calls me your husband."

Elle relaxed at the sight of Rip's twinkling eyes, his dimples cuter than a baby's. One had to relax around Rip; his charming and guileless ways had extracted them from many a fix. "Well. Just make sure you keep up that front 'til we get out of this . . . joint."

Although the red-roofed citadel of the Government House had a nicely mowed viridian lawn, it was merely an oasis in the quagmire of mud, piss, and banana peels that comprised the rest of Old Calabar. Below, the Calabar River was exotic enough in a teeming mercantile sort of way, with its barges and giant canoes loaded up with puncheons of palm oil. This part of the coast was one colossal mangrove swamp, intersected by a network of creeks. The loud morass was sensational even to Elle, who after all was jaded, having been around the world and to every port that mattered.

"Anyway. We're not near that Matardus joker so I don't need to watch my palm wine."

"Yes; I wonder what's up with that?" Elle was looking for her umbrella in the cart full of trunks, knapsacks, and photographic equipment boxes.

"More'n likely he's some lowdown varmint." Without even glancing at the cart, Rip reached in and withdrew Elle's umbrella. He was such a gentleman he even opened it before handing it to her. "Why else would Moor have given you a sealed letter of introduction? The letter probably tells him to ambush us at the first turn of the river."

"Oh, Rip." Elle looked to the cart boy, remembered she didn't know the local language, a frightening pidgin English, so just waved her arm to indicate he should start pulling the cart down the hill. "The note probably says something he's embarrassed for us to hear, like 'make sure you tighten my mother's truss.'"

They walked down Consular Hill through the magical air that caressed Elle's forearms. She had heard this part of the Niger Coast was the whiteman's graveyard and emitted noxiously mortal fumes by night, but so far it seemed like a happily tropical idyll.

"I'd like to tighten his mother's truss. That fellow is a traitorous villain if ever I saw one."

"Rip, don't be so skeptical about everyone."

"And don't you smell this air? It's got a decomposing aroma."

"It's the jungle."

They were always followed by a trail of innocently smiling children, like what America would be like without poverty. All right, it was an ignorant outlook. But it made Elle feel good, as though they weren't anywhere near the "City of Blood" yet. She wanted to see Benin City. But in another regard, she didn't.

$\sim\!\!\!\!\!\rightarrow\!\!\!\!\sim$

The leopard jumped him! Its powerful paws were around his neck, and it was sinking its incisors into the back of his head! He threw the beast off and roared to his feet. He could feel the silky bulk of his dog pressing against his thigh as she reared up in a fury of monstrous barking.

Where did the leopard go? Why was there no blood spilling down his neck? Why was Ode laughing down at him from his perch in the karite tree?

"Iwi!" the boy squealed at the top of his lungs. "You look so funny!"

Brendan now pointed his rifle at the squirming form of the boy in the tree. "Where did the leopard go?" he yelled in Edo. He saw the bait monkey still tethered to the stake, and when he slid his hand beneath his helmet of leaves, he felt no blood. A creepy feeling came over him as though he had just fallen like a thousand of brick from the karite tree, and the leopard had never even been there. The dog's bark now seemed curiously full of humor.

Ode's trilling laughter gave forth. Leaping on the tree trunk, Brendan shook it so mercilessly the small boy, hugging his bow and quiver of poison arrows to his chest, crashed harmlessly to the duff of the jungle floor. Still laughing, Brendan noted.

"Get up. Let's go home."

It was too much to hope that the little critter would disremember what had just transpired. The boy held his stomach as though his guts would fall out from laughing as Brendan jerked him along the murky path. Ode trailed the monkey on the tether, the monkey shrieking at being almost laid out flat. Could anything be more mortifying?

"You looked so funny! You went to sleep and fell off the—"

"That's right!" Brendan shouted sternly. "And that's exactly what I was trying to demonstrate to you, Ode. This is the wrong thing to do when you're leopard hunting. You must make sure to take every precaution not to go to sleep—"

The boy was merciless. "But Iwi, you really were asleep! Your eyes closed, and then you started sliding off the branch—"

"I was only pretending, boy! This is part of your apprenticeship. You are much too young to join iroghae anyway, so I thought I'd give you a few more lessons that other leopard hunters don't get. It keeps you busy when you aren't helping Ikponmwosa in the farm. Or perhaps you would rather be harvesting yams?"

That finally calmed the urchin. "No, sir. I'd rather be hunting with you." He beat the air with his quiver.

The way Ode puffed up when he said "you" made Brendan relax a little, confident the boy wouldn't tattle about the incident. After all, Brendan was Ighiwiyisi, "the hunter who shall not get lost in a foreign land." The Oba himself had given him a gift of the boy Abievbode, in return for two ferocious live leopards. Brendan wore a string of leopard teeth around his neck, and he was allowed to carry a leopard skin shield. If Ode ever doubted him, Brendan didn't think he could bear it.

After they had walked through the jungle for six hours and into daybreak, Brendan started speaking aloud in English. He knew this made Ode quizzical, but Ode's eyes had started to slide shut a long time ago. The lad stumbled ahead like a zombie, sleepwalking through the entire racket. "That leopard would've run all over me like fire in dry grass. I'm a poor worm of the first degree. This young one isn't going to respect me if I keep full of devilment."

For it had taken Brendan six hours of hard walking to admit to himself the reason he'd fallen from the karite tree. He wasn't asleep, quite. It was more like a hazy waking dream where someone dropped a gauze curtain over his head. He saw a woman, a white woman of sun-browned finery with a proud stately throat, flashing dark eyes, and loads of auburn hair shining like velvet pouring over her shoulders. The strange thing about the vision, the thing that made Brendan realize it wasn't a real memory, was that the white woman stood next to a chair of European design, yet carved with imagery from Edo. There was the Oba with his mudfish legs next to a leopard that had decapitated a critter of some kind. The most anomalous carving was a whiteman in a boat holding an oar. In the other hand he grasped a chain attached to a barrel, and behind him was a cannon. Brendan had never seen such a chair in Edo, only the carved square stools the Oba and uzama had. He knew then it was witchery that brought the vision to him, perhaps from the crossroads that morning, where the white-tailed ant thrush had called its harsh prophetic cry.

Brendan imagined a dead person was playing a trick on him. If a woman died childless with no one to bury her properly, she was stuck in this world as a ghost. Understandably, ghosts were irked with the living. A fellow from the Igbesanmwan—the ivory carvers' guild where men made glorious altar tusks, hand clappers, and ceremonial swords—had died recently, and if his children hadn't buried him with his feet pointing toward Ughoton, he couldn't take the canoe to erinmwin. He could be kicking up a fuss, not being able to travel to the world across the sea, heaven.

"But why would the ivory carving fellow be sassing me?" Brendan wondered aloud. "Why am I tortured by a vision of a white woman? There's no white woman here."

They were now emerging from the inviolate jungle cover and into the blinding chartreuse glare of yam farms. There were sacrificial yam heaps topped with cutlasses and hoes next to calabashes of palm wine. Along the road were idiogbo, three sticks planted upright in the ground to represent the ancestors who first farmed along the path. Brendan paused at a mound of red earth beneath a tree where there was a terra cotta pot of water. He withdrew a few cowrie shells from a pouch at his waist, paid for the water, and drank a coconut shell full before handing it to Ode. Ode was waking now, as he wanted to be sure everyone saw him returning from his important leopard hunting training.

Brendan was gratified to see that people stopped their work and stared respectfully. He felt silly as always in the bushy helmet, but he knew that even strangers would recognize him as the Oyinbo leopard hunter of the Oba's. He enjoyed the eclectic hodgepodge of his attire, his hunting vest of forest green duck, the brass leopard face hip ornament, and his black American river boots that just reached his kneecaps. He left his long chestnut hair free-flowing, but for hunting he applied palm oil and clamped it down with coral decorations, as a pigtail down the middle of his back. Altogether Brendan felt quite feral in his getup.

"There's a few white women in Sapele. Mary Wells, the missionary, but she's got moustaches to rival Captain Gainey's. Bradley Forshaw's wife, Caroline, but she resembles a manatee. I don't think either one of them was the one in the vision. That Victoria visiting Gainey was a peach, sure enough." His penis instantly stiffened at the thought of Victoria, her white skin unmarred by the sun, her delicate earlobes like seashells. He had spent many a pleasurable moment masturbating and thinking of Victoria, hating Captain Gainey all the more. Beneath his robust cheer, Gainey was ripe for the devil with his empire-building.

However, Victoria's hair was the color of strawberries, not lustrous auburn like the woman in the vision. Brendan's guilt at thinking of Oyinbo women overtook him, and at the next "silent market" he paid more cowries for plantains, some to eat and some to leave as tribute to his ikegobo, his shrine to his Hand. He was surprised to have been so aroused by the vision of the woman, when he thought he had put such superficial things behind him.

Onaiwu, a friendly fellow of the ighele grade, jumped in the middle of the path with one arm stiff in the air. Ode kept on toward the city gate, trailing the monkey on the leash.

Brendan and Onaiwu confronted each other near a shrine, a mound of raised rusty earth embedded with sticks upon which shreds of white cloth were tied. There were so many shrines in that land it was hard to understand them all, but Brendan knew this was a shrine to Osanobua, creator of everything in the universe. Brendan's Da would be turning over in his grave if he knew Brendan even listened to notions such as that.

Brendan made the three circles with his right hand. "Kóyo. Vbèè óye hé?" Hello. How are things?

Onaiwu was so clearly agitated he didn't even give the standard response. "Oyinbo are coming to the city!" On his forehead a vein bulged in perfect symmetry with his vertical cicatrices. Onaiwu had a retinue behind him of other ighele men who protected the city and acted as policemen. "A runner told me they left Ughoton this morning."

Brendan nodded. "So they won't arrive here by tonight. How many of them? Are they English?"

"Only two, all we know is there are Oyinbo. The runner said Mateus was with them."

"Well, ain't it precious?" Brendan exploded in English, striking the muddy ground with his pike. Mateus Barbosa was a swinish cane rat of a man who made a good way for himself playing each tribe against the other. He mainly acted as broker between Africans and whitemen in matters of palm oil, stirring up trouble wherever he went. Because he'd been born in the Oil Rivers—his ancestors were the Portuguese adventurers who stayed in Edo and intermarried—and because he spoke the secret language still understood by the top uzama and eghaevbo, he was free to come and go in Edo.

Brendan sputtered angrily, and had to turn aside and glare at the earthen city walls, seventy-five feet above the bottom of the moat from which they had been dug. He turned back to Onaiwu and his men. "Oyinbo! And just what makes them think they can come here, when we haven't allowed any others?"

"We think they must be very impudent, or else very stupid."

"If they have Mateus with them, they're not stupid. He'd enjoy scaring them with frightening stories of what they think are evil doings in Edo."

Onaiwu stuck out his lower lip. "So, they are arrogant."

Brendan exhaled. "Aren't they all? And don't worry. I have tricks that I know will work very well on Oyinbo."

The irate aura surrounding the group of men lightened as they turned as a unit and headed for the city gates, although some of the more bellicose ones continued to huff angrily through their nostrils.

Onaiwu enquired, "Will you tell me about your trick?"

Brendan knew he shouldn't be so averse to other whitemen, but he was. He had lived intermittently in Edo for three years now after jumping ship during a particularly boring sojourn on the Forcados River, and he preferred it to Akpo r'Oyinbo, the whiteman's world. That was one reason he should pay tribute at his ikegobo for thinking erotically about Oyinbo women—if he scorned the industrial crap of civilization, he should scorn the women as well. "Yes, I'll need your help tomorrow."

Ugiagbe, a bold ighele man, stuck his oar in. "We can help you now! If we intercept them on the Ughoton road, we can scare them with the deity to whom we sacrifice blood."

"No!" bellowed another. "We can kill them!"

Brendan glared at the men over his shoulder. "Do you want the entire Liverpool Army"—for that was the only town in England they knew—"coming to kill everyone in Edo? No, my plan is better."

"Ighiwiyisi knows what he is doing," Onaiwu chastised Ugiagbe.

When they arrived at the northern gate, Brendan was close to his house. He knew Ode had gone home—although given to Brendan as a slave, Brendan chose to have another family care for him. Ode was too young to hear the plans of ighele men, so he was right to have continued on without Brendan.

Brendan was in a jovial mood. What a day! He had gone from mortification to anger, and now fairly chortled with glee at the thought of those arrogant Oyinbo having the gall to come to Edo. He entered the courtyard of his house, laughing aloud at the new kora that sat atop a stool. "Hey! Ikponmwosa!" he shouted as he ducked under the lintel of his front door and into the relative cool of the red clay house. "All hands on deck!"

He wandered from room to room, sticking his head into the various chambers of the honeycomb house. "Ikponmwosa?" He passed through a freshly glazed and spacious atrium. At either end were altars inlaid with cowries, and alcoves filled with carved ivories, porcelain platters, and fine mats. He paused in one room to divest himself of the leafy hat and armament, and in another room to deposit his plantains, placing several chunks that he cut with his Bowie knife atop the brass ikegobo on its mud altar. His particular ikegobo was a monument to lofty pretension, adorned as it was with figures of warriors brandishing swords, spears, shields and ceremonial doings—and, of course, a figure killing a leopard. Only the Oba and uzama had ikegobo as elaborate as Brendan's, but they had allowed him to have it made. Folding his arms in front of his bare chest, he smiled with pride at the altar.

"What're those cops doing in the courtyard?"

Brendan jumped, and was embarrassed he had jumped. "They say smoke follows pretty folks."

"You know I don't like them. Can you get rid of them?"

Brendan snorted. "Well, you're a sight."

Evin's face looked even more lupine when he squinched it up like that, his smoke-colored lens spectacles perched atop his nose. His well-trimmed moustache and little monkish beard made up for the hair that wasn't on his head. "Maybe if you'd stop worshipping at your own shrine, you could clean and gut one of those hundreds of animals you just killed."

Brendan laughed, but moved back into the hallway to cover up his shame at not having killed even one animal. "You know I didn't bag anything, because Ode already told you."

Evin always followed him. Brendan knew he was back there, with his fancy-woven eruhan kilt, his bare feet, his head wrapped in a length of red silk. "We cancelled our lesson, I have to go back to the fields. But I can stay to give you another lesson."

"Are there still weevils in the corn? Ain't that poison you ordered from the States come yet?"

"Well, as usual it took the direct route through the South Pole on its way to bonny Old Calabar." Evin paused in the front doorway behind Brendan, pointing at the courtyard. "Look at those guys. What's up?"

Brendan waved at the ighele men, who scattered like a passel of parrots. "Come back tomorrow morning at sunrise," he told them. Evin couldn't speak but the most base of the Edo language, just enough to order things in the market. Brendan was proud of his own facility with languages. "I reckon my graphophone records got hung up in Casablanca, too. I'm waiting on that Il Trovatore."

"I'm waiting on those coon songs myself. Bill Newcomb over in Albertville's sending me Hogan's new sheet music. 'All Coons Look Alike to Me.' "

Brendan smirked. "That's a mighty ironic title to be teaching these Edo folks." For Evin had been amusing himself of late, whenever in Edo, by giving classes to men of the iroghae age grade and even some elders of edion. With his Washburn lyre guitar, banjo, mouth harp, and accordion, Evin had distilled an agreeable mix of music with Edo brass bells, ivory horns, rattles made from calabashes adorned with cowries, and the most bodacious assortment of stringed instruments known to man.

"Well, I just won't sing the words," Evin agreed. "We can jazz it with hand clappers and koras. They'll never know the difference. Are you going to tell me what those cops were doing out here?"

Exhaling mightily, Brendan took a small leap off the front mud stoop and struck for his favorite umbrella tree. "Some beefeaters are headed this way." Was Evin's mouth open to let in flies again? From an alcove in the mud wall that enclosed his home and courtyard, Brendan withdrew his tobacco box, hoping beyond hope that there were some cigarette papers in there. Smoking pipes and chewing tobacco was all right for other folks, but Brendan enjoyed a good cigarette now and then.

He heard Evin sputtering as he followed him into the courtyard. "Beefeaters are coming here? Are the cops going to kill them?"

Praise be, there were cigarette papers in his wooden box. "Keep your shirt on, Ev. I'm going to make sure no harm comes to them." Brendan took a stool. He gestured vaguely at Evin, who still stood like a scarecrow in the middle of the yard. "Pull up a stool, or sit on the ground."

Evin sat. "Do you know what they want?"

"The usual, I reckon. They want to ratify the treaty that Gallwey tricked the Oba into making in ninety-two. But of course they're going to make out like it's a mighty grave thing, stopping the bloodshed."

Evin nodded earnestly. "Flint over at the Royal Niger Company's been having it up and down with old Moor, a-hollering about who's got the right to the Edo trade."

Brendan enjoyed it when Evin became so heated he allowed his Alabama patois to slip into his speech. "Yup, between those two and the Lagos Colony making a big fuss over a city that ain't theirs for the taking, mayhap all hands'll scupper one another and leave us alone. You can bet Moor's behind sending these beefeaters over this way tomorrow."

Evin barely moved his mouth when he spoke. "Moor's on leave in London."

There was a hush, as though all the air had been sucked out of the firmament above them. All the birds were still, and it seemed as though even the trees ceased dropping leaves for one part of a second.

Then the clamor resumed, the clanging of metal against anvils from the brass casters' guild yonder, children squealing gleefully in their rock-scissors-paper game. Brendan's mouth was shaped like an O, so he flattened it into a knowing grimace. "Well, then. Let the frolics begin." Moor had earlier been an inspector with the Royal Irish Constabulary, "standing at the back of the Irish landlords, bayonet in hand," stifling rebellion. Just for that reason, Brendan and Evin loathed him.

Evin picked up his kora and set it on his knee. Brendan could tell by Evin's avuncular disapproval what he was about to say. "I'm keeping a close eye on your frolics, Captain Donivan. No sense in stirring up a lot of trouble. We don't need to give them the excuse they're looking for to come rampaging in here with all the big guns."

Brendan happily rubbed his own bare chest with his hand. He smiled the delighted smile Evin termed "saurian" as he leaned back against the warm mud wall. "Don't be afeard."

His words didn't seem to soothe Evin any, as he snorted even more fiercely and set to picking his kora stridently.

Silver Imprint
ISBN#1932815112
ISBN#9781932815115
US $9.99 / CDN $13.95
Available Now

For more information

about other great titles from

Medallion Press, visit

www.medallionpress.com